MW01181677

Who is
Peter Compton?

Who is
Peter Compton?

A Story of Military Life, Intrigue and Murder

Alex Hunt

Heather Publishing   UPS Box 481
Marana, Arizona 85658

This edition was prepared for publication by
Ghost River Images
5350 East Fourth Street
Tucson, Arizona 85711
www.ghostriverimages.com

ISBN 978-1-7333149-0-9

Library of Congress Control Number:2019909680

Printed in the United States of America
July, 2019

Contents

This book is dedicated to
Ruthie

Political Intervention

Chapter 1

The cold December drizzle had shrouded the Capitol dome in a blanket of grey. Washington seemed to be in hibernation at seven in the morning. The only sound, except for some light traffic, was his leather heeled shoes hitting the wet pavement as he approached the granite steps of the Capitol building. Ascending the stairs, he pulled his green army overcoat a little closer around his neck at the same time tightening the grip on his small briefcase clutched under his left arm. His mind kept going over the events which had taken place the past three and a half months. Finally someone was going to listen to him. He had given up hope when Senator Clifton had answered his letter, inviting him to meet him and a few of his colleagues on the Senate Foreign relation committee. He remembered Senator Clifton when the senator along with the Secretary of the Army and the NATO Commander, had visited his unit in Italy. The tall lanky senator had shown a great interest in the units' readiness posture and the soldiers' morale. His knowledge of each piece of equipment shown him had surprised many of the high ranking officers, especially when he mentioned certain limitations of a new piece of equipment recently acquired by the unit.

As he approached the huge doors at the top of the steps, a man whom he had not noticed stepped from the shadows and opened the door for him.

"Major Compton, please follow me" he said in a soft southern voice. He was in his later fifties or early sixties, and preceded Major Compton down the hallway past heavy oak doors with inscribed brass plates mounted to the left of the doors; probably the names of the various senators who occupied the offices. After a few minutes they arrived at a door which was slightly ajar. Again the man indicated for him to enter. The room appeared to be an outer office. It was relatively small with heavy furniture taking up most of the space. A door opened at the far end of the room and Senator Clifton extended his right hand greeting him.

"Good morning, Major Compton, nice to see you again. This is quite a change from the balmy breezes of the Mediterranean. Hope you don't catch a cold."

He returned the greeting. The Senator must have detected his nervousness for he put his arm around his shoulder.

"You know Major Compton; say it's Pete, isn't it? Well anyway, Pete, get your coat off and if you need to use the restroom it's through the doorway over there behind the desk." The Senator kept talking as Pete removed his coat and hung it on a coat rack and straightened his tie.

"I have five of my committee members in the next room. They know basically your story having read your report but I want to go through your story from the time the unit was formed at Fort Bragg, N.C.; leave nothing out and, of course, the alert status in Italy and especially the direct MSG's from the Secretary of State. Leave nothing out and if we have to continue tomorrow, so be it. This is serious enough to warrant the time. The boys in the next room cannot be shocked in any way. They are here because they want to see justice done and are sincerely interested in your story. Let's go in and meet them and get started." Senator Clifton escorted him into the conference room. It was smaller than he had expected. The Senator's colleagues were seated around an oval table with two empty chairs at the far end.

"Gentlemen, this is Major Compton or Pete as I have come to call him. This is Senator Burgess, Clampton, Stewart, McLean, and Rose". Each in turn shook his hand and welcomed him to the Nation's Capitol.

"Let's take our seats, Pete you sit next to me up here." Senator Clifton indicated the chair on his right at the head of the table.

"I have told Pete that we would like to hear his story leaving nothing out. If any of you have any questions, I prefer that we hold them until Pete here has finished. If any of you have anything you'd like to ask him before he starts fire away."

He told them he would be happy to answer any questions they had.

"For the sake of expediency though let's keep it to a minimum, that way we can get on with it and perhaps finish this today. Since most of our colleagues have left the Capitol for the Holidays, we should not be interrupted by outside calls. Alright then, if you have any questions before Pete starts?"

The other Senators around the table were refilling their coffee cups and getting their note pads out. Senator Burgess seated on Pete's right brought coffee to Pete and Senator Clifton.

"If you want anything in it, help yourself, Pete," Senator Burgess said with a polite smile.

"Pete" Senator Rose at the far end of the oval table was the first one to speak up.

"I have observed you since you arrived here a few minutes ago. You appear to be well decorated, Viet Nam I take". He didn't wait for Pete to reply. "I also happen to know and will pass it on for the benefit of my colleagues, that your military record can only be described as outstanding. You appear to have a bright future in the Army, providing you continue your good work."Pete nodded his thanks and smiled towards Senator Rose. "But how in the hell can you come up with a fantastic story like the one you wrote Senator Clifton? Are you prepared to call some of the highest ranking officers in the Army and God knows the State Department a bunch of liars, not to mention the President of the United States. I suggest that you forget about all this horseshit and go back to being a good soldier."

Senator Rose's voice had risen as had the color of his face. His outburst had taken Pete by surprise and he was working hard to regain his composure.

"If I might interrupt," It was Senator Stewart. "You know gentlemen, sometimes it's hard to adjust from a war time situation, like Viet Nam with its combat and excitement to a peace time situation, which many professional soldiers find a drag. They don't hand out many medals in peace time, do they, Pete?"

Pete looked around the table, all eyes were on him. His palms were sweating. He looked down at his hands and rubbed them together, slowly extending his fingers trying to collect his thoughts.

"I have come here today hoping to start a process which will eventually right a wrong." Thoughts were racing in his mind. He knew he would be alright, the nervousness had left him.

"The easiest road I could have taken was the one most of my fellow officers and some, not all, of my superiors took, namely go along with the official version of the events which occurred. I am not after another medal, being an officer in a strike unit has more than enough excitement for anyone even in so called peace time."

"Gentlemen," Senator Clifton spoke up, "Pete is not on trial here, this is not a witch-hunt, we are here to listen to Pete and question him. We here are aware of the ramification this could have if it were released to the press in the wrong manner. Heads would roll. Pete has come to us; he didn't go to the press, even when he thought the last door had been slammed in his face. He has gone about this in a dedicated and mature manner. A lesser person, one selling sensationalism, would have gone to the press long ago. After listening to his story, we here have to decide what to do about it and how best to handle it. I suggest Pete that you start off and tell it like it is or was, leave nothing out from the start of forming the unit in to the move to Italy and what transpired."

"Yes Sir, thank you." Pete took a sip of his coffee and fingered the stack of papers in front of him; finally he had gotten his chance. He briefly glanced at the first page, he knew it by heart. Pushing the papers to the side he heard himself start. "The unit was started or formed by Colonel Lawson, the Brigade Commander of the 1st Airborne BDE part of the 82 Airborne at Ft. Bragg, N.C. Division. The officers were picked first, then the NCOs and the enlisted men. Total force about eleven hundred officers and men. The competition for slots, especially among the officers, was intense. Boot licking and ass kissing were not uncommon. The unit was formed into an Airborne Combat Team: 3 Rifle Companies, 1 Artillery Unit of 105 millimeter artillery, 1 Engineer Platoon, 1 Expended Medical Platoon with a Doctor and Dentist, 1 Parachute Rigging section, 1 Recon Platoon and a HQ Company. The units NCOs and men's records had to be clean. No courts martial, etc. The Colonel would not tolerate Pot Heads. (In the 1970s it was estimated that 75% of the Army had smoked pot or some form of drugs.) Physical fitness was key; the runs and physical training disqualified many. When the assignment of Italy was made public, Colonel Lawson informed the troops that in Italy the national military police, "Carabiniers" could enter any US post and arrest anyone suspected of smoking or selling pot. As a result, about 60 men left the unit, especially when informed that in Italy you could remain in jail for up to a year or more before your case was heard. In two months the unit was down to its authorized strength. The units' proficiency steadily improved and by movement day it was the finest unit in the entire US Army bar none.

15

The unit moved in the spring of 1972 to a former US Air Base in southern Italy. The facilities were far superior to anything the unit had been used to. Housing for dependents was plentiful and lavish by Army standards. As a result, the morale was sky high. By July the unit had settled into a regular training cycle and had become part of the US Army Southern European Command. The only caveat was that Colonel Lawson was the G-3 in charge of operation. Colonel Lawson was a strict airborne soldier who tolerated no deviation from his orders or plans. There was definite friction between Colonel Lawson and the units' commander LTC Hays and some of his staff. A lot of the men felt Colonel Lawson was basically a bastard and expected too much of them. Everyone had been happy to leave Ft. Bragg and Colonel Lawson behind. Now he was at the base and would probably run the unit.

This was not to say LTC Hays was soft, far from it. The Company Commanders took to heart every order he issued them and carried out his direction faithfully. It was common knowledge among the officers that a strain had developed between the LTC Hays and Colonel Lawson the last few weeks at Ft. Bragg but no one thought too much about it since they would be leaving Colonel Lawson behind. LTC Hays almost didn't get the command had it not been for Colonel Lawson intervention the command would have gone to someone else who was under the impression that he would be the new commander. Colonel Lawson was not particularly fond of this LTC who could, along with his wife, flaunt his influence to the consternation of whichever command he was under. Colonel Lawson called LTC Hays into his office and told him that he would keep his command. Colonel Lawson was not without his own influence. I was at the time Colonel Lawson's adjutant and our wives were on very friendly terms. There were a lot of rumors circulating at Brigade Headquarters and I was under a great deal of pressure to spill the beans, so to say, of what actually was happening. But my loyalty was to Colonel Lawson who had asked me if I

16

wanted the Executive Officer slot of the new battalion. This of course went against the grain of the many West Point Majors within the command and those serving in other commands. I was not a West Point graduate.

Things were moving well in Italy and there was little interference from Colonel Lawson. I was going over a report to LTC Hays one day when LTC Hays asked me to close the door. It was just the two of us in the Lieutenant Colonel's office.

"I know that you and Colonel Lawson are good friends. However, I hope that you are my Executive Officer and not Colonel Lawson's." I was taken aback by his comment. I told him I had been Colonel Lawson's adjutant for about two years and yes we had formed a close relationship. However, I was now LTC Hays's Executive Officer and would serve him to the best of my abilities and no I would not inform Colonel Lawson on activities within the Battalion.

"I will be as loyal to you as I was to Colonel Lawson when I served him. He will not hear anything from me nor does he expect to. Colonel Lawson happens to think a lot of you. I personally have not heard him say anything about your abilities. The only thing I have heard came from the Chief of Staff who mentioned that Colonel Lawson holds you in high esteem. As you well know his wife and mine are good friends and we get together once in a while and the only thing I have heard is positive things about you and the Battalion. And there is no pillow talk in our house about you or the Battalion. There never has been, no matter what unit I have been in. My loyalty is to you and if you find that I don't do my job to your satisfaction or my loyalty is in question, fire me. I know there were a lot of outstanding WPs who wanted this slot and I'm sure you would rather have chosen your own Executive Officer and to be frank with you, had I been in your shoes I would have insisted on it. I threw my hat in the ring at a late date and it was not Colonel Lawson who ultimately chose me; he told me that my chances were slim. It was the Division Commander who called me over to the Division Headquarters and asked me if I wanted the job. His words were that you and I would complement each other. I think you knew the Division General personally having served under him in Vietnam."

LTC Hays stood up and extended his hand and we shook hands.

"I am pleased with you and I know I have your loyalty, I could not have chosen a better Executive Officer. I know it must put you in a difficult situation at times and as you know there are rumors around as to who you work for. I will put those rumors to rest at tomorrow's staff and company commanders meeting. That's it, I'm glad we had this talk; we should have had it months ago. Thanks, Pete."

True to his word, LTC Hays at the end of the staff and commanders meeting the next morning asked me to represent him at the Chief of Staff's meeting. I knew there was no meeting at the headquarters so I excused myself and departed the room. What had transpired at the staff meeting after I left leaked out that afternoon and the next morning, Captain Ryder, the S-2 intelligence officer, came into my office and closed the door.

"So you knew LTC Hays before in Vietnam." Captain Ryder looked at me waiting for an answer. "Yes, I gave him some intel when he was the S-3 in a 1st Air Cavalry. They were the only ones who acted on it and got all kinds of kudos from higher headquarters."

"Well according to the old man after you left this morning if he hears any derogative comments about you, he will personally take care of the individual. He also said that he along with the Division Commander picked you as his Executive Officer even skipping a Medal of Honor recipient. I guess we have to treat you nicer from now on."

"Unless you have solid Intel, Ryder, get the hell out of my office."

"I might in a week or so" said Ryder on his way out.

Saturday night was to be a formal affair at the officer's

club. It would be the first one since moving to Italy. Everyone was dressed in their finest, the ladies looked stunning. After cocktails and the meal, just as the music was about to start, an NCO from Headquarters approached LTC Hays and informed him that an alert had been called. LTC Hays sat there stark faced and whispered the message to me."

LTC Hays stood up and called for everyone's attention. He announced the 24 hours alert and for all the officers to go through the alert procedure and get their men into the garrison. Everyone took off leaving some of their wives and girlfriends in a state of shock. The unit had 24 hours to rig and be ready to go. Some officers who took off leaving their wives and girl friends behind, some had managed to ride home with their husbands and others were left stranded. People who worked at the officers' club offered to take the stranded ladies home. None were to see their men for the next three days.

Thirty hours after the alert was called, the unit was ready to move. Colonel Lawson directed LTC Hays to pick one company for a mission. The Co-Commander was briefed, loaded his men aboard waiting C-130s and dropped in the rugged plateau area north of the base where an opposing force of Italian Airborne troops acted as the enemy. The chosen company did well and was brought back to base after a day of skirmishes with the Italian unit.

Colonel Lawson was pleased but found many shortcomings. He directed that from now on one company would be on alert status at all times. This task was rotated every two weeks. The unit on alert consisted of about 120 men. A non married soldier had to stay on post. A married man could go home and leave a phone number where he could be reached at all times.

Three alerts were held in August, the last two met Colonel Lawson's 24 hours time limit. The rigging unit was kept busy and opened another drive through building to expand their capabilities.

The Battalion settled in to a new routine, the S-3 section,

headed by a Major wrote contingency plans for just about any eventuality. Families made the most of their time off together knowing that is could be days or weeks before they saw each other again.

Each day after the Battalion physical training LTC Hays held his 7 o'clock staff meeting. If he was absent, I conducted the meeting. One of us was always on base and on call.

"Let's get this over with, we have a lot ahead of us today" LTC Hays leaned back in his chair at the same time glancing down at his note pad, which contained unfinished tasks, which he had previously assigned his staff to accomplish.

Each staff officer in turn gave his update on the previous days actions and accomplishments. LTC Hays crossed off an item on his note pad which had been completed.

"We are using up too much ammo that has been allocated to training "The S-4, or logistic officer Captain Baird was saying. "At this rate we will be out of ammo by next month. I have briefed the Company Commanders of the situation but they seem determine to use it up."

"This is what I was talking about last night, Sir. I have discussed this with Captain Baird and the two of us talked with the Task Force G-4, to see if we can pry some additional ammo out of 7th Army. Our chances are kind of slim the way it sounds."

"I don't want to cut back the arms training; qualifications are coming up next month which for us means everything from a 45 Caliber pistol to our artillery. We have a lot of folks high up looking at us and I want this Battalion to come out on top. You dig into this and come up with something. I don't want to get into it until the last resort."

"Yes sir, I'll take care of it".

The motor officer gave his report giving the status of the vehicles and its new sand color repainting.

When each one had finished there was a complete silence in the room. This happened at every staff meeting. Each staff officer knew that the Battalion Commander kept a list of tasks on his pad. Some days he would go over the uncompleted ones asking each officer the status of the tasks. This could get embarrassing for some of the tasks had been on the list for months. It was not that the individual officers were not trying; it was often times the system which they were part of which produced slow results.

"What is the status of the two 81mm mortars S-4; they were damaged a month ago in the mass equipment drop, both Charlie Company and Bravo Company Commanders informed me they are short one 81mm mortar?"

"Sir, they have been turned in for salvage. We should have the replacement any day" said Captain Baird.

"What is any day Captain Baird, I heard that last week" The Battalion Commander was talking in his low ass chewing voice. "I want you to start calling as soon as this meeting is over and have a definite answer on my desk before I depart tonight."

"Yes, sir" said Captain Baird making notes on his own pad.

"S-1, you promised me a new personnel update three days ago. I also asked you to come up with a new way to manifest our people in the event of a real alert.

"Sir, I have the program. I have been working with the Executive Officer and Task Force and have computerized our personnel system. The reason I'm late is the computer needs maintenance after so many hours of operating and this week has been maintenance week."

"Basically for you sir and the rest of the staff, the S-1 has come up with what I feel is an outstanding manifesting procedure. The S-1 can cross load the Companies in any manner you desire. He has samples available for your perusal and can have them printed out in seconds. It's so simple it's unreal. We ran a test before the computers went down for maintenance, the only thing left to do is update the cards. I talked with the Chief of Staff, Colonel Hassan and he has promised us priority, which should happen tomorrow. The S-1 will have a printout for you tomorrow afternoon."

"Thanks, Pete. It sounds good, when you get a chance I would like to see a run of the manifest, my computer skills are limited to placing a film in the VCR and that is not always a success."

"OK let's break this up. I have a meeting with the General in 15 minutes. You had better come with me Pete; he got a message from his higher last night."

The staff stood as the Battalion Commander left the room and took their seats again.

"I'm going to make this short. Some of you start sweating as soon as the Old Man brings out his pad and starts going through his list. That to me indicates that some of you are not doing your homework. You'd better start going over some of your old projects, refresh your memories a little. When you are called on give an update on every one of your tasks finished or not before he has to ask you about them. Like I told you before it can be a slip of paper, give it to the S-1 or myself and we will put it in his evening update but get it in. If you have a problem, come and see me and I'll help you. I want these meetings to be briefings not excuse periods. If you don't like the SOP around here, remember there are a hundred officers waiting for one of you to trip up so they can get your job and that is always a possibility. Now let's get to work!"

"You're getting a little hard nosed, aren't you Pete?" It was Major Bradly the S-3 operation officer. He had followed me to my office.

"God damn it, Bob, I know most of them are busting their ass but the briefings are starting to sound like excuse sessions and I don't have to tell you that the old man is under a lot of pressure from Task Force. We have to do our jobs so that he will have the answers and not be surprised by those non-airborne "legs" up there."

"OK, OK, no speeches please" Major Bradly held up his hands. "By the way what's up with the General and Colonel Lawson this morning? It sounds important. I thought maybe rumor control had a copy of the message by now."

"Where is the S-2, Captain Ryder?"

"I saw him go into the S-1. I'll get him." Major Bradly left and quickly returned with Captain Ryder.

"What's up?" I said looking up from my desk. Captain Ryder hesitated a few seconds.

"This is really top stuff," said Captain Ryder. "And yet it may be nothing", he said glancing from Major Bradly to me.

"Cut the crap, just give me the basics so I can brief the old man on the way over to the General" I said curtly.

Captain Ryder closed the door to the office. "I just got this from my contact. It seems the Egyptians are conducting rather larger than normal exercises along the Suez Canal. Some say that all leaves have been cancelled for the past two weeks and an unusual number of Russian supply ships have been in and out of Port Said the past few weeks. There have also been more than the usual meetings between the Aligned Arab countries lately."

"What about Israel?" Major Bradly interrupted.

"I don't know what they are doing. I don't have anything on their reaction to this. I do know they have a big religious holiday coming up and they usually draw down their forces so that as many soldiers as possible can go home to celebrate."

Are you sure this is the message the General got?" I asked.

"Absolutely sir," said Captain Ryder with a smile on his face.

"OK. I've got to go. I'll see you later. I'll brief the old man on the way over.

I briefed LTC Hays on the message as we walked across the parade field which separated the two headquarters.

"Where the hell does Ryder come up with this stuff or shouldn't I ask?"

"He has a lot of friends in the intel community, some that not only owe him their careers but also their lives as well. He was with me in the Special Forces in Viet Nam for over five years. He received a direct commission from Sergeant E-6 to

1st Lieutenant at the personal direction of the Theatre Commander. Two of those five years he was detailed to the Agency on the Phoenix project and project Omega; knows everyone. Probably will never make any more rank than he has but he is happy as long as he stays in the intel game.

"Well keep a tight rein on him. He worked for a friend of mine once in Vietnam. He would disappear for days at the time and come back with enemy information that contradicted everything Saigon was putting out for that particular area, to include weapons which the VC and NVA was not suppose to have. My friend slipped once when asked by the Division Commander how come he was turning in more body counts and weapons than the other battalions in the Division combined. He told the Division Commander he disregarded all the information the Division Intel was putting out and relied entirely on his own intel officer. The division Commander almost fired him then and there."

LTC Hays paused to reflect a moment and said "What I'm saying is, don't throttle him back too much but make sure he stays within bounds."

"Will do, as a matter of fact he is scheduled to go up to Stuttgart next week for a EUCOM Conference. General Peters personally asked for Ryder to be included in the representatives we send. You approved it last week." I glanced at LTC Hayes.

"Yes, I remember; what the hell could I do, the EUCOM Commander asks for him, who am I to say no."

As they approached the Task Force Headquarters building with the massive grill work, two Italian Carabiniers snapped to attention and opened the gate for them.

"I get the feeling I'm being locked up every time I go through these gates" said LTC Hays casting a glance over his shoulders.

They walked up the wide marbled stairs to the second floor where the Task Force Headquarters was located. The building had been built originally as an officers' club for Mussolini's

Air Force officers back in the 1930s. The U.S. Air Force had appropriated it along with the airfield at the end of WWII and had only recently vacated it.

They walked into the Chief of Staff's office. LTC Hays threw his hat on an empty chair and addressed Chief of Staff Colonel Hazen who was seated behind his desk enjoying a cup of coffee. "The General asked us to come over. Any idea what's up?"

"Actually the G-3 will be with you in a few minutes. We got a message last night that he wants you to see. I also think he wants to talk to you about that incident at the officers' club last weekend."

"Look, I talked to my officers who were there. They got with the club manager and paid for the damages. They have all been restricted to the base for two weeks. You were there when I briefed the General. He seemed satisfied. Why has this flared again?"

"The G-3's wife, Mrs. Lawson happened to run into the Mrs. Burtrum at the base hospital yesterday. It seems Mrs. Burtrum still has quite a bit of pain where one of your young officers supposedly had bitten her. As a matter of fact the skin was broken and required two stitches. Mrs. Burtrum has not been able to sit or lie on her back since the incident, much to Colonel Burtrum's consternation." Colonel Hazen said with a twinkle in his eyes.

"I thought Lt. Duncan merely slapped her rear" said LTC Hays looking at me. Before anyone could say another word Colonel Lawson emerged from the General's office and gave the sign for us to follow him into his office.

"Sit down" said Colonel Lawson. Before I say anything, I want both of you to read these messages. Here is a copy for you Major Compton. Handing them the messages Colonel Lawson sat back and studied the two officers as they started reading. Puffing slowly on his cigar twirling it ever so slightly, he was satisfied with his choice in the two officers. LTC Hays had turned out a little meeker than he had expected but he was getting the job done and mission accomplishment was after all the most important thing. His officers liked him and morale was high. Yet there was something he couldn't put his finger on that he didn't care for in Hays' makeup. He had only realized it during the last few weeks prior to their move. Looking over at Major Compton his mind quickly changed to the positives. The finest Major he had ever run across. Had all the qualifications an officer should have aside from his top physical condition, he was aggressive, the most loyal officer he had ever met. Compton had been his Adjutant for 2 1/2 years. It had been Compton who had run the staff, made sound decisions but most of all was loyal. He knew Compton was the one who really ran the unit, the one who got down to the nuts and bolts of the entire operation; the one who carried out the unpleasant tasks, the bastard in the unit. LTC Hays played the good guy and Compton the bastard. That was it, he thought. This was the first time he had the chance to observe the two side by side undisturbed. That was it, LTC Hays didn't like to do things that were not popular. He wanted to be friends with everyone. Of course that was it. Compton did all the unpleasant things. He would file that in back of his mind.

The two officers in front of him finished reading the messages about the same time and looked over at him.

"Well, what do you think? Is it worth increasing our readiness posture or should we wait and see?" Having said this Colonel Lawson leaned back in his chair putting his hands behind his head, cigar still in his mouth. I knew him well enough to know he had already made up his mind on what course of action to take. His G-3 staff was probably writing directives at this very moment. He just hoped LTC Hays had read the Colonel correctly and would support the approved course.

"Well sir, the message doesn't say or even imply that we take any action regarding upgrading our readiness. It's strictly information for us not implementation," said LTC Hays.

"I have read the message Hays and understand it" said Colonel Lawson with a slight irritation in his voice.

LTC Hays sensed the irritation and knew what answer the Colonel wanted.

"What I was getting at, Sir, was that short of announcing a step up in our readiness posture, we just start going down our Standard Operating Procedures (SOP) and recheck all of our rigged air drop equipment and set up additional rigging lines in the hangers out by the airfield."

"Good, we are talking off the same sheet of music. Have everything ready in the event we need it. Might be a good idea to rehearse a couple of the contingency plans, war game them. You can use our new War Room, the new topo maps are finally mounted in place. What about you, Major Compton, any ideas on this?"

The Colonel leaned forward and relit his cigar as he spoke.

"The only recommendation I have is that we don't bring any extra aircraft. Keep them up at Aviano or Mindenhall, England. Even extra aircraft at Wiesbaden or Frankfurt will tip our hand especially the C-141s they are real attention getters."

"I see your point but we don't have much choice in that area; I'll talk to EUCOM about it this afternoon; anything else?" LTC Hays cleared his throat and asked about the Israelis. "Have they increased their readiness as a result of this buildup?"

"I just talked to General LeMay last night, he came by the house on his way back to Heidelberg, stayed over last night left early this morning. He informed me that the Israelis are down to 1/3 strength all along their lines. There is a big Jewish holiday coming up this weekend and commanders have been instructed to let as many soldiers go home as possible. They are a bit over confident I'm afraid. I guess after the last shellacking they gave the Arabs they have grown a little complacent. Enough of this work on the SOP. Keep the troops in close next week. Now that God damn incident at the club last weekend keeps haunting me. Aside from the damages which I know have been taken care of. It seems some of your young lieutenants got carried away in another direction. What I'm getting at is someone bit Mrs. Burtram in the ass. Now God Damn it, look into it and handle it. I want to know how this could happen at an officers' club with people all around. Mrs. Burtrum required stitches to close the wound. I want...."

"Sir, if I may speak frankly, Sir?"

"When the hell didn't you speak frankly, embarrassed me more than once, anyway go on."

"I checked into this for Colonel Hays. It was Mrs. Burtrum, whom we all know is quite young and at times take a fancy to the young officers especially after a few martinis."

"I don't want to hear any horseshit Compton, the General is pissed over this incident."

Sir, I have talked to the five couples at the table and they all tell the same story. Mrs. Burtrum was wearing black sheath low cut dress with nothing underneath. She kept pestering Lt. Duncan who at this time was feeling no pain and who was sitting in an overstuffed chair and asked Mrs. Burtrum to get off the arm of his chair and leave him alone. She had started teasing him by leaning over him displaying her charms. He told her once more to leave him alone and get off the arm of his chair, this time in a loud voice. Mrs. Burtrum told him in a huffy manner he could kiss her ass, she intended to sit there after all she was married to a Colonel and he was only a lieutenant. Lt. Duncan then leaned over and bit her hard enough on the ass to tear her dress. Mrs. Burtrum screamed and ran from the club with her derriere exposed. End of story sir."

"That dame has been a headache ever since Burtrum brought her over here and married her. You whisper in the lieutenant's ear Hays, if anything like that happens again, he will be up in Germany. Do we all understand?" Colonel Lawson signaled that the meeting was over.

They walked out of the building without saying a word. When they reached the parade field LTC Hays broke the silence.

"He is a strange nut. He wasn't as mad about the club incident as he appeared to be. He was probably echoing the general's words but then you know him better than I do."

"The Colonel married late or should I say when he was a Major. He has been an airborne soldier most of his career. I don't have to tell you that the airborne boys have ruled the senior promotion board these last fifteen years and Colonel Lawson will make General very soon, he is definitely one of the boys. He is at least 3-4 years ahead of his West Point class; has been with the troops just about all his career except for a stint at the Pentagon and the service schools. He understands the soldiers, was a hell raiser as a lieutenant and captain. He knows the troops think he is a bastard and too hard but he doesn't mind for he also knows that the troops know he will back them 100% should the occasion arise, in mass or on an individual basis."

"I agree he has his good points but I wish he was a little further away from our headquarters. It's difficult to command the unit with him peeking over your shoulder constantly. Getting back to the message situation, get the staff together and brief them, include the support company commander and the rigger platoon leader also. I want every effort placed on getting ready should the need arise. I want to be one step ahead of TF on this. I'm going out to observe training and will brief the other company commanders on what is going on. I have a feeling the shit is going to hit the fan this weekend. Oh, and cancel all leaves for the weekend no exceptions."

"Jesus I just remember I promised the family we'd take a trip up in the mountains Saturday and Sunday. Oh well, they are used to broken promises by now."

I briefed the staff on the situation.

"Today is Wednesday. I want a report on my desk by 1200 hours tomorrow giving me the status of the work I have outlined. I want additional rigging lines set up inside the empty hangers. That way we can rig additional equipment for air drop and store it inside. You have lights and power and it's easier than using the gantries. If you need additional help, get a detail from the line companies, per SOP."

"Sir, we are in good shape, bodies wise," said Lieutenant Lise the quartermaster rigger platoon leader. "I'll have everything completed tonight."

"Good, any questions? One more thing, S-1, put out to the entire unit that all leaves and passes are cancelled this weekend. There was silence around the conference table. Each officer weighing the impact the last statement was going to have on his personal life.

"Well shit" said Captain Ryder. "Just when I was getting used to sleeping with my wife again; when I tell her we are postponing our trip to Rome, I'll be back on the old couch again!"

"You're too old to cut it anyway" said Major Bradly, "a little rest may rejuvenate you."

"If there are no further questions let's get to work." Major Bradly stayed after the others had left.

"Aren't we pushing the panic button, Pete" Major Bradly said sitting down at the edge of the table. "After all we are doing nothing but second guessing a situation which may or may not happen. Even the Israelis are going home to celebrate whatever it is they are celebrating. We aren't going to get involved in anything other than maybe go in and rescue some Embassy people who might get caught in the middle. Why screw up everyone's weekend again. The troops have been busting their ass for the past month. The people in my section have been working seven days a week for the last month. They need a break, Pete, they are getting frayed. Do you realize we have a detail plan for thirty-two different contingencies which we could get called out on and that includes viewgraphs and slides for each mission?"

"Bob, I'm not going to argue the point with you, everyone is in the same boat."

There was a knock on the door and Captain Ryder walked in.

"Thought you might be interested in a piece of information

I just got from Heidelberg." Captain Ryder didn't wait for a response. "The Secretary of the Army, a Senator and the Army Chief of Staff, the US Ambassador to NATO and the 7th Army commander will arrive here Friday AM. Purpose of the visit is to inspect and be briefed on the unit's readiness, end of info." Captain Ryder looked from one Major to the other.

"Jesus what luck! We'll be ready for Jesus Christ himself by Friday. End of my argument Pete, I got work to do." Major Bradly departed.

"Ryder keep this under your hat until LTC Hays has been briefed and tell Bradly on your way back to your section.

The briefing and equipment demonstration for the Secretary of the Army, the NATO Ambassador and the 7th Army Commander went off without a hitch. The Secretary of the Army was particularly impressed with the caliber of the soldier and their professional knowledge. In his brief address to the unit he stressed professionalism and extolled them to carry out their responsibility as the US representatives to the NATO quick reaction force. He along with the 7th Army Commander officially sanctioned their wearing of the red European Airborne Beret as a symbol of an elite unit. Morale hit a new high!

As I watched the Secretary of Army and his parties plane depart someone tapped me on the shoulder. I turned around abruptly and looked into the eye of Colonel Lawson.

"I want you and Colonel Hays and your wives at my house tonight for cocktails. That and my treat at that famous restaurant, whatever its name is, downtown."

"I sure will try sir" I said looking at my watch anxiously.

"I'd better tell the Colonel and our wives, babysitters you know."

"I know but arrange it, I'll expect you around 1930 hours" Colonel Lawson said with a grin on his face. That way I'll have a chance to tell Nancy she is having guests for cocktails. The women get their dander up if we don't give them enough lead time."

"Yes sir, I know what you mean".

"Oh by the way that was a good show today. I have never seen a better one. I'm going to send Hays a note. See you this evening."

I saluted and took off for my own jeep, told the driver to head back to the headquarters. God I was glad it was over, everyone had busted their ass to make sure everything went right. Colonel Lawson was a strange guy, I thought as I rode back to headquarters. He knew damn well Colonel Hays would not be able to attend the cocktails and dinner tonight. He had a previous engagement that the General had asked him to attend as his personal representative. He would still have to call him and tell him what Colonel Lawson had said. I knew Colonel Lawson was not overly fond of Hays. It was a hell of a mess and I was caught in the middle.

The phone woke me from a sound sleep. I opened my eyes slowly. The phone kept ringing - why doesn't someone answer it, I thought, Betty or the kids. Then I remembered the wives tennis tournament it started today. There was no one home. The kids were probably in the pool by now. I got up and walked into the kitchen and picked up the phone.

"Major Compton, Sir" He didn't bother answering, he recognized Captain Ryder on the other end.

"Better get over to the TOC (Tactical Operation Center), there is a message Colonel Lawson wants you to read. I strongly recommend you hurry, sir."

I acknowledged and hung up. God I had a headache. Why I drank wine I would never know. It did me in every time, didn't bother me while I was drinking it. It was the next morning, it hit me. How the hell did Betty take it and play tennis but then she didn't drink very much for it to affect her. There was a message there I reluctantly admitted to myself. Captain Ryder met me at the door and buzzed me in.

"I have a cup of coffee for you, sir." Ryder said with a grin on his face.

I accepted the strong cup of caffeine without saying a word. "The message folder is on the briefing table" said Captain Ryder walking into the crypto section, leaving me to myself. The red folder looked unusually thick. Opening it I started to read, sipping absently from the cup as I turned to a new page. Well here it was the Egyptians had crossed the Suez Canal and were attacking an unprepared under strength Israeli force. It took me almost a half hour to digest the implications of the message. Captain Ryder had sat down across the table from me.

"Colonel Hays is on his way back with an ETA of about 1400 hrs. Colonel Lawson says not to implement an alert but to continue to get everything ready, he is at the handball court."

"Has Major Bradly read this?" I asked leaning back in my chair.

"Yes, he came by early this morning; you and Colonel Hays are the only ones who have not read it."

"OK, get the staff in at 1500 hours, by that time we should have a follow-up message from Heidelberg and Colonel Hays will be back by then.

"OK Major Compton, when Senator Clifton said to tell everything he didn't mean everything. This is the most boring story I have ever heard. At this rate we could be here a week, not only will I and my fellow senators here be pissed but our wives will probably divorce us. Get to the meat of this pack of shit and let's get it over with or we are walking out of here, do you understand Major Compton?" It was Senator Rose and he was pissed!

"I asked Pete to explain the unit and its inherent problems. What Pete will get into now is information he got from a military attaché at the White House and friends at the Pentagon. It's not hearsay, it's notes and recordings made available to him with the authorization from the Secretary of the Army. Go ahead, Pete, get to the meat of this situation."

"Thank you Senator Rose for getting me off the tangent I was on and back to reality, as you may realize I'm a little nervous to speak to such an august group. I'm a soldier not a politician with an agenda and up for re-election."

"What the hell is that suppose to mean? Are you saying we, my colleagues and I are not serious about this situation?" It was Senator Rose again.

"See, there I go again sticking my foot in my mouth. What I meant was in the service when giving a report you have certain guidelines to go by, in this case I was winging part of it both to show the units readiness and its inherent political problems which believe me are rampant in the military. From now on I will confine my report to actual happenings which I became privy to. I thank you again for your patience."

No alert was called when Colonel Hays had been briefed, we only continued getting ready. Task Force Headquarters alerted our resupply and storage facility in Livorno, Italy approximately an hour flight north of us on the west coast of Italy, they were given a list of supplies needed for an airdrop - top priority. They had also gotten a list from the Pentagon to have everything on pallets for Air Drop. They were not told where it was going.

The Chairman of The Joint Chief of Staff got a call from the White House to report to the Oval Office immediately. He knew what the subject would be having received numerous messages about the situation in the Middle East and had prepared to brief the President on his options. He hated to confront the State Department representative whom he disliked. He knew Sadat was in trouble however even though Sadat had gone with the Russians, he liked Sadat having met him several times, he was not only a good soldier but a great statesman as well. His 3rd Army was surrounded on the Israelis' side of the Suez Canal and was running out of supplies.

His senior aide, Colonel Hammond informed him that a Rep from the State Department, the Middle East desk, and members of the Security Council would also be present. The Admiral merely grunted his acknowledgement as they walked down the extensive corridors and headed out to the waiting car. As they drove into the White House gate and were flagged through, the Admiral tried to put a finger on why he disliked the State Department so much. They were escorted up to the Oval office. Everyone was already there except the Admiral and the President. When the Admiral walked in everyone greeted him. Colonel Hammond stood behind him. The President walked in and everyone stood up. The president took his seat and everyone followed.

"Well as most of you know the Jews have Sadat's forces on the run, after a week or so when the outcome looked dire. The problem is that Sadat's 3rd Army is on the Sinai side of the Suez Canal and is surrounded. They are running out of food, water and medicine, every time Sadat tries to send in a relief column the Israelis' shoot the shit out of them. The Russians are leaving as we speak either by air or by ship. I got a call from Sadat asking for help. I like Sadat and I told him I would try to help him - that is his 3rd Army with humanitarian help. He told me he would make airfields available to us and any support we need. I informed him I would get back to him later today."

"Excuse me, Mr. President, but surely you are not serious" said the State Department rep.

"Now don't get your head screwed up with logical thinking, if we can do Sadat a favor like this we will have him in our corner and the Russians will be out. Think of the influence we will have in the Middle East if we get Sadat aboard. Who knows, he and the Israelis might be convinced to come to the peace table. That would be a feather in the cap of the State Department."

"I strongly recommend that we not undertake this mission, Mr. President."

The President seemed to have made up his mind and turned his attention to the Admiral.

"Do we have any forces nearby that could be used here?"

"Yes sir, we have forces on standby 24/7 Mr. President. We have a thousand soldiers that could be there in hours."

"Are you saying we have alerted forces already without any coordination." the State Department Rep asked?"

"No, they are part of our rapid deployment contingent part of NATO's quick reaction force which you co-signed a year and a half ago. They are not aware of any contingency. We have not alerted them" the Admiral said in a calm voice.

We have a reaction force that can be there in hours - where is this force located?'

"Mr. President the force is located in Brindisi, Italy. One company of about 120 men can leave within about 3-4 hours, the rest of the force within 24 hours. It is a paratroop force with HALO (High Altitude Low Opening) capabilities. The main supply area - food, water and medical supplies are located at Livorno, Italy about one hour flight time to Brindisi."

"Admiral, you handle the location of the drop in conjunction with the Egyptian Generals - I'm sure we have some contacts and you with your boss (indicating the State Department rep) and you two get with the Israelis and tell them we are dropping some supplies to the 3rd Army and make sure everyone in the area gets the word; I don't want some trigger happy Jew shooting up our people who are going to secure the drop zone. Which brings up the questions how many troops do we send in?"

"I would recommend less than a company, Mr. President. If we drop too many in the Israelis might get the wrong idea."

"I agree Admiral but you and your staff do the numbers coordinating with the Israelis and the Egyptians. You work with the State Rep and when you are ready I'll call Sadat and give you the final go."

The President got up and indicated the meeting was over. Everyone rose and when the President had left took off for their respective offices leaving the Admiral and Colonel Hammond and the State Rep alone.

"I'll coordinate with the Israelis and the Egyptians to make sure we don't have any screw-up's" said the Secretary. "I'll call you when we are clear."

They departed the oval office and headed for their cars. It was easy to see the Secretary was still mad.

The Admiral and Colonel Hammond returned to the pentagon and called a meeting of the Chiefs of the Army, Air Force, Navy and Marines. He filled them in on the situation and asked if anyone had any recommendations.

The Air Force Chief was the first to speak up.

"If you, Sir" addressing the Joint Chief," will alert Livorno, I can have seven 141s at their airstrip in 3-4 hours. I just happen to have them up at Aviano, Italy about an hour away. In addition, I have 12 F-4-Es at Ramstein in Germany to give close air support should the need arise. I also know the Egyptian Chief of the Air Force. I'll coordinate with him for the use of one of his airfields and send support teams including ammo for the F-4s. I recommend we send the support teams in as soon as I talk to the Egyptian Chief of Staff. We also have transport planes at Aviano we can use for the support teams. As for dropping the airborne troops we have a couple of 141s at Wiesbaden in Germany, they can be at Brindisi in about 4 hours.

"That sounds good - go ahead and notify those crews to be on standby. Have the 141s fly to Livorno ASAP. Colonel Hammond alert Livorno immediately of what is needed and that they are about to get some 141s.

Colonel Hammond and the Air Force aide left the room together.

"What size force do we send in and where do we drop them?" was the Admiral's next question.

The Army Chief of Staff pressed a button and a detail map appeared on the wall of the conference room. He zeroed in on the 3rd Army area and it showed in detail the terrain and the ground. "I would suggest right here" a red arrow appeared on the map. "It's a slight depression but the ground is flat and easily accessible to the 3rd Army. The only thing that bothers me is the ridge to the North. Anyone up there could do serious damage to the men dropping in. Not that I don't trust the Israelis'

High Command but there is always that 10% that doesn't get the word or has communication problems."

"What about the size of the force?" asked the Admiral again.

Well, I would suggest an Air Force FAC (Forward Air Controller) would have the radio to both the C-141s and the F-4s should they get into trouble; the main force about 50 troops or less. They can smoke the Drop Zone (DZ). If they get in trouble a fellow on force is not advisable cause then it becomes a turkey shoot."

"I agree with the Army here" said the Marine Chief of Staff. "The smaller the force the better. A large force, which I know they have could spook the Israelis and it could be misconstrued."

"We have a carrier and support ships in the eastern Mediterranean. If we can be of help let me know: said the Naval Chief of Staff. "I'll move them towards the Suez with your permission, Admiral.

"I hate to overdo this, but go ahead and move the Carrier Force and coordinate with the Egyptians for use of their facilities. Move the support troops and all air assets as soon as you have talked to the Egyptians. This meeting is over, go to work and brief me as soon as the assets are in place."

The conference room emptied except for the Army Chiefs of Staff.

"What's bothering you, General" asked the Admiral.

"Well, it's nothing really, but I don't trust the State Department. They have screwed up more situations over the years then I care to remember. The Secretary is a bootlicker, he wants to be something. God knows what it is! He can't become President, he is foreign born, but that's what he wants or maybe a King. I just have this feeling in the pit of my stomach that he is going to screw this up somehow and then step in and save the day. I have nothing to hang my hat on but we have to double check with both the Israelis and the Egyptians. The 3rd Army has been without or low on rations and medical supplies for a week. They must be getting desperate."

"I agree Hal. Between you and me I don't trust the State Department. I'll call on a secure line over to the Agency and talk to my friend and see if he can't use his assets. I know he has a good relationship with both sides even though Sadat has been in the Russian camp for a while. I know the Israelis will listen and get the word out. God knows we gave them enough supplies these last weeks. Get the word to Brendisi as soon as you have determined the places and don't let anyone else pick the drop zone. You send the coordinates to Task force Headquarters over there; I know they have the new maps. Is anything else bothering you?"

"Yes, I would like all Israeli recon forces withdrawn at least 5 miles from the DZ. They are the trigger happy ones. I happen to know from our Special Forces liaison that they just had a meeting at their forward headquarters. One recon force was given 5 additional tanks to go with their half tracks which have quad 50 caliber MG on them. Their order is to put pressure on the 3rd Egyptian Army, in addition the word is they are having trouble with their new radios we sent them."

"Shit, Hal, when did you find this out?"

"Just before I walked into this meeting. I didn't want to say anything in from of the others."

"OK let me get to work. I have to call in some chips."

The admiral was alone in the conference room when Colonel Hammond walked in.

"I just talked to the G-3 at Brendisi, an old friend. He is on the same page as we are. He has 45 troops handpicked and is waiting for the FAC from Aviano - 46 troops in all. He needs one C-141 - maybe another as backup if something happens to one of the planes and would like them one hours prior to boarding. So they can top off their tanks. He has an intel officer in the unit that's going in and this guy is only a captain but with all types of resources, informed him that the Israeli forward forces are to shoot and I quote the shit out of any movement in the 3rd Army area. They have done an extensive map recon and have come up with a DZ that matches ours.

"Is this Colonel Lawson you talked to?"

"Yes sir, he is a soldier's soldier."

"I know him; he will receive his first star in two months. God I know the troops he is sending in are good - because he is a hard man. I think his wife has softened him a little around the edges but he is good. Tell him to stick with the DZ no matter who tells him different - even the President and that I agree with the manpower."

"Yes, Sir, I'll get him on the horn right away."

"The Air Force Chief of Staff walked in and informed the admiral that coordination has been made - an airfield has been designated and the support personnel are getting ready as we speak; should be in place, 4-6 hours. The F 4s are leaving Ramstein, heading for Aviano, Italy. Will be briefed at Aviano and upon the Go word will head to the designated air base in Egypt. They will be armed at Aviano, just in case something goes wrong - a KC 135 will be in the air over the Mediterranean for refueling."

"Have the instructions been given as to what they are to do in case the Israelis fire on our people?"

"Sir, that will be given at Aviano and there can only be one command, destroy the Israeli unit causing problems."

"Good - our careers might be over after this but if the Israelis attack our troops neutralize them with extreme prejudice."

Colonel Lawson, LTC Hays and Major Compton were in the briefing room when Captain Ryder knocked on the door and walked in closing the door behind him.

"Just received this from the State Department."

Colonel Lawson took the message and read it, passed it to LTC Hays who upon reading it gave it to Major Compton.

"What the hell is this crap?" Colonel Lawson said in a loud voice.

"We don't coordinate with the State Department and they don't give us DZ coordinates Ryder place these coordinates

40

on our map."

Captain Ryder took the message and scribbled the coordinates in grease pencil on the plastic covered map. Matching the coordinates with the map, he looked a second time at the location and shook his head.

"Sir, these coordinates have us dropping into a rock quarry, it will be a disaster, sir."

"God damn give me the secure phone Compton. I need to call a friend ASAP, you all stay here."

The call went through.

"Colonel Hammond please, no it's an emergency. Tell him Colonel Lawson is on the secure line. Hammond, Lawson here. I just received a message from the State Department giving me the coordinates for the DZ. No God damn it, I'm not kidding, it's a fucking rock quarry. You're in with the Old man now? Tell him I don't take orders from the State Department and if I show this to my General he'll go through the roof. I have the unit commander and Major Compton who will lead the unit in and smoke the DZ. What the hell is going on?"

"I'll wait your message, give my regards to your better half, she deserves someone better than you. I'll disregard your last statement - out."

Colonel Lawson looked around the room.

"Someone is trying to fuck this operation up and it's not the Pentagon."

Colonel Hammond briefed the Admiral on his phone call from Colonel Lawson. The Admiral rubbed his stubbly grey hair leaning back in his chair.

"Give the Air Force the go ahead to move all assets immediately and give me the word when they are in place."

The Admiral called the Secretary of Defense and asked him if he had five minutes.

"OK, I'll be right over."

The Admiral looked at Hammond and told him to stay in the office in case any more calls came in but to get the Air

Force going.

The Admiral walked into the Secretary of Defense's office and took a chair.

"What is the problem today? Are we going to war or is this an internal problem?"

The Admiral explained the situation in detail trying hard to keep his temper down.

"Why in God's name would the State Department get involved in military matters much less contact the unit involved? I am close to Moshe Dayan, the Defense Minister, let me give him a call." The Secretary of Defense pressed two buttons on his phone and waited.

"Sorry for the time difference Minister Dayan but I have a problem on my hands which requires the utmost diplomacy and discretion. I'm sure you have heard that we have received a request from Sadat to help resupply his 3rd Army with food, water and medical supplies. You haven't heard a word? Let me explain the Russians have left or are leaving Egypt. Sadat indicates that he is tired of business as usual and is ready to work with us. I see this as leading to peace between your two countries. Of course, this is between you and me. Our State Department has indicated that they were in touch with your people and that everything is set. What my concern is that your unit located around the 3rd Army does not open fire on our 46 paratroopers dropping in at the following coordinates. They are merely there to secure the drop zone and bring the resupplies in. Sadat has already alerted his troops i.e. 3rd Army or any missile batteries not to fire. In fact he has ordered his troops along the entire front to stand down. After all there is a truce in effect."

"Yes, I believe him. He has given our President his word. I'm also telling you this as a friend, that he has designed an airfield for a squadron of our fighters and support crews in case anything goes wrong on either side - yours or theirs. I'm telling you this to be upfront with you as a friend. Yes, I feel strongly that peace is in the offering, but if we get too many people involved in this humanitarian support, things could get ugly. If you agree to this please inform your Commanders of the situation. If you don't agree please let me know soonest. Thanks, Dayan, I'll await your call." The Secretary of Defense hung up and looked at the Admiral.

"It seems our esteemed State Department has not notified anyone in the Israeli chain of command of the situation and Dayan was less than happy about the situation in its entirety. Thank God we go way back, otherwise it could get sticky."

"The State Department had no intention of notifying the Israelis - at least not the ones who had the clout. We would have had a fiasco and then they would step in and rescue the situation and become the big man on campus. I don't trust them."

"Don't be too hard on them, Admiral, How far are we along on our deployment of men and planes?"

"Planes and support teams are in the air as we speak. When the President says go we are ready. If you would turn your wall map on I'll show you the airfield Sadat has given us and our drop zone." A detailed map appeared on the Secretary's wall and the Admiral pointed out the two sites.

"Any reservations?"

"The only thing that bothers me is the ridge above the drop zone. We know there is a reinforced recon unit in the vicinity with 5 tanks. It could be a turkey shoot if they don't get the word."

"I should be getting a call back from Dayan in a few hours. I'll keep you posted."

As the Admiral walked into his office, Colonel Hammond was pacing back and forth.

"What's the matter?"

"I just had a call from Colonel Lawson, they have received two additional messages from the State Department telling them to hold off any action until they hear from them. They will give the order to go or not to go. I'm getting a little frustrated. I haven't told anyone and Colonel Lawson is talking only to me."

"The Secretary called Dayan, an old friend, and he promised to get back to him in a few hours. I told the Secretary about my apprehension about the ridge and the recon unit in the vicinity. I also reiterated my feelings about our State Department, which I think he feels the same way about. I don't want to go to the President until I absolutely have to. We should be able to handle this amongst the staff. I'll give our Secretary of Defense a call and update."

The Secretary answered his phone.

"What's going on?"

"Two more messages from State to Brendisi telling them to hold off and that they will give the order to go."

"I'll call our Secretary of State and find out what the hell they are doing."

The phone went dead.

"This is the Secretary of Defense give me the Secretary of State - I need two minutes of his time."

"What can I do for you?" came the gravelly voice.

"I was under the impression that the President said for your section to coordinate with the Admiral. Our forces in Italy have received 4 messages from your office telling them not only where to jump but when. The Israelis have not heard anything from you and it's been almost 5 hours now. I'm about to go over and see the President on something else but I'll surely bring him up to date on this most unusual line of communication."

"I have been trying to get Dayan but evidently he is up at the front lines and cannot be reached."

"I just talked to him not 30 minutes ago and he was headed to their Prime Minister and Golda to brief them on the relief situation and its possible long range implications between the two countries."

"Leave the politics to me and go and play with your little tin soldiers."

The line went dead.

The Secretary of Defense was fuming. He called for his

military aide and told him they were heading to the White House now. He was escorted in to the Oval office.

"What can I do for you, George, you look flustered." The President sat back in his chair and played with his pen.

The Secretary of Defense briefed the President on what had transpired and the lack of communication between the State Department and the Israelis.

"Are you sure? If that son of a bitch is playing games again with his friends, I'll fire him. We are talking about American lives here. We have lost thousands in that stupid war in Viet Nam and are still losing them. That's all we need to do is lose some more young men in the Middle East and the demonstrators will probably burn down the White House. You handle this; I'll give Golda a call right away and explain to her what we are doing and its long range implications. When Golda was here a few days ago, she seemed receptive to new and future ideas on peace with Egypt, between you and me I think she is physically sick, there is definitely something wrong with her, the old spark is gone. As you well know, Congress is after my ass; the eastern establishment is riding the crest of the wave and is screaming impeachment. Well, we'll see about that, so I have a few things on my plate but I'll call Golda now. You handle the humanitarian relief; don't pay any attention to the Secretary of State.

The President indicated the meeting was over.

The Secretary of Defense returned to the Pentagon and called a meeting of the Secretaries of the various military branches and their Chiefs of Staff.

"I wanted all of you to be here and be brought up to date on our mission to rescue or help the 3rd Egyptian Army. The only progress that's been made as far as coordination with the Israelis and Egyptians is what we have done. The State Department is trying to muddy the waters, they have not contacted anyone regarding the 3rd Army. Where do we stand as far as our air assets?"

"The C-141s are being loaded at Livorno as we speak. The F-4s should be landing in Egypt in about two hours or less. The support troops are in place. The two C-141s at Aviano are fueled and ready for departure to Brendisi when we give them the word," said the Chief of Staff of the Air Force.

"Give them the GO for Brendisi."

The Air Force General's Aide left the room.

"One more thing" the Air Force chief of Staff lifted his hand.

"I have sent a complete crew for each of the F-4s to Egypt along with the support personnel. The French balked at our over flight of their country so the trip got longer. I wanted fresh crews in case we needed them."

"Good planning, if I live to be a hundred I'll never understand the French" said the Secretary of Defense.

"Army?"

"I have talked to the Air Force and we concur. We will fly at normal altitude and then drop to 400 feet for the troops, it will give them less exposure in the air and there will be no need for a reserve parachute and they will use M-C1 stretchable chutes to lessen the footprint on the ground. I talked to the G-3 Colonel Lawson and they are ready to go. A pallet of extra ammo will be dropped also - just in case. They are continuing to receive messages from the State Department and the Ambassador to Italy flew in and gave them hell for not notifying him. According to him he is in charge of all American assets in Italy. Colonel Lawson said he had the distinct impression that the Ambassador was aware of the mission, his departing words were that nothing was to move unless he gave the order."

"I will say this one last time and let there be no misunderstanding among you and pass the word to Lawson. Dayan will contact me, The President is speaking to Golda as we sit here. The President will call me to give the GO word and I'll tell you. Do not be distracted by anyone, I don't care who he is or his title. I have heard enough horseshit today to last me the rest of my life. Am I clear?"

There was a nodding of heads all around the table.

About an hour later Dayan called the Secretary of Defense and informed him that the word had gone out to all the units. There were some problems with some of the new radios but messengers were on the way to notify them and everyone should have the word within the hour.

"You realize of course if there is any shooting at our soldiers or planes they will be dealt with in an extreme manner?"

"I understand, that's why I have ordered commanders to send personnel to these units with radio problems so that we can avoid an unfortunate incident."

"Thanks Dayan. I appreciate your personal cooperation. I think we are on the verge of peace between you and Egypt."

"Shalom, my friend." The line went dead.

The Secretary of Defense sat there even with Dayan's assurance he had a feeling in the pit of his stomach that he had missed something. He pressed the button on his desk and his military aide came in. A One Star General with years of combat experience.

"Mike, brief me on these steerable parachutes the troops are going to use and why so low on altitude?"

"Sir, the chutes have two panels missing in the back, letting air spill out. The soldier has two toggle lines, one for each hand that he pulls on to steer his chute where he wants to land. It's a very effective way to drop in anywhere and the soldiers are well trained in its use. The low altitude is to get the soldiers on the ground faster and not exposing him so long in the air for someone take a shot at him. The normal altitude is 1200 to 1250 feet that leaves the soldier in the air a lot longer."

"Do all the airborne troops use these chutes?"

"No, only special units; the regular Airborne units have the T-10s which should have been done away with long ago."

"How low below the ridge will they exit the plane?"

"About a hundred feet above the ridge a little lower at the south end."

"All this time the C-141 is vulnerable to ground fire if it's flying parallel to the ride."

"Yes, sir, that is a concern since the recon unit in the area has quad 50 Caliber Machine guns; they could definitely bring down the C-141."

"Get me the Air Force Secretary and Chief of Staff in here and you join us.:

"Five minutes later they were sitting in the Secretary of Defense's office.

"I don't like the vulnerability of the troops and the C-141 dropping them. We have twelve F-4s ready to assist. Can we send in say 4 F-4s prior to the drop, I mean right prior to the drop and maybe wiggle their wings or whatever you call it to show the Israelis that we are friendly and not to fire?"

"There are two things we can do said the Air Force Chief of Staff. One - do a dirty pass right over the recon unit. It's dicey but our pilots are trained to do it. They come in fast on the deck lower their flaps and create a sand storm that will last long enough to get the C-141 out of the area and the troops on the ground. The other 8 F-4s will be stacked over head and if there is any firing after the sand storm clears they take the recon unit out. The second option is fly two F-4s in low do a waggle as you say and do a gentle turn over the troops while 10 F-4s are stacked and ready to attack. We call the first option a dirty pass."

"Do we do things like the dirty pass normally?"

"No, to be honest but the special forces love it and often request it. It gives them time to close with and take out the enemy."

"Do what you think works best; I just don't want any American soldiers hurt."

At the State Department, the Secretary of State for the Middle East desk made a call to an old friend who worked on Dayan's staff and informed him of the U.S. Plan to send in humanitarian help to the 3rd Egyptian Army. He informed the staff officer that he didn't think it was a good idea and wanted to know if the Israelis had units to intercept this aide. He was told that they had a reinforced recon unit that could handle it. The Secretary then briefed the officer on the U.S. plan. The officer was somewhat taken aback when told that a small contingent of U.S. Paratroopers would secure the drop zone. The Secretary gave him the coordinates where the drop zone would be.

"Just pin them down so they can't call in the planes that will drop the supplies" said the Secretary of State.

The Israeli officer was hesitant but told the Secretary of the Middle East desk he would personally send the message to the recon commander who he knew well.

At Brendisi, Major Compton went over the operation with all the men going in including the Air Force FAC who had just joined them. He emphasized that the points on the drop zone each of the five sections were to land. They had good communication in case one section needed help. He also informed them that there was an Israeli recon unit in the vicinity but that they had been told about the operation and would not interfere. The Egyptians were also cooperating and would upon the landing of the supplies send a convoy to pick them up. Upon the termination of the operation CH-53 Air Force Choppers would pick them up and take them to a U.S. occupied Air Base in Egypt and fly them back to Brendisi.

"As in any operation most of us have participated in, there is always Murphy's Law, What can go wrong will go wrong. I therefore want six extra machine guns, extra ammo will be dropped, and each man carries extra ammo in their rucksack. We should be in there approximately one day perhaps two depending on the Egyptians ability to get the supplies off the drop zone. We have Air Force support in case something goes wrong hence the FAC here. The drop zone is relatively smooth but should anyone sprain an ankle or something we have medics that will place ankle supports on you. The FAC will be in contact with the planes arriving from Livorno and myself and

Captain Ryder will smoke the DC in our sector which will signal the designated personnel in the four other sectors to throw their smoke grenades. Are there any questions, we should get the word any time now so grab your chutes. You may have noticed there are no reserve chutes. You will jump at 400 feet so get chuted up and attach your rucksacks on the plane in case you need to relieve yourselves. Again any questions? No one is confused? That's good, saddle up.

Colonel Lawson had been listening to Major Compton's briefing.

"Be sure you stay next to the FAC if there is any shooting. I just had a message from the Pentagon that F-4s will do a fly over and plenty more are on station should some Israelis not get the word. Don't hesitate to shoot back if the shit hits the fan. Brief the troops once in the plane. I did a detailed study of the map, there are some large boulders scattered along the drop zone below the ridge. It could give you cover if you need it. Good luck! Colonel Lawson slapped Major Compton's helmet as he walked to the back ramp of the C-141.

Chapter 2

Captain Hertzog of the 2nd Israeli recon force was halted and sitting atop of his half track eating his breakfast along with the rest of his troops. The tanks were dispersed and all of his vehicles had recently been refueled so he was good to go for the rest of the day. He hated Egyptians. This was the 3rd time he had been called up. Everyone who was able bodied in Israel was in the reserves. He missed his family, not to mention the business he had to run along with his father-in-law. They had just started construction their 3rd large motel along the ocean not far from Tel Aviv, where he should be instead of sitting out in this God forsaken stretch of desert.

His last briefing had been, if the Egyptians move shoot the shit out of them and keep harassing them. They had destroyed a relief column sent to resupply the 3rd Army. They had used up too much of their ammunition but they had enough, he knew the tanks were low. He had sent a message requesting re-supply but these new radios were not reliable and had not gotten a reply. In the distance he saw a cloud of dust, it was a vehicle heading towards them. When it got closer he looked through his binoculars and saw it was one of theirs. As the vehicle stopped by one of the distant tanks, it quickly picked up speed again to head quickly for Captain Herzog's halftrack. A sergeant got out of the vehicle lifted his goggles up and handed Captain Hertzog a plastic covered piece of paper. Captain Hertzog took the paper out and read it. What the hell was this, he read it twice. The Americans were coming to resupply the 3rd Army? It must be some mistake. The Americans were their friends and had supported them with planes, tanks and ammunition in each of their battles with the Arabs. This must be a mistake. A small force of American paratroopers were to secure a drop zone not a kilometer away from where he was sitting and transport planes would come in later and drop supplies to the 3rd Army humanitarian supplies it said. What was going on? It was signed by Dayan.

He started to ask the Sergeant some questions but realized this was only a messenger. He handed the paper back to the Sergeant but was told by the Sergeant to sign the message. The Sergeant handed him a pen. Hertzog reluctantly signed the message and handed it back to the Sergeant who got back in his vehicle and departed. They were not to interfere with the air drop. Why were they here? Why had he lost soldiers dead and wounded? He told his radio operator to try headquarters again, static was all they got. He was tempted to drive NE to a place he knew he could reach headquarters but that was a waste of fuel. He'd wait a few hours. His men needed to rest, they had been on the go all night. He had dozed off and was rubbing his eyes, looking at his watch he realized that he had slept almost 3 hours. His troops were still asleep except for the guards. He looked around; everything was quiet except to the NE. There was another cloud of dust. He grabbed his binoculars and looked, it was one of theirs. This time the vehicle did not stop at the tanks but headed for his tract. The same Sergeant got out lifted goggles and handed Captain Hertzog a plastic bag with a note in it. Captain Hertzog opened the bag and started reading the message. What the hell was going on? The message said to pin down the paratroopers, prevent casualties and not to fire on the transport that dropped them. It was signed by one of Dayan's staff officers. He looked at the Sergeant and asked for the pen. Captain Hertzog wrote a note on the back of the message, for headquarters to clarify the two messages and handed the paper and pen back to the Sergeant who replaced his goggles and took off. What was going on? How could he pin down the airborne troops without hurting them? These were Americans their best friends. He shot a green flare up, a signal for everyone to gather around his track. The rumble of the tanks could be heard as all units started gathering around him.

When all were assembled Captain Hertzog explained what was about to happen. He didn't mention the first message. His men looked at each other and some raised their hands. Was he telling them to fire on American paratroopers? And when were they arriving? Captain Hertzog explained that they were merely to pin them down and not to fire on the transport plane dropping them. Some of his men wanted to know where the drop zone was and how were they to pin them down with quad 50s? The Americans would fire back, then what? They are dropping a kilometer north of here and we will deploy on the ridge above the drop zone. One of his soldiers pointed out that a kilometer north was a stone quarry. They are not jumping in there. There is a flat area about 2 kilometers back there. You must have gotten the wrong coordinates. Captain Hertzog checked his map, the soldier was right. He told his men they would cover both places. They should be coming in about an hour from now. He divided his forces assigning a small section to the quarry the rest to the flat area. The Tankers wanted to know what their roll would be. Use your machine guns but not the main gun was his answer. They split up and headed north. They were barely in place when 2 U.S. F-4s came in low and waggled their wings and made a lazy turn to the West gaining altitude. A large C-141 dropped down to about 500 feet above the drop zone. They could see the pilots who waved at them.

Inside the C-141s, Major Compton had done his checks and the green light came on. He exited the plane and the rest of the men followed. Major Compton was in the air and looked around. Ryder was a little above him. He slipped the pins for the toggles and grabbed one in each hand. He steered for a rock outcropping below the ridge; he was on the ground. He collapsed his chute, Captain Ryder and the FAC landed fifty feet away from him. He looked around - the troops were on the ground in their respective places, collapsing their chutes and hitting the release mechanism on their chests. All of a sudden there was a roar of two F-4s above the ridge waggling their wings and doing a gentle curve gaining altitude over the drop zone and disappearing north. The pallet with extra ammo sat in the middle of the drop zone. The troops rushed to get the extra ammo and returned to their original positions. All of a sudden Captain Ryder grabbed his arm, blood was pooling in his upper arm. Major Compton grabbed him and yelled at the FAC to get under the rock outcropping. Heavy machine gun rounds were peppering the drop zone. Major Compton cut Captain Ryder's shirt arm open with his knife. The bullet had grazed Ryder's arm. He quickly bandaged the arm and asked Ryder if he was OK. He got the thumbs up sign. Bullets were now peppering the drop zone where the troops had no cover. Three of his sections were firing MG's at the top of the ridge. Major Compton saw several of his soldiers lying on the drop zone. He grabbed the FAC and told him to bring in the F-4s and eliminate the unit on the ridge. The FAC was on the radio and told the F-4s to come in and do their duty. Major Compton got on the units frequency and told his men to try to get to the boulders leading up to the ridge. Some of them made it but three more soldiers hit the ground. The medics were moving among them; one was hit but managed to get to one of the men.

Captain Hertzog was getting peppered with M-60 MG bullets from the paratroopers. He ordered his men to fire for effect. All of a sudden there was a roar over his head. Two of his tanks and one halftrack disappeared in flames. The roar kept coming; his unit further south was coming to his aide but was also hit. Where were these planes coming from, one of his tracks was firing at one of the planes but were soon engulfed in flames. Captain Hertzog jumped into a small gully, immediately his left leg went limp. His track had been hit and he had barely escaped. He crawled out of his gully and looked around. His entire recon unit was destroyed. Looking down at his left leg he saw a piece of metal sticking out he pulled it out and wound a bandage around his leg. This was a bad dream. He passed out.

Major Compton told the FAC to cancel the air drop and why. Even though there was no more firing coming from the ridge. He had injured and dead on his hands. He also told the FAC to contact the support airfield and get the choppers to their site. Captain Ryder was pale but OK. He walked to where the medics were working. One of the medics had a bandage around his thigh but was working on the wounded. It was the soldiers who had been on the far side of the field who were wounded and dead. Seven dead, 14 wounded said the medic as he looked up at Major Compton with tears in his eyes. Major Compton looked up to the ridge. There were soldiers moving around but appeared wounded. He asked the two medics who were not wounded if there was anything left for them to do. He was told all wounded had been treated. Major Compton looked up to the ridge again and told the two medics to gather all their supplies and follow him. They started climbing up to the ridge. As they approached a burning halftrack, a soldier pointed an automatic weapon at them,. There was a sharp order from somewhere and the soldier lowered his weapon. The one who had given the command was climbing out of a small gully hardly able to walk; one of his soldiers helped him.

"I'm Captain Hertzog" he said saluting Major Compton. Something very wrong has happened here today, I don't fully understand but maybe I was not meant to."

Major Compton asked if he had wounded that needed help.

Captain Hertzog looked around and pointed to his own soldiers working on his wounded. Major Compton told his medics to go and help. They had worked about an hour when they heard choppers in the distance. Major Compton got on his radio and told Ryder to send one of the choppers up to the ridge. Three choppers CH-53s landed in the drop zone area one lifted off and landed on the ridge amongst the carnage.

"Do you want me to take the wounded back with me or to your headquarters?" "I don't think you have fuel enough to take them to our headquarters?" Major Compton went over to the chopper and asked the pilot about his fuel situation.

"I have two external tanks; how far is this place to where you want me to go?" Major Compton turned to Captain Hertzog and asked him.

"About 30 kilometers NE they have a medical unit set up there."

"How many people are we talking about?" asked the pilot.

"About 32 wounded" answered Captain Hertzog. The dead will have to wait."

"Put them aboard and I'll come back and pick you up Major Compton." The chopper lowered the back access door and Captain Hertzog indicated to his still able troops to start loading the wounded. Captain Hertzog told his second in command that he would send vehicles back to pick up the dead and able soldiers in an hour or so. Captain Hertzog with the assistance of a soldier was the last man aboard the huge chopper. There was a dust storm as the chopper took off.

Major Compton walked around the smoldering tanks and half tracks he counted 34 dead. There were probably more inside the tanks. The second in command limped over to Major Compton and asked him what happened. Major Compton shook his head indicating he did not know.

Major Compton radioed Captain Ryder and asked for a final tally of dead and wounded. "Seven killed in action, 14 wounded - 15 if you included me," he said.

"Place as many as you can aboard the choppers and have one return. I sent the wounded Israelis back to their medical unit. He should return in an hour. Have the soldiers gather around that outcropping we used and have the FAC radio a sit-rep back to the support unit in Egypt. They should be able to get Task Force. Also have the F-4s rearm. I don't know what is going to happen here but it's a catastrophe. Better yet, have a couple of F-4s return here and circle the area, you never know."

"Roger," came the reply.

Major Compton sat down on a rock and one of his medics came over and wanted to know what had happened?

"I think its politics but that's between you and me. You guys did an outstanding job. I won't forget it nor will the Israelis.

They heard the chopper return. Major Compton tossed a green smoke grenade and the chopper settled down in a cloud of dust. The back door opened and Major Compton and the two medics walked aboard. Major Compton walked forward and told the pilot to land down below the ridge.

The pilot landed and shut down the chopper.

Major Compton and the two medics had just joined the rest of the soldiers by the outcropping when two F-4s screamed overhead. The FAC told them the situation and they gained altitude and circled overhead. They reported a truck convoy heading from the NE. Should they take them out? The FAC told them, no, they were friendly and coming to pick up the dead and the surviving Israelis.

"Roger," said one of the pilots. "We will just waggle our wings".

They heard a chopper coming. The chopper on the ground started up his engines.

Soon they were covered in sand swirling from the chopper landing. They split into two groups and boarded the choppers. A little over an hour they landed at the Egyptian Air Base. Major Compton was the first one out. He saw Colonel Lawson walking towards him. Major Compton saluted and asked about the dead and wounded.

"A C-141 is taking them to Ramstein Air Force base in Germany.

"Have their families been notified?"

"No one knows about this yet. I talked to the Army chief of Staff. He said to put a lid on it for now."

Major Compton looked into Colonel Lawson's eyes shook his head and walked over to where his men were gathering. It took all his will power to tell them this was a horrible mistake and not to say a word when they got back. They were still under the secrecy act which they had signed and it could have severe repercussions until the official version got out. This is being handled by the Chairman of the Joint Chief of Staff. His eyes filled with tears as he looked at the men and shook each one's hand. When he got to Captain Ryder he just looked at him and shook his head. He asked Ryder for the manifest and gave it to the medics and asked them to annotate by each man's name who was wounded and who was killed. They sat down on the tarmac and went down the list and handed it back to Major Compton who took it from them. He thanked the group for their professionalism and told them he had never worked with a finer group of soldiers. They all had their heads bowed.

Colonel Lawson came over and asked Major Compton to come with him. They headed for a small building and walked in. There was an Air Force One Star General there and the three of them sat down on chairs. Colonel Lawson introduced Major Compton to the General and then asked Major Compton to describe what happened.

Major Compton briefed the two officers on the entire operation. When he was through he looked at the Air Force General and told him that if it hadn't been for the F-4s no one would have survived.

"Where did you send my one chopper?" the General asked him.

"I got with the wounded Israeli Captain in charge and told

58

him to load the wounded up in the chopper and they would fly them to their headquarters' hospital and for him to send trucks back for the dead and the few men he had left. He said he would and gave the order to his Sergeant. The Captain also told me he was very confused because he had received a message by a courier to let the Americans land and set up an air drop of food and medicine for the 3rd Army; it was signed by Dayan. About two hours later he received another message signed by one of Dayan's staff officers to pin the Americans down but not to hit the aircraft that dropped them. He said he had tried the radios but could not get through. He had started his halftrack to the NE where he knew he could get radio communication to verify the confused messages but then the aircraft appeared and he turned and implemented the last message. He was confused as to why they were firing on their friends, the Americans, but the last message had been signed by a General. So he obeyed."

"What did the aftermath of the recon unit look like?" asked Colonel Lawson.

"The tanks and half tracks were completely destroyed. I'm sure there were more dead soldiers in the tanks but I had other priorities, sending their wounded back to their hospital was about all I could handle. I had my own troops to take care of."

"Was the Captain badly wounded?" asked Colonel Lawson.

"Yes, he was bleeding through his bandaged thigh. He required the help of one of his soldiers to get around."

"I have sent a message to our boss the South Com. Commander. The C-141s at Liverno are being unloaded. There will be no air drop. I'll fly back with you and your men as soon as the General here releases a C-141 for the trip. The Air Force has set up a field kitchen in one of the hangers. Have your men get a meal or drink."

Major Compton walked out and told his men if they were hungry to go over to the hanger. He had one of the medics check Captain Ryder's wound which was redressed. Well let's go over and get a cup of coffee or something. The Air Force makes real food so let's take advantage of it.

A C-141 arrived and was refueled. Colonel Lawson got the men together and told them to get aboard.

Major Compton walked over to the Air Force General saluted him and thanked him for his support and to pass it on to the F-4 pilots and the helicopter crews.

"Your men did an outstanding job today - I don't understand the whole situation but then maybe I'm not supposed to."

"I'll see you in Brendisi tomorrow," said the Air Force General.

Major Compton boarded the C-141 and they took off for home. No one spoke on the way back; some of the soldiers appeared to be sleeping but Major Compton knew better. They had lost some of their friends and tried to shut out the situation by closing their eyes.

Chapter 3

Their arrival at Brendisi was quiet; no one was there to greet them. Trucks were there to take them to the base. When they had disembarked Colonel Lawson asked them to keep quiet what had taken place. They would all meet tomorrow. LTC Hays showed up his face was white and he didn't know what to say other then "good job" and shook each of the soldiers' hands. The South Com Commander came and saluted the troops. He said he had talked to Ramstein and the wounded would return to duty. The ones who had sacrificed their lives would be returned to the states. The three who had families here - he, Colonel Lawson, LTC Hays and Major Compton would go and visit the families in a few minutes. Their families would be taken care of. The ones who were not married their families would be notified. It had been a tragic mistake by the Israelis and messages of condolences had been received from Golda Meir, Moshe Dayan and their foreign minister Abba Eban. The families in Brendisi would also have friends staying with them the next few days.

The Southern Command Commander and the designated representatives took off in jeeps and headed to the quarters of the first families to be notified. Major Compton rang the doorbell and a young woman with a child in her arms answered the door. When she saw who was standing on the stoop her face turned white! He told her there had been a tragic accident and that her husband had unfortunately not made it. He had been killed. The words did not seem to sink in at first.

She looked at Major Compton who was still dirty with a torn and blooded uniform, her eyes glazed over and tears were running down her cheeks. She tightened the grip on her young boy in her arms and asked them to come in.

"Where is Tom and what happened?" She was addressing Major Compton.

"Sue, Tom was killed by friendly fire; he did not suffer that I can assure you. His body is at the Air Force Hospital at Ramstein Air Force base in Germany. Is there anyone we can call and have them come over and stay with you?"

Sue was crying now, wiping her tears she looked at Major Compton and asked if he wanted her to clean and bandage his wound. She was an RN and had supplies.

Major Compton was taken aback. He hadn't realized he had been wounded and looked down at his left side.

"Yes, please, if you don't mind."

"Tom always spoke highly of you, it's the least I can do." She placed her son in his play pen and disappeared into another room.

Major Compton looked at the three other officers just raised his hands as if he didn't know what to do.

"Let her fix you up" Colonel Lawson said. Sue came in carrying a large metal 1st aid kit.

Don't worry Major Compton, I'm not going to operate on you, just take off your shirt and tee shirt." Major Compton did as he was told. Sitting there without his shirt made him feel vulnerable.

"It's not bad, I'll just clean it and check to see if any foreign material is in there." She swabbed the wound with Iodine and gently probed the wound.

"You were lucky it's just a graze. I'll fix it up. She applied more iodine - this time Major Compton felt the sting. Sue put on latex gloves and sutured the wound. She bandaged it and looked at him.

"I didn't know I was hit, thank you. Is there someone we can call who can come over and stay with you?"

"Thank you for letting me do that" she said trying to smile but tears were welling up in her eyes. She rearranged the kit and took it into the other room.

"I just needed something to do; I really don't know what to do now. The 1st Sergeant's wife Emily and I are close, she doesn't have any kids; if you would call her for me I would really appreciate it. Her number is in the book by the phone." Major Compton who was now dressed went over to the phone and called the number in the book. The phone was answered by Emily herself. Major Compton introduced himself and asked if she could come over to Sue and Tom's place.

"What's the matter?" were her first words.

"Come over and we'll explain."

"I'll be there in two minutes" the phone went dead.

Emily walked in and saw the people sitting there. She went over to Sue and placed her arms around her.

"Tom has been killed!" was all Sue managed to get out.

Emily looked around and asked what happened.

The General explained there had been a terrible accident and Tom had died.

"Who else?" Emily asked.

"There are several more dead," said the General.

"From my husband's company?" she asked.

"No," said Major Compton.

"We will give you the details tomorrow" said the General. "Can you stay with Sue tonight?"

"Of course I can. What should I tell my husband?"

"Tell him Sue needs you and you'll be home tomorrow,"

said LTC Hays.

Emily looked at him in a strange way. "I'll be here as long as Sue can put up with me."

The officers all rose - Colonel Lawson placed a card with a phone number on it. "If you need anything day or night call this number. Do you need groceries or food?"

"No, we are fine," said Sue taking the card off the table. "This is your home number Colonel Lawson, I recognize it."

"I said day or night, Sue, and I mean it."

They left and headed for the other two families.

"That was nice of you, Major Compton, to let her fix up your wound. It got her mind off her sorrow for a few minutes," said the General.

They met with the two other wives and this time LTC Hays took over the announcement to the two grieving wives.

"Let's go over to the club and have a drink," said the General as they left the last wife. "And talk over tomorrow's plan."

They sat down in comfortable chairs away from the few customers already there. The bartender came over and took their orders and returned with their drinks. The General paid.

"I talked to the Army Chief of Staff; the shit has hit the fan in the Secretary of Defense's office. They are in touch with the Israelis. They got a thank you notice from Golda Meir and Dayan for transporting their wounded to their headquarters' hospital and want to know the name of the officer who authorized it. It seems that Dayan sent a message to the recon unit by messenger and the commander, a Captain Hertzog, signed the message indicating he understood. However one of Dayan's staff officers sent a second message telling the recon unit to pin down the American paratroopers. He had no authorization to send this message and is now confined to quarters awaiting court martial. The Israelis, even though they suffered a devastating blow, will do everything they can for the dead Americans' families and the wounded. Our President is being briefed as we speak."

"I talked to the Ramstein General in charge. Thank God our

wounded will be able to return to duty. They are being treated. When asked what happened not one of them would talk and said it was a training accident. I will have my staff write up appropriate awards to everyone. It's the dead I worry about when they get back to the states and their families. I want you LTC Hays to be our representative. You will leave for the Pentagon tomorrow to report to the Army Chief of Staff. They will have representatives to notify the families and say the official words. You will visit the four families and stay for the funerals. Take your wife with you if you want. As of now, the Pentagon is formulating the official response. If you have any questions let me know. I will be in touch with the Army Chief of Staff."

"Sir, it will be my honor to do this and yes I would like to take my wife with me. Women seem to have a more sympathetic touch with words than we do."

"I want two meetings tomorrow one with the three widows and one with the wives of the wounded. How many of the wounded were married?"

"Sir, there are eight" said LTC Hays. "I want everything possible done for all of them. I have been authorized to fly them to Ramstein if they so desire. We also have a fund to take care of them and the widows, and the Army Chief of Staff will supplement it. I don't want any to be hindered for lack of funds. I'll brief them tomorrow."

"What about the troops that were not wounded, they deserve an explanation," said Major Compton.

"You're right," said the General. "I'll talk to them after the others; make sure they are available Major Compton. I know they are getting Israeli gold jump wings - everyone involved - what else I don't know."

Chapter 4

At the Pentagon there was a meeting with the Secretary of Defense. The Secretary was in a foul mood. All the services representatives were there.

"The first thing we have to do is keep a lid on this until I talk to the President. I have been briefed by the South Com Commander. The Israeli recon (who received two messages by carrier) the first one was from Dayan telling him to pull back and not bother the American paratroopers and the resupply. The Recon Commander signed the message indicating he understood. Dayan has the message. The recon Commander then got a second message about an hour or so later from one of Dayan's staff officers telling him to pin down the American paratroopers and prevent the resupply. That staff officer is now under arrest. It seems the American officer in charge, after he airlifted the dead and wounded American soldiers to the Egyptian Air Base where they were loaded aboard a C-141 and transferred to Ramstein Air Base in Germany, diverted one of our CH 53 Choppers to take the Israelis wounded to their headquarters hospital. Golda and Dayan both expressed appreciation and wanted to know the officer's name. Let's find out who he is, this is the type of officers we want."

"Sir, his name is Major Peter Compton, he is the Executive Officer of the battalion in Brendisi. He has a good record not only from Viet Nam but Colonel Lawson the G-3 at South Com. can't say enough about him."

"Let's make sure we follow his career and do the appropriate thing."

"Yes Sir, will do," said the Army Chief of Staff.

"Now what else do I need to know about this fiasco, I have the total dead and wounded, the ones with Families in Brendisi have all been taken care of and given a sponsor. The ones who are not married and whose parents are here in the States will be briefed by the Battalion Commander and his wife and a contingent from here. LTC Hays will arrive here this evening on a military flight carrying the bodies that will go to Walter Reed first. I want LTC Hays and wife put up in appropriate quarters, either military or hotel. I want LTC Hays and wife briefed when we have come up with the appropriate words, which I'm sure the White House is writing as we speak. The wounded I understand are not in serious condition and will return to duty at their request. When asked by the U.S. doctors what happened they all told them it was a training accident. Where in God's name do we get this caliber of soldiers from? Here we go again, it seems this Major Compton took extra ammo and 6 extra machine guns with him just in case and as a result kept the Israelis from killing and wounding more Americans. In the near future I want a low keyed meeting with this Major. Now where the hell did this second message originate? I hate to say what I'm thinking and I'm sure some of you have the same thoughts but until I talk to the President in an hour keep these thoughts to yourself. Air Force good job even though tragic;see that everyone involved are taken care of. Let's talk about compensation to the dead American families. I know there is a fund available but insufficient as far as I'm concerned.

Their children should have some kind of free pass regarding their schools and let's not forget housing. There were 3 dead with families, wives and children. The other four leave parents behind. I'll check with the Staff Judge Adjutant (SJA) to see what our limits are. I will also discuss with the president what he can authorize. Army takes care of Hays and his wife; they should be arriving at Andrews Air Force base. The Air Force will know when the plane touches down; it will be a low key arrival but with honor guards, transport is laid on Walter Reed is expecting them. Is there anything I have left out? I have a meeting with the President in one hour. OK, everyone on the same page? This meeting is over; be prepared to meet later this afternoon or early in the morning. No leaks to the media."

The Secretary of Defense was ushered into the oval office along with his General Aide. The President looked tired. He indicated or them to take a seat.

"What the hell happened? I have seven young dead soldiers on my hands and God knows how many wounded. Who dropped the ball on this?"

The Secretary of Defense briefed the president on the entire episode including the wounded and that they had claimed it was a training accident.

"Promote those soldiers when they return to duty. Your telling me that Dayan sent a message by courier to the recon Captain telling him to leave the Americans alone and let the Air lift take place and this Recon commander signed the message that he understood and then some son-of-a-bitch on his staff sent a second message telling this same recon commander to pin down the Americans and prevent the air drop of supplies?"

"Yes Sir, the recon Commander told our officer in charge he was confused but in the Israeli Army you obey your last command message."

"Had a call from Golda and she, of course, apologized but thanked us for sending their wounded in one of our helicopters to the headquarter hospital. They will all be OK but their losses were severe. Our Secretary of State is on his way to Egypt and then to Israel as we speak. The Egyptian and Israelis are to meet at marker 101, wherever that is. Hopefully some good will come of this."

The Secretary of Defense looked at his aide a little bit too long.

"What's going on?" the President wanted to know.

"Nothing we can prove but someone from the United States called Dayan's staff officer and told him to send that second message. Our Intel people are working to determine who called him."

"Shit, you're not suggesting what I think you're suggesting?"

"We have nothing yet. I'll let you know when we do." If I may, I want to discuss compensation to the families whose husband and sons were killed. We are checking with the SJA to determine our limits."

"We have latitude on an operation like this. I want the children taken care of through college. The widows will also be taken care of to include houses to raise their families. I want compensation to the parents of the unmarried and the appropriate awards to everyone involved.

Army & Air Force I'll leave the awards to you, Mr. Secretary. I want this kept low keyed - no media. I'm sure at some time this will leak out but it sounds like we sent in the right soldiers."

"Mr. President, are your people working up the appropriate words to the families?"

"Hell no, this place leaks like a sieve. If we did it the News Media would be camped on the White House lawn now. Come up with the appropriate words and I'll sign it. No one here knows a thing about this fiasco, not even my Chief of Staff and I want it kept that way. I will see to it that funds are made available either through government channels i.e. a training accident or I'll get private funds which might be the way to go. I'll keep in touch with you. I want this handled quickly. Those who want the burial in Arlington arrange it. Otherwise we will fly the bodies to whatever state they want them interned."

The President indicated the meeting was over. They rose as the president left the room.

The Secretary of Defense told his aide to call the Pentagon and have everyone in his conference room when they got back. The aide borrowed a phone and made the call. When the Secretary of Defense got back to his briefing room, all the Secretaries and the Chiefs of Staff were present. He briefed them on his meeting with the President. When he told them that the Secretary of State was on his way to Egypt and Israel, there were murmurs amongst the people around the conference table.

"That son-of-a-bitch!" It was the Army Chief of Staff.

"My sentiments exactly but let's wait until the Intel boys get back to us. The Egyptians and Israelis are meeting at Marker 101 negotiating a truce/peace proposal."

It could in spite of all this mess lead to a peace between Egypt and Israel according to the President. He wants us to come up with an appropriate message to the next of kin. He will sign it. We have some in the files. He is looking into compensation. He wants all members involved Air Force and Army to receive awards and the once wounded promoted; also education through college for the children and housing for the families. I think we are on the same page here. Condolences were received from Golda Meir and her cabinet. She wants the name of the officer in charge who sent their wounded to the hospital - some would not have made it were it not for him.

"We have made arrangements for LTC Hays and his wife and they will stay at a hotel and will be present for tomorrow's meeting. I and my aide will accompany them to deliver the news to the next of kin," said the Army Chief of Staff.

"One more thing the President emphasized. No leaks on this. That's why he wouldn't let any of his people get involved. "The White House leaks like a sieve" to quote him. Let's get to work on the details and we will meet tomorrow at 12:00 hours."

The Secretary of the Army and the Chief of Staff stayed along with the Chairman of the Joint Chiefs of Staff.

"We have discussed the situation and we have come to the conclusion that all this talk is dead in the water," said the Admiral. If we start pulling funds some bean counter is going to question the reason for this amount of money and why not the standard sum handed out to others who have been in similar situation. We need to do this fast and hide it under some contract overrun or a new weapon system."

"I agree, it could leak out that way if someone follows the trail. I have some discretionary funds; if I have to I'll clean it out. The wives will receive a sum each month for the rest of their lives. That's not a problem if it comes out of the Department of Defense. However, that is certainly not enough to live on, buy a house and educate the children. The President has promised funds either government or private but he is walking on egg shells right now so it could take time. Any large sum will be scrutinized by someone that's for sure. We can't let this leak out; we will all be sacked one way or another."

The Secretary of Defense turned to his aide and asked how much they had in their fund.

"Almost two million that you could use and no one would raise an eyebrow."

"Well, that's a start. They all have insurance that will help some which will go to their wives and parents for those not married. We need more than has been discovered so far. Let's get the finance section to expedite the money they have coming and then I'll kick in my funds to the three wives. I'll call over to Jim Tabot and stir him up. In fact, give him a call and get him over here." His aide went into the outer office and made the call.

"He'll be here in 5 minutes" said the aide. The Chief of Finance walked in and took a seat. He knew nothing about what had taken place.

"Jim we have a problem on our hands and we need your

help."

The Chief of Finance took out his wallet and placed $120 dollars on the table.

"That's all I've got; my wife and a couple of your wives are on a shopping trip today so this is all I have left."

There was a chuckle around the table.

"Put your money away, Jim, we need your cooperation not your personal money. Although, is my wife in that group? If she is, I just might borrow a few bucks. Actually we had a training accident and seven members were killed, three married with children. The Army has a list of their names, ID numbers. Is there any way we can expedite their pay and insurance plus the widow benefits?"

"Sure, I can have the paperwork and money in their bank accounts in two to three days. Was this an operational training accident or was it a case of a truck rolling over killing them, etc. If it was a rehearsal for an operation, they are entitled to a larger sum, say about $500 dollars more a month for the widows. You as Secretary of Defense would have to sign off on it."

That sounds good, Jim, get the list from the Army here and get it going ASAP and thanks for coming over."

The Army Chief of Staff gave the Finance officer the names and pertinent information and he departed the room.

The phone where the Secretary of Defense was sitting rang. He picked it up and listened to whoever was speaking. A frown appeared on his face.

"Thanks for the call and quick action." The Secretary of Defense hung up and looked around the table.

"That was the SJA. No funds, extra that can be authorized without the approval of Congress. It can be attached as a rider to a Defense appropriation bill but no funds can be handed out to any soldiers other than the normal benefits authorized. The President has the authority to hand out a onetime payment to the widows but even he is restricted in the amount. The children will be given preference to any of the Academies if they should so choose and a scholarship to other universities."

"I know some regulation would prevent us from doing what is right to those left behind. This operation came from the president, it was not covert operation from the Agency. Wait a minute, they were involved we have friends in high places at Langley and God knows they have funds." The Army Chief of Staff was fuming as he finished his tirade.

"I know how you feel Hal but let me explain. When we requested their help with the Egyptians and Israelis, George told me he would have to go directly to the Chief of Stations in those countries. It seems they have a mole or moles over there and he has requested help from the FBI. He has lost agents all over Eastern Europe and Russia. It's quite a mess and it's to be kept close hold. George wouldn't talk about it over the phone but came over to my house and we hashed it out exactly what he could do for us. I'm afraid if he pulls a large sum of money, someone else has to know about it and our circle gets larger. People talk even over there, either to impress their colleagues or pass it on to someone on the hill. I reiterate this has to be kept quiet. Let the news media find out about it and we probably won't get a penny for these good people. Let me work on it."

The meeting was adjourned.

LTC Hays and his wife arrived and were briefed and took off with the Army representatives to notify the next of kin. It was a taxing situation. Some of the parents couldn't understand how their son could be killed in a training accident. All of them requested that their son be buried locally. Arrangements were made to ship the caskets; an honor guard would be present when the funeral was to take place. It was to be sealed caskets and this in itself was difficult for the parents to understand.

LTC Hays and his wife headed back to Italy to be reunited with their family after the funerals.

True to his word, the Finance Chief of Staff had all insurance and money deposited in the individual bank accounts. All members of the battalion received automatic payments to a bank in the U.S. The days of the pay lines were history.

LTC Hays briefed the General, Colonel Lawson and the Chief of Staff and Major Compton on his briefing at the Pentagon and his travels.

"I'm not sure the widows will receive any extra living allowances except for the normal benefits. The children will get Academy or college educations. The President is adamant about keeping this secret or close hold. He is under a lot of pressure regarding the investigation going on in Congress. He promised funds but in order to get them he has to involve his White House people and he doesn't trust any of them. Even had the Secretary of Defense write the appropriate condolence messages to the people involved, didn't trust his staff. The only way to get money is for Congress to authorize it.

"Our widows are being packed up and want their husbands buried at Arlington. They are all headed home to their families for now but will require housing in the near future. I have talked to the Army chief of Staff and he has made arrangements for Arlington burials. The widows and their families will be flown in to Washington and put up at hotels. That part at least is taken care of. Is there anything else I have left out?" said the General looking around the table.

"From previous experience, which we all have witnessed, it's not now that the widows will suffer the most. It's a few weeks after they are on their own that it hits them that their husbands are not there. We need to keep in touch with them whenever they settle down and somehow organize a support group for them. I have a feeling most will settle near an Army base where they have commissary and hospital privileges. I'll tell you their husbands fought bravely and if this was a U.S. war zone they would get high medals for bravery. I personally think they are going to get screwed and get little help unless we do something. They can get VA benefits for housing but they have to pay the monthly mortgage which leaves them little money for living and don't think some shyster isn't going to find out about their insurance money they have received. It happens all the time! Once we know where they are planning on settling down we need to get them appointments with the SJA. I just don't like this whole setup. People are hiding behind their jobs both at the Pentagon and the White House. Don't tell me the President doesn't have money from his campaigns squirreled away somewhere or the Secretary of Defense doesn't have a slush fund. I for one will not rest until justice is done."

"Take it easy Pete" said Colonel Lawson. "We are all trying to make things right. Somehow those widows and kids will be taken care of."

"Major Compton, talk to the widows before they leave and make sure they contact us where they plan to settle and if they have any problems. Give them my phone number and as I told them before, they can call day or night. The Air Force is providing one of their upscale planes which are equivalent to a regular commercial plane to take them to their homes or relatives. I will also divvy up my funds into three envelops to be given to them upon their departure; it should keep them in good shape for a while. Is there anything else? I think we have covered everything and I don't disagree with you Major Compton, if nothing is done for them we can then formulate a plan. After all, we are the ones that sent them into harm's way."

The meeting broke up. Colonel Lawson, LTC Hays and Major Compton went into Colonel Lawson's office.

"I know what is going through your head Pete, don't act on it until all avenues are exhausted. That temper of yours needs to be kept under control. God knows I have warned you about it before. I feel sorry for you, Hays, to have him as an Executive officer; he probably drives you nuts the way he did me. Keep him under control and don't let him go out on a tangent."

"I personally like his attitude; he keeps the battalion in order and makes my job a lot easier, which I'm sure you have come to realize long ago. Not to change the subject, but I had a letter from one of the troops at Ramstein Hospital. They should all be released in a week or so. The Air Force is flying them back here."

"That is good news," said Colonel Lawson. "I know the General received a package from Dayan; he hasn't opened the inner package so we need to have a presentation. I assume they are Israeli gold parachute wings, what else I don't know. If there is nothing else, let's get back to work."

As LTC Hays and Major Compton walked back to the battalion headquarters, LTC Hays made a statement to no one in particular, almost like he was thinking out loud. "If I live to be a hundred, I'll never figure Colonel Lawson out. You are like a son to him Pete, he reads you like a book. You two are a lot alike."

"Are you saying I'm a bastard like him?" Pete said with a smile.

"No, but when you set your mind on something there is no changing it. By the way, I agree with you. I think we are going to get a lot of air and not much action. I have served in the Pentagon and I know the culture there. If anything does happen, it will be because of the Army Chief of Staff. He doesn't care who he has to take on. He has almost 40 years service and knows he will never get the Chairman of the Joint Chief of Staff slot. He has made a lot of enemies both at the Pentagon and in Congress. His problem is that he cares for the soldiers and their dependents. He was a one star General and a friend of the Senator from South Carolina who was Chairman of the Defense appropriation committee who together wrote the rider on to the Defense Bill back in the 60's where the Services got the same pay and raises as the Civil Service. No one thought about it until after the President had signed the bill and our pay almost tripled!"

"Well, I'm not optimistic about this but I'm not going to let it die. I picked those men and I will see to it that justice is done," said Major Compton.

"Oh, I have no doubt about that," said LTC Hays slapping

Pete on the shoulder.

The package from Israel contained gold parachute wings for all the soldiers who participated. There was also an amount of money for the ones that had been killed. Combining that with the Generals fund, it was growing but not nearly enough to sustain them for any length of time.

The President asked one of his trusted friends from the Senate if there was any chance to get some money out of Congress for a training accident which had taken place. The Senator was candid with the president and told him his days as President were numbered and he would get nothing out of Congress. He called his old friends in the private sector but was rebuffed by even those that had contributed generously to his election.

He reflected upon the Senator's words that his days were numbered. He told himself that he would not be impeached. He would resign before it came to that. He would make a deal with the Vice President who would do anything he was asked. Well he had tried; the Army or Pentagon would have to take care of the widows and their dependents.

The South Com. General got a backdoor message saying there would be no additional funds for the widows from the President.

Major Compton got some messages from his friends in the Pentagon who were aides to the Generals and Secretary of the Army' also from the President's military attaché. They were all negative when it came to funding the fallen families.

Chapter 5

It had been months now and no more funds were forthcoming. He kept thinking he was missing something. His wife was growing concerned because he was not talking about whatever was troubling him. One night he came home late from work and had a stack of papers with him.

"Would you type these up for me on that new IBM Selective typewriter I bought you?"

"Sure, I'll do anything you want me to do, let me read what you want me to type."

Pete handed his wife five hand written pages he had finally decided upon after days of agonizing over every word he had written. It had to be professional and close hold. He had not even discussed it with LTC Hays or Lawson who was now a one star General.

Pete's wife read the five pages and looked at him. "Are you sure you want to send this without clearing it with your bosses?"

Pete's wife was the former Army's Chief of Staff daughter and knew the chain of command and knew the unwritten regulations when it came to going over someone's head.

"It could cost you a promotion."

"I don't care about promotions. I have enough friends who will back me if it comes to that. Will you type it in its correct format; two copies. One to go to Senator Clifton and one for me to show to my bosses after it's sent."

"I'll do it right now. The kids are asleep. Is this what has been troubling you all these weeks?"

"Yes, I guess. I have been in contact with the widows. They have settled close to their relatives and are receiving support from them. They seem OK but I know they are not. I'm just surprised that they didn't settle around an Army or other service post where they have more privileges, although the SJA has made it easy for them to utilize private hospitals should they need them. Yes, I want that letter to go to Senator Clifton. He and I got along great when he was here. I'm the one that notified his family when his nephew was killed in Viet Nam. He was part of the 5th Special Forces, so we have a bond there."

"OK, I'll get right on it, it's a good thing I have learned to read your writing. Did you know your spelling is atrocious not to mention some of your sentence structure?"

"Yes, but I do have my good points too, don't I?"

"Don't start that now or your letter will never get done," she said with a smile.

She went into the den and Pete could hear her typing. God he had been lucky, she never questioned him about anything, where he had gone or about Viet Nam. He had never said much about it, only the funny things. He got a beer out of the refrigerator and sipped slowly from it.

He had been lucky, he had met her, after getting an ass chewing from the Army Chief of Staff after being brought back to the States to write up a summary of an action he was involved in on the wrong side of the border, where hundreds of North Viet Nam troops had been killed with only four Americans wounded including Pete. He could tell after reading the summary that the Chief of Staff's heart was not into the ass chewing but it had been loud. As he departed and was about to walk into the corridor of the Pentagon, a woman's voice had reminded him that his green beret was still on her desk. He had turned around and there sitting behind a shiny wooden desk was the most beautiful woman he had ever laid eyes on. He apologized and went to retrieve his beret when she informed him that her father was normally not that vocal and that she was just filling in for his regular secretary who was sick that day.

"You mean that is your father?"

"Yes, he is and if you plan on taking me to dinner tonight you'd better behave!"

Pete had been speechless. He looked at her and said "What time should I pick you up?"

"Oh, shall we say 1930 and I'll make the reservation and your uniform is the correct dress. I live with my parents having just graduated from college. It's over in the Generals row #3. Don't be late."

Pete had mumbled something but walked out the door.

"Your beret, Captain."

Blushing he went back to her desk and retrieved his beret.

He had rented a car and arrived at 1930 hours and knocked on the door of #3.

A gruff man in uniform answered the door and looked at Pete. "Didn't I make myself clear earlier today, Captain Compton, or do you want some more?"

"Sir, I am here".....he never finished the sentence.

Betty came down the stairs and said: "Dad, this is Captain Compton. We are going out to dinner." She kissed her father on the check and said "Let's go Pete."

There was a "Humpf" sound behind the door as Betty closed it.

They had a nice dinner and Betty was an easy person to talk to. Pete could tell she liked him, God he had been out with real prudes where you had to practically drag a response out of them. The conversation flowed and it was time to take her home. He parked in front of her house and she invited him in. He was hesitant and she could sense it.

"My Father is either in bed or in his study. My Mother is visiting her sister in Roanoke, Virginia. We can go into the kitchen and have a cup of coffee or sit in the living room and my Father is a pussycat."

"A cup of coffee sounds good," the pussycat was not something Pete was ready to swallow yet.

Betty fixed them coffee and they were sitting at the kitchen table sipping the hot coffee.

"Did you make enough for another cup?" her Father walked into the kitchen in his robe.

Pete stood up.

"Sit down, Pete, I don't know if Betty has told you but I am a human being." The General took a chair and sat down. Betty poured him a cup of coffee.

"So what have you two been up to? You probably went up to Rock Creek Park and parked and God knows what!"

"No Dad, we had a nice dinner and came right home. It was our first date, the second date I'll take him up to my bedroom and make passionate love."

Pete almost slid under the table. He didn't know where to look so he sipped on his coffee.

"You have to excuse my daughter, Pete; she is headstrong like her Mother. God knows she didn't get it from me."

"Sir, I would like to write Betty when I get back to Viet Nam, with your permission, of course."

"I can't stop you from writing to her but anyone who is in Special Forces can't be quite right in his head; don't get me wrong. I and I alone are one of the few who think we need more Special Forces in the years to come but Viet Nam has taken a great toll of your comrades, which I don't have to tell you."

"Yes Sir, that's true but I still would like to write her."

"Write her, she doesn't listen to me anyway, so what can I do. You two will probably get married anyway and you are not even a W.P."

"Dad, Pete hasn't asked me yet but after I take him up to my bedroom tomorrow night, he'll ask."

"God, what have I raised here? I have tried to teach her right from wrong but as you can see I have failed."

The General got up and left the kitchen scratching his head. He stuck his head back in and said: "That was a good operation Pete, but I have to send you back day after tomorrow. Good night and behave."

"See I told you, he is a good Dad and whether he believes it or not I have been a good girl even in college. Oh, I have dated a bunch of officers but most of them have been jerks. The nice ones only dated me because who my Father is."

"Are you working tomorrow or can I take you out somewhere?"

"No, I'm free, I only filled in today."

"Do you like to sail? I know someone down at the Naval Academy who has a nice 36 foot sloop who would let us use it."

"Are you asking me out again?"

"I'm not sure but I don't think I asked you out tonight?"

"Hmm, Pete Compton, I think you are going to be trouble."

"I hope so."

He stood up and thanked her for a nice evening. He headed for the door and Betty reminded him his beret was still on the chair.

"I guess I'm a little confused."

Betty smiled and walked him to the door.

"How does 0830 sound?"

"It sounds good. I'll make some sandwiches and bring a thermos of coffee."

Pete gave her a peck on the check but she grabbed him and kissed him softly on the lips. Pete looked at her and said his goodnight.

"He is a good soldier Betty and has a good record," said her Dad.

"I know he is and I'm going to marry him when he finishes his tour in Viet Nam. He doesn't know it but I'm going to be his wife."

"Take it easy and take your time. There are plenty of nice officers out there."

"You are not listening, Dad, you and Mom married after knowing each other for two weeks. You have been lucky Dad."

"Yes, but there was a war at that time."

"You don't call Viet Nam a war? How many thousand have we lost not to mention the wounded? Pete spent 1 1/2 years in Walter Reed after one of his tours. That young man is going to be your son-in-law, Dad. Get used to it. You like him and you know it."

They went sailing on Chesapeake Bay and had a good time.

"When you get back from Viet Nam Pete, we are getting married."

"I think you Dad might have something to say about that."

"He likes you, Pete, and he doesn't like very many people."

When they got back home, Betty put the bag which had contained their lunch in the kitchen.

"Let's go, Pete Compton." She grabbed him by the hand and led him upstairs to her bedroom. "My Dad is at Ft. Bragg for two days and won't be home for two days. He is picking up my Mother in Roanoke on the way home."

Betty started unbuttoning her blouse and soon was standing naked before him. She removed his clothes and looked at him.

"Well someone is happy to see me", she said with a laugh. She pulled the bed spread back and then went into the bathroom and came back with a thin plastic sheet and some towels and placed them over the bed sheets. Pete looked at her.

"Just trust me Pete."

She got into the bed and he followed. They kissed and touched and Betty indicated she was ready.

"Go gently in at first, this is my first time."

"Are you sure you want to do this?"

"Surer than anything in my life." Pete entered her gently and hit a wall and pushed through. She dug her nails into his back and then joined him in their lovemaking. When they were through she curled up against him and told him she loved him. There was blood on the towels under them.

"Let's do it again" said Betty. This time it was more satisfying for both. When he returned from Viet Nam they were married. Betty's Mother wanted to know what the hurry was but told Pete she was not opposed to the marriage. They had a week's honeymoon and two months later Betty announced that she was pregnant.

Betty walked in and handed him the letter. It was three pages long.

"Word perfect sentence structure correct and military format." She sat down next to him and took a sip of his now warm beer.

Pete read the letter. It was good and to the point. He knew the shit would hit the fan at headquarters but he had tried everything as had his boss. Betty handed him a stamped envelope with Senator Clifton's address and marked confidential. Betty folded the sheets and placed them in the envelope and sealed it. The second copy Pete held in his hand. That's going to cost you Major Compton!

Pete placed the envelope and extra copy in the den. He came back and grabbed Betty's hand and led her into their bedroom. When he got to work the next morning he got a larger envelope, addressed it and placed the envelope Betty had addressed inside it, used the official military stamp on it and placed it in the outgoing mail.

Pete took the extra copy and walked into LTC Hays office and placed the copy of the letter on his desk. LTC Hays picked up the copies and read them. He looked at Pete and said, "I was expecting something like this. Let's go over and see General Lawson. They walked across the parade field and headed up to the General's office. They found him in with the Chief of Staff.

General Lawson looked up and LTC Hays handed him the letter. General Lawson read it twice and handed it to the Chief of Staff who read it.

"Has this gone out yet?"

"Sir, it's in the outgoing mail at our headquarters," said Pete.

"Call over to the S-1 and have him retrieve it and have someone bring it over here immediately. I am heading to the Pentagon tomorrow, I'll personally hand carry it and see that it gets to Senator Clifton. After all he is a good friend of the family," said the Chief of Staff.

You realize that this will require you to take a trip to the hill and brief him on the entire matter. I could do it but you were there and I know he thinks highly of you."

"Thank you Sir, I know it sounds like I'm going over your heads but we have tried everything to no avail. I have a copy of the after action report in my safe. I know it by heart and can give a good briefing on it."

"I'll take this letter in and show it to the boss" said the Chief of Staff and got up and walked into the South Command Commander's office. After a while all of them were called into the General's office.

"Sit down, this is pretty serious. I hope we can back it up? I had a call from the Army Chief of Staff and he confirmed that the second message sent by Dayan's staff officer came from the State Department. The Secretary is shuttling back and forth between Cairo and Tel Aviv, Jerusalem. It looks like a permanent peace offering is in the works. Sadat is now in the United States' camp and the Secretary of State is probably going to receive the Nobel Peace prize. You got a tough row to hoe, Pete."

"So now you're here and what do you expect us to do?" asked Senator Rose with a frown on his face.

"Sir, I hope Congress can pass a bill or a rider and take care of the widows and their families. After all this was no ordinary mission, it came from the president who instructed the Secretary of State to coordinate with the Egyptians and the Israelis, which he didn't do. In fact he caused the death of seven Americans. He will probably get the Nobel Peace prize for not only killing Americans but also Israelis."

"That's a pretty strong statement coming from a Major who has an emotional attachment to this sordid affair. As for the Peace prize, the people in Oslo, Norway would have probably handed Hitler the peace prize had he won the war, a bunch of socialist near-do-wells!"

"We are getting off the track here gentlemen" said Senator Clifton. "Everything Major Compton has told us has been verified by the Secretary of Defense. It is an unusual request to be sure but it's been done before so we are not setting a precedent here. I suggest that we quietly contact our members in both houses that are on the Appropriation Committee and fast and get this taken care of. Major Compton, do you have anything to add?"

"No Sir, I know I have taken up a lot of your time when you should be home with your families and friends. I appreciate your tolerance and there will be no leaks from our soldiers who by the way know nothing about this. The members involved were given gold jump wings from the Israelis. We had a ceremony at our base. Not one soldier who was not part of this mission questioned why they were given these wings, which means a great deal to an airborne soldier.

They know that some of their comrades are gone but have not questioned it. They know their job as a quick reaction force is not without dangers and they accept it. I feel that should any of you have the occasion to visit our base in Italy, you will be proud of all of them. Again, I thank you for your time and for listening to me."

Major Compton got his papers together and placed them in his briefcase. He looked at Senator Clifton who nodded to him. He rose and left the room. Senator Clifton followed him to the outer office.

"It was a good presentation Pete. If the Army doesn't treat

you well, consider running for Congress."

They shook hands and Pete thanked him again.

As Pete headed down the hall the gentleman who had led him in followed him and let him out.

"Good day, Sir," he said in his southern drawl.

Pete headed down the stairs and was lucky to flag down a cab.

"To the Pentagon E wing please," said Pete in a tired voice. He had received a message last night to report to the Army Chief of Staff. He was not looking forward to the meeting but then he had been chewed out by another Army Chief of Staff some years ago and that had turned out fine.

He showed his ID card to the guards and asked how to get to the Army Chief of Staff's office. One of the guards said he would take him there. Why had he asked directions? He knew the way. He had a lot on his mind and having someone show him the way made the walk easier. As they approached the various flags outside the Secretary of Defense's office, a LTC stepped out and asked if he was Major Compton.

"Yes Sir, I'm here to see the Army Chief of Staff" said Pete.

"He is in with the Secretary of Defense. They want you in here," said the LTC.

Oh shit, thought Pete. This is it. They are probably drumming me out of the Army. As he walked into the outer office, he took his green overcoat off and hung it on a coat rack, removed his beret and laid it on a table. He looked into a mirror and straightened his tie.

The LTC knocked on the door and ushered Pete into a large office with four men sitting around the desk of the Secretary of Defense. Pete saluted and stood at attention. The Secretary of Defense told him to take a seat.

"So you are Major Compton," said the Secretary of Defense. He introduced the others in the room: Secretary of the Army; the Army Chief of Staff; the Aide to the Secretary of Defense, a one star General.

"We have heard a lot about you Major Compton. Most of it good but what right have you got to go over our heads to Senator Clifton's committee? Have you not heard of the chain of command? Or do you think we just sit around drinking coffee all day? I suppose I can't blame you being in the outfit you're in but we were eager young officers at one time who thought that people in the Pentagon had no idea what was happening in the real world. I want you to know that the higher you get in the defense ladder the more your hands are tied in most circumstances. The bureaucracy here in Washington is unbelievable. I could not have done what you did today without half of Washington knowing about it. I have a copy of your letter. It is well thought out in which you have explained that the chain of command has done everything in their power to help. It's the sentence that saved your bacon Major Compton."

The Secretary of the Army stood up along with the Chief of Staff of the Army.

The one star General also stood up and started reading a citation even the Secretary of Defense stood and the Chief of Staff of the Army pinned the Distinguished Service Cross on the left pocket of Pete's uniform. The General read another order and the Secretary of Defense and Secretary of Army removed the gold Major leaves and replaced them with silver leaves of a LTC. They all congratulated Pete who was starting to get a little light headed.

"All the troops received awards including the ones that didn't make it; except for you, LTC Compton, so it was decided that you should be decorated accordingly. Your foresight in taking not only extra ammo but also extra machine guns saved many American lives and for that we are grateful."

"Sir, do you mind if I sit down. I came in here expecting an ass chewing and probably getting booted out of the Army and this happens!"

"By all means sit down," said the Secretary of Defense. They all took their seats after congratulating him.

88

"First, I would like to thank you all for this but I'm not the one who did the majority of the fighting. There is a Captain Ryder who deserves this more than I do."

"You mean Major Ryder" said the Army Chief of Staff. "Things have happened in Italy the few days you have been away. However, according to the after action report and the attachment LTC Hays wrote, your action was nothing short of outstanding including sending the wounded Israelis to their headquarters' hospital. The Secretary of Defense has received glowing reports from both Golda Meir and Dayan even though their casualties were severe."

"Well, LTC Compton, there is a plane waiting for you at Andrews Air Force Base to take you back home. A car is waiting for you down stairs. It will wait for you while you pack at your hotel. Have a safe journey and say hello to the troops from all of us."

Pete shook hands with all of them. The Army Chief of Staff walked with Pete down to the car slapped him on the shoulders and told him if he needed anything to contact him. Pete saluted him and got into the car.

On the way to the hotel, Pete removed the award and placed it in the blue flat case it came in. He packed his few things and they were on their way to Andrews Air Force base. There were perhaps a dozen other soldiers already aboard when he arrived. An Air Force E-7 grabbed Pete's bag and placed it in a separate room. He then led Pete to the front of the plane and showed him his seat. The engines started and the door was closed. They were taxing for takeoff. Pete snapped the seat belt and leaned back in his seat. What a trip. He had not imagined that he would be received at the pentagon in such a manner. What would be his job when he returned to Italy? It could mean a transfer or some staff job at Task Force. They had been in Italy a year now, a hectic year at that. The Battalion was in good shape and they were starting to get replacements from the states. He had always gone down to the companies each morning to either run with them or just see them. One morning he had gone down to C Company. He always stood to the side while the company Commander took the report to show that all were present and accounted for. He had noticed a new young soldier in the 1st Platoon who looked like he had been in a fight. His face was cut and his one eye was black and blue. Pete had gone up to him and asked what had happened to him.

"I fell down the stairs, Sir," said the soldier.

"We don't have any stairs in our barracks," said Pete.

"I fell, Sir."

Pete let it go and asked the 1st Sergeant about him.

"His record is good but our troops found him smoking the wrong type of cigarette. At first he wouldn't listen but now he does. I must have overlooked that portion in my orientation when he reported in." The first Sergeant excused himself and disappeared in the door heading to the company headquarters.

Pete had discussed the situation with LTC Hays.

"I'll talk to the Company Commanders. It's good that the troops are taking care of these problems but I don't want it to go overboard. We need to make sure we cover the Italian laws and its consequences to the new replacements."

The plane stopped in the city of Milan where a few personnel got off and then preceded to Brendisi. It was still in the AM and the sun was shining. Pete was the last to leave the plane. As he got used to the bright sunlight he spotted Betty and what seemed to be half the battalion. General Lawson, LTC Hays, the Southern Command General were all there to greet him. Betty ran towards him and threw her arms around his neck and kissed him.

"Welcome home soldier" she said with tears in her eyes. She kissed him again and held him close. The others were circling around him. "Hey, it's our turn!" It was Ryder.

"If you try to kiss me, Ryder, I'll have you drummed out of the Army," said Pete with a smile on his face. They all shook his hand and congratulated him.

The Task Force/Southern Command General shook his hand. "I hear you met some high ranking people at the pentagon. I see they treated you right, LTC, two years ahead of your contemporaries, not bad, not bad at all."

Pete thanked him. General Lawson grabbed him and said, "If it had been up to me you would have been demoted or kicked out of the Army. Someone must have made a mistake. Oh well, it happens. Congratulation, Pete, you deserve it. This is going to cost you a promotion party."

"Maybe we can split the cost since you didn't have one." Pete smiled at the General.

"God, Betty, he is as insubordinate as ever. How do you put up with this guy?"

"Oh, he has his good points. I just struggle along."

"Everyone laughed and applauded him.

"There is a staff car to take you and Betty home. Meeting tomorrow morning at 0800 TF Headquarters" said LTC Hays slapping Pete on the back.

They didn't talk on the way home. Betty kept squeezing his hand. As they entered their house, Pete asked where the girls were.

"They are at Sue Hays' house until later tonight. Right now you are going to have to put up with me, soldier." She kissed him softly on the lips.

Pete placed his bag on the couch and opened it, took out the medal case and opened it.

"What do you think about this?" he looked at her. Betty took it out and held it.

"My God, no one knows about this around here or I would have heard about it."

"I was surprised; the Secretary of Defense placed it on me along with the Army Chief of Staff. I thought I was getting an ass chewing which usually happens to me when I go to the Pentagon or I get a wife, I don't know which is worst."

"Don't press your luck, Pete Compton, just because they

promoted and decorated you doesn't mean you run this house and I won't tolerate any insubordination. Come with me." She grabbed his hand and led him into their bedroom which contained a bottle of champagne in an ice bucket and two glasses. Betty undressed him, hanging up his uniform. Pete removed the rest of his clothes.

"Well, someone has missed me" she said looking at him and getting undressed.

"The champagne will have to wait. I have first priority, you know, I have never made love to an LTC."

Pete slapped her on her butt and pulled her onto the bed. It was 1730 and they were both exhausted.

"I need to call Sue and have her bring the girls home. They miss you an awful lot Pete. They are definitely Dad's girls. Go and take a shower and get into something comfortable. I showered while you slept."

It was nice to be home even though he had been gone only four days. The shower rejuvenated him. He had just gotten dressed when he heard a commotion in the living room. He walked out and the girls jumped at him. God, they were a good looking pair, two years apart. They hugged him and he kissed them. He noticed Sue and walked over and thanked her.

"I expect you to reciprocate in the near future" she said smiling.

"No problem" said Betty, "anytime."

"Help me bring the food in" Sue said to Betty. They brought in covered dishes and placed them on their dining room table. Sue gave Pete a kiss on the cheek and congratulated him and departed.

"This looks great!"

"Yes, we picked it up from the restaurant downtown," said the oldest girl now six years old. They had a nice dinner and the girls talked about what they had been up to the last few days.

Chapter 6

The 0800 meeting at Task Force headquarters brought some surprising news. General Lawson briefed everyone. He had talked to the aide to the Army Chief of Staff and he along with now LTC Compton was being transferred to the Ft. Bragg, North Carolina to the JFK Center for Special Warfare. They were both being assigned to a team that would accompany the Secretary of State to Paris to negotiate the peace in Viet Nam. Senator Clifton and his committee had promised to get the money for the widows one way or another but it would take about two months. This was good news. General Lawson and LTC Compton would leave for Fort Bragg in early January. LTC Hays would keep the battalion until General Lawson left in January and would then move to Task Force as the G-3 taking General Lawson's place. LTC Hayes was on the promotion list to full colonel which he had not known about and which made him happy. The results of the meeting was to be kept close hold until the Task Force General announced it in a few weeks. The Chief of Staff was on his way back and would arrive in two days.

After the meeting General Lawson motioned for LTC Hays

and Compton to follow him into his office. The three of them sat down and General Lawson buzzed his secretary for three coffees.

"You are going to find Hays, that you are getting a frustrating job. Basically 80% revolves around the battalion. It's going to take all your will power to not go over there and run it as you see fit. Having been the Battalion Commander "you" know the ins and outs of what is going on and you want to jump feet first into its operation. You have done an outstanding job and the battalion is probably the finest outfit in the Army. The Task Force General is being replaced, he is headed to Ft. Monroe to be in charge of Army training. I have heard that General Raton is being considered to replace him, which should make your job a little easier since you two know each other. The new battalion commander is a boot licker who I have been told will never make more rank than a Colonel if he is lucky. He has some friends but he has burnt some bridges behind him and I think this is his swan song. He is airborne qualified but has never been with an airborne unit. I'm telling you this Hays, not to degrade him, but to inform you so that you know what lays ahead of you. You Hays will become the bastard."

"I knew it would happen someday but not so soon. I was hoping that Pete here could take the battalion but I guess that was too much to hope for."

"Believe me you don't want Pete in that job. He will give you ulcers within weeks. Besides he was picked by the Secretary of Defense for this job he is getting and it won't be pleasant. We both have to leave our families at Ft. Bragg and that's not going to go over too well with Nancy or Betty. I know Pete has a nice home in Fayetteville at Cottenade right outside Ft. Bragg. I hope to buy a home there, also. I know Nancy is not going to be far away from Betty."

"I don't know what Pete and I are going to be doing at the JFK Center until we go to Paris but I hope it's something less stressful than here. Who knows, I might get to swing a golf club once in a while."

"That's all I know for now. I don't know who is replacing Pete as Executive officer. If you have someone in mind Hays start working on it. There is a Major coming in around February. I don't know anything about him. You might want to check with some of your friends in personnel in D.C. since you worked there but to save you a lot of grief make sure you put the right person in that slot. That's it, there is a lot to think over for both of you."

Pete went home and told Betty about the news. She said she was ready to go back to the States but could they spend Christmas at Cortina and ski? The girls were getting good at it having spent the last two winters in ski school for three months each winter chaperoned by her. Pete was a ski bum as was Betty, so they had decided that the girls were going to learn early in life like they had.

"I don't see why not. I'll talk to our Italian Liaison Officer. I know he and his family skis. Would you do me a favor and write or call our real estate agent in Fayetteville and tell him to make sure our house is in good order. The Air Force Colonel and his wife, our renters, are moving to Arizona or have moved at the end of November. I know they have taken care of it, but I don't like surprises nor do you. If painting is required have him get someone to paint it the way you want it."

"I'll do it tomorrow. I hope Nancy and General Lawson get a house close to ours. It's so peaceful and nice out there. I'm looking forward to being in our home again."

The Christmas was great! They had rented a condo apartment in the Dolomite Mountains at Cortina. The price was stiff but the skiing was great. The girls were starting to show off. They would both yell at Pete and Betty to ski faster because they thought they were skiing too slowly.

"I guess we are raising a couple of ski bums" said Betty out of breath.

"Yes, did you see how they handled the moguls? It looks

like their bones bend with each mogul. Ah, to be kids again!"

"You will always be a kid when it comes to skiing" said Betty laughing, "You're not saying they tire a Special Forces LTC out are you?"

"No, they don't tire me out but I hope we can take a trip out to Colorado before I'm off to Europe. We spent a lot of money on their new skis and boots not to mention their outfits. I'd hate to see them grow out of them before we ski again."

"You know my parents have a place in Vail. God knows... they have asked us to use the place enough. But I was either pregnant or you were gone."

"Oh God, Vail. I skied there when I was a Lieutenant. I almost died out there after ski hours. At least this time I'm married with kids so I have to behave myself."

"Oh! Is this a confession or a bachelor's bravado?"

"Neither. I was just horney which reminds me isn't it getting too dark for another run?"

"Do you have horns, Dad?" It was the almost 7 year old daughter.

"No, he doesn't have horns" said the 5 years old. "We would have noticed it with his hair so short."

"Your Dad has different kinds of horns which don't show" said their Mother flipping some snow at Pete.

"Let's go in and get warm and go to have our supper," said Pete.

"You have to be careful what you say Colonel. There are little ears that are getting big and before you know it you are going to have to explain certain things to your teenage daughters."

"Let's go and get something to eat. I'm starving!" said Pete and skied toward the condo.

Their two weeks at Cortina were great but it was time to start organizing things for the packers who were coming in a week's time. They had only bought a few pieces of furniture since their house furniture back at Ft. Bragg was in storage, so things went smooth.

Pete had called a couple of friends and neighbors and asked if they would get their things out of storage. When they arrived home everything was in place including beds made and food in the fridge.

"Oh, those wonderful people; we will have to throw a party," said Betty, when she saw her house. It was late and the five year old was asleep in Pete's arms as he walked towards her room with her. He placed her on her bed and Betty got her clothes off. The seven year old was dragging and was sent to lie down on her bed.

Pete brought their suitcases in and placed them in the spare bedroom. Betty came into the family room wearing a robe as Pete started a fire in the fireplace. He went into the pantry and found a bottle of cognac and poured two tumblers 1/3 full.

"I'll be right back."

When he reappeared, he was wearing a robe and sat down next to Betty. They toasted to being home again.

"Hmm this hits the spot," said Betty taking another sip.

Pete looked at Betty's robe which had opened at the top.

"Why you hussy," he said pulling her robe apart and started kissing her.

"I was wondering how long it would take you to notice. I'm naked underneath."

"It's great to be home soldier. Let's go to bed."

General Lawson bought a house less than a block away. Nancy and Betty went on a buying spree to furnish the new home.

The kids were in school and Nancy and Betty played golf and tennis. Ft. Bragg had all the facilities and the weather was good.

Chapter 7

General Lawson and Pete got their orders for Paris. They were to report to the American Embassy.

Their suitcases packed, they headed for Paris. There was no indication as to how long they would be there.

They arrived and reported in. A Member of the Embassy staff took them to a hotel about a half a block away. Their rooms were adequate nothing fancy. They were to report to the Embassy the next morning in civilian clothes at 0900 hours. They unpacked and decided to get some rest.

Pete woke up at 6 PM and was hungry. He got dressed and knocked gently at General's door, no answer. He walked down stairs and asked about a restaurant. The woman behind the desk explained that it was a little early for a good restaurant to be serving but recommended a bistro around the corner. Pete found the bistro and General Lawson having a meal. He was asked to take a seat at his table.

"You would think these people spoke English with all the Embassies around here," the General was not in a good mood. A waiter brought Pete a menu and he ordered a meal in French and a cup of coffee. General Lawson looked at him and shook his head.

"I guess I should have known you'd speak the lingo, where did you learn?"

"High school, college and Ft. Bragg," Pete replied with a smile.

"Why French, you're Norwegian; I know you were born over there."

"When we did our area study at Ft. Bragg prior to deployment to Viet Nam, the Montagnard tribe we were assigned to had only 1100 words in their language and no written language except for a few words; but some of them spoke French as did many Vietnamese, so I took a refresher course in French."

Pete's meal arrived and it was good. General Lawson ordered a cup of coffee and waited for Pete to finish his meal.

They arrived at the Embassy and were shown into a conference room. They were briefed on the procedures along with about seven other people. The Secretary of State was the spokesman and negotiator. The other people were from the State Department. The negotiations got off to a rocky start. The South Vietnam delegation would not go along with some of the demands from the North Vietnamese. The South Vietnamese wanted a neutral Cambodia without any North Vietnamese in that country which they had been using as a sanctuary. The North Vietnamese wanted South Vietnam to pull back from the 17th parallel and make that a buffer zone.

In one of the sessions, the Americans still missing were brought up. The North Vietnamese denied they had American prisoners. As for the missing in action they admitted there could be Americans who had been killed, i.e. in air planes shot down and were hidden in the jungle and mountains in North Vietnam. But as far as prisoners, they had been returned.

One day after leaving an unfruitful session regarding MIA's from both North Vietnam and U.S., Pete was walking down the hall to the bathroom. As he opened the door to the bathroom, a person behind him came in and slipped a piece of paper in Pete's jacket pocket. The person was a North Vietnamese who shook his head when Pete went to reach in his pocket.

"Read later," was all he said and went into one of the stalls.

As Pete and General Lawson went to get something to eat before their evening sessions with the other U.S. Representative s, Pete took the paper from his pocket and read it. He handed the note to General Lawson who read the short note twice.

"The North Vietnamese sent over 1500 U.S. prisoners to Laos? Where did you get this?"

Pete explained.

"How do we handle this? The Laotians are not willing participants and have sent only a few observers who haven't even been formally recognized. They want nothing to do with these negotiations. The Communist's will end up controlling Laos. We need to give this info with an explanation to the Secretary of State's "second man tonight".

"That's what I was thinking. Pete replied," I just hope he gives it to the Secretary of State. These negotiations are dragging on and people are getting tired and frayed. I know the Secretary of State wants to come up with some sort of peace deal even if the South Vietnamese are not happy with it. I heard he is meeting with the head negotiator from North Vietnam, Politburo Member, Le Duc Tho, although from what I understand they are not making much headway. The North Vietnamese are not happy with the U.S. refusal to help restore North Vietnam with all the damage that the bombing raids have done. They want compensation in the billions of dollars."

"Where are you getting this from Pete? I have heard nothing about his and now this note?"

"I listen to the lower echelon North Vietnamese talking. I understand a little Vietnamese although the North Vietnamese or should I say some have a little different dialect, than the South Vietnamese. A few are giving me a little gossip. I sort through the bullshit and try to determine what is real and what is bull.

Some of these South Vietnamese want to come to the U.S. and live. They see the handwriting on the wall."

"Be careful. However this note is a bombshell and could set this negotiation back years if the politicians in Washington and the President choose to press it. I wish I had access to a secure phone. I know I can't use our Embassy communication?"

"May I ask who you are trying to get in touch with?"

"Yes, I only trust one and that's Colonel Hammond. I talked to him before we left the States."

"I might know someone at the Canadian Embassy. Let me go over right now and see what I can do."

"Be careful, Pete, this could blow back in our faces if we handle it the wrong way."

Pete went to the Canadian Embassy and asked if Colonel York was available. The guard looked at him. Pete showed his military I.D. and the guard had Pete ushered into the building where another military, a captain, sat behind a desk. Pete asked for Colonel York. Pete showed him his I.D. and explained that they were old friends. The Captain behind the desk lifted his phone and pressed a button. He explained that LTC Compton was in the lobby and requested to see Colonel York. Pete stood there and looked around. The Embassy building was a lot better appointed than their own Embassy. An elevator opened and Colonel York came out of it with an extended arm.

"Good to see you, Peter. I saw in our memo that you were in town. I have been wanting to get in touch but I know it's dicey for you over there."

"Not so dicey that two old friends can't have a talk." Pete shook his hand.

"Let's go up to my office."

The elevator took them up to the third floor. Colonel York preceded him down the hall to a half opened door. There was a woman secretary sitting behind a desk.

"I don't want to be disturbed." Colonel York informed her, as he opened the door to his office. He ushered Pete in and told him to sit down and joined him across a small table.

"What have you been up to since our school days at that wonderful institution at Ft. Leavenworth, Kansas? Or shouldn't I ask? I know you had a problem with the Israelis."

Pete was taken aback. He tried to smile but didn't think he was successful at it.

"I'm afraid I don't follow you?"

"This section is the equivalent to your Cultural Affairs Section in your embassy so very little happens to our neighbor to the South that we don't know about."

"Well, it was a fiasco with yours truly in charge but it was a case of lack of communication. Or, should I say counter communication by a certain person in our State Department who has his sights set on bigger and better things. All is well now except for a few minor details."

"Politics are the same all over, Peter, but we soldiers have to clean up their messes one way or another."

"How are Pam and the family?"

"Fine, thank you, and I hope Betty and the girls are happy and in good health."

"Yes, thanks, not happy about being left alone back at Fort Bragg but that's the life of an Army wife.

"Ok. You didn't come over here to say hello and chit chat. What can I do for you, Peter?"

"We, and a comrade of mine, have a serious problem that has developed as a result of our quote "Peace Negotiations" and I need some help. My comrade is General Lawson, a good friend. We need a secure line to the Pentagon and can't use our own Embassy communications."

"How serious is this problem?"

"Extremely."

Colonel York looked at Pete for a moment and went to his desk and picked up a pad of paper writing down something and handed it to Pete.

"Come to this address tonight with your friend and you'll

have a secure line."

"There is a time difference so give me a time when we can reach a certain person."

"How about 1800 hours? That will give you time to make a call and make sure that person is in his office."

"Thanks. I appreciate this and I won't forget."

Pete stood up shook hands with Colonel York who escorted him downstairs.

When Pete got back to his hotel he knocked on General Lawson's door. The door opened immediately.

"Come in."

Pete, brief General Lawson on what had happened.

"General Lawson picked up his phone and told the hotel operator he wished to make a long distance call to the United States. He gave the number and in a few seconds he had his wife, Nancy, on the phone. He made pleasant comments.

"I want you to call my best friend and classmate and tell him to be in his bosses office at 1800 hours our time over here. I will call you back in 1/2 hour to confirm. Tell him Oxbow, yes Oxbow."

Hanging up he looked at Pete. "I hope Hammond is in. I don't trust anyone else. Let's have a beer." He went to the small refrigerator and got two cans of Heinekens.

"I don't know what Hammond can do other than to tell his boss."

"Well, they can start sending a blackbird over Laos. It shouldn't take long to pick something up."

"Yes, I suppose that's one way to verify this message. It's time to call again. He called Nancy and was told that his friend would be waiting for him. She also had someone who wanted to talk to Pete. General Lawson handed the phone to Pete. It was Betty.

"I miss you Pete. How are things going?"

"Oh, I miss you too. Things are going just wonderful, just wonderful. Give the girls a hug from me. I have to go. Love you." Pete handed the phone to General Lawson. He made small talk with Nancy and hung up.

"Well, we are set. We have 45 minutes to get to that address. Let's go."

Back at Ft. Bragg, Nancy looked at Betty.

"What's wrong?"

"Pete and I have this code word, when something is wrong. He used it twice which means something is really wrong."

"Let's have a glass of wine and hope for the best," said Nancy.

They arrived at the address Colonel York had given Pete. A guard asked for identification. He then let them into a courtyard and opened a door for them. Colonel York was there to greet them.

"Welcome to my home away from home."

Pete introduced General Lawson to Colonel York, who took them into an almost barren room with a desk and four chairs. On the desk were two phones, one red and the other blue.

"The blue phone is at your disposal, General Lawson. You can dial direct to Washington D.C. I'll leave you alone. Oh, press the #2 button and dial your number." Colonel York departed the room.

General Lawson took out his small book and sat down in the desk chair and dialed the number. He waited a few seconds and started talking to Colonel Hammond. Colonel Hammond informed General Lawson his boss was listening in on the call.

General Lawson briefed them on the situation.

"Yes, I'm one hundred percent sure it's true. No, I have not briefed anyone else on this. The Laotians want nothing to do with these talks and no one else knows about it. I don't know what you can do with this but then that's why you people get the big bucks. I don't know what I can do with this information. I'm calling on a secure line courtesy of our neighbors to the North. I couldn't use our own Embassy - too many ears and questions. If you want me to give this information to our glorious leader here, let me know. You can use our own Embassy for a yes or no answer to me personally. In the mean time I'll keep this close, unless you have an answer now."

"I got this from my partner whom you know and recently decorated. He feels the same as I do. If we do the math, the numbers correspond close to what we are looking for."

"OK, I'll keep it close for now. Have a good day."

General Lawson hung up and looked at Pete.

Colonel Hammond looked at the Chairman of the Joint Chief of Staff.

"I don't think our Secretary of State has this information or even if he did he would ignore it in order to speed up this treaty with the North Vietnamese."

The Chairman leaned back in his chair and stared at his fingers.

"When I went through Ranger school in the 50's we learned "leave no man behind". Here we are talking about over 1500 U.S. Prisoners of War. What as a nation are we coming to? The President won't lift a finger that we know. He needs this Treaty badly. We don't want this to leak. We need to get the Agency to start flying their bird over Laos as soon as this treaty is signed which I think will be soon. We will give away a lot and screw South Vietnam!"

"The CIA Chief is in with the Secretary of Defense. Let's see if we can grab him and bend his ear for a few minutes." The Chairman of the Joint Chiefs of Staff pushed a button on his phone and asked them to give a note to the CIA Chief and have him stop by his office. In less than five minutes there was a knock on the door.

Colonel Hammond opened it and let the CIA Chief in.

"Got your note. What can I do for you?"

"We have a situation and we need your help."

"This is not my day, the Secretary of State is giving the store away over in Paris and according to the Secretary of Defense, the President won't lift a finger as long as we get a peace treaty.

The Chairman of the Joint Chiefs of Staff briefed the CIA Director on the latest intel.

"We know that the North Vietnam were sending some prisoners of war to Laos but we didn't know how many. Where did you get this information or shouldn't I ask?"

"It comes from a very reliable source. We just got it about an hour ago. Can you use one of your Blackbirds to start making runs over Laos? I know you have that new system that can just about pick up an ant pissing."

"You know we are not supposed to be doing anything to upset the peace process and the withdrawal of U.S. troops from Vietnam. You know and I know that there will be no peace until North Vietnam has conquered the south and it will happen. It's a civil war for Christ sake. We had our civil war. The domino effect will not happen. If it does, it will not last. Will there be bloodletting, you bet, but Vietnam has too many resources and will someday become an economic factor. Well this little speech will give you two credit hours in international relations should you choose to go back to school. What can we do? Yes, I can authorize some flyovers but it has to be a silk purse operation. It can't be advertised in my section. I have a man on station that can put it in motion and if anyone finds out about it "we are doing it to make sure the North Vietnam are complying with the ongoing peace treaty." We will start unobtrusively and go from there. Was there anything else?"

The CIA Chief departed.

"You know what we need to do Hammond. We need to start drawing up plans for a new special ops force. One that is secret and draw people from all the services and establish a new Joint Task Force down at Ft. Bragg. Ease the command section down there over a period of months. They have the facilities down there. The Green Berets can run the school, training and interviewing. I don't want a bunch of knuckle draggers. I want an elite unit that can think. If they pass the training, I want them to go before a board of officers and senior NCOs to determine if they are fit mentally. I know it will take some time to get a force together, probably a couple of years. I don't want the men recruited for this force to know anything about it other than if they pass they are part of something special. We draw people from SEALS, Green Berets, Rangers and Marine Force Recon. It has to be voluntary. The Air Force can start or keep doing the special flying down in Florida only ratchet it up a notch or two. Call a meeting for the Chiefs of Staff for day after tomorrow.

The Paris peace accords were coming to a conclusion. There were last minute changes or disagreements but North Vietnam knew they had what they wanted. The South Vietnamese were not happy. The United States would back them should the North Vietnam attack. The world was told that there was peace in Vietnam. In the United States, the President declared peace with honor. The Secretary of State was declared a hero. The troops were coming home only to be met with hecklers and demonstrations.

General Lawson and Pete arrived in Washington on their way back to Ft. Bragg. They had received a message while in Paris to report to the Army Chief of Staff. They entered the Pentagon and walked into the Chief of Staff's outer office. Colonel Hammond was there to greet them. He briefed them on what was going on. They were to see the Army Chief of Staff and then come down to Colonel Hammond's boss, the Chairman's office.

"I'll see both of you in a few minutes. Go in and see your boss and get briefed.'

They knocked on the door and entered. "Good to see both of you. I haven't seen you, Lawson since Vietnam. Congratulations on your promotion. Get comfortable. I have something to discuss with both of you. Help yourselves to a cup of coffee." They both got a cup and sat down in comfortable chairs.

"How was Paris or shouldn't I ask?"

"We gave away the store, I'm afraid."

"Well, we all know that but I want to tell you both about a

new force we are about to organize at Ft. Bragg. It's strictly a secret force where we get volunteers from all the services. There will be a unified command located at Ft. Bragg. You, Lawson will be the Army representative. You, Compton, will work with an old friend of yours, "Charging" Charlie Beckwith. Pete put down his cup and was about to say something when General Lawson placed his hand on his arm.

"I know how you feel about him but I need someone to keep me informed and see that he doesn't wander too far off his target and stack the force with his old buddies from the Delta Force in Vietnam. By the way, the new unit will be called the Delta Force. Its objective is to be our force for anti-hijacking of passenger planes and a few other missions. It will be an extremely high caliber unit and no one who tries out for it will get a free pass. We are getting volunteers from the Green Berets, Rangers, SEALS and Force Recon. Each class will start with about 75 men. If we can get 25 to 30 graduates per class, we will be lucky. It will take us about one year to get the force we need but the training will continue. There is no ceiling on the total force but only a few people will know the exact strength. Let's head down to the Chief of Staff's office and get some more information."

They both rose and followed the Chief of Staff out and into the corridor. A short walk and the Chief of Staff opened the door to the Joint Chief of Staff outer office. There were the Chiefs of Staff of all the military branches waiting. Introductions were made. Colonel Hammond came out and ushered them into the conference room. They all took a seat. The Joint Chief of Staff walked in and they all stood up.

"I have just talked to the Secretary of Defense and he is in complete agreement with our plan. Before I start, I want to say to General Lawson and LTC Compton, "That problem we had has been taken care of by the Budget Committee in Congress and it has passed. The President signed the bill three days ago. Good work Compton."

General Lawson poked Pete in the ribs with his elbow. "Now when I tell you this: it's classified - I mean its classified! The name of the unit will be Delta Force. Each of you will designate a Colonel or General to be your representative at the Unified Command to be established at Ft. Bragg, N.C. It will be a PCS (permanent change of station). You will put out to your respective services that a new unit is being formed and it will be strictly voluntary. However, I want the best people you have. Each class will consist of about 75 people of which according to the initial training program I have read, about 25-30 men will graduate. This is not a confidence course. This is serious. It is physical but mostly mental. Your men have to have the right mental attitude or your men will not make it. At the end of the basic training, they have to appear before a board to determine if they are mentally qualified. This board will have on it qualified Military Psychologists as well as CSM and senior officers who have been associated with the type of operations this unit will perform. I would leave it to your Sergeant Majors in case of enlisted personnel and Company or Battalion Commanders for officers. There is no rank when a person goes through this course. This will be stressed at Ft. Bragg's unused old walled prison when they get there. Put out to your commands that I don't want anyone who volunteers to be turned down if he is an exceptional soldier that they can't do without. Believe me, you want to send the best damn soldiers you have when I'm authorized to tell you the missions they will have."

"Air Force, I want you to up your training with your Special Ops units. You have been issued the new guidance/radar systems available. If something new comes up, you won't have to ask for it. Your planes for the next two years will take a lot of abuse, don't worry about it. New or refurbished planes will be available to you and your training budget is unlimited. You will have your authorization tomorrow. If someone comes up with a new concept, try it. When I was a young lieutenant, I used to think "what are those old generals thinking? We can accomplish the task or mission in a more efficient and easier way." If someone has a better idea, try it.

"Are you saying that out of 75 men only 25-30 will make it? What's to keep us from stacking our quota so that a few of our men make it?" It was the Navy Chief of Staff.

"Fist of all, there is no quota. Second, if I see a service sending only a few men, we will have a talk. I have discussed this exact problem with the Secretary of Defense and I have his blessing. The class can be 76 or 80 but the optimum would be 75. Talk to your senior officers. I can guarantee you that if the right message is conveyed to your men, you will have no problem with volunteers. If they don't make it, it is no stigma on their careers. They can go back to the unit they had been part of before volunteering."

"Who will be running this school or who is in charge?" It was the Chief of Staff of the Marines.

"It will be Colonel Beckwith with a cadre of officers and SGM both on active duty and retired; people who have been involved in covert operations in Vietnam. Some are ex-MACV-SOG personnel. The school will run two test groups through to iron out any problems or unforeseen situations. You can start sending volunteers in a month and start sending your joint staff within the same time. Ft. Bragg has already allocated office space and some housing. There is BOQ for any single lower grade officers or aids. Any more questions?"

There were none and the Chiefs of Staff started leaving.

"General Lawson and LTC Compton, please stay a moment."

When everyone had left except for Colonel Hammond, General Lawson and Pete, the Chief of Staff leaned forward in chair and starred at General Lawson and Pete.

"You have probably guessed why or one of the reasons why we are forming this unit. Your intel better be right because we are spending huge sums of money to get this force trained and continue this course. When the Secretary of Defense asked how certain I was on the intel, I staked my career and reputation on it. Is there any doubt in your minds about this info?"

They both answered "No".

"I would not have called Colonel Hammond had I not been sure. The only problem I have is that I wish we could go in tomorrow and free those poor bastards. However, I see your point in delaying this operation until we have trained personnel and know exactly where they are. The Green Berets have suffered heavy casualties of the highly trained personnel in Vietnam. We have highly motivated people but lacking training. There will be casualties among the POW's if they have to wait more years; either by working them to death or dying from starvation. I can tell you that the Laotians, the Paet Loas are not friendly towards the U.S. or the Army we trained and equipped over there. It's only a matter of time before they have the entire country under their control."

"Don't think we haven't brain stormed this situation but we need a cohesive well trained smart unit to go in there and get them all out. Blackbird flights are starting next week. One thing I want to tell you is that I'm under great pressure to reduce the Special Forces (Green Berets) units and there are factions who want to do away with them completely. We have abandoned the Montagnard in South Vietnam. The Special Forces are training Cambodians and South Vietnamese regular forces as we speak. However, their future is in jeopardy. They have been tasked to death by Generals who are still fighting WWII. I foresee a day coming and not too long off when the need for Special Forces will be paramount. I want you, Compton, to go out on test runs of this course. See where improvements are needed. I don't want this course to be a Paris Island basic training course. We treat the people with dignity and we don't degrade the ones who don't make it. There will be officers and enlisted, all ranks come off the uniforms when starting the course. Officers don't pull rank on enlisted soldiers. If I hear of it, that officer or commander will have a one on one with me. You go through General Lawson and report on the course. Do either of you have any questions? This meeting is over."

Colonel Hammond walked them out into the corridor. "The old man is very serious about this. I hope Beckwith has calmed down a bit. Keep us informed on the commander and training. Have a good flight home."

General Lawson and Pete collected their luggage in the Army Chief of Staff's outer office and headed down to a staff car waiting to take them to Andrews Air Force Base. The ride home was quick. They took a taxi to Cottonade where they lived.

"We have two weeks off. Enjoy yourself, Pete, and my best to Betty."

"Same to Nancy, you know she could have done a lot better than picking you for a husband."

"Why you insolent pup; I'm going to tell her exactly what you said. No, I better not. She will probably agree with you. Have a good one."

Pete rang the door bell and was greeted by Betty and two beautiful girls. It was great to be home. There was a chorus of "Did you bring us anything from Paris?"

"You'll have to wait until I unpack my bags."

Betty put on her usual sultry act.

"Hey soldier, have you got plans for tonight?"

"Yes, as a matter of fact I have. If I don't get more hugs and kisses from all of you, I'm going to a motel for the night."

"You always say that Dad when you come home. How many do you want this time?" It was the oldest girl.

"At least a thousand from each of you"

"We don't have that many but we will give you all we have."

Pete sat down in a comfortable chair and took his jacket off. The two girls hugged and kissed him until they said they had run out.

"OK, open that small bag; there is a package for each of you. Your names are on them."

The girls grabbed the bag and unzipped it in record time

finding their packages and ran to their respective rooms.

"Now then soldier, how about their Mother? Do you have something for her?"

"I have several things for you."

Betty sat on his lap and gave him a nice homecoming kiss.

"I have missed you, Betty" he said between kisses.

"Are you saying those French women aren't as good as I have heard?"

"Naw, they are way overrated."

"Be careful soldier. Talk like that could get you a dry spell. No I take that back I'm tired of dry spells. Good to see you home. I do think you have lost some weight and you look tired. Was it that tough over there?"

"It wasn't tough physically but mentally it was a disaster in spite of what you read in the newspapers. The whole thing is or was a disaster. The only good thing is we are going to be in our home here for quite a while, meaning years. Lawson and I have both been assigned to a new task force here."

"Oh, God, our prayers have been answered. Nancy and I were just talking girl talk today and saying how nice it would be if we finally had a states side tour. Not moving for at least two or five years."

"We'll be here. I just hope you don't get bored?"

"Not as long as you're here I won't be bored."

Chapter 8

The new assignment was not without its bumps. The staff was in the process of being assembled and had no idea what was being planned. Colonel Beckwith was busy contacting old friends and getting his inner circle together. The exact starting date had not been determined and there was confusion to say the least. Pete found Colonel Beckwith in his temporary office and reported to him. To say Colonel Beckwith was less than happy to see him was an understatement. Colonel Beckwith informed Pete that he had just gotten a memo assigning Pete to his staff/ cadre signed by the Army Chief of Staff. Pete had been standing in front of Beckwith's desk. He looked around and saw a folding chair leaning against the wall. He went over and got it and sat down in front of Beckwith who was somewhat taken aback by this unauthorized gesture which he had not offered.

"I see you haven't changed much since the last time I saw you in Vietnam and you are now a LTC. Let's see the last time I saw you, you were a Captain. That's a pretty fast promotion and the Distinguished Service Cross. I heard a rumor you were in Italy. I didn't know we had a war going there? What happened?"

Pete was wearing his class A green uniform with the Gold Israeli's parachute wings and his decorations.

"It's all classified, Colonel Beckwith, but you can check with the Secretary of Defense or the Army Chief of Staff. I'm sure they will inform you sir."

Colonel Beckwith's face turned red and Pete was sure he was about to get one of his famous outbursts but he just sat there and looked at Pete.

"Well, I guess I'm stuck with you."

"No, we are stuck with each other. I can assure you that I will be loyal to you and carry out your orders. I can further assure you that I want this project to work more than anyone. A lot of people depend on it. I'm sure you have been briefed on it."

"I haven't been told a fucking thing about anything other than there is a taskforce forming here at Bragg and I'm supposed to be in charge of training some volunteers. I think it's a Joint Task Force: Army, Navy, Marines and Rangers, of course. No one has briefed me."

"General Lawson is in his office in the main JFK Building, he might have the authority to brief you."

"Are you saying that Colonel... er... I mean General Lawson is here? Holy shit, I think I'll retire. He is the biggest bastard I know. I don't know if I can work for him."

"He is a lot like you" said Pete with a smile on his face.

"I'm going to take that as a complement even though I don't like him. Talk about a hard ass! Do you know him?"

"I have worked for him and I have worked for you and you are a lot alike. I'll tell you one thing, he is very intelligent. He doesn't miss a thing. If I were you, I'd go and see him."

"Yeah, I guess I'd better. Do you know what this is all about and why the big secrecy?"

"I do, but Sir, I'm not the one who should tell you with all due respect. I'd go and see General Lawson."

"Here is a list of staff personnel I have come up with. Some you know and some you don't. You will be my second in command. Look at the list and see what you think at least about the people you know. I'll be back in an hour."

Pete sat there looking over the typed list of personnel. Beckwith had stacked it with his old buddies. Pete crossed off about eight individuals; one a Major who was an ass kisser and Beckwith's errand boy. There were some names he did not know. He had an SF book with him in his briefcase. He looked some of them up in the index. They were all there. He cross referenced them and eliminated four more. That brought the staff down to seventeen. That should be enough. If they needed more they might utilize some of the people who washed out because of injuries or some unforeseen incident.

Beckwith came back looking like a whipped puppy. He sat down behind his desk and looked at the list of staff members. He was about to say something but changed his mind.

"General Lawson hasn't changed a bit. He informed me I was completely in charge and he would not interfere in anything including the selection process. Tomorrow when you come in, wear fatigues. We will go over to the old Jail which has walls all around it and see what we have to do to get it in shape for training and establishing a shooting range. I have identified a lot of ammo that no one wants. We need guards 24/7. What do you think about hiring some retired SGM who are wasting valuable talents sitting around their homes or drinking beer at the NCO club?"

"That sounds good but they have to be briefed and sign the secrecy act. There can be no leaks about this to their friends."

"I agree. After listening to Lawson, I'm kind of surprised they gave me this project. I'm not particularly popular with a lot of high ranking officers. Lawson promised to support me 100% which almost floored me. He has a lot of clout. I see you have crossed off some people. You would have gotten an argument from me had you done it before I saw Lawson. I'll see you tomorrow. I'll get the people left on the list. They will go with us to the Jail. Come up with some basic ideas, just jot them down and be prepared to brief the people over at the Jail tomorrow."

Beckwith held out his hand and Pete shook it.

They started fixing the old jail complex. It needed some work. A shooting range was completed and guards were posted. The retired SGM were happy to be part of the organization and earn some extra money. Pete had come up with a training schedule and Beckwith had added some of his ideas. The finished schedule was submitted to General Lawson and the rest of the Joint Task Force. It came back with changes, some of which were incorporated. The volunteers were starting to show up and helped with modernizing the jail. Living facilities had been set up along with a first class mess hall. All training gear which had been requested showed up. Nothing was denied them. The volunteers brought their own uniforms and gear and they were confined to the Jail. Nearby Camp McCall was also available to them and when not at the jail, Camp McCall was their home. The cadre had gone through a rehearsal and Pete had gone with them. It was tough! The 48 hours map and navigation up in the North Carolina mountains was a ball buster. It was timed and checkpoints were established where a volunteer had to be at a certain point by a certain time. The course was laid out like the Star of David (the Israeli symbol), As a result of the first rehearsals by the staff, it was decided to increase the staff with eight more people. The second trial went smoother and they were ready to start.

The first class of 77 students was formed up for a group picture. CSMG Mays took the picture and told the group to look around at their fellow classmates. The next picture he informed them would be of the graduating class and most of them would not be present for the picture. The volunteers all laughed because they were not ordinary volunteers. They had proven themselves time and time again and no course would keep them from making it. CSMG Mays just smiled at them and walked away.

Although the hours were long and some days and nights he was gone, Pete was home most evenings. It was a good assignment and Betty and the girls were happy.

The first class graduated: 26 of the original 77. CSGM Mays took their picture and congratulated them. They had all passed the selection board. Those that were not HALO (High Altitude Low Opening) parachutists were sent to the course. The others started marksmanship and other training. There was a one week break between classes giving the cadre a chance to go over changes to the course, adding or fine tuning it. Colonel Beckwith was back to his old self. He was enjoying his role and the fact that he got every piece of equipment he asked for. At one of the meetings with his cadre, he admitted this was the toughest course he had ever seen and he was proud of the work the staff was doing.

When Pete got home one evening, Betty told him the Secretary of State had received the Peace Prize. Pete looked at her and shook his head.

The phone rang. It was General Lawson. "Have you heard who got the Peace Prize?"

"Yes, Betty just told me. You and I talked about it - we knew it would happen."

"Yes, but the North Vietnamese Le Duc Tho refused by saying there was no peace and he is right but our politicians are happy. See you tomorrow." The General hung up.

The training was going great. Colonel Beckwith amazed Pete. He was really into it and kept the staff on a short leash and Pete was enjoying working for him. Some of the early graduates had performed missions both in the Middle East and Africa. They were getting up to strength where they could start planning for the POW mission. The Joint Task Force was pleased with what they saw.

There was a new President in the White House who was very controversial. He had placed a Navy Admiral in charge of the CIA and people/agents were being cut in favor of satellite imagery. The morale at the Agency was low. The Blackbird program had continued and the POWs were located. However, an unforeseen incident happened that changed the focus of the POWs. The American Embassy in Tehran, Iran was taken over by students at first and then the new regime in Iran took over and the embassy staff became prisoners. The Embassy was looted. There was a lot of diplomatic effort spent on freeing the prisoners but to no avail. A few managed to escape and some were killed. It was a presidential election year and the American prisoners in Iran became a major issue. They had been prisoners for over four hundred days and the President decided to do something. The Delta Force was assigned the mission to free them, however, all the branches of service wanted a part of the action and it became confused. The Air Force Special Ops Unit was put on alert. They had the large helicopters available with the latest navigational equipment and were well trained. However, the Navy insisted that they had helicopters on Air Craft Carriers in the region and wanted to use them. The President was a Naval Academy graduate and his CIA Chief was Navy, so it was decided to use the Navy choppers whose maintenance was iffy and its pilots less trained than the Air Force Special Ops pilots. The Navy was betting that the operation would not happen so no special training occurred. When the order to go was given the Navy was surprised. One chopper on the way to a rendezvous point in Iran had mechanical problems and turned around. Colonel Beckwith was put in charge of the Delta Force which was prepared. They landed at the rendezvous point in C-130s. However, the mission turned into a fiasco during a refueling mission for the choppers and a fire broke out causing severe damage to the choppers, C-130s and personnel. The rescue was a disaster. Pete had stayed at Ft. Bragg and continued the training. The news of the disaster made the headlines both in the newspapers and TV. Each Service claimed the other service was in charge of the overall operation.

A new President was elected and the prisoners were released

by Iran. There was a reshuffling of the CIA and other agencies. Agents were placed back on the ground again and the morale and intel was reestablished. The Joint Task Force at Ft. Bragg was reshuffled. It became bigger and more cohesive. The new Chairman of the Joint Chief of Staff and the Secretary of Defense kept a closer eye on their operations. General Lawson was now a two star general and was in charge of the Army Section. Colonel Beckwith retired. He had too many Generals gunning for him and with the old President out of office, a fellow Georgian native, Colonel Beckwith, was hung out to dry.

Pete had a talk with him before he retired and Beckwith said he hoped Pete would take his place but he had not recommended him or anyone else because his word meant nothing anymore. Pete was sorry to see him go. They had gotten close over the last year. There were people who hated Beckwith and then there were the ones that really liked his bravado and tough stance on things.

Pete was at Camp McCall in his office when the door opened and in walked General Lawson.

"Got something for you, Pete" General Lawson said with a smile on his face. Pete had come to attention when General Lawson walked in.

"Sit down and take a look at these." Pete opened a large envelope and took out aerial photos which had been enhanced. They showed new pictures of the POWs. They had scratched a huge POW sign in the dirt in their compound with their feet.

"There are at least 1500 prisoners here. We need to rehearse fast. This time there will be no fuckup. Get back to Bragg and report to the Joint Staff headquarters. I'll see you there in an hour." General Lawson grabbed the photos and departed.

Pete drove back to Bragg and walked into the Joint Staff headquarters. He headed for General Lawson's office but was diverted by a Captain to the Conference Room. As he walked in a large crowd including Betty and Nancy were there. He didn't know what was going on. General Lawson told a Major to read the orders. LTC Compton was promoted to full Colonel. General Lawson pinned the Eagle on his collar. Betty and Nancy each gave him a kiss. Colonel Compton was also told he was now in charge of the training of the new force. There was coffee and cake and everyone congratulated him. Someone yelled "speech".

"I don't know what to say."

"Don't say anything. Just cut the cake. I'm hungry!" said General Lawson.

Pete cut the cake, someone else took over the cake cutting and Betty and Nancy served coffee.

"Well Colonel, how does it feel?" It was Command Sergeant Major Mays.

"I still don't know what to say. It's a complete surprise. You're the one that deserves this Eagle. You have been the backbone of the entire operation.

"Naw, I wouldn't be in your shoes much less an Officer. You people are too much like politicians."

"You're right and we have a lot to do in the next weeks."

We're going to the club tonight." Betty informed him when they got home. The General and Nancy arrived and they all had a drink and toasted Pete again.

General Lawson confided in Pete of the events preceding his promotion to full colonel. "You know you are three years ahead of your contemporaries now. I got a call from the Army chief of Staff. He is about to retire. He asked if there was anything he could do for me before he left. I told him there was an LTC who should be promoted immediately. He got angry and asked if you were still an LTC and I said "yes". You will have his orders tomorrow and I want him taken care of. He should be wearing your stars. He is working his ass off and if Beckwith tells me that, I know it's true. Give him my regards. I have put a letter in his file and the previous Secretary of the Army endorsed it."

"So you see you are not forgotten."

"I appreciate it, believe me. Betty will probably go on a shopping spree again. It happens each time I get promoted."

"I have to look like a Colonel's wife. What do you expect?"
"We'll pick you up in two and a half hours. Civilian dress."
The General and Nancy departed.
"The girls won't be home for at least an hour. It's tennis lessons today and I have never been to bed with a full Colonel. How about it soldier? He grabbed her arm and took her into the bedroom.
"General Lawson and Nancy picked them up and they went to the main Officer's Club. When the General and Pete went over to another table to say "hello", Nancy looked at Betty.
"You look like a newly plucked chicken tonight, eyes sparkling and a glow in your face. Is it the Colonel?"
"You mean it really shows? I don't know what the SF put in the coffee but Pete is unbelievable! You would think he would slow down but he is as good as ever. I have to be careful and not smile at him so much it triggers something."
"I'll have to remember that, although I'm not complaining. Generals can be brutes and I love it."
The training continued and all rehearsals for the freeing of the POWs increased. The Air Force had gotten new and refurbished planes with the new GPS systems and was ready to go. Choppers were stationed in Thailand with full support crews. Pete came home late one night and tired and went in and kissed the girls good night. He went out and sat down next to Betty who had fixed him a cocktail.
"You look like you could use one tonight" she said kissing him softly on the lips. "I suppose you have heard the news?"
"What news?"
"A retired Colonel Gritz and a team of men are on their way or are in Thailand and are going after some American POW in Laos."
Pete almost spilled his drink. Gritz had done some good work in Vietnam in '67 or '68, covert action in Cambodia but he was not in shape. Pete had seen him not too long ago and it was apparent that he had let himself go. He had been living up

in Idaho, Coeur d'Alene, or some such place with a bunch of ex Green Berets, loose cannons. Where the hell had he gotten the intel and funds to stage a raid at his age?

"Excuse me, I have to call General Lawson."

Pete got him on the second ring.

"A little late isn't it, Pete?"

Pete explained what Betty had just told him.

"If this is a joke, it's not funny. I'm going to make a call and I'll be right over."

Betty had been looking at Pete all this time. She had never seen him so upset.

"Did I say anything wrong? What is the matter?"

"Turn on the TV and see if there is anything on the news?"

Betty turned the TV on and sure enough the TV news anchor was explaining that a Green Beret Colonel and a team of men had located American POWs in Laos and were on the way to free them. There would be more news about them once they came back to Thailand.

The doorbell rang and General Lawson walked in.

"Betty, I'll have whatever Pete is drinking." I just talked to the new Army Chief of Staff. They are in a meeting with the Secretary of Defense as we speak. To say the shit has hit the fan is an understatement. It seems this Gritz had been contacted some time ago by the State Department and asked if he was up to a mission and was briefed on what it would entail. Of course, Gritz jumped at it and said he would furnish the men but he needed equipment. It seems a rich Texan and a conservative movie star had come up with the money for just about everything they needed. The State Department had authorized a hefty sum to pay these raiders as they were referred to. They are in Thailand as we speak and Gritz is being interviewed by a local Thai TV station. They have been over there close to a week now and are getting ready to cross the border into Laos."

Sure enough the TV anchor informed them they had a News Alert. Betty turned the TV up.

There was Gritz, in all his glory overweight and in tiger camouflage suit, telling the Thai TV station about their mission. It was unbelievable! He practically told them when and where they were crossing and that he had the full backing of the U.S. State Department. The news anchor informed them that was all but was sure there would be some updates in the next few days. After all this was a classified mission.

General Lawson looked at Pete.

"How the hell did anyone find out about this? The State Department again! I'll lay you odds that our old friend who screwed up the Israeli operation is behind this. He doesn't want any POWs freed. It would make him look like a fool. After all the hoopla about the peace Treaty, he still has his friends. We will have a meeting tomorrow morning and get the latest. Doesn't Gritz realize that the Laotians watch TV also? Someone is paying a lot of dollars for this. The contributors probably don't know about our program. Well, I'll see you tomorrow morning in the conference room. Thanks for the drink, Betty."

After the General left, Betty looked at Pete and frowned.

"Is this what you have been working so hard and long hours on?"

"Yes. It's been held real close. We knew over a year ago where the POWs were but we didn't have the force to go in and get them. Now we do and now this fiasco. They won't get a half a mile into Laos before they are hit, if they get that far."

At the meeting at Ft. Bragg, the Joint Task Force was told by the Army Chief of Staff via a secure line, that the operation was cancelled. New photos from Laos showed the POWs were being split up and taken to different locations by trucks. The Blackbird recon would continue.

Pete sat next to General Lawson and knew who was behind this fiasco. Gritz and his team had been ambushed as soon as they hit Laotian territory and they had escaped by boats back to Thailand.

General Lawson stated that the Delta Force had many more

missions to perform and the training would continue. The force would continue to grow but its classification and mission was to remain secret and that the troops who had been training for this mission would receive other missions.

After the meeting, Pete went back to Camp McCall where CSMG Mayes had gathered the force which was to go in and get the POWs.

Pete informed them what had happened. Most of them knew already but to hear it officially was a letdown to say the least. He described new missions by groups of two or more and nothing had changed as far as classification.

"Continue to hone your marksmanship for you are going to need it. Some of you will take refresher foreign language courses. We have more missions than we can fulfill at this time. Hence, new people will continue to expand the force. Nothing changes as far as Delta Force is concerned. It will remain a highly trained elite force and few people will know about it. OK, that's it. Get back to training. In the next few days you will check with me for your next mission. Nothing will be written down."

Pete returned to his office. General Lawson and a man in civilian clothes were waiting for him.

"Pete this is Bob Miller."

Pete looked at Miller and at General Lawson.

"Did I say something wrong," quipped the general. "Both of you look like you are about to laugh."

"General Lawson, let me explain," said Miller. "Pete, here, rescued me and my partner in Cambodia in '69 right before we were about to lose our heads, literally. We were young, just out of training, and Vietnam was our first posting. We wanted to impress our boss and fell for an old trick. Pete here briefed our boss afterwards and made us look like heroes."

"Why am I not surprised; I have worked with this young Colonel for years. In fact, he was my adjutant when I was a Colonel in the 82nd Airborne Division. He caused me more headaches than you would believe. He still hasn't changed. Is there more I should know?"

"No, there is no more, although this is the first time I have heard an agency person tell the truth" said Pete.

"Well, what I was going to say is that Mr. Miller here is our agency liaison officer at JFK Center now and he will be working closely with you and the Joint Staff. I have work to do." The General left.

"I'm sorry to hear about the POWs, Pete. We have been following closely your training here and the events in Laos. We think we know where the leak was but unfortunately it's over and until we locate some of them again, we have been told to hold it close as I'm sure you have also.

Endnote: The Delta Force continues to expand. It is engaged in Special Operation in contested areas. Its size and mission is known to few. It continues to train in the Ft. Bragg area and is overseen by a Joint Military Command.

A Little Favor

When the sun shone on a summer day and the temperature was in the 70's or 80's, Norway was a beautiful place to live, but it happened so seldom and people knew that tomorrow could bring showers. One had to take advantage of days like this and that was exactly what Pete Compton was doing. He was sitting on the large wraparound porch about 300 feet above the ocean outside the village of Os, on the west coast of Norway, about 30 miles south of Bergen, the second largest city in Norway and at one time its capital.

Pete's father and mother had retired and moved back to Norway and built a nice comfortable house on property given his mother by her father years ago. He owned the largest farm in the area and also had a large mill where he milled the grain from his farm and other farms in the area. The family was large and was related to most of the people in the county one way or another. Pete's father passed away in the 80's. His mother was surrounded by sisters and brothers and was able to maintain the house and property.

In 1997 at the age of 94, Pete's mother broke her left thigh bone and needed help. Pete's older sister flew over to take care of her; however it was not working out. They just didn't get along. Pete and his wife Betty retired and moved to Norway to take care of his mother. His sister left the next morning for the U.S. after their arrival. Betty got along with her mother-in-law although his mother had a mind of her own and could be demanding and stubborn. His mother had been told by Pete's sister that she would never be able to walk without a walker and this was a major concern for her because she had always been independent and up until now had been in excellent shape. Pete informed her the first day they had arrived that if she listened to him, she would be walking without any assistance to all the Christmas parties in the family six months from now. She had been reluctant at first but when Pete walked with her on the extended porch each morning and afternoon she regained confidence in herself and after a few weeks informed Pete she didn't need him to hold her hand anymore. She could do it herself holding on to the porch railing. Pete extended her walks to an hour in the morning and afternoon. At Christmas she attended all the family parties without the use of even a cane.

In March of 1998, Pete's mother suffered a stroke and was placed in the hospital section of the village nursing home. She passed away in May of 1998. Pete bought his sister out and now owned, along with Betty, a beautiful house overlooking the fjord and across from one of the largest glaciers in Europe. The view was extraordinary even when it rained.

So it was on a sunny day in July as Pete was relaxing in a comfortable lounge chair on the porch when Betty came out and handed him the phone.

"Who is it?" he asked holding his hand over the mouthpiece. Betty shrugged her shoulders indicating she didn't know.

"Pete speaking, how may I help you?"

"This is Bob Miller. Don't tell me you have forgotten me already?"

"The Bob Miller, Viet Nam and Fort Bragg?"

"The one and only who along with his partner got caught on the wrong side of the border many years ago, only to be rescued by a snake-eater (a nickname for the Green Berets) named Pete. How are you and Betty doing?"

"Fine, enjoying retirement and the good life."

"I'll be right behind you, have two more years, unless they extend me. Sorry to hear about your mother. I saw her paperwork since she was a U.S. citizen."

"Where are you and what are you up to?"

"I'm at the U.S. Embassy in Oslo and you know what I'm doing! Listen, I'll be in Os tonight staying at your famous Solstrand Hotel. I'd like to talk to you tonight if at all possible and invite you and Betty to lunch tomorrow. I know it's short notice, but that's the nature of the beast."

"No problem. I'm free tonight. Betty is going out to one of her hen parties with her girlfriends so plan on it. What time?"

"I'll meet you in the lobby of the hotel at 1800 hours if that's OK and don't eat cause from what I understand they serve the best food in Norway."

"Not to worry Bob, bring plenty of money because they are not cheap."

"Fine, see you then, my best to Betty."

The phone clicked off. Pete looked at Betty who was sitting in the lounge chair next to him soaking up the sun.

"What is that all about?" she asked keeping her eyes shut.

"Damn if I know" said Pete.

"Don't commit to anything that will mess up our retirement and remember we don't intend to live over here too many more years."

"Oh I know, I'm sure it's just a small favor or something. After all he was instrumental in getting me that job after I left the Army."

"Pete, no one flies from Oslo to Bergen and stays at one of the top five rated hotels in Europe just to ask you a small favor. Your cousin is married to the Chief of Staff of the Norwegian armed forces. You have two other cousins involved in the government, not to mention your uncle who just retired as the Secretary of Agriculture after thirty years. The small favor is not going to be small and you know it."

"We'll see tonight. By the way when do you leave for the States for your check-up?"

"This Friday, I'll probably be there about three weeks. I'll stay with my Mom. Why?"

"I was just thinking about our townhouse over there which you had renovated and furnished. It would be nice if you could sell it while you were there. I hate to keep asking your brother to check on it and we always stay with your mother when we are there. Sell it furnished so we are rid of it. After all we have decided not to live in Florida when we move back."

"I'll see what I can do. We sold our main house the first day we advertised it and for the asking price! Maybe we will have the same luck. Back to your meeting with Bob. Don't commit to any long term deals; you of all people know how they work."

"Not to worry, however, this is something we need to keep strictly under our hats. Don't mention my meeting tonight to your friends."

"I won't but you know the size of your family. I hope it's not something we have to sneak around about?"

"Yeah, I know, but Norway and the U.S. are close allies so it can't be something covert. Besides, I'm getting too old for that bull."

Pete met Bob Miller in the lobby of the Solstrand Hotel and they greeted each other as long time friends.

"I hope you haven't eaten yet because they have a fantastic spread laid out in the dining room" said Bob steering Pete down the long hallway decorated with antique furniture and period pictures on the walls.

When they got to the dining room receptionist, Pete asked for a table by the window so Bob could enjoy the scenery as they ate. It didn't get dark in Norway at this time of the year until about 1230 and then the sun barely set before it came up again. The waitress came and took their drink orders. Pete ordered a light beer while Bob had a scotch on the rocks. Bob looked questionally at Pete after the waitress had departed.

"I'm driving" said Pete.

"This village is as tough on drivers who drink as anywhere in Norway."

"That's right. I sometimes forget" said Bob.

They asked about each other's families and got caught up on the latest news. Their drinks arrived and they were told by the waitress to please help themselves to the food laid out on long tables in the middle of the large dining room. Pete recognized and nodded towards some people he knew but did not introduce them to Bob. As they were sitting at their table savoring the variety of delicacies on their plates, Bob held up his glass and touched Pete's beer glass with his and they toasted.

"To the good old days" said Bob and he took a sip.

Pete held his glass up and said "No, to the present and future good days" and sipped his beer.

Bob didn't say anything as the owner of the Hotel came over to their table, a striking looking lady, and asked if everything was to their satisfaction. Both Pete and Bob stood up and Pete introduced Bob to Borea, the owner.

"We have already met, I always greet Americans. It gives me a chance to practice my English. Please sit down. Where is Betty tonight or shouldn't I ask. Is this a boys night out? You know, Mr. Miller, I have been trying to get Betty to join our staff here. She would be a wonderful addition and could show the wives of visiting business men Bergen and the many interesting sites around our area. Most of our clientele here are business groups from America and England who hold their conferences here and of course the rest of Europe, too; Germany especially. The reason I haven't really pressured her is because I know she has some health issues which she has to go back to the states for. Our wonderful socialized medical care is not what I would wish on anyone. Give my best to her Pete and you two enjoy the food." Borea departed.

"She is quite a Lady, has renovated and upgraded this hotel and wants to make it the official number one hotel in Europe. Her husband died some years ago so she has done the planning and expansion in addition to raising three beautiful daughters who could be models or screen stars. Two are at Wharton Business School and the youngest is at Cornell studying Hotel and Restaurant management. Their mother keeps them humble and on a strict budget."

"She sounds like a woman who knows what she is doing" said Bob.

"So tell me about the little favor you want me to do. Don't screw with my retirement."

"It's easy really. All you have to do is monitor a situation once a week down in Bergen. It will be more of a treat for you and you can bring Betty with you. Do you know the restaurant called Brygge Stuen?"

"Sure, out on the docks and serves the best food in Bergen. In fact the entire area where it's located is on the World Heritage list, goes back to the 15 hundreds - a real tourist trap."

"That's the one. We have a ship, actually two, they alternate, that come in every Wednesday. You can see them dock from the restaurant. They are listening and monitoring ships stationed up in Northern Norway. Their cover is Marine Biology surveying vessels."

"Are you talking about those huge grey hulled catamarans that do about 50 knots or more, bristling with radar and antennas? Listen, we were out sailing and came to the entrance of the Bergen's Fjord when one of them came by us full power and almost capsized us and we were on a 45 foot sloop built for rough seas. I had the helm and was lucky to steer into the wake at the last second; otherwise our mast would probably have snapped. God don't you guys ever learn. It looks about as much like a research vessel as an SR-71 spy plane looks like a 747 passenger plane. Use fishing boats like the Russian's do."

"I know it is a little overdone but we are getting good results or should I say we were getting good results. We have a man or rather two men who alternate. They fly into Bergen each Wednesday morning and meet a crew member at the restaurant where they have a meal and the crew member hands over or rather exchanges briefcases with our man. They sit next to each other at the table and sometimes our man brings a woman friend or one or two men that they have become acquainted with in Bergen and treat them all to a meal. Sometimes it looks like a chance meeting other times they walk in together. We have gotten reports that the Russians are reading our mail."

"Can't you send Burst messages? I know they can't read those."

"We tried but there are some atmospheric conditions up there that garble the Burst messages. So once a week we get hard copies via our people. Believe me it's expensive to run those ships up and down the coast of Norway."

"So your man flies into Bergen Wednesday morning, gets the briefcase, and flies back to Oslo:"

"That's about it. I have a cellular phone in my pocket that I'll show you. If you need to get in touch with me, you just press one button and it will get me."

"I haven't signed on to your project yet and what are my benies?"

"You will be on contract basis, $10,000 a month plus any expenses, cash to you or we can arrange a bank transfer to you in the States or Norway."

"To me, I pay enough to Uncle Sam and I'm surely not going to subsidize the Norwegian Socialistic system."

"OK no problem, a bonus if you solve this predicament."

"You are more generous than you used to be."

"Norway is expensive and if you had any idea what this operation cost us to establish, you'd get an Agent to negotiate the terms for you."

"What time does your man arrive at the restaurant?"

"Between 1230 and 1:00."

"OK, I'll take Betty to lunch on Wednesday."

Bob signaled for the check and paid leaving a generous tip.

"Let's go out in the lobby and I'll show you how the phone works."

They found two adjoining overstuffed chairs. Bob took out

the small cell phone with a small imbedded antenna that could be pulled up to about 6 inches.

"All you have to do Pete is press this white button and you get me."

Bob handed the phone to Pete who looked it over, depressed the antenna and placed the phone in his pocket.

"I have some paperwork to do so we'll call it an evening. I'll walk you to your car" said Bob getting to his feet. "Looking forward to seeing you and Betty tomorrow, say 1:00 PM."

"I know you and Borea is an attractive woman. She is in excellent shape so I hope you have been jogging over in Oslo, otherwise she will give you a heart attack!"

Pete explained the proposition to Betty when she got home. She listened attentively while stroking their Shetland sheep dog "Heather" who was comfortably ensconced on her lap. Pete handed her the envelope Bob had given him in the parking lot of the Hotel. She opened it and took out the U.S. bills and counted them.

"Is this a onetime payment?" she asked.

"It's a monthly retainer strictly under the table deal."

"I'm beginning to like Bob. It looks like I'll have some nice shopping trips when I get to the States."

"Be my guest but place some of it in our bank box or deposit it."

"I'm kidding - but my trips to the states are getting expensive and this comes in handy. Don't worry; I'll take care of it. Besides how long do you think this little favor will last? Did Bob mention anything?"

"No but we'll go along for a while and see what happens."

"OK, I'm tired. Oh, I did get a complement on my Norwegian language tonight. I know they are being kind but the fact that we speak Norwegian most of the time at home helps a lot. Your mother was right in insisting on not speaking English unless we had to. One of the girls at our get together said there is a Norwegian course starting this fall. It's free and begins at

8:00 AM each day and ends at 3:00 PM four days a week. She is one of the teachers. It seems no one can get a work permit here unless they pass the test at the end of the school year which is in May of next year. I think I'll sign up for it so I can at least learn the correct grammar."

"You do fine. I can't believe how well you do."

"Oh, I know I make a lot of mistakes, especially at the stores but people here are so nice and never laugh at me, not even your family and that's saying a lot cause you have some crazies who like to kid. However I think it's because of you. They think a lot of you, Pete, and wouldn't think of criticizing me for fear of your wrath. They have heard too many of your war escapades from your sister so they behave."

"I don't know what she could have possibly told them. I have never said a word to anyone and that includes you, other than the funny incidents."

"Oh, they see all your medals which I found stuffed in a box and had them framed by that nice old picture framer in the village. They look nice hanging in your den."

"Well, it attracts too much attention as far as I'm concerned. It must have been Hank who told you how to place them when he and his wife Floe came over for Mom's funeral."

"I can't tell you, it's strictly on a need to know basis." Betty laughed.

"Come on to bed, we have a lot to think about the next couple of days. I'll just take Heather out for her final airing", said Pete getting up and calling to Heather who was eager to inspect her domain.

Betty had packed her suitcase and got organized for her trip to the States. She was a planner and Pete considered himself lucky, he hadn't packed his own suitcase in years. Betty seemed to know what he needed.

Wednesday morning Pete placed the breakfast dishes in the dishwasher and cleaned up while Betty was getting ready for their trip to Bergen. It still amazed him how long it took a woman to get ready, whether it was just dropping in on one of his cousin's houses or going to a formal party. Oh well, his mother had been the same so it must be a female genetic thing, he thought to himself.

They walked down to the village bus station. It was a warm sunny day. The bus arrived and they made themselves comfortable for the one hour ride to Bergen. From where the bus stopped, it was only a fifteen minute walk to the restaurant, however, Betty had to window shop at each store they passed. So by the time they got to the restaurant it was 1215. Pete had called ahead and reserved their corner booth near a large fireplace. If you hadn't been there before you would not notice the booth. It was rectangular and had room for six people if you used the two chairs at one end of the table. The hostess recognized them and showed them to their booth. They had a good view over the entire restaurant. Only a few tables were occupied but that would change in the next minutes. Tour guides steered their charges to the restaurant for lunch and dinner. Their waitress came and took their drink orders and left them each a menu. Betty sat around the corner of the short end of the table and Pete sat in the middle of the longer side.

"Here comes three of them" whispered Betty as three men dressed business suits, one carrying a black brief case with a zipper section running the length of its top. The hostess placed them at a table against the far wall at a 45 degree angle to their booth. Although there were two tables in the middle of the restaurant at Pete and Betty's level, their view was not obstructed. There was also a large seating section to the rear and up a few stairs where tour groups usually were placed.

Their drinks arrived just as another man a little more casually dressed carrying an identical black briefcase greeted the other three at their table and joined them. A waitress brought them four large glasses of beer. They all held up their glasses and said something which Pete and Betty could not hear. The group drank heavily from their glasses and picked up and studied their menus. The two with the briefcases were sitting next to each other.

Betty was transfixed by the men across the room and didn't realize the waitress had asked what her choice to eat would be. Pete tapped her with his foot under the table. Betty came out of her trance and apologized to the waitress. They both ordered Medallion of Reindeer. The waitress thanked them and departed with their menus.

"Skaal" said Pete raising his glass to Betty who gently raised her glass and said "Skaal".

"Nothing has happened yet", said Betty in a low voice.

"Don't stare directly at them" said Pete. "Just glance once in a while. I can see their briefcases but they can't see me."

"Let's not do this again" said Betty, sipping her drink.

"This is worse than spotting a well dressed woman and trying to figure out how I would look..." Betty did not finish her sentence. She starred across the room and said "They switched briefcases."

"I saw it" said Pete.

The man who came in with the two men reached into the zipper section of his briefcase and handed one of the other two men a medium sized manila envelope. He placed the envelope inside his suit jacket. He must have had a gigantic pocket sewn into the liner of his jacket.

The waitress brought the four men each another large glass of beer while her helper brought their meal. Again they all raised glasses and drank.

Pete and Betty's meal arrived and it looked delicious! They started eating but for Betty the meal could just as well have been the soles of her shoes. She had no taste in her mouth. She took a large sip of water but her mouth was still dry.

"I'm going to step outside for a second" said Pete.

Just as he got up a large group of Japanese tourists came in. The hostess escorted them to a large table in the back of the restaurant. Pete slipped out the door and reached in his pocket for the cell phone, extended the antenna and pressed the white button and immediately Bob's voice was on the other end. Pete explained what had happened and that the group had just started eating and drinking several large glasses of beer. They would be there at least twenty minutes more.

"You and Betty stay where you are. I'll take care of it from here on".

Pete heard a click as Bob hung up. Pete returned to their booth. Betty's face was pale.

"Everything is fine" Pete assured her. "Enjoy your meal."

Betty started eating and had just finished when two large taxi station wagons pulled up outside their window. Three men in suits and ties came into the restaurant and sat down at one of the tables in the middle of the room. One of them went over to the waitress station and pointed over his shoulder with his thumb. He then returned to the table and said something to his two partners. The waitress he had talked to brought a bill on a small silver tray and started to leave. The man who had talked to her told her to stay. He reached into his pocket and brought out his wallet, looked at the bill and extracted three large denomination Kroners and laid them on top of the bill. The waitress told him she would be right back with his change but he told her it was her tip. The waitress blushed and did a small curtsy and departed. The three men walked over to the table where the four men were sitting. Words were exchanged but in the end all four got up escorted by the three men out to the taxis and departed.

"Oh my God!" said Betty. "One of the briefcases is still under the table." Betty got up and walked over to where their waitress was standing and said something that Pete could not hear. The waitress smiled and disappeared into the back. A large group of tourists came in and the hostess escorted them to the area in back of the restaurant. Betty appeared at their booth and slid the black briefcase under their table to Pete.

"Nice going" said Pete reaching under the table and giving

Betty's knee a pat.

"What were you talking about with the waitress?" asked Pete.

"Oh, I just ordered desert for both of us."

Betty had just finished talking when the waitress brought their ice-cream with whipped cream and cloud berries on top. Pete asked her for their check. She informed them she would be right back. They were digging into their delicious dessert not saying much. When their check arrived, Pete paid the waitress immediately giving her a generous tip. She smiled and thanked them.

"I think I'll start waitressing after seeing the large tips down here."

"Let's get out of here" said Pete, getting up, waiting for Betty to precede him out of the restaurant. He carried the black briefcase in one hand and reached into his jacket pocket and extracted the small phone. He pulled the antenna up with his teeth and pressed the white button. A few seconds went by and Bob answered. Pete informed him that he was walking south from the restaurant towards the Funicular Station (which carried people up to Mt. Floyen where tourists and local people could view the city of Bergen) and would be there in five minutes.

"Oh, by the way, I have the second briefcase", said Pete in an almost afterthought comment.

"Stay in front of the station with your arm around Betty. A black 4-Door Peugeot, with a small green triangle sticker inside the right side of the windshield passenger side, will be there in less than ten minutes. Open the passenger door and the driver will say "Rain is reported for tomorrow." Place the briefcase on the passenger seat and slam the door."

There was a click in the phone as Bob terminated the call. The car arrived in about five minutes and the exchange was completed.

"I have to pee so bad I can taste it, in fact I almost wet myself back at the restaurant. Let's not do this again Mr. Compton."

"There is a Tourist Information building right down the street. Let's get you there fast. People haven't peed on the sidewalks in Bergen in years, so let's go!"

"Very funny mister" Betty grabbed Pete's arm and they headed for the International Information building.

Pete asked the woman behind the counter for the ladies facilities. She pointed across the room and Betty headed for it.

"Do you have any openings on the Fjord Tours in the middle of August" Pete asked the pleasant woman behind the counter.

"Let me bring it up on the screen, it's the height of the tourist season and we have what we refer to as the German invasion at that time. "How many people were you thinking of?"

"Two ladies, my wife and her mother."

"I have two rooms; let's see, on the 14th of August. One room is down towards the car deck and the other is a deluxe suite on the top deck with balcony. It's truly deluxe and so is the price."

"I'll take the deluxe one" said Pete.

"Let me call the Ships Line to confirm it."

The lady talked a few minutes and hung up the phone.

"You have it!" she said with a smile.

"You know there are not many Norwegian men who would treat their mother-in-law to such beautiful accommodations."

"I have been in America too long" said Pete with a smile.

"I'll print up your confirmation and your tickets."

Pete gave her the passenger names and his Visa card and thanked the lady for being so helpful. Betty came up to the counter as the lady handed Pete the envelope containing tickets and luggage tags.

"Can we have a brochure on that Fjord trip? I believe it's a 12-day trip" said Betty.

"I'll be happy to" said the lady smiling at Pete.

They thanked her again and walked out on the sidewalk.

"I swear the Norwegian people are the nicest and friendliest we have ever met in all our travels."

"Well that's true, we probably are the nicest people in the world" said Pete.

"I know I should not have said that. I'll be paying for that remark somehow."

Pete yelled and held up his hand. A taxi pulled up to the curb and he ushered Betty into the back seat joining her.

"Up to Os, please" Pete said to the driver in Norwegian. "You can drop us in the Centrum."

Pete turned to Betty and told her in a low voice not to talk about today's events. He took the envelope out of his jacket pocket and handed it to Betty. She opened the envelope and read the names on the tickets and a diagram showing her their suites on the ship. She stared ahead, tears welling up in her eyes.

"Well, no comment".

"You are the best man in the world. I'll show my true appreciation tonight". She dabbed her eyes and leaned over and gave him a soft kiss on the cheek.

"Not a word to your Mother when you go over there. I know she is dying to come over. She thinks you live in an old log house with grass growing on the roof and outdoor toilets."

"No she does not. I told her we use a hole in the ground. This is so nice Pete and such a surprise. My mother was after my father for years to take her on this trip. He thought it was too expensive but he did take her to other places."

"We'll be in Os in a few minutes. Do you need anything at the store, food or anything?"

"No, I think we are fine."

After Pete paid off the taxi from Bergen, they walked over to the village taxi stand and had a taxi drive them to their house.

"Why didn't you have the taxi from Bergen take us the rest of the way to our house?"

"Well, I'm sure by now someone saw the events at the restaurant and tongues are wagging. I didn't want the taxi driver to know exactly where we lived. Bergen is not that big and we have used taxis before. We probably should have taken the bus back."

Heather was waiting for them as they walked into the house and Betty took her out.

"I'll meet you on the porch just as soon as I get the princess here aired out and I expect a good drink waiting for me."

"Yes Mam" said Pete, giving her a mock salute. He changed into a comfortable jogging outfit and made them each a drink which he took with the phone onto the porch. He had just settled into a lounge chair when the phone rang.

"I have been trying to get you for the last half hour. Where have you been?' Bob said sarcastically.

"We just got home. Why did we miss another object that someone over-looked?

"No, I wanted to say thanks. The old man actually praised me, can you believe it?"

"Probably the first time in 30 years."

"Listen it's costing you a trip for two up the coast of Norway for Betty and her mother in August when she gets back."

"I don't care if they want to go around the world; you thank Betty properly for me. Listen when is she leaving for the states?"

"Early Friday morning. Why?"

"Why don't you go with her to Oslo and make sure she gets on the right flight to the states."

"OK, what's up?"

"Friday morning stop by the SAS counter in Bergen and pick up plane tickets. You're booked in adjoining seats in Business Class and you return to Os Friday night. What will you be wearing?"

"Let's see, navy blazer and dark gray slacks, brown loafers, light blue shirt. Do you want to know about my underwear also?"

"No, that's fine. When Betty is on her way, go to the airport Building exit. A car and driver will be waiting for you. We are having a little meeting Friday and I would like you to be there. Nothing exciting. See you Friday."

There was a click in the phone as Bob hung up.

"Who were you talking to" asked Betty as she sat down in the lounge chair next to Pete, taking a sip from her drink.

"I'm escorting you to Oslo Friday to make sure you get on the right flight."

"That will be nice and after I leave I suppose you are seeing Bob?"

"Yes, he asked me to attend a meeting Friday. By the way, he arranged adjoining seats in Business class. I pick up the tickets at the SAS counter in Bergen Friday morning."

"I'm just going to say this one last time, Pete, don't get into any long time deal and leave me out. They are treating us right but I can't handle any more restaurant situations. I think my heart stopped for a while today."

"I'll be careful. I will pick the assignments. Here, Skaal" said Pete touching his glass to Betty's.

Heather was barking at her arch enemies, a pair of Magpies who were hopping around on the lawn by the apple tree.

"She thinks she owns this entire area around here. She sure has adjusted well and likes her surroundings. I fed her but she didn't eat much. I wonder if our neighbor was over with table scraps."

"Ha, table scraps, Kristi gives her meatballs and gravy. She eats better than we do." Pete said laughing. "It's a good thing she has a large area to run around; otherwise she would look like the pigs up on the farm."

Heather, who was standing by the porch railings, turned around and gave Pete one of her disapproving stares.

"It's been a day, hasn't it? It's a good thing we have this place to come home to and relax," said Betty.

"I'll pack your oversized briefcase with clean shirt and toiletries, socks and underwear just in case."

"Thanks. I don't think I'll need them but with Bob you never know."

"I know it's still early but let's go to bed, pull the shades so no one will stop by."

"Good idea and there was a promise made earlier which I'm looking forward to"

"Me too", said Betty laughing.

True to his word, Bob had made arrangements for them on Friday morning. It was a smooth flight over the mountains and the sun glistened off the snow covered peaks and glaciers. Pete escorted Betty to her flight which had just been called. They flew Iceland Air, business class, when going to the States. The services and food were superb. The flight stopped in Iceland and then direct into Orlando, Florida. A limo would pick Betty up and take her to her mother's house on the east coast of Florida.

Pete headed for the Terminal Exit and saw a light tan Mercedes sitting in the No Parking Lane directly in front of him. A young man came up to him, opened the back door of the Mercedes and asked Pete to please enter.

The drive to the U.S. Embassy took about forty-five minutes. Traffic was heavy at this time in the morning. A Marine guard stopped them and checked the driver's badge and waved them on. The driver pulled up to the entrance of the Embassy, shut the car off and came around and opened the door for Pete. The driver escorted Pete into a large entrance hall where a Marine Sergeant was sitting behind a desk. The driver explained to the Sergeant that the gentleman was here to see Mr. Miller. The Sergeant pressed a button on his phone and a Marine Corporal appeared out of nowhere. He was instructed to escort the gentleman to Mr. Miller's office. The Corporal said "This way, Sir," and took Pete to an elevator. They got off on the third floor and the Corporal opened a door for Pete and indicated for him to enter. Pete entered the office alone and audibly sucked in air through his mouth. Behind a mahogany desk sat the most stunning middle aged woman he had ever laid eyes on.

"Mr. Compton", the woman said with a slight Southern American accent. "Mr. Miller is expecting you. Would you like me to bring you a cup of coffee or something else?" she asked holding Bob Miller's door open.

"A glass of cold water, Mam" said Pete not taking his eyes off the woman.

"Call me Ann, please" she said closing the door.

"You haven't changed a bit" said Pete extending his hand to Bob , who came from behind his desk. Bob laughed taking Pete's hand. He indicated for Pete to take a seat in one of the two stuffed chairs with a small table between them. Bob sat down in the other chair.

"First, I again want to thank you for the fine job Wednesday. There is a rumor at Langley that the "Burma Fox" actually smiled when he heard the news but then it's only a rumor so one never knows for sure."

"I find that hard to believe", said Pete with a smile. "I didn't think his face had the muscle structure for a smile, it surely would be a first. But in all seriousness, why haven't you used your assets here or nearby to solve that simple problem?"

"We have tried but each time came up empty. Either the people were tipped off or were using a different place. The Norwegians have been more than helpful but nada. I think we have a mole at our upgraded RADAR station up North in Bodo. The RADAR station coordinates with the ships and somehow the crewman has been tipped. We have secure contact with the RADAR station so maybe we have gotten careless in our talks, which by the way is the reason for the meeting today. The Russians were grumbling about the station, saying it violates our treaty. Our story and the Norwegians have told them that we merely exchanged some worn out old equipment. The station is the same as it was. Have even invited them to inspect it but so far they have refused. If the truth be known we have spent about eighty million on the latest technology and know what the Kremlin is having for breakfast. But like I said "Someone up there is feeding the Bear our information and the Bear has stopped grumbling." The Press has not mentioned it again, although there were only two articles about it, both from the two left leaning representatives in the Norwegian Parliament."

Ann brought Pete a glass of water with ice cubes, setting it down on the small table between them. Pete thanked her. She smiled and departed.

"Do you think this is related to the ships intel and does the Radar station have contact with the ships?"

"The answer is no and yes. I think the ships intel loss was a separate operation but yes the RADAR station does have burst commo with the ship when they pass close by going South to Bergen, especially if they have any timely hot intel. The ship then makes a hard copy and it's included in the briefcase hand-over. Otherwise information from the RADAR station is sent over a secure line to us. The secure line is our main means of transmitting."

"So what's the scoop with Ann? No wedding band on her finger. Do you live together or what?"

"We have been together since about a year after my divorce. Jean didn't want to move anymore. The kids are out of college and on their own. One is married. God I couldn't blame her. I have dragged her all over the world and to some lousy places but I was given this plum and she said no. The divorce was amicable. We are friends. She has a friend, a retired agency man, and seems happy. Ann is a widow. We plan on getting married when we both retire in a couple of years. She is great and we have developed a special relationship. She takes good care of me, knows what I'm thinking and acts on it."

"I think she is the most beautiful woman I have ever seen but then you have always had beautiful women. My God, Jean could have been a model."

The intercom buzzed. Ann reminded them they had less than 5 minutes before the meeting.

"Listen, I'm going to introduce you as Alex Lien, a GAO representative from Washington, over here to inspect the RA-DAR station to make sure Uncle Sam got his money worth."

"How long will I be up there and what am I looking for?"

"You know what you are looking for but as far as the RADAR facility, I have an extensive list for you. Just walk around with your clipboard."

"I warn you I don't know a damn thing about electronics."

"You don't have to. Each new piece has a number and it corresponds to your list and there are numbered pictures which correspond to the numbers. Let's go."

There were four other people in the conference room, all in civilian clothes. Pete took a seat next to Bob. Bob introduced him as Alex Lien from the GAO in Washington and went around the table starting with John Garvik, head of the Norwegian section. George Kennedy in charge of the U.S. section and two Embassy employees whose job Bob never mentioned.

"Alex will join you up at RADAR station making sure we have the equipment we paid for and that it is operating properly.

"Are you an expert in electronics, Mr. Lien?" It was John Garvik, the Norwegian.

"No I'm not and please call me Alex. To be honest with you I have just mastered the VCR on our television, so maybe you could call me an electronic expert."

There was laughter among the participants.

"Some years ago when my mind was sharper and younger, I did work on the famous IODIT computer where you could type in English and the hard copy came out Chinese. It was well published. It was a government built machine but it took IBM to work out the bugs. I might add that after thirty years, it's still working but like all electronics it has been upgraded several times. That, gentlemen, is the sum of my experience. At your site, I will merely check off the equipment against my list. I will not bother your people. If I have any questions I will come to you two, if that's agreeable. I would like to leave with a complete check list, otherwise my boss will probably send a real shithead over, and we have many who fit that description, and set your program back months. I promise to be very cooperative but I will ask you two questions if I hit a brick wall."

"I'm sure I speak for my Norwegian counterpart, John, when I say you are more than welcome. We have a close and cooperative group up there. How long do you expect to be with us Alex?" asked George Kennedy, the American representative at the site.

"About two weeks give or take a few days. I would like to learn as much about and see the facility on a normal day's operation.

"So Alex wouldn't hear it from someone else, I briefed him on our leak so he wouldn't be surprised. He has the same clearance as you but everything is on the need to know basis," said Bob.

"Which brings me to the real purpose of this meeting. Is there any fraternization that you have been able to detect, either one of you?"

"There is something going on between Jens Tronsrude and Jane Gallaway", said John. "It started about 6 months ago, about a month or so after Jens arrived. He traded his week off with someone else up there and was together with Jane at least four nights at our apartment here in Oslo. He stayed overnight each time. We have had our people keep track of him. The rest of the time he spent at his parent's house on the outskirts of Oslo. He has an apartment over their garage. His girlfriend spent the other nights with him at his apartment. He had two men visit him one evening at his apartment. The visit lasted about 20 minutes. One of the men was his friend from the university days. They have been close for many years. The other man we are not sure of. He was dressed like a skier. Could have been Jen's girlfriend's coach; she is a top candidate for the National Biathlon team. In fact, she took off for Littlehamer training site the next morning and was gone two days."

"Is there any military regulation, George, which prohibits them from fraternizing?"

"Only officers and enlisted personnel and civilians who work directly under them. The latter case is only frowned on and the officer is given a warning and if it continues is made a permanent part of their file. As long as national security doesn't come into play......frankly I would have to look it up in our regs. Jens would constitute a foreign ally and we have the same equipment as the Norwegians. In fact, we alternate at times on the equipment. So it is a gray area, to use an old cliché.

"Would it be wise to transfer Jane back to the states?" asked Bob.

No one said anything for a few seconds. Then John spoke up.

"I don't think that's a good idea until we have solved this problem. She is divorced and Jens is not married. Under Norwegian military regulations if one of them was married, we would have a case but as it stands we have nothing to hang our hats on, as you Americans are fond of saying."

"I agree with John" said George. "It's not a secret up there that they are involved but no one is saying anything about it. No one cares to be honest with you."

"Well, we care" said Bob. "We haven't spent 80 million to upgrade that place only to have two lovebirds that might be compromised over an entirely different issue, sell or give secrets to the Russians. Shit it wouldn't be the first time and why wasn't I notified about this situation."

"You work closely with our people Bob. I would have thought something would have been said. Maybe they are waiting for more information. I don't know. I didn't know until last night that they were watching Jens."

"Well, keep your eyes open" said Bob.

"Could Alex perhaps work on this as long as he is up there," asked George.

"Let me be clear on this. If Langley found out that a "bean counter" from the GAO is trying to solve this case, the shit will hit the fan. I didn't even want Alex to know about the leak or have him sit in on this meeting. Nothing against you, Alex, but I was overruled by my boss who figured he would hear rumors when he was up there. Alex, you stay out of this. Check the equipment and make your report."

"No problem, I'll have a tough enough time checking off the equipment and pretending I know what I'm doing."

"Are you and John satisfied with the complement of people you have up there?" asked Bob in a more calm voice.

"Yes, John and I have discussed that at length and we both agree that more personnel would only complicate things. The unit is for all practical purposes automatic. It runs itself. The only thing John and I do is collect the data and transmit it either over secure lines or hard copy," said George.

"OK then, everything we have discussed here is Top Secret. Thanks for your input John. It's good to hear your people are trying to get a handle on this. I'll make contact but your name will not come up."

Everyone shook hands. George told Alex that they were flying up to the site Monday at 12:00 hours. If he could be at the Embassy by 11:00 hours, he could get a ride.

Alex (Pete) followed Bob back to his office. Ann was not at her desk. They found her in Bob's office arranging their lunch on his conference table.

"Will there be more than the three of us," she asked Bob as they walked in.

"No" said Bob. "And thanks, this looks great."

"Just trying to do my job", said Ann laughing.

"She is just trying to impress you, Pete. She will probably demand a bonus at the end of the year."

"The bonus I had in mind better not wait until the end of the year!"

"I'm henpecked and we aren't even married yet," said Bob chuckling.

"Wait until you get married, Bob, you'll be automatically demoted to a common husband although from what I see that would be a pleasure."

"Thank you, Pete, Bob has told me much about you. You are really smarter than I would have thought working for Bob and all."

"Let's eat," said Bob.

"What did you think of the meeting, Pete?"

"We know where the leak is. What surprised me were John's comments about watching Jens and his coming and goings. The Norwegians are a lot better at this game than I thought. Very low keyed. If you asked an educated Norwegian if they had an Intelligence Service in this country, they would say no and that there was no need for one. They have their National Police, our FBI, but they have bungled so many cases as you well know. You know my cousin is married to the Chief of Staff of the Armed Forces. He and I talked about their intel program and the problems they face in Norway. The people do not want a KGB or a CIA so only a small select group is aware of them. With the Russian Bear at our door step, we can't afford to not have an intel section but the problem in Norway is recruiting people and it's very expensive. The average agent has a PhD. and can often be found at the University teaching courses from International Relations to Botany. Medical doctors constitute a high percentage of the group. The background checks are so extensive that it can take years for clearances to come through. They learned the hard way in WWII that the ones who were eager to get into sensitive positions in the underground were Nazis or Communist plants. It was dicey in Norway after the war. We had to get English planes and soldiers on the ground and American battleships in the major harbors cause the communists wanted the top spots in the government. At the present there are two left leaning or communists representatives in the government and they are usually the most vocal."

"I thought Labor was left leaning," said Bob.

"Oh, they can be. It all depends on how bad the U.S. screws up, Viet Nam for instance, but generally they are Nationalistic in their voting. If one word describes them it is "Socialistic" i.e everyone should have a nice house, a cabin in the mountains and a boathouse with a nice boat. Unlimited vacations all paid for either by their employer or the government. I almost forgot several girlfriends or boyfriends depending on the gender."

"I like them, good ideas all of them," said Bob.

"That couch of ours is not comfortable to sleep on, Bob. Keep that in mind when you make comments like that," said Ann with a raised eyebrow.

"I was referring to the houses and cabins," said Bob.

"What am I to do with this guy, Pete?"

"Love him and take good care of him. There aren't many dedicated people like him around."

"Yes, I know so I'll do what you say, Pete."

They discussed Pete's travel up to Bodo and his getting a lift from John and George. Ann would arrange for his travel from Bergen to Oslo Monday morning.

"Be careful up there Pete. None of them are stupid. I got the file on Jens Tronsrud and he is not what he seems. There was no way we could block his assignment up there with his uncle being the prime Minister. His parents are seriously rich. He fell in with a small but dedicated left leaning group at the University. I'm not saying Jane is feeding him information but there is smoke there so play the role. Stop in here and see me before you head up there Monday."

"Do you need me for anything else? Otherwise, I'll take an earlier flight back to Bergen."

"No, go ahead, Ann can arrange flight changes and have the car waiting for you downstairs. Thanks for coming!" said Bob and stood up from the table shaking Pete's hand.

"It's been a pleasure meeting you, Ann," Pete gave her a kiss on the cheek.

"Same here, Pete, I'll get your flight changed. Give me your tickets."

When Pete had departed, Ann sat down in a comfortable chair while Bob poured her a cup of coffee.

"He is everything you said about him. I hope he can pull it off up north without too much publicity."

The only thing we need to do is put some aviation assets for him up there. Have the military branch here place a helicopter and a plane at the airfield at Bodo. They like to get their flight pay and have an adventure. God this country is too civil! People get bored here. Have a contact for Pete should he need a fast extraction. They are to be on a 24/7 notice. I have a funny feeling about this one. We may have to move some people fast and this is strictly a silk purse operation. The only thing the Military Liaison needs to know is I need these assets up there for the next three weeks."

"No problem, your loyal servant will take care of it," said Ann.

Bob leaned over and gave her a kiss on the lips. "More when we get home," he said getting up.

Pete was in Bob's office at 10:00 hours and was getting a last minute briefing on the assets that would be available and a list of code words in case he needed an extraction fast. They know where to land in the compound up there. Bob handed Pete a leather shaving kit with all the toiletry implements. Pete looked at it and felt the weight. It was heavy. He grabbed the inside of the box where the shaving implements were laid out and lifted it up. Underneath was a small 380 caliber handgun with two clips of ammunition. Pete looked at Bob who just nodded his head. Handguns were frowned upon in Norway. One could buy all kinds of dynamite but handguns were illegal unless you belonged to a shooting club and then after extensive background checks. Pete place the shaving section back covering the gun and closed the lid on the box.

"You have my phone so if you need anything, press the button."

"Is the item sterile?" asked Pete.

"It's a German SigSauer, no serial number, registration or any paperwork. You are familiar with it - 7 round clip, automatic."

"Thanks. I was wondering about having one. I always feel

better. It's hard to overcome old habits."

"You will be leaving from a military base. George will pick you up in about 15 minutes."

Pete placed the shaving kit in his oversized briefcase and locked it. As he was leaving Bob's office, Ann gave him a kiss and stuck a piece of paper in his left jacket pocket. Pete didn't know if Bob saw the exchange but thanked Ann for her help. A Marine Corporal was waiting outside the door and escorted Pete down to the Embassy entrance.

George's vehicle pulled up and the driver opened the trunk and placed Pete's suitcase in it and slammed the trunk. Pete held on to his briefcase and joined George in the back seat. They exchanged greetings and headed out of the city. They were inspected at the entrance to the airfield and passed through. Bob had given Pete new identification papers to include a passport. John was already aboard their military version of Citation Jet. A steward asked if anyone wanted coffee or a soft drink. They declined, George telling him when they were airborne to check again.

The takeoff and flight was smooth.

"We'll be there in about two hours or less depending on what's going on at the airbase. We run a lot of NATO fighters and cargo plane traffic up there. Norway provides the fuel so our people and other countries take advantage of them especially if the weather is good."

They landed and were picked up at the airfield and were at the RADAR compound in a few minutes. Pete was amazed at the number of guards, both American and Norwegians. The RADAR itself was huge and comfortable looking houses surrounded the perimeter fence. George took Pete to his quarters. It was like an upscale hotel, plush was a good description. There was a fully equipped kitchen, living room, two bedrooms bathrooms and a large TV.

"Why a kitchen when you have a mess hall?" asked Pete.

"The staff is allowed to bring the families up here. So far

none have but it's better to be prepared. All the units are basically the same. The guards live in the duplexes. Each one has his own unit. We did not spare expenses when it came to the living quarters. It gets pretty grim up here in the winter."

"Well this is great. I don't think anyone complains about their living conditions."

"Not so far. I'll leave you to unpack. Chow is at 1800 hours and while we are there I'll have security sweep your quarters. They have done it in the last two days but I don't want to take any chances. I'll also have everyone but two people there (the ones monitoring the RADAR). Give a short little talk to the people about why you are here."

"No problem," said Pete.

George left and Pete unpacked. He had a bulky zipper jacket that had zipper pockets on the inside. He slipped the gun and magazines in the left inside pocket of the jacket. He would wear that to supper. No one could tell the gun was there. He didn't want to leave it in the shaving kit when they swept the rooms. Pete sat down and went over the check list Bob had given him. It was twenty-five pages long and also had a section with clear pictures of the items he was to inspect.

Pete went to the mess hall and was immediately waved over to George and John's table. There were about 35 personnel already seated. Pete saw that some were guards.

George stood up and asked them for a few minutes before they went through the line for their food.

"I want to introduce a new member or I should say a guest to our compound. We have Alex Lein from Washington DC here. He works for the GAO (Government Accounting Office). In the US when we spend a certain amount of money, the GAO is required to make sure we spent it on the equipment and facilities we requested. Alex the floor is yours." George sat down.

Alex (Pete) got up and said, "You know a lot has changed in the military when you can call Colonels by their first name." The people in the mess hall laughed and seemed to relax.

"As George said, I'm here to inspect the equipment and facilities. I'm what is called a bean counter. In other words Uncle Sam wants to be sure the equipment he paid for is the equipment that was contracted for and that it works. I'll be as unobtrusive as I possibly can. I have a check list which I'll go by and when I'm in your section checking off items, I'm not going to question you. However, if you have a computer or items that are not performing as they should, I would appreciate it if you tell me about it so we can replace it. I know you had tech reps here when the work was first done but they work for the manufacturer of the item and that is not always a reliable source. Again, I'll stay out of your way but please bring problems to my attention. Does anyone have any questions?"

One hand was raised; it was a young Norwegian.

"How long will you be here, Alex?"

"You know I was under the impression that the Norwegians were warm hospitable people and welcomed visitors. To ask them how long they were staying was something a true Norwegian never asked."

This time there was loud laughter including the questioner.

"Seriously though, it should take me about a week or two and I'll be out of your hair. The thing I want to emphasize is that the report I submit to my boss and his committee is complete and detailed. Otherwise, they send a team over here and I don't want those people here and neither do you. As in any bureaucratic government agency there are always people who want to get noticed and promoted and I'm afraid we have plenty of those."

There were no further questions and the food was being served.

"Good talk, that was Jens that asked the question," said John.

Jane and Jens had started their affair about 6 months ago, about 6 weeks after Jens was assigned to the Norwegian team. They had both been to Oslo for a week of R&R. Jens had switched schedules with another Norwegian since he had not been there long enough to warrant a week off. Jens had asked if he could call on her one evening. Jane was pleased since Jens was much younger than her. He had called her the second night she had been in the apartment the Americans rented and agreed to go out with him that night for dinner. He had emphasized that it was not a fancy place so dress casual had been his recommendation. He had taken her down towards the ocean to a small but cozy restaurant.

The food had been great and Jane had asked Jens up to her place for a cup of coffee. There had been no coffee but they ended up in each other's arms and in bed. Jane who had been married until her divorce two years ago had never experienced sex like she had that night! Orgasms came one after the other, a first for Jane and she could not get enough. They had been together four nights with Jens leaving late in the Mornings. Jane was delirious when they made love. She seemed to melt and she was transformed out of her body.

Jane had dated in High School but nothing serious or physical. At the Air Force Academy it was frowned upon to get involved with fellow cadets or anyone for that matter. Upon graduation Jane had been a virgin and was one when two years later she married an Air Force Captain. They had both been assigned to the same section at NORAD: at Cheyenne Mountain complex in Colorado Springs. The wedding had been a big affair at the Air Force Academy Chapel and later at the Broadmoor Hotel in Colorado Springs. They had spent their wedding night at the Broadmoor and it had not been a rousing success. When her husband had penetrated her she had screamed in pain. Her husband thinking it was an enjoyable pain had continued pushing into her as fast as he could, finally climaxing. Tears were flowing down her cheeks. He had rolled off her turned on his side and went to sleep. She eased out of bed and was startled at the amount of blood on the bed sheet. She headed for the bathroom and sat on the toilet using toilet paper to stem the flow of blood. She had cleaned herself and took some large towels spreading them on the bloody sheet; her husband was sound asleep. As she laid there her mind wandered. Surely there had to be more to sex and lovemaking than this. She dozed off and was awakened in the morning by her husband mounting her. She turned her head to the side so she didn't have to look at him. It didn't hurt this time. He kept pumping and finally came. She felt nothing although she pretended and kissed him. He pulled out and was about to head for the bathroom when he noticed the towels; picking them up he looked at all the blood on the sheets. Looking at her, he smiled and said "You really were a virgin or are you having your period?" She informed him she was not having her period. He looked at his penis and saw blood. Again he smiled and said "When you screamed last night I knew you were enjoying it. Pure ecstasy, I guess. I'd better take a shower. We ruined the sheets and it will cost extra. It's a good thing we are leaving today. This could turn out to be an expensive honeymoon." As he headed towards the shower Jane turned her head and cried softly into her pillow. It had to get better than this but it didn't. Jane divorced her husband after a year of married frustration. Jane was transferred to Norway after four years at NORAD.

Her times with Jens fulfilled all her dreams of lovemaking. They had talked about how they could meet when they returned to their compound up North. Jens had assured her that it would not be a problem. Jens had come to her house at night and so their lovemaking continued.

It was a week after they came back and Jane had the night duty in the American Secure room when she heard a knock on the outer door. She thought it was strange since only persons with coded key cards could enter. She went through the blackout curtains and opened the door. It was Jens. He pushed through and she quickly shut the door. They were standing in the blackout section.

"You can't be in here," she told him.

"I missed you, I couldn't sleep. I had to see you."

"OK, come in but just for a few minutes."

They walked through the curtains and into the operation room.

"I have something coming in so give me a few minutes."

Jane took her place at the console and pressed a button and a printer started spewing out hard copies. Jens pretended to be looking at a magazine while the printer collated the copies. He was glancing over at the hard copies and caught snatches of its contents. Jane told him they changed disks at midnight and had to bind the hard copies. She got up from her desk grabbed the hard copies and went into a small room where she told him she would prepare the report. Her old disk was still in the computer. Jens grabbed a blank disk from the shelf to the right of the printer and inserted it into the copy section and pressed the copy button on the computer. Twenty seconds later he had the disk and placed it in a plastic case and slipped it into his left pocket.

Jane came out with two spiral bound copy folders. She then ejected the disk out of the computer and placed it in a hard plastic case writing the date and time group on it. She then placed a new disk in the computer and entered a series of codes and gently touched the record device.

"OK, all set for another 24 hours," she said, getting up and walked over the Jens. "If someone finds you in here we will both go to prison. You know that don't you?"

"It's worth the risk Jane. I've missed you." He pulled her in close and kissed her softly on the lips. She responded and soon they were caressing each other; Jens led her to the table between the two monitoring stations and stared to unzip her slacks. He turned her around where she faced the table and pulled down her slacks and panties.

"Bend over the table" he told her. As she did he lowered his pants and underpants and placed his erection against her vagina and with his hand caressed her swollen lips. He inserted his erection just inside the lips and withdrawing it. Jane started pleading with him to insert it deeper; he kept this teasing up and withdrawing and there was a sucking sound each time. Jane was now begging. She could feel the tremors in her body and knew she was about to climax. She could no longer hold it back and she shivered feeling her wetness spill out and on to her thigh.

"You are like a mare in heat," said Jens in a husky voice. It always amazed him the amount of wetness that Jane expelled when she had an orgasm. He started inserting his erection further and further in and Jane was responding. He grabbed her by the hips and pulled her hips hard to him. A cry emitted from Jane's throat. He was now pushing and pulling as fast as he could. He felt her body shivering again and again. He came hard. She felt his semen squirting inside her and she felt the faintness enveloping her. Jens stayed bent over her, massaging her breasts while still inside her. Jane was lying with her face on her arm, nothing like this had ever happened to her before. It was a good thing she had started taking her birth control pills for the amount of semen he deposited in her would have had her pregnant months ago. Jens pulled out of her and pulled her underpants and slacks up to her waist. He then dressed himself. Jane remained bent over the table.

"This is going to have to do for tonight," said Jens. She raised her head and fixed her slacks pulling her sweater down.

"I don't know what you do to me, Jens, but it's wonderful. I have to sit down at my console.

"Let me out first". Jane led him to the blackout curtains and reached up and kissed him on the lips. She let him into the alcove and carefully opened the door. Jens looked out and disappeared. She walked to the console and sat down. She had been sitting there staring at her console when she felt wet between her legs. She felt with her hands and her slacks were wet. Great, what a way to spend the rest of the night with wet pants! Oh well, it was worth it. She knew she had made a mistake letting Jens into the American secure section but she didn't want to lose him and he seemed to more than just like her. He was handsome and he was big and drove her wild when they made love. They had done things she had only read about or had heard her Academy girlfriends talk about. She had always thought they were just exaggerating their affairs. Certainly nothing like this had ever happened to her during her short married life. With her husband it had been just one position and although he groaned and came, it left her lying there unsatisfied with his wetness between her legs.

She had the night duty the whole week and if Jens came she didn't know what to do. If they got caught she knew she would be court-martialed and probably kicked out of the Air Force. She had worked too hard for that and had a promotion coming up. She knew she was in good shape and was a good looking woman but there were so may beautiful Norwegian women much younger. Jens could have his pick yet he had chosen her and the sex was unbelievable. She would have to be careful.

Jens had gone back to his quarters and had printed out the disk. He could not believe what he was reading and seeing. The Americans had a secret section at the station that he was sure the Norwegians were not aware of. He placed the hard copies in a large envelope and addressed it to his old friend in Oslo. He would have to visit Jane each night she was on duty. She liked the sex that was obvious but she was not that great. He would have to spice it up a bit to keep her interest. He saw her walk out of the mess hall the next morning. He walked up to her and walked back toward her quarters with her.

"Are you alright? he asked.

"You know I'm alright" she smiled at him. "But we took a big chance last night."

"John and George will be gone the next three nights. They are going up to the border area to see about establishing small unobtrusive RADAR and they are the only ones making inspections at night so we don't have anything to worry about."

"I don't know" said Jane, "We got away with it once maybe we shouldn't press our luck?"

"Are you getting tired of me?" asked Jens in a hurt voice.

"Oh, you know I'm not. I adore you Jens."

"Well then?"

"OK, I'll see you tonight," said Jane unlocking her door to her quarters.

"I'm late for my shift," said Jens giving her a hard squeeze and walked towards the Ops Center.

George had given Pete a key card and explained to him the workings of the American secure center and explained that John was the only Norwegian aware of it. He had also explained that it ran 24 hours, seven days a week. They changed disks at 2400 hrs. Each night and also printed hard copies. He informed Pete that he and John would be going up north for three to four days and if he wanted to check out the equipment in the secure center it would be a good time to do it while they were away.

Pete had gone through the regular operation centers and the personnel had been very cooperative. In fact, much to his surprise he had discovered a piece of equipment in the American Ops center which although it was working did not correspond to his list. He had notified Bob at the Embassy who had been very surprised and promised to inform the proper people. Bob had asked how it was going and Pete informed him he was going to inspect the secure section the next few nights.

Pete had watched Jane and Jens and it was no secret that they were having an affair. He had been there a week now and it was time to start digging. The people were getting used to him and from what he observed it was a professional group working the RADAR station, including the guards.

Pete was sitting in his quarters going over the rotation schedule at the secure section and noticed that Jane was on duty for the next four nights, having already pulled three nights. Pete decided to go over there around midnight and check the equipment and Jane since she was one of the operators he had not gotten to know well. Pete waited until 2400 hrs. He had shut off the lights in his quarters about one hour prior. He didn't want to be seen going into that section or arouse any suspicion. He had his zipper jacket on and a clipboard in his hand. He eased his door open and slipped out. He was about to head for the secure section when he noticed Jens leaving his quarters heading for the secure section. He watched the door open quickly and Jens disappeared inside. Pete noticed that there was no light coming from the inside. That would mean a blackout curtain or separate entrance room. Pete knew the card key was noiseless and he could at least get into the outer section undetected. He looked around. No one else was out and he headed to the secure section. Listening for any noise and not hearing anything he slipped the card into the slot and the door opened noiselessly. He stepped inside closing the door. He could barely see, heavy black out curtains had been installed and he was hidden in the dark alcove. Pete peeked through the slit in the curtains and could hear two people talking. By widening the slit he could see Jens standing to the right of Jane who pressed a button on her control console and hard copies started spewing out of the printer. Then the printer stopped and Jane gathered the copies up and headed for another door in the secure room. He heard Jens tell her to hurry because he didn't know how long he could wait for her. She informed him he knew it would take her at least 4-5 minutes to spiral the hard copies and get them ready. While she was in the other room, Pete watched as Jens took a disk and inserted it into the computer pressing a button. He is copying the disk thought Pete. Sure enough about 20 seconds later Jens extracted his disk placed it in a hard plastic cover and placed it into his jacket pocket. Pete was starting to sweat. He had a gun with him but he needed better evidence and a witness. He didn't know if Jens was armed.

Jane came out of the other room carrying two thick spiral documents. She went over to the computer pressed a button and her disk ejected. She placed the disk in a hard plastic case and wrote something on it. She then selected a new disk from the shelf to the right of the computer and inserted it into the computer punching in some numbers. She told Jens that they were set for another twenty-four hours. She walked over to Jens who had been leafing through a magazine and placed her arms around his neck.

"You drive me crazy keeping me waiting like this," Jens said to her dropping his magazine and kissing her on the lips. Jane undid his belt and pulled his trousers and underpants down and took his penis in her mouth and started performing oral sex on him. Jens pulled her up and moved Jane over to a table and unzipped her slacks lowered them and her underwear. He bent her backwards over the table lifting her onto it. She kicked one foot free of her clothing and spread her legs. Pete though he better get out for he knew what was coming and it would obscure any noise he made getting out.

Jane was moaning and making small cries. Pete moved quickly and quietly opened the door and went out shutting the door carefully. He looked around and saw no one and headed towards his quarters. He let himself in and sat down in a comfortable chair. The scene had his heart pumping when he settled down he thought about what had happened and was convinced that Jane did not know that Jens was copying the disks. What did Jens do when Jane was not on duty? How did he get the information if he got it at all? She was the only female there or was she? Kirsten Olsen from the Norwegian section was a stunner. Was she seeing Don Miller or Earl Frey or both from the US section? Pete didn't think the Russians were satisfied with only part of the information, especially now that their ship source had dried up. Pete decided to talk to George when he got back. Meanwhile he would go to the secure section earlier the next evening.

Pete entered the secure section at 2300 hours sliding his card and walking in. To say that Jane was surprised and startled was an understatement. Pete held out his hand and introduced himself. "I have not had the privilege of meeting you before. I have been meaning to talk to you but something always came up."

"How may I help you" said Jane retrieving her hand from Pete's firm grip.

"There is little I require of you, this being the secure section; it's basically kept from the Norwegian personnel. To your knowledge have any Norwegians been in here?"

"No, this is strictly a secure American operation. The equipment here is the latest technology available."

"Any problem with the equipment, atmospheric or otherwise?" Pete was now looking at Jane who now had moisture on her upper lip.

"No, everything is running smoothly. We run hard copies every 24 hrs changing disks approximately 30 minutes from now."

"I'll just check the equipment against my list."

Pete went to the opposite end of the room and started checking serial numbers and verifying them against the pictures.

"I didn't realize you were cleared to be here", said Jane, now wringing her hands. Pete was about to answer when the vibrator in his phone went off.

"Excuse me" said Pete turning away from Jane.

Pete pushed the receive button and listened. It was Bob and Pete was told not to say anything and for Pete to go back to his quarters and await further instructions. Pete clicked off the phone and turned around and faced Jane.

"I'm sorry but I have to leave. Can we do this tomorrow night instead?"

"Sure come back anytime. If you come a 0100 hrs., you can see how we print and collate the hard copies getting them ready for shipment."

"Great, I'll see you then." Pete let himself out and headed for his quarters. He did not turn on his light inside but stood peeking out his curtains so he could see anyone approaching the secure section. Sure enough after waiting about 5 minutes, he saw Jens knocking on the secure room door and was let in.

When Jens walked into the secure room he noticed Jane's

demeanor. Her complexion was white and she was sweating.

"What is the matter?" he asked taking Jane by the shoulders and looking into her eyes.

"Alex was here as a matter of fact he just left about 10 minutes before you got here."

"What did he want at this time of the night?"

"He was just checking equipment and wanted to see how we operate."

"Did he seem suspicious? What did he ask you?"

"He was very friendly, wanted to know if we had any problems with the equipment and started checking the far side of the room when he got a phone call."

"What did he say to the party on the other end?"

"Nothing. He just listened and then excused himself and asked if he could come back tomorrow night."

"What did you say?"

"I told him if he came at 0100 hrs. and he could see the collation of the hard copy and how we do the transfer."

"0100, isn't that kind of close?"

"No, I'll just switch disks and explain how the operation works. We'll have time."

"That's cutting it close Jane. Maybe you should make two copies, one normal and do one when he gets here. Tell him you had a problem downloading, he won't check the log."

"Good idea. God I'm glad to see you Jens". Jane placed her arms around his neck and gave him a soft kiss on his lips. "Let me get this collated and I'll be done."

Jens was nervous. This had been too close. He didn't like the idea of Alex snooping around. However, Alex seemed like a nice guy and like he had said on his first night at the mess hall, if his report had flaws the next group they sent over would be vultures, leaving no stone unturned. Jane went into the other room and Jens copied the disk.

Pete turned on the lights in his quarters. He was sitting thinking about the situation in the secure room. He phoned Bob and brought him up to date on the events. Bob informed him to be careful and that he did not need someone else to observe what was happening in the secure room. He would be in touch with George. Pete went over to the mess hall and got himself a cup of coffee.

"Would you like a sandwich or a real American hamburger loaded?" It was one of the cooks leaning on the counter.

"I didn't realize you served food here at night."

"It's a 24 hr. operation. We have smoke salmon, any type of Norwegian food or American."

"Thanks! I'm not going to press my luck. I'll be happy with a good old fashion artery clogging hamburger. Oh, can I have cheese on it?"

"No problem."

"Where are you from in the states?" asked Pete, as the cook was getting thin plastic gloves on.

"Ely, Minnesota, you have probably never heard of it. It's on the Canadian border, beautiful place if you like to fish."

"Myself and three other guys used to go up there from Chicago each summer before high school started in the fall and rent canoes and buy staples at the Wilderness outfitters in Ely. We would paddle in and spend three weeks fishing and exploring, taking hundreds of pictures. It's truly God's country up there," said Pete.

"If you rented and bought food at the Wilderness outfitters you bought from my family. My Dad and Uncle ran that portion and my Mother and Aunt ran the lodge which I'm sure you stopped at on your way in and out."

"Oh! That log lodge was beautiful. I spent the last night each year there before heading home. How did you end up here in Norway? Are you military?"

"Yes, this is my domain. I had to get out of Ely, joined the Air Force and when Colonel Kennedy asked if I would be interested, I jumped at it. My family on both sides are Norwegian and I have heard stories about Norway since I was born. They treat you great here and I have 1 1/2 years for my 30 year retirement. This is the 8th tour I have had with Colonel Kennedy and he has taken good care of me."

"What grade are you? Somehow you don't fit the typical mess Sergeant mold."

"I joined when I got out of high school and I'm top step E-8 and when I get out I take over the lodge in Ely. It's still in the family. I'm a cross country skier and run to stay in shape."

"You refer to George as Colonel; you are the only one I have heard refer to their rank instead of the first name."

"The first time I met the Colonel, he was a 1st Lieutenant. Of course, in those days it was strictly Lt, Capt, Major, etc. This assignment is the first we have gone by first names and civilian clothes. I will always call him by his rank. I don't know, it's something the service breeds into you."

"So you are the mess sergeant here. How come you are working the night shift?"

"One of the youngsters had a chance to go away for a week with his Norwegian girlfriend and her family, so I told him I would do his shift for him. He is in love and far be it for me to interfere with those emotions."

"How about yourself, you married?"

"Yes, 28 years, high school sweetheart, two boys both in college, Air Force ROTC scholarship. My wife is back in Ely supervising the building of our first house. She is of Norwegian decent and knows exactly what she wants, not stubborn but determined you might say."

All the while the Sergeant had been talking he had been frying the hamburger and heating the bun, slicing tomatoes and onions, etc.

"Do you want mayo or ketchup on it?"

"I'll take ketchup, thanks."

The Sergeant slid the burger with cheese on the bun and added the accoutrements and placed it on a plate.

"This is great," said Pete chomping down on the burger.

"It's been a while since I had one of these. It's great!"

"Anytime the cooks will fix you anything you want."

As he ate Pete noticed that he was the only one in the mess hall along with the Sergeant.

"Everyone seems to get along pretty well up here."

"Yes, it's a good group but we have special cases if you know what I mean."

The Sergeant had grabbed a cup of coffee and had joined Pete at the table.

"Oh, you mean they are not happy with the food?"

"No, but between you and me there is one here that thinks he is special and is not a team player, has political connections."

"You are talking about Jens now I assume. That, by the way, was the best hamburger I have ever had. Thanks!"

"Like I said anytime and by the way you are quick. You sure you are a bean counter?"

"Yes, I'm afraid so but it doesn't take a rocket scientist to spot a jerk."

"Good description. Between you and me he threatened one of the Norwegians the second week he was here and had him change his R&R time in Oslo, so Jens could go. Hell, he had only been here two weeks. There was a lot of rumbling amongst the Norwegians."

"Well there is always one", said Pete wiping his mouth and hands on a paper napkin, settling back in his chair and taking a sip of his coffee.

"How long are you pulling double duty?"

"Monday I'm back to my regular shift."

"Doesn't it get lonely up here without female companion-ship?"

"Well some of the people go into town but it's frowned upon although one or two have fallen in-love with local girls and it seems serious. Then there is the R&R down to Oslo and we have nice accommodations there. My wife and I have been separated so many times that you get used to it. Besides, my wife is worth waiting for. She will be over here for a couple of weeks this fall and that's how most of the Americans are working it out. We have some fraternization here in the compound. A couple of officers but no one cares; they are either single or divorced so I guess it's OK."

Pete reached into his pocket and felt a piece of paper. He withdrew it and realized it was the note Ann had slipped into his pocket when he left Oslo. He quickly read it, folded it up and placed it back in his pocket. He wondered why he had not read it before. He looked at the mess sergeant and asked if his name was William or Bill Petersen. The mess Sergeant put his coffee cup down on the table and looked at Pete.

"What gave me away?"

"Well, Ann gave me a note when I left Oslo and the fact that you fried the hamburger on a frying pan instead of using the grill. Although to be honest with you it was the note. I'm to contact you if I get in trouble."

"Everything I told you about Ely is the truth except I attended the University of Minnesota for four years and was recruited by the agency when I graduated. The Colonel doesn't know and it's been tough keeping it from him."

"Why the mess sergeant cover?"

"You would be surprised what you learn from the talk going on in the mess hall. I have had other covers but mostly it's been the mess hall when the U.S. has a joint venture with a foreign country."

"What do you know about what is going on up here?"

"Everything, including the leak; by the way, Jens has a pistol so be careful."

Pete's head was spinning. Why was he up here if they already had someone who could do the job?

"You carry on with your inspections. If you think you need my help, let me know, but try to keep me out of it if at all possible. This is a pretty sensitive station and the fewer people involved the better."

"Did Bob brief you about me?"

"Not much, only that you saved his and his partners life during the Vietnam War and that you are not a very nice person."

"Oh shit, he would get into that."

"Don't get me wrong, I think he meant it as a backhand compliment," said Bill smiling.

"I think I'd better turn in. I have a lot to do the next few days. Thanks for the hamburger and I'm glad to know I have a partner up here."

Pete held out his hand and shook Bill's hand and said good night. Pete's phone rang in his quarters the minute he walked in. It was Bob.

"Thought I'd get you on the secure line; listen, let it play out, the secure section meeting until Jane is off her shift. We are intercepting everything Jens sends down here before his friend gets it. Carry on with your inspections." There was a click at the other end of the line. Pete sat and thought about the call. He would check on Jane tomorrow night and would then watch her quarters when her night shift was over. The following night he let himself into the secure section. Jane seemed nervous.

"I'm just collating the hard copies for the past 24 hours. It takes me a few minutes to bind them and then place them in the safe."

"Does George read them before they are sent out?"

"Usually everything is turned over to him. He makes the final dispatch."

"He is away now. Do you hold the hard copies until he returns?"

"No, his assistant goes over them and makes a copy for George and dispatches the other copy to Oslo. When George has read his copy he shreds it."

"I appreciate your time and cooperation. Let me check the rest of the equipment and I'll be out of here."

"No problem, everything in here is working fine."

"Good, thanks."

Pete checked the rest of the equipment and let himself out. Pete figured he had 3 days left of work. Jane was coming off her shift in the morning.

George and John were back and Pete had breakfast with them.

"How are things progressing?" asked George.

"Fine, found one piece that doesn't match but it's working OK. I gave Bob the report otherwise things are fine. I should be out of here in 2-3 days."

"That sounds good", said John while giving George a strange look. Pete pretended he didn't notice and got up to get himself another cup of coffee.

"If it's OK with you two, I'd like to spend a day in each section from morning through the entire day just to observe how the sections operate without having to check the equipment. That portion is completed."

"Be our guest," said George. "There are extra chairs and consoles in each section not in use."

Pete spent the first day with the Norwegians. They were businesslike and real pros. They invited Pete to observe an incident or unusual incident. Pete figured the Russians didn't have a chance with them looking at every facet of their operation, unless they had the same equipment.

The American section operated in the same manner that the Norwegian section had. Jane was now on the day shift and Pete nodded to her as she walked in. She looked tired and headed towards her console.

Jane was having a hard time concentrating. She and Jens had argued in her quarters. He wanted her to request another week of night duty. She would have to go to George today and ask for another week in the secure section. Why was Jens so insistent that she work the night shift? If she stayed on days they could spend the nights together and she had been looking forward to that. Was Jens getting tired of her or was it something else? She noticed George over at the far end console talking to Earl Grey. That was strange. Grey was supposed to start the night shift tonight. It should be his day off. They were both heading towards her.

"Has everything been running smoothly at the other section at night?" George looked at her with a frown on his face.

"Why yes", Jane retorted quickly. "No problems at all. Is something wrong?"

"No, not with the section but Earl's wife had a miscarriage and is at the hospital down in Oslo. I need to send him down there this morning. There are some complications with his wife.

He came in to clean up his section this morning and I need someone to cover the night shift."

"Oh, Earl, I'm so sorry to hear about Liz. I know how much she was looking forward to this baby. Is there anything I can do?"

"Would you mind covering his night duty? I know I'm asking a lot but Miller has a project going and the higher-ups are pressuring us for the results so I hate to pull him off."

"I'll be happy to cover it and here, I want you to buy Liz some nice flowers from me." Jane pulled a 1000 Kroner bill from her pocket and gave it to Earl.

"Thanks Jane. I won't forget this," said Earl as he headed for the door.

"Take the rest of the day off Jane and I appreciate your attitude on such a short notice. I'll cover your section here."

"No problem George, I'll get out of your way," said Jane picking up her handbag and heading for the door.

At the mess hall Pete joined George at his table. George informed him that Jane was back on the night shift and the reason why. Pete looked at George. George told Pete he knew what was going on and asked Pete to just monitor Jens' movements at night and not to interfere. Pete told George that Jane had no idea that Jens was copying her disks. George informed Pete he knew and that he had talked to Bob. Tomorrow night we are arresting Jens when he leaves the secure section and will ship him to a safe house outside of Oslo. Pete informed George that Jens had a gun. George knew that also and he and Pete would take Jens out. No one else knew about it.

"What if he pulls his gun?" asked Pete.

"You and I will each have a weapon with silencers. If it comes to that we shoot for one of his extremities. Try not to kill him as he is too valuable. You will find a gun and silencer in your shaving kit when you return to your quarters."

"What about Jane?"

"She stays for a couple of weeks or so and then we'll see. We will talk later."

George left the mess hall. The mess Sergeant came over with a cup of coffee and wanted to know if everything was OK. Pete told him to contact Bob and see what roll he would play tomorrow night. The mess Sergeant held his cup up and gave an OK signal. Pete left the mess hall and returned to his quarters and inspected the gun. It was a .22 Caliber Ruger. He screwed the silencer on and dry fired it to get the feel of the trigger. He looked at the magazine ejecting two of the bullets; he discovered a small hole in each bullet. He had never seen such a small caliber hollow point bullet before, if that's what they were. With the silencer it made for an awkward weapon. He put the gun in his right jacket pocket. Thank God it fit! The slash pockets were extra large. He could fire it from his pocket but then he would have to go for center mass and George had said to go for the extremities. Well, that made it necessary to aim. He went to the mess hall for the evening meal, sitting with George and John.

"I understand you are leaving us tomorrow or the next morning," said John in a low voice

Pete looked at George who nodded his head.

"I think we have wrapped this up," said Pete. "It's been interesting. I get better food here than I get at home but all good things must come to an end."

John and George smiled. When they were through eating and got up, the mess Sergeant came over and asked how the meal was. "We were just talking about that", said Pete. "Is there any chance of just taking a vacation over here and eating at your mess?"

They all laughed and the mess Sergeant slapped Pete on the shoulder slipping a note in his pocket at the same time. When he got back to his quarters Pete reached in his pocket and read the note. "Chopper will be here at my call around 1245 hours. Have your bags packed." OK, that settled that. There was a knock at the door. Pete opened it and George walked in. He asked Pete what time Jens usually left the secure section.

"About 1230-1245" answered Pete.

"There is a shadow by his quarters and he will be coming out of bright lights so it will take a few minutes for him to get his night vision. It's only 25 yards from the secure section door to the door of his quarters. You will stay in the shadow of the secure section and I will be by his quarters with a rifle with night scope and silencer. You will have a cloth soaked in chloroform.

As he exits the door, he will have his back to you. Place the chloroform over his nose and mouth. It has to be fast."

"I have used that before. We are about the same height so I may have to hit him between his head and shoulders. That should collapse him and it will make the chloroform easier."

"The guns will be the last resort. We'll use handcuffs. There will be a chopper here to take you and him out of here. Can you think of anything we have left out?"

"You have to explain to the people here why Jens is missing."

"Yes, John has a replacement ready. Jens suffered an appendix problem so we had to evacuate him to Oslo and you will make your exit speech tomorrow at supper. Make it light and short."

No problem," said Pete.

George let himself out. Pete packed his things. It was going to be a long day tomorrow. He was getting too old for this type of work. He would have a chat with Bob when he reached Oslo.

At lunch the next day, George told him they would use a car for the transfer to the airfield. He, George, would drive them, less noise and commotion. The car would be parked next to George's quarter which was not unusual. Pete looked over at the mess Sergeant who gave him a thumbs up. At supper Pete stood up and asked for the people's attention. He told them that his report was completed and thanked them all for their cooperation and congratulated them on their professionalism. Seldom had he observed such a dedicated group. I told George here that "I have probably gained ten pounds eating here." The food is better than I get at home, however that is classified." They all laughed. Pete sat down. On his way out he went over to the mess line and thanked them all for the fine food. He shook hands with the mess Sergeant who was standing a little apart from the rest of the cooks. The mess Sergeant told him he had talked to Bob and suggested a car instead of the chopper. Bob had agreed and had informed George. A plane would be ready at the airfield. Pete thanked the mess Sergeant and said he would definitely head up to Ely in the next few years. Walking back to his quarters, Jens came up to him and walked along with him.

"Will we receive any more visitors from Washington?"

"I don't think so. I have been working on the final report all day and it's tight. I think they will be pleased with it and the professionalism I have observed here. You Jens, you are lucky to be working with this group. I can tell you from my personal experience that the quality of the people is superb. I have worked with some real Neanderthals in my life and most of my current workers don't come close to what you have here."

"That sounds good. I was lucky to get this assignment and I agree they are good especially when you consider there are no problems having two nations working together. It is, as you say, unusual. I hope you have a good trip back. Jens shook Pete's hand and headed for his work station.

Pete had measured Jens up as they talked and walked, he was in good shape, young and tough. He would have to review carefully tonight's assignment.

Pete watched Jens going into the secure section. He walked out, no one was in sight. The car was by George's quarters. He could not see George. He had a bottle of chloroform that George had given him and a padded cloth and his gun was in his pocket. He took up his station to the left of the secure door. There was no moon so it was dark. After what seemed like hours the door opened and closed swiftly. Pete had just poured a good amount of chloroform onto the cloth and capped the bottle placing it in his pocket. Jens seemed to be about to turn towards Pete maybe smelling the chloroform when Pete brought the edge of his hand hard down on Jens between the head and shoulder. Jens went to his knees and Pete placed the chloroform pad over his nose and mouth. Jens struggled a little trying to get to his feet but Pete kept the cloth over his face. Jens sank to the ground and George was there with the car. They handcuffed Jens and placed him in the back of the car on the floor. Pete's belongings were placed over him. George and Pete got into the car and slowly headed for the gate where George showed his ID card. Then they drove towards the airfield. Pete had removed the disk and gun in Jens' pocket. Inside the secure section Jane thought she heard some noise outside but kept sitting in her chair feeling the wetness flow out of her. She was a lucky woman, she thought.

At the airfield the twin engine jet was ready to go. A man Pete did not recognize came down the plane stairs and helped them carry Jens aboard. Even though his hands were handcuffed the stranger placed irons on his legs and secured them to an iron loop in the plane's floor. Jens was placed sitting up and strapped in with the seat belts. George shook Pete's hand and left. The stairs were pulled up and the door to the plane secured. Pete recognized the stranger as one of the men in civilian clothes who had been at Bob's briefing in Oslo several weeks before. Pete gave the chloroform bottle and cloth to the man who placed it in a plastic bag and sealed it. Pete also gave him Jens gun and his own with the silencer. These the man placed in a briefcase. When they had gained altitude, Jens was starting to wake up. He threw up a little spittle which the other man cleaned up with a cloth and placed it in another plastic bag. Jens was now awake and spoke in a hoarse voice wanting to know what was going on. He asked if they knew who he was. No one spoke. Jens realized he was handcuffed and secured and laid his head back and closed his eyes. Pete went into the bathroom and washed his hands thoroughly with soap to get the chloroform smell off. He returned to the cabin with a soaked towel and wiped Jens' face. Jens opened his eyes and starred at Pete not saying a word. Pete returned to the bathroom and threw the towel in the trash container. Returning to his seat he was handed a cup of coffee by the man. They both sat behind Jens and sipped their coffee not saying a word. The plane started descending and half an hour later they landed. The man opened the door and the stairs descended. He nodded for Pete to take his baggage and leave. Pete walked down the stairs with his bags and was greeted by Bob.

"Throw your things into the back of the car and get in." Bob got in and they drove through the airfield gate. No one stopped them.

"Nice job and congratulations. I knew I picked the right guy for this ops."

"I'm getting too old for this," said Pete. He briefed Bob on the weeks up there as they headed in to Oslo.

"You will be staying with us for the rest of the night. You can write up your after-action report in the morning and head home."

"That sounds good. You sure I'm not putting you out? I can get a hotel."

"Not on your life! Ann is waiting and has the guest room made up. Don't disappoint her."

"I wouldn't do that," said Pete smiling. Ann seemed happy

to see him, giving him a hug when he entered their apartment.

"The warrior returns", she said smiling. Pete was told which room to put his bags in. When he came out, Bob and Ann were sitting on the sofa holding a drink in their hands.

"What will it be" asked Bob.

"Oh, tonight I'm ready for anything."

"Good, I fixed three of these," said Bob getting up and going to the kitchen and returning with a glass of Scotch he handed it to Pete.

"To a successful mission," said Bob holding up his glass. They all took a sip of their glass. "I had a talk with George"; he related what transpired up there. The last thing he said was "don't let this guy go; he is good!"

"I have heard a lot about you," said Ann. "But I didn't know you were a voyeur?"

Pete laughed and told them he didn't peek long enough to see the action but did hear some sounds.

"I know I'm getting old but I will admit my heart was pounding when I got back to my quarters." They all laughed.

"Are you blushing?" asked Ann.

"I probably am, she was a looker."

Bob told him he would write Betty a letter and tell her what a lecherous husband she had. Pete told them she had known that for a long time.

"Speaking of the looker, what will happen to her?" directing his question at Bob.

"That's up to the Air Force. She has a spotless record up until now. I know she is on a promotion list. She did violate a pretty sensitive security breach. She could get a Court Martial but then a lot of sensitive information might get out. She is a ring-knocker (a term used for anyone graduating from a military academy) which is in her favor. To be honest I don't know. The Air Force will have to deal with it and from past experience that branch of service has a tendency to sweep things under the rug."

"God, we have invested a lot of money into her, she is

bright."

"Would you feel the same way if she was ugly?" asked Bob with a smile on his face.

"Yes, I probably would. It was a mistake of the heart or loneliness from what I understand. She had a short and less than fulfilling marriage."

"Loneliness is what has caused us numerous breaches at our Embassy around the world. We can't afford them. You are getting too soft for this type of work. I can remember when you would have shot both of them."

"You are right and the thought entered my mind up there. But the enemy is too far removed now and besides Betty has made a human being out of me, at least a nicer one."

"This is getting too serious," said Ann. "Not to change the subject but how was your food up there?"

"The food was great and when I get back to the States I'm going up to Ely, Minnesota and do some fishing like I used to do when I was in high school."

"It sounds like you made a friend up there," said Bob.

"Yes, a very helpful one."

They went to bed and Pete slept until 10:00 o'clock, something that had not happened in years. Bob and Ann had left a note and the password to their computer so he could write up his after action report. There was a pot of coffee and cereal on the kitchen table. He took a shower, got dressed and had some coffee. Then he got his notes out and wrote up his report and placed it in an envelope. He got his gear together pressed the button on his phone which was answered on the first ring. Bob informed him there would be a car to pick him up in 15 minutes. "Come by here and drop off your report and I'll leave you alone for a while."

When Pete arrived at the Embassy, he was ushered into Ann's office.

"Good morning," she said with a smile. "Can I get you a fresh cup of coffee?"

"Yes, please."

"Bob will be here in a few minutes. He is in a meeting with our Norwegian counterparts."

Just then Bob walked in and told Pete to follow him into his office. Pete took a seat and tossed the envelope on Bob's desk.

"I want to tell you the Norwegian intelligence are really pleased with the operation last night. They know about our secure section: have known about it since we upgraded the site. They are working with us and have received copies of everything we have gotten. They are a tight little group - very professional."

"Do you need anything further from me?" asked Pete.

"No, Ann has made travel arrangements for you. A car is waiting."

They shook hands and as Pete was heading out the door, Bob asked for the shaving kit. Pete opened his briefcase and extracted it, handing it to Bob who weighed it in his hand and informed Pete that he appreciated his handling of the situation up North. Pete gave him a wave and headed into Ann's office. She gave him a hug and a kiss on the cheek. She handed him his ticket and said "We will be seeing you snake eater" then ushered him out the door.

The flight to Bergen was uneventful with nice weather over the mountains. Pete took a taxi home. He went next door to pick up Heather their Sheltie. She was sleeping with her face on an old slipper. His aunt explained that Heather had not eaten much of her dog food that he had brought over. Pete knew what her meals had been; fried fish cakes with buttered potatoes and meatballs. He woke her and she gave him the evil eye as if to say "where have you been and where is my Mother". He collected her bowl and dog food and she reluctantly followed him. He gave his aunt a nice bottle of cognac and thanked her. Back at the house Heather followed him around while he changed into his jogging suit and running shoes. He gave her fresh water and a bowl of dog food. She drank but just sniffed the food. He made himself a drink and went out and sat on the porch. Heather went out and inspected her property. Someone was walking on the road about 150 feet below the house and heather let them know they were not welcome. She finally came up on the porch and jumped up on the other lounge chair and closed her eyes. Pete was getting the silent treatment but she would come around just like all females. He sat thinking what had transpired up North. He had not had a chance to talk to Bob but he would let him know that he was reaching a point in his life where he was losing coordination and reflexes that he once had. It had been exciting and brought back memories. He would not tell Betty about his adventure. Bob had stuck an envelope in his briefcase and it was double his agreed upon fee. He would walk down to the village bank and place it in his vault box tomorrow. The phone rang and he went inside and grabbed it. It was Betty.

"Where have you been? I have been worried about you. I have called day and night. Have you found a younger model or have you been playing games with Bob?"

He told her he had been in Oslo and had just gotten home; no he had not found a younger model. At his age it was too hard to train a new woman and besides he was happy and loved the woman he had. That seemed to calm her down. She asked if his relatives knew he had been away and how was Heather? He told her to work on her priorities. She had not asked how he was but was worried about their dog. She apologized and asked how he was. He told her he missed her and asked how she was doing and feeling. The doctors were happy with her and said Norway seemed to be agreeing with her. She had sold the townhouse and gotten the asking price they had agreed on. There should be an express letter at the post office in the village and for him to sign it and send it back to her by Express mail. It was the only thing holding up the sale. He told her he would drive down to the post office as soon as he hung up. He asked about her mother and told her to say hello. She told him she would be home in a week and could they take a vacation when she got home. OK, I have to go and see the lawyer and make sure the paperwork is on track. I'll place the money in a Certificate of Deposit. No I can't do that because I need your signature. Send me a limited power of attorney in the Express envelope.

She told him she loved him and hung up. It was a good thing he hadn't touched his drink because he would drive down to the village. He drove down to the mailbox and amongst the mail found a slip of paper indicating he had an Express letter. He took the slip and drove down to the Post Office and handed the slip to the woman behind the counter. He took the envelope and walked across the street and up two flights of stairs to his attorney's office. He explained what he needed and while he waited for the attorney to fill out the paperwork he read the sales contract and signed it. He signed the power of attorney and headed back to the post office; he mailed an express enve-lope to Betty with its contents. He was the last customer. They locked the door when he left.

When he got home one of his cousins was parked by his house. Pete drove around him and into the garage. His cousin got out of his car and greeted Pete.

"So where have you been my friend? You know you can't make a move around here even going to Oslo weeks ago and disappearing!"

Pete told his cousin he was in the wrong business. Instead of being a lawyer he should be in the intel business.

"Well, when one of our cousin's wives, who is an airline stewardess, walks down the aisle of the plane and says hello to you and you don't answer, she figured you were up to no good!"

"Oh shit, come in and have a drink. I have had a tough couple of weeks."

Heather was happy to see Pete's cousin but was still giving Pete the silent treatment. Pete fixed a drink and took his out of the refrigerator and they went out on the porch and sat down.

Pete took a long sip of his drink and told his cousin he had been at the U.S. Embassy in Oslo. He asked his cousin if he had read in the newspaper that there were rumors of a big demonstration by the Norwegians, especially the University students protesting the U.S. invasion of Iraq. His cousin nodded his head. Pete explained that he had a friend there and he had asked Pete to come to Oslo and write an Emergency SOP in case something happened as there was no written instructions on what to do.

"Is this the same person you had dinner with almost a month ago at the Solstrand Hotel and the next day you and Betty had lunch with him?"

"You are in the wrong business."

"Why?" asked his cousin "Don't they have people who can write up something like that?"

"I used to do things like that in my former life before I retired and they knew about it."

"The rumor around the family was that you had a woman stashed in Oslo or the vicinity and does Betty know about this?"

Pete told him she knew and since they didn't have a demonstration, at least they knew what to do. His cousin smiled at him and told Pete he better get in touch with his cousin's wife, the airline stewardess, and apologize. Pete assured him that he would.

"Did you write this paper in Oslo or somewhere else?"

Pete looked at him. This cousin was his best friend. They even owned a cabin cruiser together. Their wives were inseparable.

"What do you mean?" asked Pete.

"Well, you took off from a military airfield heading north the same day you arrived in Oslo."

"Who else knows about this?"

"I talked to the Chief of Staff, our cousin's husband, two days later. He thought it was kind of strange."

"Does anyone else know?"

"No, he only mentioned it but told me to keep it to myself

and not mention it to anyone else. I haven't told anyone."

Well, all I can say is I did an old friend a favor which affected Norway as much as the U.S. I would like to leave it at that."

"OK, but I think you are up to your old tricks again but that's between you and me."

After his cousin went home Pete sat on the porch. Heather had now licked his hand and jumped up in the vacant chair and was keeping watch over the road below the house. It was her way of making up. He thought about what his cousin had said. Betty was right. You had to be careful. His family was involved in too many things. How the hell had they seen him depart the military airfield? Was there a camera or some type of surveillance device there? He picked up the phone and called Bob and explained what had just transpired. Bob said he would look into it and not to worry. The bird Pete had brought back had sung and was still singing, didn't want to bring any shame to his family or uncle. He had asked who Alex Lien was. Of course, no one knew a person by that name. "Say hello to Betty." The phone clicked off.

The money was good. He had gotten a bonus for the ship affair plus the passage up North for Betty and her mother. He would have to talk to Betty when she got back. Maybe it was time to sell his real estate and boat and head back to the good old U.S. They would have a party and invite his cousin and her husband the Chief of Staff. Well, it was time for Heather's walk and her meal.

Betty arrived a week later. Pete had painted the outside of the house so everything looked nice and bright. Betty was in a good mood and it was a good reunion. They decided to take a trip down to the Greek Island of Mykonos where they had been several times before and knew the hotel owner. The hotel furnished a car to take them to a secluded beach but not an empty beach where clothes were not worn. Betty had maintained her shape and looked good. It was delightful to swim without clothes and there were people of all ages, most from Germany and northern Europe.

This sure is relaxing," said Pete looking around at the scenery.

"Well you are not too relaxed" said Betty looking at him. "See something you like?"

"No, thank you. I have everything I like lying next to me."

"Right answer" said Betty smiling.

It was raining and cool upon their return to Norway. They had decided to give a party the following weekend. About 20 cousins and their spouses showed up. Betty always organized a nice party. Pete got the Chief of Staff into the den and had a chat with him. It was agreed that what had transpired would go no further. However, the Chief of Staff informed Pete to be careful because the family was everywhere. The Prime Minister was grateful for the low exposure; politically it could have been a bombshell. Pete called Bob the next morning and gave him an update. He took it in stride and asked Pete if he and Betty could take a trip to Oslo the following week. Bob informed him it was a social call and there would be tickets waiting for them at the Bergen airport. Pete told Betty about the phone call and awaited her response. She wanted to know what it was all about and Pete told her what Bob had said. Betty agreed and said she could be ready by Wednesday. Pete relayed the decision to Bob who informed them that a car would be waiting for them at the airport in Oslo.

The trip to Oslo was uneventful. Betty was impressed with the nice car and driver waiting for them. They were ushered into Ann's office. The two women had never met and Betty made the comment that she knew now why Pete was making trips to Oslo. Ann laughed but claimed that she had already handcuffed Bob and he was stuck with her. They both laughed. Ann opened the door to Bob's office where a nice spread had been laid out. Bob was behind his desk and stated it was about time they showed up. Ann had gotten all this food and he was famished. They had a nice lunch and the girls seemed to get along. Ann wanted to know if Betty was interested in a shopping trip. She knew these stores that she thought Betty would like. Bob informed them that the Embassy had these guest apartments and one was reserved for them.

"I would love to go shopping" said Betty. "Our little village is limited in clothes selection so you lead the way."

"This is going to cost Pete when Ann shops she shops!"

"Well, I know her sister," said Pete.

The girls cleaned up the dishes and said their goodbyes. "Ann, remember we made those reservations at that little restaurant down by the ocean for tonight so be back in time."

The girls left giggling like a couple of high school girls.

When the door closed Bob told Pete that there was a small problem up on the border with Russia. It seemed there was a high ranking Russian officer that wanted to defect. "Oh! Didn't you learn from your Viet Nam tour and who is going to the rescue this time?"

"Jesus that was a close one wasn't it. They were ready to chop our heads off when you and your men showed up."

Pete informed him that he was much older now and didn't have people he could count on to back him up. "I'm too old to get in a pissing or shooting contest with the Russians. Does anyone else know about this?"

"The Norwegian Intel is aware and has promised a backup of their Jager unit (our Special Forces) in the event of problems. They will be well hidden but within range and they are good!"How did we hear about this?"

"One of their tourist boats swamped on the river separating the two countries and the Norwegian border patrol helped in the rescue and this Russian General stuffed an envelope into one of the Norwegian officer's pocket. It was addressed to the Norwegian Intel service and the U.S. Embassy. Here is the letter or should I say note."

Pete read it carefully and read it a second time. It seemed

legit but one had to be careful.

"Has the Burma Fax read this?"

"He has and said to tread lightly. It could be a coup for us which means if something goes wrong he knows nothing about it. The usual backup he tells everyone."

"Do we know who this General is and what his job is?"

"Yes, we ran him through our computer. He is the head of Army Intel for Northwest Russia."

"Holy shit; do we have a way to contact him?"

"Yes, he will be up on the border for the next week where the river and the Arctic sea meet."

"There is little vegetation there. In fact, I can't remember any vegetation except for some scrawny trees," said Pete with a frown on his face. "We will have to do it at night and about a mile down the river. If you can get a message to him to that effect, tell him there will be a small boat waiting for him and whoever he wants to bring along to get into the boat and hang on."

Bob looked at Pete and smiled.

"I want about 1/2 a mile of rope and a four wheeled drive vehicle with plenty of horsepower and the Jager unit. I'll go up there in the next few days dressed in a Norwegian border guard uniform. I'll recon the area and find a suitable crossing."

"Thanks" said Bob slapping Pete on the back.

"Don't thank me yet. I want Ann to take Betty to Paris and show her around, especially the Louvre. I'm sure you have guides at the Embassy down there who can guide them and protect them. Not a word to Betty. Talk to Ann and make it seem like a spontaneous trip that Ann has always wanted to take. Betty has been after me for a year to take her down there. A week should do it but Ann has to spring it on her tonight."

"No problem, Ann will jump at it. I'll make it sound like we got invited and have to act on it soon. I'll get on the phone right now to our Embassy down there and make arrangements. Get yourself a cup of coffee and relax."

Bob got on the phone and asked for a certain person. Bob outlined the trip and at the end said it was a request from the Burma Fox. He was assured that a car would pick up the ladies and that they would be well taken care of. "Not too well!" Pete heard Bob tell the person at the other end as he hung up.

"All set. I just have to tell them what flight they are coming in on and when."

The girls returned from shopping and were in a good mood. Bob informed Pete and Betty that a car would take them to their apartment and would pick them up for dinner. "Dress casual. It's not a fancy restaurant but the food is great. We'll meet you there at 8 o'clock."

On the way to their apartment, Betty could not say enough good things about Ann. "She is just like us, down to earth. I could really be friends with her."

The driver took them and their small suitcases up to the apartment and informed them he would pick them up a 7:45PM. The apartment was luxurious. Betty showed Pete what she had bought. The last item she went into the bedroom and put on. It was sheer black lingerie with open spaces so that it left nothing to the imagination. "Ann bought one just like it. How do you like it?"

"I don't think we will make dinner nor will Bob and Ann," said Pete rising out of his chair, steering Betty into the bedroom.

"Don't rip it," was all Betty said as they settled on the bed.

"Wow" said Betty afterwards as she snuggled in Pete's arm. "I should have gotten one of these outfits long ago."

Pete looked at the clock; it was time to get ready. He slapped Betty on the butt and told her to take a shower. Betty had dozed off and stumbled out of bed. "I don't know what you do to me Mr. Compton but do it again when we get back."

He rinsed off in the other shower and was dressed and ready when Betty came out in a nice pair of slacks and sweater. The restaurant was timbered and looked old but it was crowded. Bob came and steered them to a corner booth. Ann looked happy and was in an excellent mood..

"I can tell by your face, Betty, that you showed Pete the black outfit."

Betty just smiled and said "I think Bob was treated also". The waiter appeared and took their drink orders. The dinner was superb. Ann had ordered for all of them. While they were having their dessert Ann asked Betty if she had ever been to France."

"Well, I have a good deal coming up but we have to leave in two days, all expenses paid for six days tour guide included," said Ann. Betty looked bewildered. She looked at Pete and Bob. No one said anything.

"Are you inviting me to go to Paris?" asked Betty.

"Yes, if you can stand my company for six days. I know a very expensive couture that makes the most beautiful clothes; of course, it would also give us a chance to stroll around the Louvre for a few days also."

"Wait a minute" said Pete with a frown on his face. "Didn't you two go shopping today? After all we have to put away some money. There is a limit to what we can spend on luxuries."

"Did you and Bob go to the same school or are you related? Don't tell me you didn't like the black outfit Betty brought home today? It would give you a break Pete. You wouldn't have to wander around Paris. I know you have been there several times and you are not that fond of the place."

"Bob are you OK with this? I will soon have to go out on the street corner and sell pencils. This woman is going to bankrupt me."

"Hell, its only money! Let them go down and enjoy themselves. It would save you and me the agony of going to look at all those pictures again not to mention shopping."

"I guess I know when I'm outnumbered. This is going to cost you!" said Pete.

"You mean the black outfit again tonight?" said Betty with a straight face.

They all broke out in laughter.

The next morning Pete and Betty flew home and Betty packed for her Paris trip. Pete would take her to Oslo and the Embassy and see her and Ann off to Paris.

"Don't get into trouble while Ann and I are gone," said Betty as they entered the Embassy.

"Don't worry. Bob asked if I would write up a security SOP for the Embassy which I'm not looking forward to."

"Be nice and remember this trip is not costing us anything so cooperate with him. Ann said that Bob thinks a lot of you."

"Yea, but I'm getting old and my mind is not clicking like it used to do."

"It sure clicked good at home last night!"

"I'm going to burn that black outfit of yours. I'm beat today! I hope there is a bed here in the Embassy where I can catch up on my sleep."

Ann was waiting for them at the office. She looked at Betty and then Pete. "You look tired Pete. You know you can wear it out! Bob is not too peppy today either. I think our trip will do both of you good and give you a rest. I have the tickets and a car is waiting downstairs to take us to the airport. You and Bob get some rest and you'll feel better."

Bob came out of his office and kissed Ann goodbye and gave Betty a peck on the check and told them to behave themselves. Pete said his goodbye and followed Bob into his office.

"Everything is a go. The things you wanted are waiting for you up at the border-guard headquarters. We made contact with the crosser and have two men up there who can contact him when you are ready. A plane is waiting for you at the airfield. It's making one stop to drop a person off at the RADAR site and then it's all yours."

Bob went with Pete to the airfield and gave him another phone. "It's more powerful. Keep me advised."

Pete got his bag and headed for the plane. As he walked up the stairs and into the plane, his eyes couldn't believe who was sitting in one of the seats. It was Jane from the RADAR site.

He put his bag in an empty seat and took a seat next to her. She said hello and Pete returned the greeting.

"Are you headed up to the RADAR site?" she asked in a muted voice.

"No, I'm going further north. Are you OK?" he asked as the plane taxied out and took off.

"Yes and no. I have been trying to locate Jens while in Oslo but it's like he has disappeared. I know you must have realized that we were more than friends when you were up there."

"Yes, I guessed as much but then George came and got me and told me Jens was in a bad way. He thought appendix or something. Jens was in pain. There was a military ambulance waiting when we arrived at the airfield. Did you call his parents?

"Yes, I finally got in contact with their residence but a housekeeper answered and said they were on a trip to Germany. I asked about Jens but she said she didn't know where he was."

Tears were running down her face. "The maid told me that Jens fiancé had gone with them."

"I'm sorry, I didn't know Jens that well but he seemed like a nice person."

"Yes he was" said Jane wiping her eyes with a hanky.

"Anything going on at the RADAR site? It seemed like a good group of people up there. I enjoyed my time there. Unfortunately I sent my report to the States and was told to check on a site further north. It's just a two or three days stop and then back to the good old U.S. Norway is great but people here are too civilized for me; their government too socialistic. I like more action."

"I know what you mean. I'll probably be heading back soon myself. I got promoted and I'm waiting for orders."

"Congratulations," said Pete, tapping her gently on the shoulder.

"Thank you, but unlike you I like Norway and would have stayed here for the next two years but it seems the Air Force has other plans."

"You mean you liked Jens. Let me tell you, I was in love with a girl and we planned to get married when I returned from my last tour in Viet Nam. However, I got a Dear John letter from her about half way through my tour. It just about destroyed me. We were compatible in every way. It devastated me. She had found someone else. End of story. So I know how you feel."

"Did you find someone else when you got back to the states?"

"Yes, I did. I found the nicest girl and have been married over thirty years, have two children both girls. We still act like a couple of newlyweds."

"A nice story, I hope I have your luck."

"You will. You are a good looking woman Jane. Don't sell yourself short. The fact that Jens had a fiancé tells me he was not as nice as you think. If you and I had a relationship, I certainly would have cut any ties to anyone else. He was lucky to have you but he was cheating not only on his fiancé but also on you and you deserve better. Someone in the Air Force thinks highly of you, otherwise you wouldn't be sitting on this plane today newly promoted, considering your indiscretion at the RADAR site. But that's a secret between you and me."

Jane blushed and looked at Pete.

"Who are you?"

"Let's just say I'm your friend and let's leave it at that."

"Do you know where Jens is?"

"No, I don't and it would not do you any good to go around moping about him because he almost got you court-martialed and ended I think not only your future but also your future happiness. So let your indiscretion be a lesson to you otherwise life could be miserable for you. I didn't lie to you about my love affair; if it hadn't ended I would never have known what true happiness really is."

Jane looked worried. The plane was starting to descend.

"One more thing Jane, don't tell anyone at the RADAR site that you saw me. The case is closed and you are a beautiful and lucky woman with a fine career ahead of you. I know there is a guy waiting for you back in the States but take your time."

Jane smiled at him and said "I owe you whoever you are and I won't forget it."

After dropping Jane off, the plane continued north and landed at NATO airfield not far from the Russian border. Pete was met by two Norwegian military men and was escorted by jeep to the Norwegian Brigade's North headquarters where he met a Colonel Holm. They shook hands and went to a briefing room with a large map of the border area. "Please take a seat and we will brief you on where you are and the border area."

A Major oriented Pete and explained that the only good crossing point for what he had in mind was located one and a half miles south on the river. He recommended that the crossing take place during the night on or about 03:00 to 04:00 because that was the graveyard shift for the guards in the tower who were at minimum efficiency at that time. The Major also explained that the ground was solid at this sight and a vehicle could easily traverse the area at this point. A man in border uniform without insignias took over the briefing and explained that contact had been made with the Russian General; he would have one other person with him. Both would be in civilian clothes with one bag between them. The Jager unit is here on standby should they be needed. He went over the list of equipment that Pete had requested. The boat was a 13 foot skiff with a small keel and reinforced in the area where the rope was to be attached. The inside of the boat was lined with a rubberized material which was self sealing in case of rifle fire. The boat would be taken across the river by two men from the Jager unit with scuba gear. A doctor and corpsmen would be on site in case of injuries. If the general can't make it on the night in question, the boat will be returned to the Norwegian side.

"Is there a plan "B"? asked Pete. "There is," explained the briefer. The river is approximately 12 feet deep and a little over a quarter of a mile up from Plan A location. Two scuba divers will swim across and place masks on the General and his companion and attach a rope to them which will be attached to a jeep and dragged across. The plane you came in and landed in such a way that the Russians are not aware of its presence. It is fueled and ready to go."

"I want two Jagers on the plane in case there is any trouble and I want an automatic pistol. I like Plan B. Is there a problem getting the two scuba divers across current etc.?"

"No, there shouldn't be. The guard towers are a little further apart at that point. The current is weaker upstream and it increases further down. Upstream is where the small tourist boat operates so it might be the best spot."

Get word to the General that we will pick him up at the Plan B sight and that he will get wet. Also get me a scuba outfit and a sealed pistol. I'm going with the Jager men."

The briefer looked at Pete with a frown and at the other men in the room. "Do you think that's wise?"

"I have been involved in these operations before."

"I think I'd better make a call," said the briefer.

"If you are calling who I think you're calling, he is alive today because of exactly such an operation where I saved not only his life but also his partner's. So forget the call. I assure you I'm well qualified with scuba gear. I just need to see the regulators because they have changed.

"OK, it's your game. Bring in a suit and tanks - the works." Two minutes later two young men brought the gear in. One of the men explained the new system to Pete. "No problem," said Pete. "Get the message to the General that we will get him in the morning at 03:30 hours." Pete went over to the map and studied it. When he got outside he extended the antenna on his phone and pressed a button. It was answered immediately, "A OK plan B" and Pete clicked off. Pete got with the Jager unit and briefed them. He wanted two snipers at the nearest towers not to open fire unless the Russians did. The other Jagers were to be camouflaged and feed the rope out as the swimmers went across. When they felt two hard pulls on the rope, they were to gun the vehicle on its prescribed route as fast as it would go. When they got the two people on land, they were to search them, get them to a concealed area, strip them naked and put on some large border uniforms on them.

"What if they put up resistance?" asked the Jager who appeared to be in charge.

"Subdue them with your hands, place cuffs on them, blindfold them and gag them. Place their clothes and personnel effects in a bag and get to the airfield. Do not board the plane until I get there. Snipers watch the opposite bank of the river carefully with your night scopes. The range should be OK even with the silencers on your rifles. Anymore questions? Do not discuss this with anyone else outside this group. This is "Top Secret".

The Jagers took off to make preparations. Pete went back into the briefing room. "Have the rope attached to the vehicle and make sure it has a clear path to go when given the word. Is there a mess hall around here? I'm starving!"

The two who had been standing by the map told Pete to come with them. They headed towards the airfield and then descended a steep slope and opened a door which Pete had not noticed. The mess hall was underground. They walked into a neat spacious room where some boarder guarders were eating. Pete recognized the mess sergeant immediately. He smiled not saying anything. All three of them went through the serving area and took a stainless steel tray with compartments in it. As they went along the serving line, the cooks asked what they wanted.

"Can I have an American cheeseburger with everything on it?" asked Pete. "I'm sorry," said the mess Sergeant. "We don't have cheeseburgers but we do have fresh fish. I can fry it up in a few minutes."

"That will be great" said Pete, "I'll just grab a cup of coffee and wait."

"I'll bring you a cup, take a seat."

Pete sat down and the mess Sergeant brought the coffee

over to him before the others joined them. "You do get around!"

"I was told to go up here and keep an eye on you. I'll have your fish to you in a few minutes."

The others joined Pete, their trays laden with food. "The food is great up here," said the briefer digging into his food.

"I would like to take a look at the river."

"That's no problem. I think you will find it a little wider than you thought it. Good thing we have a large spool of rope."

Pete's fish arrived with boiled potatoes and carrots. After the meal, Pete and one of the border guards walked to the river's edge. There was no sharp embankment but the river was flowing faster than Pete had been told. It would not be an easy swim across with the bag containing the two tanks and masks. He asked the guard if he had ever been in the river?

"Yes, but we use the underwater self propelled scooter or boards."

"Can you show me this equipment?"

"Sure, we have a small equipment place where we store them. They are always ready. We have three types." The guards said, leading the way back towards the mess hall and a little beyond. This storage area was also buried underground. The underwater scooters or boards were lined up. Pete had not seen this type of self propelled underwater crafts before.

"Can these boards take us across the river and back?" Pete was interested in the bigger ones.

"The bigger ones are faster but they all work on the same principle. They are powered by an air breathing engine. The bottom portion is fuel. The pipe extends above the water and catches the air. It is expandable and barely makes a ripple in the water.

"Do they make any noise?"

"No, they are made by Konigsberg and are designed for covert operations. They can actually carry a small torpedo or two people laying side by side. As you can see they have a gyro for direction and a joy stick for steering, a small keel and rudder keeps them on course.

"I don't see a propeller?"

"It uses a water jet whose pipe circles the engine keeping it cool. Once it starts you can't hear anything. The only ripple is the air intake.

"Are they ready to go?"

"Yes, let me check the fuel lever. Yes, they are full. The joy stick works by pushing it forward for speeds 10-15 KM per hour. Turn the joy stick to the side for turning, straight up is stop."

Pete thought about it. They would use them and carry the rope and tanks with them. There would be no moon in the early morning and according to the briefer the weather would be cloudy: mist or rain. Pete thanked the guard and made his way to the briefing hut. The briefer and the Jager leader were standing outside talking. Pete joined them and told them what he had just seen in the storage area. They both agreed that the boards would save them time and energy. They had been talking about them when Pete walked up. The boards were heavy on land but no problem in the water. They had a trailer for them that hooked up to a jeep. We should launch a little further up cause the Tower on the Russian side burned down two days ago and had not been replaced.

"Let's plan on that" said Pete. "I'd better get some rest. Can I assume that where you took my bag is my quarters?"

"Yes, it's all set," said the briefer. Pete went to his quarters and laid down fully clothed. He had just gone to sleep when someone shook him awake and told him it was time to go. He was told they had contacted the General and it was a go. He rubbed his eyes and looked at his watch. He had slept longer than he thought. Pete felt around in his bag and found his K-bar knife and departed for the briefing tent.

Everyone was assembled in the briefing tent. The briefer went over the plan. The boards were in the water. The Jagers seemed anxious to go. They were all in their camos except the two that would go with Pete. He was informed that they had rehearsed the operation. The rope was attached to the jeep. Everything was ready. The Jagers brought in three wetsuits plus a one piece undergarment which would keep any sweat away from their bodies. It was decided to start dressing in one hour. After going over their wetsuits and tanks, Pete noticed that the other two swimmers carried a short automatic 9mm weapon which was attached to the wetsuits. It was time to get dressed. The suits had feet in them and rubber gloves that fit tightly around the wrists. Pete attached his weapon at the waist of his suit and the K-bar above his ankle. They carried their tanks and fins and walked out to the waiting vehicle. No lights were used on the vehicles. They were on their way to the river.

The fins were placed on their feet. Two guards were waiting by the boards. Pete was #2 to take off. He got on the board and sank down starting the engine like he had observed the first swimmer do. It took a few seconds to get used to the board and then it was like a toy. The first swimmer had the rope; the third swimmer had the bag with the tanks and masks. There was an illuminated strip attached to the back of each board so you could follow the leader. They were making good time. They were moving at an angle down to the pickup point. The current was strong and the river was deep. Pete kept watching his gyro and the board ahead of him. He glanced at the watch attached to his wrist. They had been in the water about 15 minutes when he noticed he was getting close to the board in front of him. The lead board had stopped and Pete pulled alongside of him. The third board moved to the other side of the first board. Pete pulled the joy stick to the upright position and shut down his board. They surfaced slowly together.

They spotted their two passengers about twenty feet further down. It had started to mist. The two people walked in a crouch towards them. The two came up and gave a signal and one of the swimmers placed the tanks and masks on them while the other swimmer attached the rope to them about 20 feet apart. They started their engines and the #1 swimmer grabbed the passenger's bag and gave two sharp jerks on the rope. There was a few seconds before the rope started moving. One of the Russians fell and made a splash in the water. The three boards sank as a light hit the water about 10 feet from them. It was the tower. The Russians had just made it under the water when a hail of bullets hit the water around them. Pete raised his board to the surface. The Russians were moving on top of the water instead of under it. He heard a familiar thud as a bullet found it mark. Pete started moving his board under when his leg went limp. Shit he should have stayed in bed. He was hit! He pushed his joy stick forward and caught up with the Russians trying to convince them with sign language pointing down and under the water. Another round hit near his board. He looked at the tower as the light exploded. There were voices from the river's edge and gunfire. Another round found its mark. The two Russians were now swimming on top of the water. There were shouts from the Russian's side as the sniper's rounds found their mark. The #3 swimmer came up alongside Pete's board and indicated for him to go under. A round slammed into the swimmers back and he went under the water as did Pete. The Russians hit the Norwegians side before the swimmers. They were grabbed and taken away. The swimmers hit the soft riverbank and people were there to grab their boards and their tanks and took the masks off them. Pete and the #3 swimmer remained in the water indicating they were wounded. They were dragged ashore and carried to a vehicle. The boards were lifted out and tied to a trailer and disappeared.

Pete and the #3 swimmer were brought to the dispensary. The two Russians were stripped and much to the surprise of the Jagers, one was a woman who was not too happy at being treated in such a manner. Border uniforms were placed on them. The General had been hit twice in the back of his left thigh and left buttocks. The doctor fixed him up for the flight to Oslo. None of the wounds were serious. The Russians were split up; the woman in front and the General on a hospital mattress in the rear. Both were handcuffed and sedated. Pete and the wounded swimmer were able to sit in the seats. The Gulfstream jet roared off and headed south. The flight was long and Pete was tired and sore when they landed outside of Oslo. The two Russians were taken off first along with their bags. Pete and the swimmer were taken to a military hospital and operated on.

When Pete woke up, Bob was standing at the foot of his bed talking to a doctor.

"Well, it's about time you woke. I have important work to do and can't be hanging around a hospital all day. From what I understand we have a very mad woman on our hands but she will get over it. The other person is fine and he is who he said he was. However we have other problems. We have two ladies coming back in three days. The doctor says you can be up and around by then but you will probably require crutches.

"Oh shit. Betty will be furious!" said Pete with a frown on his face.

"Not to mention Ann. All she knows was that you would be looking for a ground RADAR sight up there. She knows nothing about the snatch. I'll be sleeping on the couch for the next month. By the way your wound is not bad. They had to debred it and you'll be taking antibiotics for the next 11 days. I'll be back to see you later. Do you need anything?"

"I'm starving; any chance of some food?"

"Coming right up," said Bob and left.

A nurse came in about half an hour later with a tray of meatballs, potatoes and carrots and a large glass of water. Pete thanked her and dug in. He ate everything, laid back and fell asleep. The next thing he knew someone was shaking him. It was Bob.

"We are not paying you good money to sleep. I just wanted you to know the General brought over a treasure trove of information. The lady is his Chief of Staff and is finally settling down. The General's wounds have been taken care of but will require an extended time to properly heal. They also brought a bag of diamonds and platinum. The woman is talking while the General sleeps. I might add kudos from Langley. They will both be transported to the States within a week."

"Well, I can tell you this will be my last assignment."

"Don't worry about that. We will make it well worth your effort. I have instructions from Langley to be generous. They are reading the documents the General brought and are studying the maps as we speak. I have brought your clothes plus accessories. They are hanging in the closet here. I will pick you up tomorrow. The doctor here will check you over and the Embassy doctor will take care of you from there. I talked to Ann. They are having a great time. I didn't say anything."

"I need to use the bathroom; you can help me up; I never could use those bedpans."

Bob helped him into the bathroom. The leg seemed OK. He could probably get around without crutches. That would be great and less noticeable. He was a little light headed but that would disappear by tomorrow. He called for Bob to help him back to bed but instead a nurse opened the door and took his arm. He asked the nurse what happened to the guy that was here. He was told he got a phone call and had to leave. Pete asked if she would help him walk around. She was hesitant but agreed. They walked around the room until Pete could feel his leg talking back to him. It was time to get into bed. The nurse helped him get comfortable and told him not to try to get out of bed by himself. She asked if he was in pain and he told her no he was fine.

He didn't want that pain pill they stuck up your butt in Norway. He didn't know if they were behind the times or ahead of the U.S. when it came to controlling pain. The nurse left and Pete fell asleep. He woke when he heard voices in the room. The nurse was serving supper; meatballs, potatoes and carrots. Bob came around the bed and asked if that wasn't what he had to eat earlier? "Hospital food is hospital food," said Pete. The nurse pushed a button and the back of the bed raised up so Pete could eat more comfortably. As the nurse left Bob said they had a problem. Pete looked at him holding a fork full of food half way up to his mouth.

"The girls are coming home tomorrow at 1:30 PM. It seems the Embassy in Paris is getting a delegation of Congressmen and women from the States and like Ann said they are both ready to come back. She said the Frenchmen are way overrated and they were both looking forward to a good old American man!

"Holy shit," said Pete. Well it will be good to see them and hear their exaggerated lies. I walked around the room with the nurse and it was no problem. Can you get me out today and over to the Embassy clinic? I know they must have a bed there."

"I guess it could be arranged if you think you are strong enough. I'll go and see what I can do."

"Arrange for an American cheeseburger, French fries and a vanilla milk shake" said Pete as Bob walked out of the room.

Two men came and got him a few hours later. They dressed him after the doctor had looked at his leg and re-bandaged it. It was a short ride to the Embassy and up to Bob's office. Pete sat down in a comfortable chair. Bob was looking hard at him. He asked how he felt and was told fine. There was a knock at the door and a marine brought in the large paper bags and departed. Bob took out the cheeseburgers, French fries and vanilla shake for Pete and the same but a coffee for himself. They started eating not saying anything until the food was consumed and Pete slurped the last of the milkshake through the straw.

"Now that was good," said Pete as he settled back in the chair. They discussed what to tell the girls tomorrow. After many scenarios, they decided to tell them the truth or part of it. They had both been up North and a border guard had accidently fired his weapon trying to clear it before going into the mess hall. The round had creased Pete's leg but it was nothing but a scratch.

A bed had been brought into Bob's office and Pete slept there that night. A doctor came in first thing in the morning and un-bandaged Pete's wound. He added some more antiseptic and re-bandaged it saying it looked good but for Pete to take it easy for a week or so. Pete felt good. He shaved and cleaned up and got dressed. Bob brought in breakfast and they sat around and enjoyed it. Bob made some phone calls while Pete read the newspaper. A marine knocked on the door, stuck his head in and said the car was on its way to the airport to pick up the ladies. Bob cleared the dishes and put them in a small kitchen next to the office. Pete got up and went into the bathroom and brushed his teeth. When he came out Bob told him he looked good except for being a little pale. He also handed Pete an envelope. Pete peeked inside and let out a low whistle.

"It will help pay your divorce settlement when Betty finds out what you have been up to.

"God, I hate to lie to her but this will be a little white lie."

Pete lay back in his chair while Bob had the bed removed from his office. He must have dozed off for the next thing he heard were the girls busting into the office. Two marines carried their luggage and packages, deposited them and left. Bob came around and gave Ann a kiss and welcomed them home. Betty stood there and looked at Pete as he slowly got out of his chair and came over and gave her a kiss. Betty looked from Bob to Pete. Bob told them to sit down and told them the story they had agreed on. Betty looked hard at Pete and wanted to know if he was alright. He assured her he was fine, just a little stiff he told her.

"Now that's what I like to hear" said Ann. "How about you, Bob, a little stiff?" she asked trying to lighten the mood.

"Tell us all about Paris and don't leave anything out. I'll get us all a glass of wine," said Bob.

The girls related their adventure with enthusiasm and informed them that both Bob and Pete would have to go to the bank and get a loan to pay off their credit cards.

"Didn't I warn you, Bob; we will both be out on the street corner selling pencils."

"Are you sure you're OK? You look pale," said Betty.

Pete assured her he was fine. In a day or two he would be back to normal. Ann stole a glance at Bob but didn't say anything. There was more to this story she told herself.

Pete and Betty flew home two days later. Betty went over to Kristi's house to pick up Heather. She was told that Heather had started passing blood again. She had taken her to the vet who had been treating her for the last two years for an ailment common to Shelties when they reached 11 or 12 years of age. Pete had agreed that should Heather start bleeding again to put her down. The vet had told Kristi that there was nothing she could do for her and had put her to sleep. Betty came back crying and informed Pete. It was a shock! Heather had become part of the family. Pete called down to the vet and asked her to have Heather cremated and wanted her ashes in an urn. The vet told him she would take care of everything.

Betty was sitting in the living room teary-eyed. Pete told her it was time to sell their holdings in Norway and move back to the good old U.S.

"It's time to visit our girls and their families even though they have been over here. We have a grandchild we have not seen."

"Well we should look for a home first. The area outside of Tucson, Arizona looks nice and it's warm out there. We can go up to Colorado from there and visit the girls and maybe get some skiing even though we won't be able to ski the black trails anymore at our age."

"Speak for yourself" said Pete. When I go skiing, I go skiing. However, it sounds like a plan. We'll settle in one of the gated country clubs outside of Tucson with all the amenities: golf, tennis and swimming pool."

He went over to Betty, sat down next to her and gave her a kiss.

"It's been a hell of an adventure over here hasn't it?"

The Turner Incident

They were coming up the fairway of the 9th hole. Pete had the shortest drive off the tee, so he was first to hit. He took his 3 iron (his favorite club) out of his bag and took a couple of practice swings. He mentally went over the steps, keep your head down and don't try to kill the ball, let the club do the work. It was a long, uphill shot to the green, about 170 yards. He felt good as he brought the club up and swung it through the arch. The club head's contact with the ball sounded good and he followed through with the swing.

"Why you sucker." It was his partner, Ken, who was the first to react. The ball rolled within 2 feet of the pin. The other two players kidded Pete good-naturedly. They were all good friends, lived next door or across the street from each other. Ken's ball hit the sand trap next to the green. Ken's frustration elicited a well-used phrase from him when he saw the others had hit the green – although far from the pin.

"Whose mother are we talking about?" asked Stan, as he headed his cart across the fairway to the cart path. Pete tapped in for a birdie. The others parred the hole. "I think I'm going to call it a day", said Ken. "It's too damn hot today."

"Are you going to continue playing Pete?" asked Stan.

"Yes, I'll drop Ken off at his house, and I'll be right back."

"We are going to get some water. Meet us at the Pro shop."

As Pete pulled up to the Pro shop and walked in the door, the Assistant Pro walked over to him and whispered quietly. "Those two men over by the new clubs are asking about you," he said and walked away.

The men he referred to were wearing dark suits and ties. "That's odd," thought Pete, "nobody in Arizona wears ties, especially on a hot day like today." He walked into the bathroom, washed his face and hands and was drying them off when Stan came in and said they had to get going or they would lose their place. "You better go without me. I got a couple of gents waiting to talk to me." "Not the ones over by the golf clubs I hope?"

"Yes, as a matter of fact, they are the ones."

"FBI" was all Stan said and left. Pete went over and introduced himself, holding his hand out.

"Tom Reed" said the older of the two, shaking Pete's hand. "This is agent Tony Connors." They shook hands all around.

"Is there a place where we can go and sit down and not be disturbed?" Tom Reed asked.

"Yes, let's go into the library. It's usually empty this time of the day. By the way, you want a coke or something to drink?"

"Yes, diet cokes would be fine," said Tony. Pete gave the order to a waitress and told her they would be in the library. He led them into the circular library and they found three comfortable chairs and sat down.

"This feels good," said Pete, as he stretched back in the overstuffed chair facing the two agents. "You saved me from sheer torture. It's too hot to play today. Nine holes were enough."

"I hope we didn't ruin your day," said Tom.

Their drinks arrived and Pete signed for them.

Tom and Tony both took out their FBI badges and showed them to Pete. "What can I do for you?" asked Pete. "We are here about the Turner woman's death. We were hoping you could shed some light on it. I know it's been a while since it happened but it seems the state's attorney is getting some pressure, so we were asked to step in and help. The Marana police have run into a stone wall, so here we are," said Tom.

"I'm not sure how much I can help. I briefed the Marana people about what I know, which I'm sure you have in your files. However, before we go any further, please turn off your recorder in your briefcase, Tony, until we have established some ground rules."

Tony was about to say something but Tom cut him off. "He is right, Tony. Shut it off," said Tom.

"I'll tell you all I know about Mrs. Turner and when I'm through you can ask away. Is that fair?" Tom said, "That's fine."

"You can turn your recorder back on Tony," Pete said with a smile.

"Mr. Turner was in the state legislature for years, over twenty, and was thinking of running for Congress. However, his wife of almost 35 years died of cancer and it sort of took the wind out of his sails. He decided to stay in the state legislature. About a year after his wife's death he married a wealthy widow, a Marge Petersen, whose family had something to do with Coca Cola. Marge Petersen became Mrs. Turner, about 25 years younger than Mr. Turner, and they seemed happy. I say that 'cause I met them here at the club and we got together socially at each other's houses. Mrs. Turner had or has a house here. Mrs. Turner joined the ladies golf team, known as the ladies niners. She and my wife and a lady friend of ours became good friends so I got to know Mrs. Turner better than I knew her husband."

"Excuse me Pete but what year was this?" interrupted Tom.

"Oh I'd say late '04 or early '05."

"Go on," said Tom.

"Mrs. Turner preferred to stay here when Mr. Turner's legislative duties called. I don't know if this was a problem, if it was I never heard about it. I do know that they talked about moving up to the Gallery – an upscale country club about a quarter of a mile from here, bigger and more expensive homes. How shall I say this without casting dispersions? Mrs. Turner was what my dear departed mother used to call *full of life*. Not only was she full of life, she was a damn good looking lady."

"Did she have any close men friends here?" Tom asked in an even tone.

"If she was stepping out of the circle she was very careful about it. This is a small place and word gets around. She and my wife were good friends and there was never any pillow talk about Mrs. Turner in our house."

"Is there any chance of talking to your wife?" asked Tony.

There was a long silence. Tom looked uncomfortable and was staring at his fingertips.

"Tony! Both of you know who I worked for the last few years of my service. Am I correct?"

They both nodded in the affirmative.

"There was an unwritten rule in my organization, and that was to know as much as possible about the person you are going to question or interrogate, in other words do your homework. Obviously you came half prepared to this session or you would have known that my wife died less than a year ago."

"Pete, I'm sorry and I apologize. I was aware of your situation and yes it's written in your background file. I'm sorry Pete, you're right. I should have known," said Tony.

Tom looked at Tony and their eyes met and a lot was said in that look.

"OK, moving right along," said Pete. Mr. Turner died in June of '06. After her husband died, Mrs. Turner continued to live here. She got over his passing very quickly, at least that was the appearance she gave, and was back with the ladies playing golf within two weeks of his death. There was no more talk of moving, she seemed to be happy, and was at our house for dinner several times. Let's see, she was killed in the fall of '07. That about wraps it up, at least for what I can think of. Fire away any questions you have."

"Was she dating anyone here?" asked Tom

"Not that I know of, you have to remember this is a 55 and older community. We have people up to 93 years old. Is there any back door slamming, you bet there is. There are people living together and it's accepted.

"What about outside this community?" It was Tom.

"You are now getting into a sensitive area and I'm not sure I want to go there. Have you talked to anyone else in this community or do you know if the Marana police have talked to anyone other than her neighbors?"

Tom looked at Tony who was about to say something, and cut him off.

"The Marana police gave us the neighbors' statements and that is where we got your name Pete, looking here at my notes it was actually your wife's name we got but since her demise we figured you might know something; we did a background on you and well, here we are."

"Have you read the autopsy conducted on Mrs. Turner?" Pete looked at both of them.

"Yes she was shot at close range by a 22 cal. bullet, forensic stated that a silencer was probably used, determined by the grooves on the bullet which was recovered in extremely good condition. Their conclusion is that the shooter was a pro, other than that nothing else stands out about her death, no struggle, probably knew the shooter since the gun was held close to the back of her head – powder burns etc.," said Tony.

"There was nothing else about Mrs. Turner's autopsy report that was odd or rather unusual, anything that struck you as maybe odd, maybe a little unusual or not normal?" Pete was looking from one to the other.

"I think you better go over the autopsy report again, and while you're doing that I'm going to make a quick phone call. I'll be right back," said Pete, getting up quickly and going out to the admin office to ask if he could use a phone for a few seconds. He was told there was a phone in the next room and he would have privacy. Pete thanked the lady and proceeded to the next room. He dialed his old friend and partner Hank Wadsworth. The phone was picked up on the third ring.

"Hank here."

"Listen Hank, it's Pete, I've got two FBI agents asking me questions about Mrs. Turner; how far do you want me to go on this?"

"Use your own judgment Pete, the bitch is still dead isn't she?"

"Yes she is dead, Hank. I was thinking about Hank Jr. and they might want to question you."

"Tell them the truth; you and I are clear, the stupid detective from Marana didn't know what to ask. I'll talk to them if they are interested but don't volunteer me, let that decision be theirs."

"OK Hank, I thought we were through with this crap, one of the agents is sharp, and the other needs to go back to school. I'll let you know what happens." Pete hung up the phone and returned to the library. The two agents were just finishing up the autopsy report.

"Well I see what you mean Pete, herpes and HIV. Is this going somewhere Pete?" asked Tom.

"Mrs. Turner became involved with an 18 year old high school senior" Pete said looking at both the agents.

"And you think he killed her or had something to do with killing her?" Tony asked, giving Tom an odd look.

"No, I don't think the 18 year old killed her or had something to do with her death, but she did give him a present before she was killed."

"And what was this present?" asked Tony, somewhat irritated.

"She gave him genital herpes," Pete answered quietly.

"I don't think people kill other people because they give..." Tony was told to hold it by Tom.

"We are going too fast here," said Tom, giving Tony another one of his looks.

"Pete - is this getting a little sensitive or too close for you?" asked Tom in a low friendly voice.

"Yeah, it's getting close, but I have been given permission to brief you on it, with the stipulation that it be kept in close hold for now."

"Shut off the recorder Tony."

"But Tom, this might have a bearing on the case."

"Shut off the damn recorder."

"It's off," said Tony letting out a long sigh.

"OK Pete, give us what you have and it will be stamped confidential if we write it up."

"Hank Wadsworth Jr. was an outstanding senior with a straight A average, captain of the football team (set a new passing record in the state of Arizona), and selected to the all National High School football team. He had every college scout in the nation making offers, but there was only one school he wanted to attend and that was West Point, where his father graduated. He was accepted. During his last semester in high school he was introduced to Mrs. Turner at a party at our house. His father was with him. They live at another development near here. His father and I have been friends for over 30 years – served in the Army Special Forces together for years. Mrs. Turner was quite taken with Hank Jr. What woman wouldn't be, a strapping 6' 4", 210 lbs good looking all American boy getting ready for the greatest adventure and biggest dream of his life?

"He started seeing Mrs. Turner; in fact she bought him a new car. Hank Jr. drove it home and his father met him in the driveway, didn't pay much attention to the car, figured it belonged to one of his friends. His father had a letter from West Point in his hand and handed it to Hank Jr. as he got out of the car. Hank Jr. opened the letter; it was a notice for his physical to West Point to be given the following week at an Air Force base outside of Phoenix. Hank Sr. had to go to Boston the next day (his parents were divorced) and wouldn't be home until after Hank Jr.'s physical.

"When Hank got back from Boston, he pushed the garage door opener and just sat in his car. His son Hank Jr. was hanging from a 4 x 4 in the ceiling of the garage. He called me on his cell phone and I got over there within 5 minutes. I was stunned. Hank could not talk. I took his cell phone, left him sitting in his car and called 911. I went into the house to see if there was a note or an envelope. I found an envelope addressed to his father which I stuck in my pocket and went out and got Hank out of the car and brought him into the house through the front door. I sat him down on the couch and started talking slowly to him.

He came around and asked me to call his ex-wife; she lived with her sister in Phoenix. I called and told her there had been an accident and asked if she could come down to Hank's house and to have here sister drive her. She wanted to know what was going on and was starting to get hysterical. Her sister got on the phone and wanted to know what was going on. I knew her well, and asked her to please drive Nancy down to Hank's house and that I would explain later.

The police, fire engines and ambulance arrived a short time later. They cut the body down and sealed off the house. An officer in plain clothes came in and identified himself. He asked Hank if he could get some preliminary information from him. Hank answered all the questions put forth. The officer informed them that they would have to seal the house and wanted to know if Hank had another place he could stay for a couple of days. I informed the officer that the victim's mother was on her way from Phoenix and asked if we could stay until she arrived. "No problem," was the officer's response. "Just don't touch anything in the house. Do you have firearms in the house?" the officer asked Hank. He told the officer there were a 12 gauge shotgun and a .380 caliber handgun in his bedroom. "Could you show me where they are?" Hank got up and I followed him to his bedroom. Hank opened his closet and took out the shotgun and went over to the nightstand drawer and handed the officer the .380 handgun.

"I thought you told me you were divorced," the officer said looking around the closet.

"Well it was a friendly divorce," said Hank, looking at some of Nancy's clothes hanging in the closet. "You'll find some more of her things in the dresser over against the wall."

"We will try not to disturb anything in here. Can I assume

that your son's room is down the hall?" Hank nodded. "You can go to the living room and wait," the officer said.

"Where will you take the body?" I asked.

"The Pima County Coroner's building. Here is the address and phone number."

The officer stayed in the bedroom while Hank and I went to the living room and sat on the couch.

"This is a tough one" Hank said looking away. "I don't know how I'm going to explain this to Nancy."

I placed my index finger across my lips and told Hank in a whisper not to say anything until we were alone in my house. "When Nancy gets here she can follow us to my house."

Hank looked at me and nodded, tears were streaming down his face.

They heard a car pull in to the driveway. I took Hank by the arm and led him out of the house. It was Nancy and her sister. I signaled for them to stay in their car and to follow us. Nancy lowered her window and wanted to know what was going on. The ambulance had departed along with the fire engine, but there was police tape across the house. I didn't answer her, but got a hold of one of the uniformed officers and told him we were going to my house and that the plainclothes officer had the address and phone number. I told Hank to lock his car which he did with his automatic key by pressing the button on it.

I opened the door of my car and helped Hank into the seat. I got behind the wheel and drove out the cul de sac with Nancy and her sister following. When we got to my house I pulled into the garage and Hank and I got out and indicated to Nancy and her sister to come in through the garage which I then locked. We proceeded into my living room where we all took a seat.

"If you are going to tell me what I think you are going to tell me Hank, I don't want to hear it," said Nancy in a controlled voice. Tears were streaming down her cheeks. Her sister gave her a tissue and she wiped her eyes and cheeks.

Hank turned towards her, took her hands in his and started

to say something.

Nancy cried out and asked Hank not to say anything. She was starting to get hysterical. Hank pulled her to him and held her.

I motioned for her sister Jane to follow me into the den and told her to take a seat in one of the comfortable chairs. I sat down in the desk chair. I told Jane that Hank Jr. had hung himself and that Hank found him when he got home today.

Jane started crying saying no it can't be true, he had everything going for him, and he was going to conquer the world. She wanted to know when it had happened. I told her I didn't know. Hank had been up in Boston for five days and that Hand Jr. had a two day physical for West Point. I think the physical started Tuesday, so my guess would be some time after Wednesday.

I told her we would get a report from the coroner's office. I asked her if she wanted a drink. I informed her I still had some of that nice brandy that she had liked the last time she was at my house. Her face flushed turning a bright red; she wiped her tears and looked at me like a school girl who had gotten caught cheating on a test.

I got a couple of glasses and the brandy when I remembered the envelope I had found in Hank's kitchen. I walked into the living room. Hank and Nancy were sitting apart, Hank talking in a low voice, Nancy was crying softly. I apologized and handed Hank the envelope and returned to the den. I poured a healthy shot into each glass and handed one to Jane. To better days I said, and we both took a sip. "Do you have any idea what could have triggered this?" Jane asked looking at me. I shook my head and said it could have had something to with the physical but that's just a wild guess.

Hank walked in and asked if he could have two of whatever we were having and said that Nancy was settling down. It looks like you are going to have company for a few days Pete.

"Stay as long as you want. We aren't exactly strangers."

"I need to run to the shopping center and pick up a few

things for Nancy and me. We left in kind of a hurry." " I think Nancy has what you need at my house, if the police will let us back in," said Hank.

"Oh!" Jane gave Hank a strange look. "You didn't read your final divorce agreement too closely, you are not to bother her, or something like that."

"Who is bothering whom?" It was Nancy that came in to the den.

"Nothing, we were just discussing the finer points of the law," I told her.

I handed them each a drink and they sat down.

"Here read this." Hank handed me the letter I had given him. I put my glasses on and read it and then handed the letter to Jane. Nancy started crying again.

"That bitch could at least have told him she was a walking mine field, he found out at the physical he had genital herpes and was disqualified for West Point. His life's dream down the drain over a roll in the hay. I wonder how many others she has infected. Oh that bitch." Nancy was getting worked up.

"That poor young man," said Jane as she placed the letter on the table.

"I'm awful tired; will you take me into the bedroom?" Hank took the letter and put it in his pocket and took Nancy by the hand and departed.

"You know where everything is, help yourself," I told them.

After Pete finished his statement, Tom and Tony continued with the questioning. "That had to be tough," said Tom.

"What kind of a relationship did Hank Jr. have with his mother, and could we turn the recorder back on?" asked Tony.

"Sure, and did you read the autopsy on Hank Jr.?" asked Pete.

"We read it; in fact we tore it apart to check for any trauma to the body thinking it might not be a suicide. There is nothing about genital herpes in our report. From the statements we got from the Marana police, neighbors and friends statements, the guy seemed like an all American kid. No problems in school, liked by everyone, had not let his fame go to his head. Was dating a girl pretty steady until he met someone else and I can assume that was Mrs. Turner, at which time he broke off his relationship with the girl."

"I'd check with the coroner on the autopsy report if I was you; and as far as his mother went, they had a good relationship. It was a friendly divorce and Hank Jr. stayed with his father so he wouldn't have to change high school in his last year. He got along great with both parents.

"Do you have any idea why his parents got divorced?" asked Tony.

"Hank had been a career army officer for thirty years having been gone to various parts of the world most of the time. He had promised Nancy that when he got out at thirty they were never going to be separated again. We were both in the same outfit and when we went to work in the morning we didn't know if we were going to see our families again that day or in 6 months. It was hard on the wives and most of our people had been divorced at least once. When Hank got out he was offered a very good job with the CIA, who we both had worked for off and on during our career. Nancy said no, she wanted to settle down in Arizona where she had a sister whom she was very close to. My wife and I had already bought a house in this gated community, lived on the golf course and had all the amenities of an upscale golf and tennis club. Nancy fell in love with our set-up. However, there was only one problem. They had a son of high school age making them ineligible in our 55 years and older community. They bought in a nice development across the boulevard from us. Things seemed fine but there were no golf course or tennis courts and Nancy was an avid player of both. Hank Jr. found new friends and was making good grades both on and off the football field. Hank Sr. took the job with the CIA and planned to buy a house in our community and quit working when his son graduated in 2 years. Hank Sr. was gone quite a bit and one day he got back home, Nancy had left and moved in with her sister in Phoenix along with papers for a divorce. While they were working out the divorce, Nancy spent quite a bit of time at Hank's house and although the divorce went through it was friendly to say the least. It was just that Nancy felt that Hank had not lived up to his word, i.e. retiring and finally staying home.

Whenever Nancy was down from Phoenix she and my wife Betty spent a lot of time together, playing golf and cards at the club. When Betty was diagnosed with cancer, Nancy stayed down more than before and nursed Betty to the end. It was a difficult time for all of us.

"In your mind do you think that either Hank or Nancy could have had Mrs. Turner killed?" Tom asked not looking up but jotting some notes down on his pad.

"No, not Hank, that I know for a fact," said Pete.

"How can you be so sure?" Tom asked in an even voice.

"Hank and I have no secrets from each other. I saved his life in Viet Nam and we were just close. I asked him if he had killed her and he said no, but there was a time when he said he had thought about it. Nancy wouldn't know which end of a gun to point at anyone. She thoroughly dislikes guns of any kind."

"What about some of your friends in the DECAD Association? Both you and Hank belong, and from what our people tell us, there are some pretty loose cannons who are members," Tony said with a smile, as if he had scored a point.

"There are several DECAD Association units in each state and I believe about 5 foreign countries. These are people who served with the Special Forces at least 10 years. Headquarters for the organization is at Ft. Bragg, and we have people from all walks of life, i.e. judges, lawyers, doctors, businessmen and even FBI agents," said Pete.

"You ran into some of them at Ruby Ridge in Idaho," said Pete in a calm voice.

"Well let's not go there," said Tom. "If, as you say, there are

223

loose cannons, that's where they are located – up in the Coeur d'Alene area. They feel the government let them down after they performed some pretty amazing stuff over in Laos, Cambodia and Viet Nam, and that we left over 1500 American prisoners over there, that could have been freed. However you have to remember that these people are getting old, although there has been some infusion of younger blood in the last twenty years. I can't speculate on any ties there."

"Well you have been more than helpful, and we appreciate your openness. Can we call on you again if anything turns up? I have your phone number so we'll call before we barge in on you like today."

"Sure, I play a little golf and do some writing, and best of all I'm retired and enjoy it. Call anytime," said Pete getting to his feet and shaking their hands.

Pete left with them, got into his golf cart and headed home which was less than two minutes from the club. He pressed the garage opener and pulled in next to his car, plugged the charge cord into the cart, and took off his golf clothes and hung them on the washer and dryer and walked naked into his bedroom. He grabbed his swim suit and phone and went out the back door, put the umbrellas up, placed the phone on the table and went into the pool. God it was refreshing. He laid back and floated, dunking his head under the water and walked up the pool steps to the patio. The back yard had been one of his wife's pride and joy. It looked more like a fancy spa than a private home. He walked over to the outdoor kitchen and took a cold Coors light out of the built-in refrigerator and went back to the umbrella table, took a seat in one of the four plush chairs, put his feet up and cracked the top of the beer – taking a long sip. It had been an interesting morning. He didn't think he had tipped his hand too much, had answered their questions but not volunteered everything. He scrolled down on his phone and pressed Hank's number, it was answered on the first ring.

"I can tell by the incoming number that you are not in jail, so let's have it."

"Grab your suit and come over. We have to talk," said Pete and hung up.

He thought this bullshit was over with, he grabbed a pair of sunglasses and put them on; the sun was tough at this time of the year. Oh well it would all shake out.

He heard Hank come in; he had keys for the house as he had keys for Hank's house.

"Damn you have a nice set up back here."

"Yeah I spent many a sleepless night mentally planning each detail," said Pete, as Hank headed for the pool and immersed himself.

"Listen if it hadn't been for your better half, you'd have a dirt hole in the ground and no plants around the fence," Hank mumbled as he headed for the refrigerator and grabbed a can of Coors and went over and sat down in one of the chairs opposite Pete.

"Let's have it, what happened?"

Pete recounted what had transpired as Hank stared at him. When Pete was finished, Hank leaned forward on the table and asked, "Did you tell them about our place up at Coeur d'Alene?" Pete shook his head negative, "They didn't ask."

"They will find out, and next they'll want to search it," said Hank. "I'll give them a week and they'll call."

Hank finished his beer, grabbed Pete's empty can and headed for the fridge where he took two new ones and deposited the empties in the small waste receptacle. He opened both cans and handed one to Pete.

"I have to go up to Spokane in three days. I'll go over to Coeur d'Alene while I'm there and go through our cabin and make sure it's straight and sterile."

"We could ask Brian to go over and clean it out. Hell he lives in the small cabin rent free, all he does is guard the place and ride around on the John Deere SP lawnmower and do a little trimming, he is not exactly overworked.

"No, I need to brief him and make sure he has his place squared away, a housekeeper he is not. He had a woman living with him last time I was up there, seemed nice enough but I want her and her stuff gone in case we get visitors. Brian knows the game and I trust him but the fewer people the better."

"You're right, we'll be ready for them, the barn could probably stand a little sweeping, a good job for Brian," said Pete taking a drag from the beer.

"Hey! How about staying and grilling a few steaks, baked potatoes and a salad, I just got the Omaha steak specials yesterday – they look good."

"Nancy and Jane are coming down for the weekend, I wouldn't want to intrude."

"Call them and tell them to bring their suits, we need a little diversion."

"You sure?"

"Of course I'm sure, it's not as if they are strangers."

"OK give me your phone."

While Hank called, Pete went in to the kitchen and made sure he had everything. As he was taking his place at the table Hank was hanging up.

"Caught them just in time. They were walking out the door and happy for the invite, no need to mention our visitors today," said Hank with a frown on his face.

"I agree and it sounds like a plan. If you want me to go up there a few weeks earlier than I normally go each year let me know – it's not a problem – it's starting to get hot here so I would welcome a little cooler weather."

"No, I'll be using a company plane and it shouldn't take me but a few hours to straighten out the Spokane problem."

"Thanks for offering dinner tonight Pete, I have had a rough week and I know the girls are ready to relax."

"My pleasure, any time, you know that, we'll turn on the spa. I'm the only person who has not left for the summer for five houses on either side, and we have the golf course and the

Catalina Mountains to the back. It's about as private as anything you could find."

"I'm looking at a house here on the 5th fairway – not as plush as this but nice. Nancy likes it, so I hope we'll get back together again."

"That's the best news I have heard Hank. I'm not going to say anything so if the subject comes up I'll be surprised."

They both headed for the pool again and had just opened another can of beer when the doorbell rang.

"That's the girls," said Hank. "Jane is going to get a ticket one of these days the way she drives."

Pete went in through the house and opened the door. They were both standing there giggling like a couple of school girls.

"What's so funny?" asked Pete.

"You are," said Nancy giving Pete a kiss on the cheek and walking past him into the house. Jane looked at him and gave him a soft kiss on the lips.

"Now that's better," said Pete, as Jane walked into the house. He closed and locked the door.

"Some people are getting kind of cold lately," directing his comments towards Nancy.

"We have plans so things could get pretty hot before the nights over," said Nancy twirling her two piece swimsuit on her finger.

"I have heard that before, promises, promises. Oh Nancy, change in the guest room. Hank's clothes are in there, and you young lady can change in the master bedroom. I'll show you the way, you might not remember," said Pete with a grin on his face.

"It sounds like someone has been into the Coors beer already," said Nancy.

"I never complain. I just do what I'm told," said Jane. "And I know where the master bedroom is thank you."

Pete went out and sat down next to Hank.

"Well, they are in a good mood," said Pete. "It's good to see them like that for a change."

"Amen," said Hank.

They both came out together and each gave Hank a nice kiss. They looked good, were in good shape and had not let themselves go. Both went into the pool.

"Oh my God, this feels good, I hope I can have a pool someday," said Nancy. "Some people know how to live, and to think that none of these lonely women around here have gotten Pete into a relationship. I guess they are not sending out the right scent," said Nancy laughing.

Jane didn't say anything but was looking around like she hadn't seen the place before.

Pete went in and got them both gin and tonics in fancy plastic glasses. Real glasses were dangerous around a pool. "Cheers," said Hank, holding up his can of beer, they all joined in.

When everyone was feeling good, Jane grabbed a towel and wrapped it around her. "I'm going to get the salad ready," and departed for the kitchen.

Pete got up and followed her saying the steaks needed tending to.

Nancy started to get up but Hank held her back.

"I just got you a fresh gin and tonic, besides we need to talk."

Pete walked into the kitchen and started preparing the steaks.

Jane came into the kitchen with a towel wrapped around her. Must have been to the bathroom thought Pete. As Jane started to walk around him, Pete circled her waist with one arm and drew her close. He looked into her eyes and kissed her softly on the lips and drew her in tighter. Jane returned his kiss with urgency, Pete placed his other hand in the fold of the towel; there was no swimming suit bottom. He rubbed her behind and pulled her in tighter. His hand found the folds of her lips and inserted a finger, she was already wet. He found her clit and gently massaged it. Jane moaned and grabbed Pete's erection working it out of his bathing suit. She turned around presenting her rear to him, bending over the kitchen table. Pete grabbed her breasts as she guided him inside her. Pete thrust it in, withdrawing it slowly and thrusting it farther in. Jane was moaning pushing her rear into Pete. He let go of her breasts and grabbed her by the hips pulling her tight into him. There was a cry as Jane wiggled her rear into Pete as her whole body shivered followed by another cry. Pete exploded at the same time. They just stayed that way with Jane leaning on the table her head resting on her arms.

"God Pete Compton, how do you do that? I have never had orgasms like that before."

Hank and Nancy were talking when they heard the first cry.

"I guess the steaks are going to be extra flavorful tonight," said Hank.

"Maybe he has found the scent, which would be great. Jane loves that guy more than either of us realized. It's been four years since her husband died and she has not been out with anyone except for Pete."

"Take it easy, Pete is a loner, he can live without the attachments, it hasn't been a year since she died. I don't think Pete will marry again, at least not in the near future, and he has some things to take care of before he gets serious about anyone."

"Oh I know but they make such a good couple and I think Jane has the scent he likes."

"It sounds like it from the kitchen," said Hank. "And if she makes cream colored dressing on the salad, check it out. Hank laughing jumped into the pool. Nancy followed and splashed Hank as he came up for air.

The dinner was delicious. Pete lit the fire in the kiva next to the table keeping them warm.

"Is that spa warm by now?" asked Hank.

"Anytime you're ready," said Pete.

Jane had been rather quiet during the meal, and as she and Nancy were cleaning the table and placing the dishes in the dishwasher, Nancy looked at Jane and asked if everything was OK.

"It's more than OK, that guy makes me have orgasms over

and over again. It has never happened to me before. I'd do anything for him" Jane said with a far away look in her eyes.

"Take it slow little sister; we are going to be around for a long time. Hank and I are going to buy that house up the street and get back together again when his contract is up."

"Oh Nancy that's the best news I have heard in a long time. I always knew you would get back together again."

They joined the men in the spa, taking off their swim suits.

"This is nice," said Hank, fondling Nancy's breasts and her mound.

"It looks like a sleep over," said Hank.

"I hope so," said Pete giving Jane a kiss on her neck.

They all petted and kissed, talking and pretending that they were not arousing their partner.

Finally Nancy claimed her skin was wrinkling up and she was tired and needed to go to bed. Hank followed her drying her off as he walked behind her.

"It was nice of you to have us for dinner, us barging in here like we did," said Jane cuddling up under Pete's arm as he was stroking her nipples.

"I enjoyed it," said Pete, "especially the hors d'oeuvres."

"I don't know what you do to me Pete, but I like it, I hope you feel the same. It has never happened to me before. I'm turning into a brazen hussy."

"We better get out of here or everything will shrink into wrinkled skin," said Pete with a laugh.

"I wouldn't want that to happen," said Jane getting out of the spa.

She was walking ahead of him to the towel rack, her naked skin glistening. They dried each other off.

"Not everything has shrunk," said Jane toweling Pete off.

They headed for the bedroom where Jane took over and finally collapse on Pete.

They all slept late and it was Nancy who walked in on them and shook them awake.

"Hank has a phone call for you Pete."

Pete mumbled something, got out of bed naked and headed for the bathroom.

"Nice buns," said Nancy as she walked out of the bedroom.

"Yeah," said Jane rolling over on her back shading her eyes with her hand. She was so sore she didn't think she could walk. Pete came out of the bathroom wearing a pair of shorts, kissed her on the forehead and left. Hank was holding the phone out to Pete, who took it and said "Pete speaking."

"Sorry to bother you on a Saturday but a few things came up." It was agent Tom Reed. "We came up with a couple of things that we were not aware of, and by the way we did check with the coroner and Hank Jr. did have herpes. What I wanted to talk about was your place outside of Coeur d'Alene up in Idaho and your man who lives on the premises."

"Sure go ahead," said Pete. "In fact I'll fill you in on Brian Huff. Retired Command Sergeant Major (E-9), worked with him about 16 years in the Special Forces. He was my Operations Sergeant on a couple of tours until he got promoted; kept in touch for years after. I believe he was born in Columbia, South Carolina, or at least he was raised there. His father was a Colonel in the Army, his mother died when he was about 12 years old; has a sister married to a General. Brian wanted into the Army as soon as he was through high school but not as an officer although he had numerous chances during his career for both OCS and a direct commission. Wanted to be a grunt. He used to say officers were too much like politicians, didn't care for either.

His wife died about 6 years ago and his two kids are grown, boy and a girl. The boy is a lawyer the daughter a doctor. Talked to Brian at his wife's funeral. At the time he was retired with over thirty year's service. I was looking for someone to look after the place up in Idaho and he jumped at it, wanted to get away from the Ft. Bragg area. Wouldn't take any pay, said he knew how tight officers were with a dollar, so it wouldn't be worth it anyway. Oh! His wife came from a wealthy family and upon her death he inherited a good sum of money. There was a small cabin on the property and he had it renovated, looks after the property, does a little hunting and fishing and is happy. Has some old friends in the area so he is not lonely."

"Well Tom has your tape run out?" Pete said with a laugh.

"No I still have plenty left," Tom said with a chuckle. "When was the last time you talked to or saw Brian?"

"Let's see, about two weeks ago. I usually give him about two weeks warning before I go up there so he can get someone to dust and knock down the cobwebs. I go up there this time of the year before the heat sets in here. I spend about three to four months up there fishing and working on the place. In fact you were lucky you called today because I'm flying up there tomorrow."

"Who was the guy that answered the phone when I called?"

"That was Hank. He came over to clean out my refrigerator and any liquor and beer I'm leaving behind. A true friend especially when he can get something for free. He is typical of what Brian described about officers and how tight we are with a dollar."

"Are you kidding Pete, liquor doesn't deteriorate if properly sealed."

"No just kidding Tom, there is very little in the house. I just made that remark because he was passing by with a cardboard box as I was talking to you."

"Oh! I see," Tom was chuckling again.

"That's about all I can think of," said Pete. "If you have any questions fire away?"

"How long have you owned the place up there?"

"Well, let's see, we bought the place about 15 years ago from the widow of our old boss General Flanagan, she wasn't much for the outdoors and she offered it to Hank and I for a pittance, she just wanted to get rid of it. "I see, so you and Hank own it together. How large is it?"

"The deed says 42 acres 10 acres open pasture, the rest woods, has a small barn, the main cabin and the cabin I told you about that Brian uses. There is a nice stream meandering through it. It's a nice rustic place."

"And you are going up there tomorrow?"

"Yes, got my tickets, all set."

"Do you mind if I come up there? It would be towards the end of the week. We have a mandatory meeting in Washington the first part of the week so I'm looking towards a Thursday-Friday time frame."

"That's fine – give me a call on my cell phone when you land and I'll give you directions."

"Fine thanks Pete. I'll see you then."

As Pete hung up he looked at Hank who was sitting on a chair looking at him.

"Listen buddy, that old gumshoe is going to have the local FBI up there snooping around today or tomorrow. I'll go over to call Brian from my house and give a heads up, and tell him to get rid of any visitors he has. What I can't figure out is why he is so interested in us," said Hank getting up.

"Yes, good thing I have these open tickets. I'd better confirm. You know they will check the airlines."

"Do you want company?" It was Jane nursing a cup of coffee.

"You know that might not be a bad idea," said Pete. Hank nodded affirmative. "I'll take care of your tickets" said Pete.

"Give me a heads up on your flight, Pete, as soon as you confirm."

"God, what am I saying?" said Jane. "I can hardly walk after last night."

"Self inflicted wound. Ask Nancy what she uses. It might help in the future."

"OK, I'll drive home and pack, be back tonight."

Nancy and Hank left.

"Can I at least get a piece of toast or something to eat before

I go? After all, you can't just have your way with me and send me away hungry."

Pete laughed and kissed her. "Hmm, you've got a funny taste on your lips."

"Well my eagle scout, that happens to be from you in case you're interested," said Jane snuggling up to him.

"Fix us some eggs and bacon while I confirm the reservation."

"Yes sir," said Jane saluting with her left hand, and turned around and flipped up the back of one of Pete's shirts she was wearing with nothing underneath.

"Hey, hang on. I don't have to call this minute," said Pete laughing and reaching for her.

"Oh yes you do mister. I'm so sore I may need a wheelchair," said Jane moving towards the refrigerator.

Hank grabbed her and bent her over the kitchen table, spread her legs and dropped his shorts and entered her from behind.

"You're still wet," he moaned leaning over her taking a breast in each hand and gently caressing them.

"Oh God Pete, put it in further, hurry."

Pete went in and out with gentle strokes until they both climaxed.

"You are definitely taking me with you. I'm not letting you out of my sight."

Pete withdrew, pulled up his shorts and sat down in a chair and started dialing the airlines.

"It will be a few minutes before breakfast now. I definitely need a shower before I can do anything."

Pete blew her a kiss and started talking on the phone. He made reservations for both of them. Hank would drive them to the airport. Pete went to the fridge – took out bacon and eggs, got the frying pan and stared the bacon. It was sizzling in a few minutes. When the bacon was done he placed the slices on a paper towel to drain.

Jane came in wearing a pair of shorts and buttoning her

blouse.

"Thanks for starting the breakfast; my knees were so weak I had to hold on to the shower bar. You go and shower and I'll finish up the eggs and toast."

Pete kissed her and said "We are leaving at 11:00 tomorrow and I promise not to make you weak in the knees before we leave!"

"Wait a minute mister; did I say I minded weak knees? I'll be back this afternoon and tonight I'll show you something that will make you sleep like a baby."

"Christ I can go to sleep right now, but I better shower and eat something or I'll drop."

Pete headed for the shower and as he was toweling himself off he heard singing coming from the kitchen, which sounded nice. It had been a long time since he had heard it and he missed it.

They ate without much talk, when they were through Pete cleaned up the table and placed the dishes in the dishwasher and turned it on.

Jane came out of the bathroom and gave him a soft kiss on the lips.

"I'll get on the road, you get some rest and I'll see you around four o'clock."

"You drive carefully now. There is no hurry!"

"I know, I'm picking Nancy up and she'll keep me straight."

"Ha!" said Pete and slapped her on her rear as she walked out.

He called Hank and told him about the flight arrangement and that Jane was on the way to pick Nancy up.

"I don't get it Pete. Why are the FBI interested in us and our place up in Idaho?"

"Beats me but I just want to make sure the place is straight and looks homey, if you get my drift."

"Yeah I know but it doesn't make any sense. Anyway I'll pick you up about 0900 or a little before. See you then." Hank hung up.

As he placed the receiver in the cradle Pete's mind was in deep thought. Mrs. Turner had been killed at close range by someone who knew her and knew what they were doing. It had to be someone she was close to —maybe one of her lovers that had caught something from her and had confronted her. Herpes could be controlled, he thought, but HIV was a death sentence if it was advanced, although he had read somewhere that they had discovered some kind of vaccine for it. Oh well, there for the grace of God go I, he thought. There were times when the Turner woman had made it plain to him that she was available, but there had always been something in the back of his mind that stopped him from pursuing her invitations. Whoever her other conquests had been, she had kept it close hold. He wondered if his deceased wife had known. They had been good friends. It wasn't anyone he knew of, that was for sure. Then why the snooping by the FBI?

He heard the dishwasher click on to the drying cycle. He'd lie down and get some rest. Damn that Jane was getting to him. Was he falling in love with her or was it just the good sex? He kicked off his loafers and lay down on the bed. Jane had straightened it out and made it before she left him, another point in her favor. He drifted off to a deep sleep.

Hank shook him awake. He heard someone in the kitchen.

"What's going on?" he said groggily.

"It's your wakeup call dear," Hank said in a coddling tone. "The girls are in the kitchen putting dishes away and cleaning up. Christ, do I have to tell Jane to go easy on you? You slept for almost five hours. Go take a shower or whatever you have to do. We are barbequing at my place. The girls have made potato salad and regular salad and I'm in charge of grilling baby spareribs."

"I must be getting old," said Pete, heading for the bathroom.

As Hank returned to the kitchen, Nancy and Jane looked at him.

"What's the verdict?" asked Nancy.

"He mumbled something about getting old," said Hank.

"God, I can verify that he is not. In fact, I hope he gets old one of these days. If it hadn't been for Nancy I would have fallen asleep at the wheel and I'm 15 years younger than he is."

"Well you can wear it out," said Nancy at the same time ducking a towel Jane had in her hand.

"What can you wear out?" asked Pete coming through the door.

"Her welcome," Nancy retorted quickly.

"Nah, she is a good woman. I got plans for her tonight," said Pete with a grin on his face, placing his arm around Jane's waste.

"You know Pete, I think we better let it heal awhile and I think you need a rest."

"Stop this talk. I'm starting to get horny again and Hank has to grill ribs," said Nancy placing both arms around Hank.

"Let's go, enough of this talk," said Hank. "I'm thirsty and hungry. Then we'll see."

They all left Pete's house and headed for their cars.

"Get in with me," said Jane to Pete. They drove to Hank's house in silence. As they were getting out of the car, Pete asked if she was all set for tomorrow. "All packed and ready, even brought my flannel pajamas," said Jane linking her arm in Pete's.

"You could have saved that space for something useful," said Pete with a grin, leaning over and kissing Jane on the neck.

"Man that could lead to something tonight, something gentle," said Jane, kissing the side of his face.

Hank had made Margaritas for the women and had iced down beer in a cooler for him and Pete. Pete went out and asked Hank if he was ready for a cold one, but Hank held a can of beer over his head with one hand and had a giant set of stainless steel tongs in the other and was in the process of turning over ribs on the grill. He indicated for Pete to come closer.

"How about basting these ribs and making yourself handy?"

Hank looked at Pete with raised eyebrows.

"Sure, I always end up doing the work over here. I thought I was a guest."

"Do you think it's a good idea to take Jane with you?"

"Hell, she can lend a woman's touch to the place. We haven't been up there in about 7 – 8 months."

"It could muddy the water with her there if the FBI comes calling."

"Why, I thought you agreed earlier," said Pete.

"Well it's just someone else for the FBI to check out, not that I think it's really going to make a difference. It's just one more person they are going to ask about."

"Well, I got her ticket and reservation and besides I'm probably selfish but I'm really starting to like her company."

"So I've noticed, but remember the old saying about the little head ruling the big head," said Hank with a chuckle.

"Hey? Start basting with that sauce and make sure you put plenty on. I have a reputation to uphold when it comes to baby spareribs."

"Hell, I can remember when they tasted like charcoal. The meat was burned to a crisp."

"Yeah, well I had some bad ribs that time and besides my beer is empty so do the honors will you?"

Pete grabbed his empty can and got two fresh ones from the cooler.

"Now Hank, don't overdo these. Remember that time they tasted like charcoal?" Nancy had appeared and was looking at the ribs.

"You make one mistake in your life and people won't forget."

It was a good meal and the girls and Pete heaped kudos on Hank and his ribs. They were all in a good mood and Nancy and Jane cleaned up while Hank and Pete cleaned the grill.

"We'll pick you two up at about 0830," said Hank as Pete and Jane were getting into her car.

Pete gave Hank a thumbs-up sign and they headed for Pete's house.

"I think they are getting back together," said Jane as she concentrated on her driving.

"I hope so. They should never have gotten divorced in the first place. The only one who made out on that deal was the lawyer," said Pete.

When they got to Pete's house, they walked in and took off their clothes and got in bed. Jane curled up with her head on Pete's shoulder and was gently snoring before Pete closed his eyes.

The flight up was uneventful. Pete rented a car at the airport and drove up to Coeur d'Alene and stopped at a grocery store and they bought what they thought they needed for a week. They could always come back and replenish. Jane continued to comment on the scenery. She had never been up there before.

Twenty minutes later, they pulled through the arch of Pete and Hank's place which announced that they were now entering the Snake Ranch.

"I'm impressed," said Jane.

"Well, don't be. It's only about 40 acres and Brian, the guy who looks after the place, had one of his friends make the sign."

"Why Snake Ranch?"

"Well back at Ft. Bragg, the Special Forces were known as the snake eaters, hence the Snake Ranch."

After a few minutes they saw the main cabin and then the small cabin came into view.

"Is that small cabin new?" asked Jane.

"No and yes; Brian had it completely renovated. Wouldn't take a dime, said the officers were too tight with a dollar and he wanted it done right."

As they pulled up to the main cabin, a tall burly man with a trimmed beard appeared, slowly walking towards their car. He had one hand behind his back. He walked up to the car and Pete got out.

"You can stick that hog in the back of your pants, away" said Pete, holding a hand out in greeting.

"I knew you were coming but I didn't expect you for a few days," said Brian, giving Pete a handshake.

Jane had stepped out of the car and was coming towards them.

Brian looked at her carefully, taking in the entire woman.

"Brian, this is Jane, Nancy's sister. Jane, Brian." They shook hands. Jane's hand disappeared into Brian's huge hand. She felt coarse calluses on his hand. It was obvious Brian didn't sit on his rear all day. They exchanged pleasantries.

"Do I see a new log fence circling the property?" asked Pete.

"Well, it's not completed yet, but it will be soon. You have all these lodge pole pines around so I though I would put them to good use."

"It looks great," said Pete.

"They pay me such high wages that I feel guilty not fixing things a little." Brian was directing his comments to Jane.

"That's hard to believe," said Jane. "I usually have to go Dutch treat whenever Pete takes me out."

"Well I can understand that," said Brian laughing. You probably had to pay for your own air ticket up here. Don't be taken in by these two, tight they are, stole this place from Mrs. Flanagan."

"Okay you two. I know when I'm beat," said Pete.

Brian followed them into the main cabin.

"Hey! What happened here? It looks brand new. Someone has sanded and oiled the inside lumber," said Pete.

"Well, if I left it to you and Hank, the place would have fallen down," said Brian in a sarcastic tone.

The stone fireplace had been redone and made larger.

"Hope you don't mind but a mutual friend of ours whose name will remain unmentioned took one look at it and started tearing it apart. After he was through I had to do something about the rest of the place."

"I want a bill for this," said Pete in a firm voice.

"Well I can't do that, Pete. Our memories go way back and we figured we owed you a hell of a lot more."

"Oh! So big Bill was your partner here," said Pete with a far look in his eyes. "You invite him up here? How is his wife doing?"

"She is fine now, healthy as a horse, which reminds me - the lady Hank saw up here last time is now my wife so if it's okay, I'll just keep her here."

"No problem," said Pete congratulating Brian and Jane joined in.

"Is that cabin big enough for both of you?" asked Pete.

"When you two get settled, come on over and we'll pop a few. I think you will be surprised," Brian said heading for the door. As he turned, Jane saw a huge pistol sticking up out of the back of his pants. When they were alone, the first thing Jane asked Pete was, "Would he have pulled that huge gun if we had been strangers?"

"Well I can tell you if those strangers had made trouble, they and their car would have disappeared forever. Brian is very careful who he befriends."

"God I hope he likes me," said Jane with a shiver.

They put away the groceries and the perishables in a huge refrigerator.

"That has to be the largest refrigerator I have ever seen."

"Brian and his friends got them cheap when they tore down the old Bison Hotel in town. As a matter of fact, if the electricity goes out, we have a huge generator over in the shed by the barn, another find by Brian and his friends. It kicks in automatically."

"It sounds like Brian has some good friends around."

"Yes and plenty of them," said Pete with a grin. "So he remarried. I'm happy for him."

"Someone has dusted and cleaned around here and I'm sure it wasn't Brian," said Jane.

Jane was taking a nap, so Pete went out and looked around.

The barn was straight and ready for inspection. Pete walked around. The grass had been trimmed and cut. It was a neat looking place. He saw Brian walking towards him. He was chewing on a blade of grass.

"So what's going down?" asked Brian looking straight into Pete's eyes.

"You remember me telling you about Hank, Jr. and then the death of that Turner woman?"

Brian nodded his head. "Well the FBI has gotten into the case and is asking a lot of questions which doesn't make any sense to Hank and me. We thought it was a closed case. They found out about this place and want to come up and look around, for what I don't know. That's why I came up a few days early to brief you and make sure the place looks presentable."

"And does it?" asked Brian.

"Does it what?" asked Pete.

"Does it look presentable? We spent some time on it knowing you usually come up around this time."

"Hell yes, the place has never looked better. It just baffles us why they want to look it over."

"The DECAD Association and all the old Special Forces people around, you know the FBI has never forgotten Ruby Ridge. Hell the Congress paid Tom about $7 million and chewed the FBI out publicly. So there is that to think about," said Brian looking seriously at Pete.

"Yeah, Hank and I have mulled that one over, but Christ it's a stretch."

"How was that Turner woman killed?"

"Shot at close range in the head, 22 caliber, looked professional, could have been one of her other lovers who caught something from her, but we are just guessing. What I don't want is the Feds stirring up the old Special Forces community. God knows we have some border line cases up here."

"Yeah, I guess we have, but their heart is in the right place. What role do you want me to play?"

"Tom is the older of the two agents; smart, low key. The other needs to go back to basic. Still wet behind the ears, asks questions without engaging the grey matter. Hell, I don't know, just tell them what you know about Hank and me. I don't know what else they can want."

"You want me to tell all I know about you?" Brian had a broad grin on his face.

"Nah, just the straight stuff."

"Have Hank and Nancy gotten over Hank, Jr.? They were pretty broken up about it. Never saw Hank that way before."

"I know, the good part is that he and Nancy are getting back together again."

"How about you, doing OK? By the looks of Jane, you have gotten out of your funk. Like you used to tell me, life goes on, got to live each day, you never know. That's why I got married again. Met Cathy at a Special Forces picnic, husband got killed in Nam in '72 and was with MACSOG. Had to ask her for six months before she would go out with me. Has a son, an LTC, works in the Pentagon now, good man. I meant to tell you before, but yesterday there was a government sedan cruising by here. You can spot them a mile away, didn't stop but slowed. I was out by the road working on the fence. So they are getting the lay of the land and for what?"

"That's what Hank and I can't figure out. I know I'm not going to get overly excited about this. I have a good rapport with Tom and I have been honest and up front with him. He will probably be up here Thursday or Friday. Brief Cathy that we will have visitors."

"Brief her yourself. I was on my way over to tell you and Jane we are having an early supper, aged elk meat, been in the crock pot for about eight hours. Cathy is a great cook with a good sense of humor which she needs putting up with me. We eat at 1700 hours, dress casual, shoes optional."

"Hey, come on. No need for that, we have plenty of food."

"Are you arguing with a former SMG? You know I never

took any crap from officers."

"Okay, we are happy to come and Jane will be especially happy knowing she won't have to cook. Thanks, we'll be there."

When Pete told Jane, she put her arms around Pete and kissed him.

"Is there anything we can bring? I'll be happy to make dessert or a salad."

"No, I have some nice wine and a bottle of Brian's favorite bourbon. That will make Brian happy. I don't know if Cathy even drinks, so we'll chance it with wine for her and bourbon for the good SMG."

At 1630 they knocked on the door and Cathy answered. To say she was a handsome woman was putting it mildly.

"So glad to finally me you," Cathy said with a welcoming grin on her face. She shook their hands and invited them in.

"We love company," she said in a loud, friendly voice.

"That's not company; it's a former officer looking for a free meal." Brian appeared, shook hands and told them to proceed to the living room.

"My God, you have built a new house here," said Pete, looking around in astonishment. "I think we'll switch cabins," said Pete laughing.

"Not on your life," laughed Brian. "Come with me. I'll show you around." The cabin had three bedrooms, obviously a new section added on, which was hidden from the main cabin, beautiful bathrooms and a rustic but obviously expensively decorated living room with a huge stone fireplace. The kitchen was country tasteful, decorated with a large dining area.

"This is really well done," said Jane. "Who is the decorator and where did you get this furniture?"

"Brian has a lot of friends and a lot of it was made by them. It has taken us about two years to get it the way we want it."

"Hell, be honest Cathy, you wouldn't marry me until everything was the way you wanted it."

"Well, that's partially right, but Jane, you should have seen it: Army footlockers for tables, rifles all over the walls, old army trays to eat off of – it was what you might call nostalgic army motif."

"God, we spoil our women Pete. A lot of sweat has gone into this place," said Brian with a laugh.

"And a lot of love," said Jane, giving Cathy's shoulder a squeeze.

"Well, here is something for both of you. Hope you can use it," said Pete.

"Well, I can see by the labels on these bottles that old Pete here is changing. It must be your influence Jane," said Brian, placing the bottles on the kitchen counter and turning around and giving Jane a hug.

"Thanks a lot," said Brian. You don't forget much, do you Pete," holding up the bottle.

"Well, sit down and make yourselves comfortable," said Cathy. "The dinner is ready but it's a simple fare, so it can wait."

"What can I get you Jane? I know what Pete likes before a meal."

"I'll have whatever Cathy is having."

"Good, 'cause I just mixed a pitcher of martinis." Cathy brought in glasses with olives in them and Brian poured.

"If you want to change your mind Jane let me know, but I think you'll find this very smooth."

"Heavens no," said Jane with a smile.

They toasted and Pete and Jane congratulated Brian and Cathy on their marriage.

The meal was fantastic. The meat was so tender, knives were not needed. Cathy obviously knew her way around the kitchen. They had coffee and homemade pie for dessert.

"You know, Cathy, you could have done a hell of a lot better than hooking up with this old snake eater, although I will say that if Brian likes you, he is the kind of guy that will take good care of you, no matter what. I can personally attest to that," said Pete squeezing Cathy's hand.

"Oh I know and he is very persistent. Once he makes up his mind about something, that's the way it's going to be."

"Jane, do you want to go into another room and talk?" said Brian sarcastically. "They are carrying on a conversation like we aren't even here."

"Nah, let them talk," said Jane laughing.

Jane helped Cathy clear the table and clean up. The men went into the living room.

"Brian told me Pete took the passing of his wife very hard. He was very glad to see you when you arrived today. I hope you spend the summer up here. It would be nice to have another woman around to talk to, not that I don't see any other women, but they live a distance from here and I miss not having a cup of coffee with another female without driving forty five minutes to see her."

"I think I'll be here, Cathy – it would be great to solve all the problems that the men have created and talk strictly girl talk," said Jane giving Cathy a hug.

"You know I think you and I could get into some real mischief," said Cathy. "Wouldn't that be nice when the guys go fishing or work on the fence?"

"I'm looking forward to it," said Jane giggling like a school girl.

"You know when Pete said Brian lived in the small cabin, I pictured a one room shed about ready to fall down, not this beautiful place. I'm not complaining. The other cabin looks wonderful and someone has really spruced it up."

"Brian and friends. At times there were about twenty friends fixing it up. They think a lot of Pete and Hank. They are close, very close," said Cathy with a faraway look on her face. I wish I had friends like that."

"You know Cathy; I think you have found one. I think you and I will become special and drop in on each other whenever we feel like gabbing. I don't know if Pete and I will ever settle down together. It's early for him. I lost my husband over four years ago so any time I spend with Pete is truly special. I love the guy so much and we are compatible, but I'm not going to push." Tears were welling up in Jane's eyes. "Oh, silly me," she said wiping her eyes. "I am like a school girl. You and I are going to have some intimate talks."

"Oh I hope so," said Cathy hugging Jane.

It was an enjoyable evening. Brian and Cathy were good hosts and company. Jane was surprised at Brian's good humor. For such a big brute of a guy, he told some pretty funny stories and usually he was the scapegoat. His stories about when he first worked with Pete up in the mountains of Viet Nam had everyone with tears in their eyes, they were laughing so hard.

They bid their farewells and Jane hugged both of them, thanking them for such a good time.

"They sure seem happy," said Jane on the way back to their cabin.

"Yeah, I can't get over how nice their place looks. Hank and I are going to give them a deed to their place. Hank must have been up here when they were fixing both places up, cause Cathy is a good housekeeper and has changed Brian into a human being. Believe me, he used to be a hard nut in the old days."

They went into the bedroom and got undressed and looked around at how nice the place looked. A lot of work had gone into refurbishing their cabin, small details in the bathroom which had been enlarged with both a shower and a huge old fashioned claw bath tub. It was modern yet had that rustic feel. They had not turned the heat on so there was a chill in the cabin. When they were both done with their toiletries, Jane started laughing.

"Where is the commode?" she asked Pete. "Don't tell me I have to go outside."

"Nah, see that door with the quarter moon cut out on it? That's the throne," said Pete laughing. Jane who had thought it was a linen closet opened the door and was surprised at the size of the room and that I also had a bidet, another of Brian's surprises.

She jumped into bed naked and put her arms around Pete. They laid there for a while just enjoying the clean smell of the sheets and pillows, not to mention the huge down comforter.

"When the FBI comes up here, keep them out of the two bedrooms and attached baths. If they have to use the john, let them use the half bath in the hallway. I don't want them thinking that we are rich or something. I don't know if you looked but the other large bedroom is a duplicate of this one. Brian probably figured Hank and I would fight over the biggest and the one with the most amenities."

"You know, Pete, Brian and his friends have done a lot and spent some money getting this place looking like it does. They must think a lot of you and Hank."

"Yes I know, but knowing Brian, he probably had his friends in shackles and a whip in his hand getting them to do what he wanted," laughed Pete. "He was not this way when we worked together. He was very quiet but got things done with few words. When his wife died, he was devastated. I think this place saved him. He was left a small fortune from his wife. He also has a good retirement from the Army. However, I think Cathy has been the one to bring him around. Believe me, Brian wouldn't have renovated his cabin and done all the work in this place on his own. Cathy has as many friends as he does in the Special Forces community. Her husband was well liked and was put in for the Medal of Honor posthumously but we had General Abrahams as the MACV Commanding General and he had no use for the Special Forces, so it was down graded to the Distinguished Service Cross, over the protest of many high ranking military and civilians."

"I like both of them," said Jane cuddling next to Pete. You know when we came up here I was just planning on staying a few weeks, but if you can put up with me I'd like to stay the summer."

"You obviously didn't see the closet with the shackles, where Hank and I lock any damsel who tries to escape."

"Hmm, that might be interesting; can I take that as a 'yes' then?"

"Just as long as you don't get bored," said Pete.

"Well, let's see, I have been reading this book on different things to do in bed," said Jane climbing on top of Pete and removing his underpants. "I think you'll like what I'm going to do."

"Oh God, you are turning into a hussy. Just what was it you used to do before I met you?" At that, Pete let out a yell, "OK. OK. You can stay and I'll behave."

Those were the last words spoken except for some moaning before they both fell into a deep sleep.

Jane woke up to a soft knocking on the back door by the kitchen. She grabbed a robe and padded barefoot out to the kitchen and opened the door. Cathy was standing there with a freshly baked loaf of bread wrapped in a white towel.

"Here, something to go with your bacon and eggs," she said getting ready to leave.

"Come in and have a cup of coffee," said Jane thanking her for the bread and pulling her in at the same time.

"Are you sure? Brian is still sleeping, but I have the automatic bread making machine, so I had two loaves smelling up the cabin when I woke up."

"Pete is sleeping. Let me go and close the door to the bedroom."

Jane came back and Cathy was filling the coffee pot and placing it on the burner.

"I woke you, didn't I?" said Cathy with an embarrassed look.

"Yes, you did and I want to thank you. Pete gets very romantic in the morning, in fact in the middle of the day and evening and I need to heal a little. I'm not complaining mind you but the guy is ready all the time," said Jane blushing.

Cathy laughed. "You know I think it's something they put in that Special Forces coffee, because my first husband was just the same and with Brian, I have to be careful not to smile at him too much or I'd never get out of bed."

"Thank God for the Special Forces," said Jane giggling.

"Did we hear a yell or a scream last night?" asked Cathy with a slight twinkle in her eyes.

Jane blushed to a bright crimson.

"Oh my God. I thought the cabins were far enough from each other so one couldn't hear. It was Pete teasing me in bed, so I did what any red blooded American girl would do and I squeezed his most vulnerable parts and he promised to behave, but it was not a serious wound 'cause his parts were in fine working order afterwards.

"Let's have some coffee and fresh bread with butter on it," said Jane getting up and pouring two mugs of strong, black coffee. Slicing the bread made the kitchen smell like a bakery. They both buttered a slice and sipped their coffee.

"Do you want some milk or cream, Cathy?"

"No, I like it this way, thanks."

"That was a wonderful meal and a good time last night. We both really enjoyed it."

"I'm so glad you and Pete are here. Sorry for barging in on you this morning, but I thought you'd enjoy the fresh bread, and I enjoy a little girl talk," said Cathy reaching across the table and squeezing Jane's hand.

"That goes both ways," said Jane smiling.

"We'll have to slip away and go shopping. They have some nice old stores in town – old antiques – I just love roaming around them."

"You know I want to buy Pete something to hang on that long wall in the living room, but I have to be careful. I don't want him to think I'm trying to snare him."

"Listen, the first time I saw Brian, I knew he was the one for me. I held out six months before I agreed to go out with him and that was it. We ended up in bed that night and then I definitely knew I was going to trap him even if I had to threaten him with a gun."

Jane giggled. "Maybe I'll buy a gun."

They both started laughing.

"I swear Cathy, I have only been here about 13 – 14 hours but I haven't talked about things and laughed so much in years. I think you and I think alike."

"That's good to hear. The same goes for me."

Pete took her around and showed her the property. There was an all-terrain vehicle in the barn and a cleared trail ran inside the fence on the property line. Two rough bridges had been built over the creek. It was a beautiful piece of property as far as Jane could see. A sprinkle of Ponderosa and blue spruce but mostly lodge pole pines. They took their time and waded barefoot in the creek. The water was freezing and Jane was glad when she got her socks and shoes back on. They came upon Brian and another man cutting down lodge poles and stacking them.

"Could use a little help tomorrow," said Brian in greeting them. Wayne here has things to do so I'll be short."

"Hank will be in tonight, so I'll bring him also," said Pete giving them a salute and giving the all-terrain vehicle gas as they departed the area.

"You weren't exactly friendly towards Brian and his helper," said Jane as they slowly followed the trail.

"Brian was sweating and was in no mood to chat. Besides, his helper and I go way back."

What a strange group these people were. It was almost like they could read each other's minds.

Hank's arrival brought Oh's and Ah's. He was visibly impressed by the upgrading of the cabin. Pete told him the story of Brian and Cathy while Jane fixed spaghetti and meatballs.

"The FBI will be here Thursday; I gave them directions and my cell number," said Hank.

Jane announced supper and they dug in. It was a pleasant meal.

"I have until Monday morning here," said Hank pushing

away from the table. "What about you and I going out to help Brian, and the girls can give them directions where to find us," said Hank.

"Sounds good; Brian and company have done a hell of a job. The least we can do is help finish the fence. If we work tomorrow, Wednesday and Thursday, we should have it done by the time our company arrives."

"Jane, you're up to date on these FBI people, aren't you?" asked Hank.

"Yes. Cathy and I will give them a friendly welcome," smiled Jane.

"Hey! Not too friendly," said Pete with furrowed brows.

"Not to worry," said Jane.

Hank begged off and headed for his bedroom. He looked tired. Obviously the Spokane business had been more taxing than he thought.

Pete and Jane cleaned up and went out and sat on the screened porch, enjoying the cool breeze.

"I don't know if I can't handle all this fresh air but I'm tired," said Jane. "It's so quiet and peaceful up here. I could stay forever."

"When winter comes you might change your mind. As for the quiet and peacefulness, that I agree with, but you'll have to stop that rough sex or Brian and Cathy won't get any sleep. I need Brian to finish the fence."

Jane got up and stretched and gave Pete a kiss on the top of his head.

"See you in a few minutes," said Pete.

Brian drove them hard on the fence project. Sweat was running down Pete's and Hank's faces and back. Their shirts were soaked.

"We have about another hour and we'll be done," said Brian notching another lodge pole. Hank was digging holes for the fence posts and was barely keeping ahead of Brian and Pete who were setting the fence poles and then attaching the long lodge poles. There had been no sign of the FBI and they were almost up to the gate so they had not entered the property.

"Should I put a hole next to the gate posts, or are you going to attach the lodge poles to the gatepost?" asked Hank, wiping sweat from his face.

"No, we need a hole about a foot away from the gate post. Don't get too close to the gate post or you'll undermine the gate," said Brian with a slight grin on his face.

Hank and Pete set the last fence post as Brian was notching the last pole. They had just completed the fence when a government vehicle ran over the cattle guard and stopped inside the fence.

Tom stepped out and greeted them. Tony remained in the car. Pete made the introductions.

"Christ, couldn't you have come earlier and helped with the fence?" said Pete, taking off his work gloves and shaking hands with Tom.

"Would have been here sooner but my navigator steered me on to the wrong road and we almost ended up in Bonner's Ferry. Scenic drive though," said Tom with raised eyebrows.

"Well come on, you're in time for lunch. Just follow the road and you'll run into the cabin. We'll just gather up our tools and will be along in a few minutes," said Pete.

The vehicle took off and they placed their tools on the all-terrain vehicle and hopped on. Brian drove without saying a word. They pulled into the barn and put the tools away and headed for the main cabin. There was a sink in the mud room where they washed off the sweat and put on their dry shirts, walking around the front of the cabin to the screened porch where the girls had laid out a meal and were chatting with the two FBI agents.

"Well I see you found the place," said Brian in an even tone. "I don't know if we ought to feed them. They haven't done any work."

"How about if Tony and I do the dishes?" said Tom, getting

a laugh from everyone.

After the meal, the girls cleaned up and left the men on the front porch.

"I'm not really sure why we are here," said Tom. "But I felt we had to cover all the bases which weren't done on the first go around."

"Is there anything I can do for you," asked Brian, "even though I have never met the woman, Mrs. Turner?"

"There are quite a few loose cannons up in this area," said Tony. "Do you know if anyone has been down in Marana, or have you heard any talk?"

"'Loose cannon' is a relative term, Tony. Any one of us here, including the two of you, fit that category, maybe not knowingly but certainly by reputation. We have a community up here that is in the autumn of their years and has become more laid back and forgiving as the years go by. To answer your question, I have not heard even an innuendo. In fact, I'm probably the only one who knew about it until yesterday when I told my wife that we might have some visitors."

"When did you first hear about Mrs. Turner's death and who told you?" asked Tony.

"Well, let's see. About six or seven months ago when Hank stopped by, we discussed Hank Jr.'s tragedy."

"Are you telling me that these two friends of yours didn't call you and tell you that the woman Hank Jr. had been dating had been killed? Is that what you want me to believe?" Tony was getting worked up.

"Actually, yes, Tony, that is what I'm telling you. We don't communicate much except when Pete here is getting ready to come up. He usually gives me a heads up about two weeks prior so I can go over and knock the cobwebs down. It's also a good idea, Tony, when asking questions, to do so in an even voice 'cause when you get a little excited your finger has a tendency to tighten on the trigger, which can have unexpected results: one, the people who you are talking to have a tendency to clam up and not help you along in your investigation; or two, you fire prematurely which can have devastating results."

Tony was fuming and looked to Tom for help which was not forthcoming.

"Can we take a walk around and take a look at your place here," said Tom, "so in case we talk in the future and you tell me you are heading up here, I have an idea what it looks like?"

"Come on," said Hank, "Ill give you the tour.

Hank and the two FBI men took off and headed for the barn.

"Brian really takes care of this place. Like Pete says, it probably saved him after his wife passed away. He was really down and jumped at the chance of getting away from Fort Bragg. There were too many memories there and not enough to keep him occupied. Here he can do what he wants, work as little or as much as he wants. He remarried and is happy as a kid. This is the barn, nothing exciting. We store some mowers and a vehicle, tools, etc. I don't think there have been any animals here, at least not in our time here. The hay field you see out there is cut by our closest neighbor – the hay is rolled when it's dry and left in the field for deer and elk – it can get kind of harsh here in the winter and the wild animals run out of food. We also chip in and place salt licks out for them"

"Salt licks. Are you saying the deer and elk eat salt?" Tony asked in a skeptical manner.

"Yes, they need salt in their diets just like we do. There are areas where there is natural salt in the dirt or around dry areas, but this makes it easier for them."

"This is Brian and Cathy's cabin. He renovated and enlarged it. It's quite comfortable now."

"How does an enlisted man get enough money to renovate a house, or a cabin?" asked Tony.

"Well," said Hank looking at Tom, "when his first wife died of cancer, he inherited quite a bit of money. Her family was wealthy."

"What was her maiden name?" asked Tony, taking out a

small notebook and pen.

"That you are going to have to ask Brian. I always knew her as Mrs. Huff. I don't think that ever came up in all the years I've known Brian. It just wasn't something you asked. I met some distant relatives at her funeral but I don't recall their last names. It was sort of a first name type introduction, since both Pete and I were close to Brian."

"The woods around here belong to us. When we saw you today we were just finishing up a fence which encircles the property. Actually, Brian and some friends did the work. Pete and I just helped with the last hundred yards or so."

"Is there any way to drive around the perimeter?" asked Tony.

"Sure we have to take the all-terrain vehicle though, a car can't make it."

"I think I'll join the others on the porch," said Tom. "My nephew has one of those and they scare me to death."

Hank and Tony got on the vehicle and drove out of the barn.

Tom knocked on the screen door and Pete told him to come in.

"It looks like you lost some of your company," said Brian.

"No, I didn't lose them; Tony wanted to ride around the perimeter of your property, so Hank obliged him. I wanted to straighten out what was said earlier. Tony is an intelligent guy on paper, but street wise he would get lost in his own neighborhood. He doesn't always engage the gray matter before asking a question or making a statement, so you might say he is an OJT as you Army folks call it. I'll straighten him out on the drive back. Hope no offense was taken."

"No, drop it," said Brian. "He is right. We have some loose cannons, but most of them are in wheelchairs now, missing limbs here and there. There are some who haven't got much money, so the organization holds raffles, skewed towards those that are in need. They wouldn't take an outright gift but a raffle or bingo is different. We who can chip in and we petition our headquarters at Fort Bragg for a good chunk each year. We hold a barbeque each 4th of July and a Christmas party.

We have guest donors who send us money so all in all everyone is taken care of. We have a van that takes some of them to the VA or over to Spokane where there is a military hospital, actually, a glorified clinic. So you see Tom the days of drum beating have passed now. We make sure our brothers are cared for."

"Well, since both Hank and Pete are members down in Arizona, a couple of names have come up as possible suspects - a Billingsly and a guy by the name of Hanks," said Tom.

"Know them both well and so does Pete here. Hanks had his other leg amputated, diabetic; let's see about 3 or 4 years ago. He is confined to a wheelchair. Lost the other leg in Nam, '72 I think. Billingsly lives in Australia with wife #3, an Aussie. Raises chickens, lots of them, and is from the rumors a multi-millionaire. He not only raises them, he processes and freezes them, has a modern operation going. His wife owned the land and was raising a few chickens when Billingsly met her. Has one son, three star General, head of Army Intelligence in the Pentagon. Hanks had two sons, both killed behind the lines in Desert Storm. You might have remembered Billingsly from Ruby Ridge. He was helping Bo Gritz calm everyone down, and managed to get Tom to give up after the unfortunate incident. That's the only Hanks and Billingsly that is or was here."

"Tony must have gotten the names wrong, but what we don't want to do is go running around up here getting your friends all excited. What I would appreciate is if you hear anything to let me know. There is one other thing I should let you in on. I saw no reason to come up here in the first place. Tony's uncle is our number three man in the Bureau, and he convinced his uncle it was part of a conspiracy by old grudge bearing Special Forces personnel. I'm inclined to go with the theory that what happened to Mrs. Turner had to be someone she knew, perhaps one of her other men friends – no struggle or blemishes on her body so it had to be someone she knew – no forced entry to the house. When are you heading back to Tucson, Pete?"

"I usually stay here to the end of September, first part of October. That gets me out of the worst of the hot weather."

"Did you meet or hear anything about Turner expecting any out of town visitors around the time of her death?"

"You know Hank and I have been racking our brains about this case, Hank being the more experienced in intelligence matters. My wife got pretty bad and passed away after Mrs. Turner was killed, but I never told her. She couldn't understand why Mrs. Turner never stopped by to see her. They had been good friends. I came up with excuses for her and so did Nancy, Hank's wife, for she was taking care of my wife towards the end, being an RN plus her best friend. Mrs. Turner did have friends in Washington, D.C., which was one of the excuses we used, that she was in D.C. Now that I reflect back, I don't think I mentioned that before. It was a bad time, like I said, and if anything else shakes loose, I'll let you know."

"Thanks," said Tom. "I see our friends are back so we better get moving. Our pickup time at the airfield is in an hour or so, so we better hustle." Hank and Tony appeared as Tom was walking out the screen door followed by the others.

"This is a nice set up," said Tony. Nice creek with trout. I could get used to a place like this.

"Do you want something to drink before you leave?" asked Pete. Tom waved him off.

"Please give our thanks to the ladies for a fine meal," said Tom.

The two FBI men got into the sedan and departed.

"What did you say to Tony to get him in such a good mood?" asked Brian.

"Oh his ego needs stroking," said Hank with a smile.

"I'm going in to see what the girls are up to and bring us a much deserved drink," said Pete.

As he walked in he heard laughing and giggling coming

from the kitchen. It was music to his ears. He was glad the two women were getting along.

"What is so funny? You two sound like school girls, up to no good."

"Oh we were just talking girl talk," said Jane, still laughing.

"Would you like something to drink, or aren't you of age yet?"

"We're of age alright, what did you have in mind mister?" said Cathy with a smile on her face, eliciting another laugh from Jane.

"Have you two been into the firewater already or do you want something else?"

"Something else," said Cathy, both of them bursting into a laugh.

"OK, I'm fixing something for us, if you need something, sound off."

"We need something," both of them echoed in chorus.

Pete got some beer and shot glasses and a bottle of bourbon and headed for the porch. He poured three shots and gave them a can of beer each.

The girls appeared each holding a can of beer.

"Can we have some of that firewater?" said Cathy.

Pete poured a shot into the two empty glasses.

"What's all this laughing about?" asked Brian.

"You'll find out later," said Cathy, taking a glass from Pete.

They all said "cheers" and downed the bourbon. They all took a sip of beer and leaned back in their chairs.

"That was in interesting day," said Pete.

"They are way off their mark," said Brian sipping his beer.

Meanwhile, George Hamilton sat in his corner office on the 4th floor in the J. Edgar Hoover building. He leaned back in his chair interlocking his hands behind his head. What a goddamn mess, he thought letting out a sigh. He should never have let Tony talk him into sending him and Tom up to Idaho in a company plane. They were on a wild goose chase and he knew Tom was aware of it. If they stirred those Special Forces people up, the shit could hit the fan again, like it had at Ruby Ridge. His only justification had been his sister, his only sister, who had gone through a sordid divorce and his nephew Tony who was assigned to his division. He had assigned Tom as his partner a seasoned FBI agent with a good head on his shoulders. He should have listened to Tom's reservations. After all, they could have closed the case and made it go away.

Tony was smart but had little common sense. He had given in to Tony thinking he might learn something and, yes, tag the killing of Mrs. Turner on one of those weirdo Special Forces relics up there. After all, there was a tie in with Pete Compton, a member of the DECAD Association. Well it was too much to hope for, or was it? Tony had a good imagination, about all he had.

His intercom shook him out of his reverie. Susan, his secretary, came on and wanted to know if he needed anything before she left for the day.

"Thanks, I'm fine. I'm just finishing up some paperwork. I'll be out of here in a few minutes."

"Is it anything that needs typing? I haven't shut my PC down yet."

"No, it's just notes I need for my briefing in the morning."

"OK then, good night." The intercom light went out.

George Hamilton stretched and got up. He reached for his suit jacket and put it on, locked his desk and headed towards the door. Opening it, he saw Susan putting on her blazer and retrieving her purse from her desk. Locking his door, he turned around. Susan was holding the hall door open for him.

"Thanks, I should be the one holding the door for you."

"After all these years, it really doesn't matter, does it?"

"No, I guess not," he said and walked out the door. He heard Susan locking it. God she was a good looking woman, widowed, no children, no baggage.

He pressed the button for the elevator. It opened immediately. He waited for Susan to go in first. There were alone in the highly polished paneled elevator.

"Are you feeling OK, George? You seem a little distant lately," said Susan as they descended to the parking area in the basement.

"Yeah, I'm OK; just have a lot of things on my plate, what with my sister-in-law dying and my wife up in Maine taking care of her, and the normal bull around her. It gets to you after awhile."

"Oh I know, but I have missed you George. Is it something I have done or haven't done?"

"No I have a little medical problem. In fact, I'm heading over to Dr. Hollingworth now."

"Is it anything I should be concerned about or aware of?"

"No, it's just a man thing that happens when you reach a certain age. I want it taken care of before it does become a problem."

They had reached the garage and the elevator door opened.

"If you need anything, you know where to reach me and good luck at the doctor." Susan headed for her car.

"Thanks, I will, you know that," George said half-heartedly and headed for his car.

Christ, he had been seeing Susan for over five years and they had never had any secrets from each other. She had gotten him out of potential jams with his Director by being on friendly terms with his secretary. He owed her that was for sure. He would have to come clean with her one way or another. Then there was his wife. He had to have an explanation for her when she returned. She was a needy woman and would probably be home soon. She had spent almost seven months nursing her sister up in Maine. She had appreciated his understanding and had told him more than once; she would make it up to him when she got home.

He reached the underground parking at Dr. Hollingsworth's office, took the elevator up and arrived in the plush reception room.

"Good evening, Mr. Hamilton. I'll let the doctor know you're here. Please have a seat." He took a seat and leaned back, resting his head against the wall. What a goddamn mess, he thought.

Dr. Hollingsworth appeared in the door.

"Come in George," Dr. Hollingsworth said with a grin, closing the door behind him.

"Sit down, George. I have some news for you. The test results for genital herpes and HIV came back negative. What you had were genital warts which I removed. Drop your pants and let me take a look at the little guy."

George was almost in shock with joy and excitement. He undid his trousers and let them fall to the floor, and took out his penis. Dr. Hollingsworth shone a blue florescent light at the head, examining thoroughly.

"No sign of them reappearing. Hell you're as good as new. Stop by in about six months or sooner if you see anything. My secretary will make an appointment. You know George, you and I have been friends for a long time. When you came in here and told me the story about your partner, I was a little surprised. We have been to each other's houses over the years and our wives are good friends. I'm not lecturing you. I'm giving you some friendly advice. If you need to step out, use precaution if you don't know much about your partner. There is no cure for genital herpes or HIV. OK, enough lecturing. Have a good evening." Dr. Hollingsworth got up and escorted George to the door.

"There is no chance that the lab made a mistake, is there?"

"No, I had a friend of mine run the tests and he is the best – in fact he ran those three times."

"Thanks Doc and I'll remember what you said."

Jesus Christ, he was ready to shout as he headed for the garage. That fucking bitch sure as hell had infected a friend of his. He needed to talk to Tom and Tony, but first things first. He dialed Susan's place as soon as he got in the car.

He heard a cautious hello on the other end.

"George here. I have been thinking about our earlier conversation. Are you tied up tonight?"

"No, as a matter of fact, I was just thinking of you. I've missed you."

"I have missed you, Susan. I'll stop and get the champagne you like and I'll see you in half an hour."

"Looking forward to it, George."

There was a click at the other end as she hung up.

It had been weeks, no let's see, months, since he had sex. When his friend Roger had come down with herpes and HIV, he had panicked. He had no desire for sex and the damn tests had taken months, at least it seemed that long. He pulled over to the curb and walked into the liquor store. Hell, the prices here were twice what he would pay at the other stores, but its customer base didn't mind so they charged. Hell, he'd pay ten times the going rate, he was so happy. He also picked up a bottle of Bailey Irish Cream. Susan liked that with her coffee.

When he reached her condo, he knocked gently on the door.

Susan opened it wearing a white slip, nothing under. George reacted at once like a teenager. God what a hunk of woman.

He handed her the bag with the bottles and Susan placed the champagne in the freezer and placed the Bailey's on the kitchen counter.

As she turned around, he took her in his arms and nuzzled her neck, running his hands down her buttocks, spreading them apart. She grabbed his erection and squeezed it.

"You better get out of your clothes or there is going to be a wet spot on your pants."

Susan led him into the bedroom and started undressing him, being careful to hang his jacket and pants on a hanger while he took off his shoes and socks. He removed his tee shirt and underpants, lying down on the bed.

"Hmm, little George is ready to burst," she said removing her slip.

God she was a real woman, firm breasts, flat stomach ending with a loose protruding mound covered in a mass of black hair, hard shapely legs with a hint of hair on the inside of them where they joined her lips.

"Didn't have time to shave my bikini line," she said noticing his look. Hasn't been any reason to for a long time."

She snuggled into his arms as he gave a huge sigh. God she had missed him, but she intended to make up for it tonight.

"How about a little champagne to celebrate?" she said, looking up at his face.

"I'll get it," he said, getting out of bed and heading for the kitchen. He took the bottle out and untwisted the wire holding the cork in. Popping the cork, he filled two glasses half way and brought them into the bedroom. Susan was sitting up, leaning against the headboard of the bed.

"You look good George. Working out has certainly kept you in shape."

"You are the one in great shape. I don't know how you do it. Running is one thing but your body is toned all over."

"Well now that we are back exercising again, it should improve even more," Susan said accepting a glass from him.

"Here is to us and a good evening," he said touching his glass to hers.

They finished the champagne and placed them on the night stand and made love.

They lay on the bed holding hands.

"Christ, you take it out of me Susan. I feel whipped, out of practice I guess." He placed his arm around her and drew her close.

"You have no idea what you do to me Susan. I have never experienced anything like this before or have enjoyed it so much, which reminds me you better set the alarm clock. I have to go home and put some fresh clothes on for tomorrow. God, I haven't even asked you if I can spend the night."

"George, I love it when you stay. I just assumed you knew

after all this time. I love snuggling up to you. Besides, I've set the alarm already so you will look fresh tomorrow at the Director's meeting."

He kissed her and snuggled down in bed next to her. The next thing he knew the alarm was going off. Susan moaned and turned her face for a kiss, reset the alarm and went back to sleep.

When George got to the office Susan was there, coffee ready and a fresh Danish. He smiled at her and went into his office. God he was tired. He would have to start jogging again, besides his workouts. Susan walked in with coffee and a plate of Danish, setting them at the edge of his desk.

"Talked to Betty. The Director had to go down to Quantico this morning, so the meeting is canceled."

"Thank God. I'm not sure my mind is on my work today."

"You do have a confidential fax – it's just coming in. I'll bring it in. Are there any priorities this morning, or should I finish up that draft study you gave me yesterday?"

"Yes, get that done. You never know when he is going to ask for it."

Susan left and closed the door behind her. God, what a woman, good looking and smart. She could have done a lot better in the job field, but she said she enjoyed her work, and he had seen to it that her salary had increased to the highest step which gave her a comfortable life. She owned the condo, free and clear, and had taken his advice and invested her husband's life insurance in some very profitable stocks. She was wealthy and could have retired a few years ago with a full pension from the FBI, but decided to stay on.

There was a slight knock on the door and Susan walked in with sheaves of papers in one hand placing them on his desk. He had just finished his coffee and a Danish and was wiping his hands on a napkin.

"The faxes I told you about. Another cup of coffee? I just made some fresh."

"Thanks, you must have read my mind. It tastes particularly

good this morning," he said with a smile. Susan returned with a silver decanter and poured him a fresh mug and departed.

The faxes were from Tom and Tony, giving him a detailed report of what they had learned, or more specifically what they had not learned. Those former Special Forces people up at the cabin had been very helpful but they were as puzzled about the Turner death as the FBI. It had to be someone she was close to, considering the coroner's report and forensics. The two names Tony had come up with proved useless - one was a paraplegic and the other was and had been living in Australia the past 10 years. The only new piece of information was that Turner had friends in D.C. and they were in the process of trying to find out from her extended family, which was scattered, whether they knew anything.

George threw the papers on his desk and took a sip of the coffee - God it tasted good - and ate another Danish. He was starving. OK. What to do?

Roger Dunbar had met Mrs. Turner at a party in D.C. He had also visited her in Tucson a few times but usually she had come to D.C. on weekends, which had not been a problem for Roger, even having a wife and family, although the kids were both in college. Roger, being a lobbyist and living the high life, was often called away on weekends, and his wife understood. They were both members of Burning Tree Country Club, and his wife was into the Country Club set both as an avid tennis and golf enthusiast. However, when she came down with genital herpes, the shit hit the fan. Her gynecologist had told her he wanted to run additional tests on her and had asked her about sex partners. She had informed him the only person she ever had sex with was her husband. The doctor had recommended her husband go and see his doctor. Roger had been sitting by their pool sipping a drink and going over some papers when he heard his wife coming up behind him. He had given her a friendly greeting without taking his eyes off his paperwork, when she had struck him in the head with her purse with such force that his paperwork fluttered into the pool and his drink crashed to the stone slab patio. Roger was literally stunned. She wanted to know who he had been fucking and for him to go and see his doctor immediately. He had no idea what she was talking about. Their maid had come out when she heard the glass break but retreated back into the house when she heard the conversation. His wife had sat down in a lounge chair and started crying. He had asked what the matter was. She had told him. She wanted to know if he had any symptoms. He had immediately said "No" and tried to turn the tables on her wanting to know what she had been up to. The best defense is a good offense he had learned long ago. When she told him through tear filled eyes that she had never strayed on him and asked him to go see his doctor, Roger had pulled out his cell phone and called and was told his doctor would see him within the hour. The initial results had been devastating, but positive results would take a while. Roger was not prepared to reveal his other partner to the doctor and had left with the promise to contact her. The doctor told him he would let Roger know the results as soon as he had them. Roger had noticed some redness on his penis, but had chalked it up to over use. When he reached home he had sat down with his wife and talked. She was furious. He had asked her if she wanted a divorce. Hell no, she had retorted. Who was she going to have sex with, he knew her needs; no, he was going to take care of her for the rest of her life and speaking of life, it was going to cost him that new home they had seen with acreage around it. When the news came that Roger not only had genital herpes but HIV also, it was a shock to both of them. They both had a stiff drink. How much money do we have, had been her first question. Roger had told her they had approximately four million, everything was paid for. She wanted to know how much in offshore banks and that he better not bullshit her. He had informed her they had another five in three different banks. She had then informed him that they would stay in their house but buy a winter place in the Caribbean. He had agreed to all her demands. Who had infected him was her next question and had any of his friends stuck their dicks in her. If so he should let them know. She had excused herself while he dialed his cell phone.

The only one he knew of that had seen her was George, whose phone was now ringing.

"Mr. Hamilton's office," said a voice on the other end.

"Susan, Roger here, let me speak to George. It's important." She had patched him through and George was on the other end.

"George, I got some news, you better be sitting down."

"Go ahead Roger, you're on a secure line."

"Remember that Turner woman I introduced you to? Did you sleep with her?"

"Well, yes, she was very nice and I appreciate the intro. Why?"

"She gave me genital herpes and I'm also HIV positive." There was a silence at the other end of the line.

"George, are you there?"

"Yes, I'm here. How do you know it was her?"

"She is the only one I have been to bed with."

"Jesus Christ, Roger. How did you find out?"

"I infected my wife and she confronted me. I just got the doctor's report back today confirming it."

"Holy shit, Roger, I'm sorry. Is there anyone else?"

"I'm sure there are but you are the only one I introduced her to. You better go see your doctor ASAP."

"Thanks, Roger. I will. I'll talk to you later."

George sat in his chair. His life was over. What a goddamn mess. He called his doctor and made an appointment. What the hell was he going to do? Revenge was the first thing that cropped into his mind. He had noticed some strange red spots, almost a growth on several places on the head of his penis. Shit, he was infected also. What to tell Susan and his wife. Let's see, it was Thursday. He called Mrs. Turner in Tucson. The phone was answered on the fourth ring.

"Turner residence, how may I help you?"

"This is George Hamilton in D.C. How are you?"

"George, yes I remember, bad boy. Are you in town?"

"No, but if you are not tied up I have business there tomorrow and this weekend. I was wondering if we could get together."

"But of course. How about dinner at my place tomorrow evening? I'll meet you outside the first gate you come to on the left side of Dove Mountain Boulevard. You have to cross the median there. It's easy to find. You'll be coming off I-10 at marker 240, Tangerine Road. Go east to the first stop light. That's Dove Mountain Boulevard. Take a left and go north approximately 1.5 miles. You'll see my red car. I'll be there at 7:30 p.m. sharp. I'll get you through the gate. I have an automatic opener. That way no one will know you're in town or visiting me.

"That sounds great. Looking forward to seeing you."

"Me too, George, I have been thinking about you, a naughty boy who needs a spanking."

George had hung up. He would make his own travel arrangements, using his authorized alias name. That bitch would get the surprise of her life. Naughty boy, eh! Well he would see.

Susan had asked as he was leaving if she would see him this weekend. He had told her he needed to go out of town, but would probably be back Saturday night. He would give her a call. She had seemed pleased and assumed he was going up to Maine where his sister-in-law was dying of cancer and his wife was taking care of her.

"Do you want me to make flight arrangements for you?"

"No thanks, I'm hopping a ride with a friend on his plane, you know Alex Kimbell, he has a home up there. I'm leaving for the day, like I said, and should be back Saturday night if it fits Alex's schedule."

"OK, have a nice trip – hope you're back Saturday," Susan said with a smile.

269

The flight to Tucson had been uneventful. He had to show his ID in order to bring his weapon aboard, but he had telephoned ahead and a friend at security at Dulles airport had made it smooth – didn't have to take it out of its leather case. He was whisked through. Business class was not what it used to be. He had a drink and leaned back shutting his eyes. He rented a car and drove north on I-10. He was early but got off at marker 240 and headed east on Tangerine road. The first stoplight he came to was Dove Mountain Boulevard.

He drove past several developments until he spotted the locked gates on the left side of the boulevard. He had an hour to kill before he was to meet her. He kept driving and saw the main entrance to Heritage Highlands and kept driving. He saw the entrance to the Gallery Country Club and pulled in. Parking his car in a reserved slot, he walked into the club, sat down at a table in the bar and ordered a beer. He asked the waitress if he could get a sandwich in the bar and when she answered in the affirmative he ordered the day's special. The place was nice, upscale and the sandwich was good. He looked at his watch. He had ten minutes until his meeting with Mrs. Turner. He paid his bill, left a generous tip and departed. He started driving slowly towards the south gate. It was getting dark, but he noticed an expensive red car emerging from the gate, making a U-turn and stopping at the entrance gate. He blinked his lights. The other car saw his signal and returned the signal. The gate opened and he followed the other car through the gate. They drove past one street and took a right on the next street, drove to the end of the block and a garage door opened revealing a large empty garage. Mrs. Turner pulled in to the left in the garage and he pulled in along side of her. As he shut the engine off, the garage door closed. He took out his pistol which had a silencer attached and stuck it in the back of his pants. It was uncomfortable but it would do. He got out of the car and was greeted by Mrs. Turner.

"Good to see you again, George," she said giving him a

kiss on the cheek.

"Been looking forward to this," said George as he followed her into the house. It was expensively decorated. She led him to a large couch and they both sat down. He asked her how she had been. As she was about to answer, she turned her head away and looked at the wall to her right. George pulled the gun out and placed it at the bottom or her skull and fired. A word had partially been said but it was unintelligible. Blood was starting to flow down her neck to her left shoulder. George got up, looked at his jacket. There was no blood splatter. He picked up the spent shell. The silencer had muffled the noise.

He walked to the kitchen not touching anything, took a kitchen towel, wet it, and wiped the door and door knob leading to the garage. He opened his car door and placed the gun with the safety on in the passenger seat. He walked to Mrs. Turner's car, opened the door and took the garage door opener off the sun visor, closed the door to the car and got into his car, put the safety belt on and opened the garage door, starting his car at the same time. Backing out he closed the garage door and headed down the street turning his lights on. He would get rid of the towel and garage door opener at the airport. While he was driving he ejected the magazine and unscrewed the silencer. He ejected the round that had automatically chambered as he had fired. When he got to the airport, he sat in the car and wiped down the gun with the damp towel. He placed the spent casing and towel in a trash receptacle. The garage door opener he placed in another trash receptacle.

He placed the gun and silencer in his leather gun case and placed it in his briefcase. He drove the car down to the Avis section and cleared the car with the Avis agent check in person at the curb.

He had just enough time to get the flight to Atlanta and go through security. He had to show his gun permit and identification at security and headed to his flight which was already boarding.

When the plane was airborne he ordered a double vodka on ice. He slept most of the way to Atlanta and caught his flight to Dulles. It had gone smoothly. He had not left any finger prints behind. He felt good. George took his time driving home. His telephone was ringing as he walked in the door. He picked it up and said "George here."

"I have been calling all evening. Is everything alright?" his wife asked.

"Yes, we had a late meeting. How is your sister?"

"Oh George, she is so thin. That's why I called. George I have to stay with her. She can't handle it herself. I know I'm asking a lot, but George I promise I'll make it up to you when I get home."

"Listen hon, you stay and do what you have to do, but I'm going to hold you to your word. We'll probably have to get new sheets, but what the heck, it will be worth it."

"Oh George, you are so understanding. I'm so lucky to have you. I have to hang up. I hear her calling for me. I love you, George."

"I love you too, and give your sister my best wishes." There was a click and then the line was broken.

That was close. He was glad she was staying a while. He called his doctor and left a message on his answering machine that he needed to see him first thing Monday morning instead of later in the week. He also left a message for Susan at the office that he would be late due to a doctor appointment.

He got undressed and took a long, hot shower. He put a white terry cloth robe on and poured himself a healthy glass of vodka on ice. Settling into his comfortable chair in his den, he turned the TV on flipping channels until he found an old movie. He woke up and there was a newscast on. He turned off the TV, went to the bathroom, got two aspirins out, swallowed them with a glass of water and went to bed.

He woke late Saturday morning, got the paper off his lawn, and made a strong cup of coffee. Jesus that had been an efficient operation yesterday; like the old days when he had worked in Central America for the agency. It was an adrenalin rush. That bitch. She was or had been a cool one. Had never asked if he had come down with something. The adrenalin rush turned to dread. What the hell was he going to tell his wife and Susan? He had told her he probably would be back today. He wouldn't call her, nor would he answer his phone unless it was his wife. He spent the weekend catching up on some paperwork and read a new paperback, "Lonesome Dove". It got his mind off things.

Early Monday morning he showed up at his doctor's office. The secretary was on the phoned and waved him into a chair. Dr. Hollingsworth came out from his office and waved George in.

"What's the panic, George?" Dr. Hollingsworth asked, taking a sip of coffee.

George blurted out the story, except where he had spent Friday. Dr. Hollingsworth just stared at him. When George was through, the doctor told him to drop his pants.

"Out with him, George."

George reached in his underpants and showed the doctor his penis. Dr. Hollingsworth put on some latex gloves and examined the penis. He went over to the counter and brought back a bottle which has a protrusion attached to it. The doctor put a drop of the solution on each spot, and told him the little warts should disappear within a day. The doctor drew some blood and informed George he would send it to have it analyzed. It would take some time. In the meantime, the doctor informed George that from his exam he did not detect any genital herpes but that didn't mean he didn't have any. They sort of flared up from time to time, and for George not to have any sex until he heard from him.

George left the doctor's office in a dejected mood. How would he explain it to Susan? They had gotten into a routine which he looked forward to each week.

When he got back to the office Susan greeted him with coffee and Danish. She asked how his sister-in-law was doing.

"Not good," said George. "It was kind of depressing being up there, didn't get back until late Sunday night."

"You have a meeting with the Director at one o'clock. I typed up your notes the way you like them. Tom and your nephew finished the case they were working on – want to come in and brief you when you have time. Said there was no hurry. It won't go to trial for at least two months, included that wrap up in your notes."

"Thanks, the old man has been pushing for a conclusion on that one, could have widespread implications and a feather in the old man's hat."

"If you can hold my calls, I need to get familiar with my notes and see if you can schedule Tom and Tony to come in tomorrow afternoon if the schedule permits."

"You're fine for tomorrow, but from then on you're booked solid to the end of the week."

"Sounds good. Sorry about Saturday but it's not a pretty picture up there. I would much rather have been here."

"No problem. I had things to do. Good to see you back, George. I think you better get some rest. You look tired and drawn."

"Yeah, well, I better get at these notes."

Susan left and closed the door. He had to get his mind on his work. The Director, or as most called him "The Old Man", was a stickler for details.

Over the next weeks and months, he had avoided Susan, staying late at work and had helped Tom and Tony with their case. It was a terrorist case and the ACLU had gotten involved so they had to be sharp. Susan never confronted him, but he could tell by her looks that she was expecting some kind of explanation.

One day he took a call from the State's Attorney from Arizona. He asked if George could send a couple of agents out there to clear up a murder case. The local FBI agents were swamped with border issues and he needed help. He briefly outlined the case to George. The local police down in Tucson had screwed up, hence the call for help.

George promised him help. The agents would be there in a day or two.

He pressed the intercom. "Susan, get hold of Tom and Tony and have them report to me ASAP. They have been basking in their glory for their last case long enough. It's time they started earning their pay."

"I just saw them downstairs. I'll get them up." There was the usual click from the intercom.

Fifteen minutes later there was a slight knock at his door. Tom and Tony entered, took a seat and waited for George to finish reading some papers.

"We have been asked to help solve a murder case out in Arizona. I believe it happened right outside Tucson, Marana is the town. It seems this lady's husband – deceased – was in the state legislature for a long time and some months ago his wife got shot in her home. The newspapers are putting pressure on the State's Attorney. The local FBI office is tied up with border issues, so you two are going to sunny Arizona. Check in with the Marana police and get everything they have on this case, which isn't much according to the State's Attorney. You know how to handle this. Use diplomacy with the local police, you know how they hate for us to get involved.

"When do we leave?" asked Tom.

"Susan will make the travel arrangements. There will be a government car waiting for you at the Tucson airport – the keys are at the Avis counter. Try and get out tomorrow, next day at the latest. Weapons will be located in false compartments under the back seat.

"OK, said Tony. "We're on it; shouldn't take too long."

Tom glanced at George, their eyes meeting, no need for words. Tony was his usual self.

Susan had the travel arrangements taken care of when they left George's office. "I wish I could go with you," she said as she handed them the paperwork. "I hear it's dry out there, no humidity. It sounds like a nice place to live."

"You can go," said Tony. "It's just a little, simple case. I can handle it. Tom can stay here."

Tom rolled his eyes. Susan saw it. She smiled at Tony. She knew he had a crush on her, even though she could almost be his mother.

"Who would take care of your uncle?" He can get very cross at times and has a lot of things riding on his shoulders."

"Yeah, I guess you're fright. I'll take Tom here; do him good to get a little sun."

They left the office and checked in with their section. Tom told him he'd see him at Dulles, next morning. He walked into his office and sat down. Why in hell had he been shackled with this juvenile? He had almost jeopardized their last case. If it hadn't been for George, he would have transferred out of this division, but he and George went back many years. George had always taken care of him and had promoted him to the highest grade. He had even been asked to take over a division, but he liked the leg work, with the stipulation that if he should change his mind, he'd have his own division.

Arizona was hot at the end of May. They drove out I-10 to Marana, got off at marker 240 and drove into town.

They reported in to the Marana police station. A secretary showed them in to an office and told them Detective Howell would be there in a few minutes. They took seats, but had barely settled when the door opened and a middle-aged person in civilian clothes came in with an outstretched arm and introduced himself.

"I knew you were coming so I have the files ready. I'll give you a brief synopsis and then you can do what you have to do. If you need anything, any kind of support, let me know. This is a very peculiar case. We usually solve murders in two – three weeks, but this one has us stymied. Forty one year old woman shot at the base of the skull in her own home, no struggle – no marks, no fingerprints, no blood spatter, no witnesses, and no enemies. Husband died about a year ago – state legislature, well-liked. Checked the neighborhood. No one saw or heard anything. Looks like a professional job. There is a list of friends on the first page. Have background files on two people – thanks to your office. But to be honest, nothing to hang your hat on.

Tom took the files.

"Was she seeing anyone after or before her husband died?" asked Tom.

"She got involved with a young boy – senior high school – all American, sad case. Hung himself long before she was killed."

"Are his parents in the files?"

"Yes, nice people – he works for the agency, in fact he found his son hanging in the garage."

"Thanks for your help, Detective Howell. I'm sure we will have questions but let us do a little ground work," said Tom.

They left the Marana police station and headed towards Heritage Highlands.

Tom and Tony reported to George and gave him a verbal report on their trip to Idaho. George had their faxes spread out on the desk. After they were through, he asked about Hank, Pete and Brian.

"Brian is a cocky enlisted man," said Tony with a sneer. "He needs to be taken down a peg."

"It says here he was a command SMG. They don't hand out those grades with their daily rations. I wouldn't say too much about SMGs around here. The Director was an SMG in the Special Forces before he went to get his master's degree in criminology. He is very proud of that rank and has all kinds of medals and citations hanging on his walls. He always says that it's harder to become a command SMG than it is a four star general and he knew he would not make it so he got out."

"What I meant was, he was sarcastic."

"Whatever he said that hurt your feelings, Tony, I hope you

learned from him."

"You don't even know him and you're sticking up for him." Tony was getting hot.

"I know his breed, Tony. He is the kind of guy you want at your six o'clock when you get in a jam. All I want to know is if either of you think he is a suspect who was doing his friends a favor."

Tom and Tony looked at each other and shook their heads in a negative way.

"What about Pete Compton?"

"Could have done it; lives about a block and a half away with his wife, and it was she who was a friend of Mrs. Turner who was in the last phase of cancer at the time. His mind was elsewhere, didn't even tell his wife about the kid hanging himself or of Mrs. Turner's death. He was very cooperative, as was Hank, the agency man. He said there was a time he thought about it. His son had been accepted at West Point, a dream come true, and when he went for his physical, they found he had genital herpes and there was only one person who could have given it to him. There is a copy of the letter to his parents in those faxes. No, I don't think either one was involved. They in fact helped us with the coroner's inquest, items we had missed. No, I think our person is an out of town guy."

"According to Pete, she had friends her in D.C. and could well have friends elsewhere. We got a lead on some of her relatives so we'll get on that, if you want to pursue it," said Tom.

"Yes, we should make an effort, but for God's sake, use public transport. I got called on the carpet and had to justify using one of our planes up to Idaho. Unless it's a national emergency, don't even think about it."

"What if we get a hot lead in this case?" asked Tony somewhat downcast after the lectures his uncle had given him.

"Borrow a couple of horses from the 3rd Infantry Guard at Arlington. Does nothing I say sink in? For Christ's sake, the Director seldom uses those planes. Now get the hell out of here.

I've got important things on my desk!"

When they had departed, George sat back in his chair. He felt bad saddling Tom with his nephew. He would talk to Sam Bolton down at Quantico to see if there was a job Tony could do and not cause any damage.

As they departed George's office, Susan looked up and gave Tony the once over.

"You look depressed Tony. Are you OK? Maybe you should take that good looking red head Diane I saw you with the other night, out for dinner and a romantic evening. It does wonders for you and her."

Tony blushed a deep crimson and for once he had no comeback. He departed out the door.

Tom looked at Susan and smiled. "Are you telling me that our Tony is dipping his wick? Maybe there is hope yet."

"Well, she works on the next floor down and you know us girls. We are always comparing. Yes indeed, he is but between you and me, not very well. It seems to be equipment failure most of the time."

Tom laughed and then got serious, "I wonder how long George is going to have me nurse maid that kid?"

"I have a feeling it's coming to an end," said Susan, "but you didn't hear it here." Tom thanked her and left.

He had wanted to ask Susan out over the years, but had a feeling she had a steady guy. Her husband had died during the latest Iraqi war, a colonel in the Special Forces. Maybe she could give him an insight to the DECAD Association. He would keep that in the back of his mind.

The phone on Susan's desk rang. It was George's private line.

"Mr. Hamilton's office, how may I help you?"

"Susan, this is Ann. Is George in?"

"Yes, Mrs. Hamilton, I'll connect you – please accept my deep sympathy regarding your sister."

"Thank you Susan, that's very kind of you, but there is only one way now. I got my niece and her husband to come down for a week so I'm home and believe me I need a break. It's a 24 hour job."

"I can't imagine and I'm glad you're back for a while. Here is George."

George picked up and was surprised his wife was on the phone. She was home and waiting for him. He told her how happy he was and assured her he would be home as soon as possible.

He buzzed the intercom. "Susan, come in here will you?"

Susan entered and sat down.

"My wife is home for a week," he said, looking at her.

"I know. I had the florist send a dozen red roses with an appropriate note. It should be there in about 20 minutes."

"Thanks, I didn't even think about that. I was thinking about something else."

"I know, George, but she is your wife and you and I have been apart before and we'll make up for it. We always do. I have never pressured you, nor will I. I'm happy and content with the way things are. You're such a brute of a man. I need time to heal from our little get-togethers."

"You're something. I won't forget. Thanks." Susan departed.

God, it had been months since he had made love to his wife. She was needy, but a Susan she was not.

He drove up his driveway. It was a fashionable part of Virginia. He'd bought it years ago from an old couple that was moving to Florida. He had spent a ton of money fixing it up and having shrubs and trees planted. He owned the house and 5 acres free and clear. It was a beautiful place; the kids had grown up here, a lot of memories.

He drove into the three car garage. He parked next to his wife's car. The other space was taken up by a John Deere SP lawnmower with all the attachments.

He pressed the button inside the garage and entered through the kitchen. Ann was standing there in a see through negligee, with a martini in her hand. He walked up to her, took the martini from her, took a sip and set it down on the counter. He grabbed her by the shoulders and gave her a long, deep kiss. She was still a good looking woman, even after two kids, and she worked on staying in shape.

"I have a pitcher of martinis up in the bedroom. Is that alright?"

"You bet it is, let's go."

He led her up the stairs to their huge master bedroom. He took off his clothes and was naked in a few seconds. He poured two martinis and handed one to Ann, who was also naked by now.

"I can tell you're horny and glad to see me. My, it's been a long time since I have seen little George so robust."

They clinked their glasses and downed them. It was their ritual.

They lay next to each other and stroked each other. He entered her, kept thrusting it in and he felt her come. He didn't care; he kept thrusting until he exploded inside her. He withdrew quickly and she let out a cry. George lay on his back and pulled her to him. She cuddled into his arms.

"George, I thought I was going to have a heart attack. What has happened to you?"

"I've missed you, Ann. It's been a long time."

"I didn't realize you were that needy. I felt like I was being raped."

"It wasn't good for you then?"

"Yes, it was great; let me get us another refill."

Ann got up and filled their glasses. George didn't know if it was the martini or the fact that he thought Ann was Susan when he got that hard.

They sipped their martinis, not saying much. She cuddled up in his arms and fell asleep.

Christ, he had to be careful. This was not Susan. He had to be gentle with her. Ann was passed out and he knew she would not awake until morning. He still had an erection. He placed her on her back and gently entered her. He thrust in gently. She was small and narrow and soon he climaxed in her. She moaned quietly with a smile on her lips. He covered them with a sheet and fell asleep.

The next morning Ann was up and had breakfast going when George came down dressed for work. He gave her a kiss on her neck and asked if she was alright.

"Yes, I'm fine. My body is still pulsating. I guess I'm not used to sex. It will take me a while to get used to it, just bear with me. You know it's been almost seven months and you know how needy I am. You know I forgot to properly thank you for the roses. They are beautiful. I'll thank you properly tonight."

George gave her a long kiss and told her he looked forward to coming home. She told him she would be a little more co-operative tonight.

Susan had coffee and Danish for him as he walked in. She brought it into his office, and asked if Ann was happy to be home. He had looked at her, and told her he had to be careful, there were times he thought it was her he had in bed but it was not the same. Ann was leaving Saturday morning. Could they get together Saturday night? Maybe go out for a nice dinner first and then to her place? Susan smiles at him. Can we go down to Maryland to that lobster and crab place we used to go to? He informed her that whatever she wanted. She left smiling and closed the door.

Christ, he had a good life. No one knew that he and Susan had an affair going. They had been discreet. In fact rumor had it that Susan was involved with her deceased husband's boss, a one star general.

The intercom buzzed. "You have a meeting at Quantico starting at 10 o'clock and ending at 1500 hours. No briefing required. It's some security briefing."

"Thanks, lay on a car and a driver for me unless someone has room for me."

"I'll arrange it." The intercom shut down.

Five minutes later the intercom came on.

"You have a seat on the Director's helicopter."

"Thanks."

He worked through his paperwork when he noticed Mrs. Turner's name on a fax. "Shit!" He hadn't even been thinking about that bitch. Tom and Tony had located some of her relatives who were trying to get their hands on her estate. One had indicated that one of her friends was a high profile lobbyist and was trying to remember his name. Mrs. Turner had confided in her over several drinks that her friend was way up there and was very rich – real rich. She knew the general area where he lived but the name had escaped her. He worked for a Japanese consortium and a Polish agriculture corporation. She would recognize his name if she saw it or heard it.

George called Roger Dunbar on his private line. His secretary answered. "Dunbar and Dunbar, how may I help you?"

"What's this Dunbar and Dunbar? Who is the other Dunbar?"

"Who is this?" asked the secretary.

"Tell him George is on the line."

"Yes sir, Mr. Hamilton, just a second."

"Roger, here. How are you doing? Well, are we secure?"

"Hell, yes"

"Medium to rare," said Roger.

"Listen, meet me at our usual place in one hour. I'll be at our regular table." George hung up.

It took George just about an hour to get to the Inn in Virginia. Roger was waiting for him.

They ordered a drink and a dozen oysters. After their order arrived, George took a hard look at Roger. He didn't look too good.

"Roger, did you have anything to do with Mrs. Turner's death?"

Roger, who had just taken a long sip of his drink, went into a coughing spell. The waiter appeared but George waved him off.

Roger regained his composure and looked directly into George's eyes.

"What the hell is this? I think you know I wouldn't know which end of a gun to point at a person. Besides, I was in Tokyo when she supposedly was killed. Which brings me to another question, are you infected?"

"No, I'm not infected, but things could get sticky for you. Mrs. Turner identified you as her friend in D.C. and you visited her in Tucson. The FBI is hot on your trail. They know who you work for but not your actual name yet."

"Holy Christ, George. I swear I didn't have anything to do with it. You and I have been friends for a long time – I have given you stock tips and make you a rich man. My wife is over the shock and we are living a normal life again. She only has herpes, no HIV. I'm getting out of the lobbying business. Sold it to a law firm here. We are buying a place in Aruba, in fact we close on it in a week or so. Of course, we are keeping our place here also. I swear I didn't have a thing to do with her death. I told my wife the whole sordid story, didn't mention you. She didn't want to know, only that I contact others that might have had a relationship with her so they would know and take the proper protection."

George had finished off the oysters while Roger talked. He signaled the waiter for another dozen, which arrived within minutes.

"Listen, you and Ann are welcome down to Aruba, especially in the winter. It's a beautiful place, has its own private beach. In fact use it whenever. We are going down in the winter; life is too short, if that isn't a cliché. The doctor says I'm HIV positive, but it hasn't progressed, so we use condoms, like we were high school kids. Roger had finished his drink and ordered another.

They left the Inn thirty minutes later. George was upset. He called Susan and asked if there as any reason to come back to the office. She had reminded him about the meeting in Quantico, the helicopter was departing at 0930. Otherwise everything was fine. George drove home. He entered the house and saw no one and headed upstairs.

"Is that you, George?"

"Were you expecting someone else?" His wife appeared naked from the bathroom.

"You look good enough to eat," said George.

"I hope so. I have anointed my body for you. Do you want supper before or after?"

"After. I just had a dozen raw oysters and I was told they were special, so I want to see if they all work."

"Oh George, I don't think I could do it twelve times. I'm still tender from last night."

"Just a joke, Ann, just a joke."

"The martinis are in the freezer, just the way you like them. I'll get them."

She walked downstairs naked, damn she was still a desirable woman.

He got undressed and laid on the bed as she arrived with frosted martini glasses and the pitcher. She poured them each a glass and left the pitcher on her night stand.

"How would you like to spend next winter in Aruba?"

"That sounds great. You will be with me, won't you?"

"Of course I will. I'm thinking of retiring. I'm at the highest step as far as pay and I know I won't be made Director. I have more than enough time in and with our stocks, we can cruise the world."

"George, that sounds nice. I'm looking forward to it."

They saluted and downed their martinis. Ann got on top and inserted him into her.

"Oh my God, George. I think he gets bigger each time he gets erect."

She moved her hips and he grabbed her buttocks pulling her down on him. It wasn't long before she started to shake, a sure sign she was about to have an orgasm. She leaned back and he thrust in.

"Hold me deep," she moaned, and she shook like she was having a convulsion. She collapsed on him, pulling his erection out of her and squeezing it.

"God George, in all our married life I have never had orgasms like I have had the last two days – but sometimes I don't even know where I'm at when they come over me."

"Hmmm, you are getting to be a hussy."

"Oh, I hope so." She caressed his erection. He massaged her buttocks and spread her knees. He grabbed her hips and pulled her into him with each thrust. Ann was screaming and moaning at the same time. The screaming aroused him more. He kept thrusting. He felt her shiver and knew she had an orgasm. He squirted in her right after. He held her, still hard inside her and then withdrew.

He left her and went to the bathroom and washed with disinfectant soap.

She was still crying softly when he returned. He turned her over and poured her a full glass of martini and gave it to her. She downed it in one gulp. She was sitting with her pillow on the headboard, leaning on it with her knees pulled up. The sheet under her was bloody and stained with semen.

"George, we have never done that before. I have talked to the girls about anal sex and they are split about even – some love it, others just put up with it. I guess I have joined the club now. It's different but not unpleasant. As long as you like it, it's fine with me. You were right about the sheets. Look between my legs. Its blood and you all over, but we have other sheets. Who cares?"

They had made gentle love and had fallen asleep.

When George came down there were eggs and bacon, toast and coffee waiting for him.

"I like this," he said. "It's nice to have you home, not only for a good breakfast but other things as well."

"She gave him a kiss on the cheek. He told her he was heading down to Quantico this morning, should be home early evening. He kissed her goodbye and headed for the small air field.

Ann took a long shower and dressed carefully. She drove to George's office. She hoped Susan was around. She passed security and entered the outer office.

Susan was sitting sideways, inputting some documents on the computer.

"Have a seat," she said not looking up.

She glanced up and recognized Ann.

"Mrs. Hamilton. I'm sorry my mind was on your husband's briefing. I didn't look 'because I thought it was one of the other secretaries wanting to go for coffee."

"No problem, Susan. I know George is down in Quantico, so I came by. I need to talk to you."

Susan's radar clicked on – there was no way Ann could know anything.

"Is it personal?" asked Susan.

"Yes, I'm afraid it is."

"Let's go into your husband's office. That way we won't be disturbed. Would you like some coffee?" asked Susan.

"Yes, that would be nice."

"Go right in. I'll bring the coffee."

They sat in comfortable chairs, sipped coffee and looked at each other. The silence was maddening for both of them.

"I don't know where to start, but I have known you, Susan, for a long time and you know George. Has anything happened to him while I have been away? What I mean is, is he under a lot of stress here at work?"

"No, nothing unusual. It's the same old crises one day and doldrums the next. Why, is he not feeling well?"

"Oh he is feeling well. He is feeling too well. As you know, I have been at my sisters for almost seven months straight and have not – how shall we say it – well, we have not had sex. I hope you don't think I'm too forward and I don't mean to dump on you, Susan, but I feel I can trust you to keep it between just us."

"You know you can, Mrs. Hamilton."

"Please call me Ann."

"Well, George is insatiable. He is doing things to me that have never happened before in our entire married life."

"Is it good for you – do you enjoy it or is he hurting you?"

"Both," Ann started crying.

Susan handed her a Kleenex.

"Can I speak frankly?"

"Anything you say does not leave this office," said Susan.

"Well, the other night he used his belt on my backside. It hurt so bad I screamed and asked him to stop, but he became almost enraged and penetrated me really rough. Oh, I'm not saying it was all bad. My orgasms came one after the other. Then last night he took me anally. I thought I was going to die. I bled so much after I thought I had to go to the doctor but it stopped. George thought nothing of it. He was his usual self after."

"When you said it's been almost seven months since you were together, you don't mean that."

"I haven't seen George in seven months – in fact I'm heading back Saturday morning. I needed a break, but now I need a break from George."

"George hasn't been up in Maine on weekends?"

"Why no. Night before last was our first time together in seven months. I haven't seen him."

"You know my husband used to go away for months at a time. When he came home, he was like an animal. I guess men are different, but I tell you I wish many a times that the animal was back. I miss him so. I guess what I'm saying is we women have to take the good with the bad. My husband used to say he would dream and fantasize about us. He would arrive back at Fort Bragg, go through debriefing and get the first shower and clean clothes in months and then come home and we wouldn't leave the bed for days except to eat and drink and get back in bed. There were times I didn't' think I could ever walk again,

I was so sore, but I got used to it."

"Don't you have a friend now that can take care of your needs?"

"Well, there is someone who was my husband's boss whom I see every so often, but we women do get spoiled and it's not the same when it's someone you love."

"You are a very attractive woman, Susan. There must be all kinds hoping to date you."

"I'm not interested and I work out and run. That takes some of the needs away."

"I am so glad we had this talk and that you listened to silly me. I guess I should consider myself lucky to have George."

"Well, sometimes we all need someone to talk to and make sure we are normal. I think some of your friends would be happy to have George around."

"Thanks, Susan, and this is all on the QT."

Ann picked up her cup and saucer and walked into Susan's office. Susan followed and bid her farewell and good luck with her sister.

When Ann was gone, Susan tried to get back to work but something was bothering her. She couldn't quite put her finger on it, but her nagging mind would not let go.

She went to the file cabinets and dialed the code. She looked up the Turner case and read the faxes. She had been killed the weekend George said he was going up to Maine. She checked out the expense reports, but nothing showed. She went into her computer and entered the classified section. George's alias had used the card on that weekend for a ticket to Tucson, Arizona. The bill would be paid automatically without going through her office. He had only stayed in Tucson a few hours and returned to D.C.

My God. What was she reading? It couldn't be, could it? Had George been infected by Mrs. Turner? No, he had gotten a clean bill from the doctor. He had acted strange for awhile, but that night he had called he was his old self.

She had to get Tom up here and talk to him, about something else. She knew he had been on the verge of asking her out, but nothing had come of it. George didn't have many close friends. When he had advised her what to do with her money, she had been introduced to a Mr. Dunbar, Roger Dunbar. He had called often for a while and she had thanked him and chatted with him while she was waiting for George to get off the phone. One conversation stuck with her. Roger had asked if her boss seemed happy lately. She had answered yes; he does seem in a good mood. Well a little change is good for a man; he appreciates his wife more then. So George had not only gone out on his wife but on her also. He could have infected both of them. Her conscience had bothered her the first few times she and George had been together, but the sex had been great and it had gotten her out of the funk about her husband's death. When Ann had shown up today she was sure Ann had learned about their affair. After listening to her story, she really didn't have any sympathy for her. Ann lived in a privileged society and if she couldn't handle a little rough sex, too bad. She knew George was rich. Ann was like a lot of Washington society women who wanted everything nice and gentle.

Susan sent a hand printed note to Tom - "Roger Dunbar" was all it said. She addressed it, and dropped it in the US Postal mail box a block from the building.

She would not tolerate taking the chance of some infection by George or anyone else. She was not going to say anything to George.

The meeting at Quantico was a bore and he was glad to be back in his office sitting at his desk. George had finished going over the faxes when he went into the secure section of his computer. At first he didn't notice the small yellow warning light blinking down in the left hand corner of his screen. He was about to scan farther when it caught his eye. Someone had accessed his space. The only person who had the code was Susan. Why had she gone in the classified section? He buzzed

Susan. When she answered, he asked her to come in.

"Do you want me to bring a cup of coffee for you?"

"Yea, that would be great."

Susan entered with a cup of coffee, placing in on his desk. "Sit down."

Susan took her regular chair and looked at George.

"Have you accessed the classified section on my computer?"

"Yes I did, two days after you returned from Maine. Mr. Kimbell called. I left a note on your desk.

"Why?" said George in a calm voice.

"Mr. Kimbell made some small talk and I asked how Maine was. He informed me that his plane was down for maintenance and he hadn't made the trip but was planning one next weekend."

"What has this got to do with you accessing the classified section?

"George, I hadn't received a bill for your flight up there. I figured you had gone commercial and you know Mr. Bloom in Finance. If I don't submit the bills within two days, I have to go over and explain to him why we are late. He is a pig George. He hits on me and other secretaries. He is a crude and repulsive fat slob. He forced himself on Betty Anderson's 18 year old daughter and got her pregnant."

"Who told you he forced himself on Betty's daughter?"

"Betty did – her daughter had an abortion. Anyway, when I didn't see any bill, I went in the secure section to see if you had used that mode to pay the airlines and I found it. It gets paid automatically. So I was relieved."

"Did you see anything else?"

"No, it was the first thing that came up on the screen and I shut it down, why?"

"I trust you, Susan, you know that. We haven't kept any secrets from each other. It was just when I saw the yellow light on my screen I couldn't figure out why you had accessed it."

"If you don't want me to access it, change the code George."

"No, it's okay. So Bloom is overstepping the line is he?"

"Yes, definitely. You wouldn't want me to tell you some of the things he has suggested to me."

"Thanks, that's all I wanted to know."

Susan left the office and her knees were trembling. She sat down in her chair and saw that her hands were shaking. That had been too close.

However, she made an appointment with her gynecologist for the next day.

When George came to work the next day, she asked him if it was alright for her to take an extra hour off in conjunction with her lunch.

"Is everything alright?" George had asked.

"Yes, I pulled a muscle running last night. I guess I didn't warm up properly or else I'm getting old," Susan had said smiling.

"Let's not talk about getting old, please. I fell asleep at the briefing yesterday. If it hadn't been for a friend jabbing me in the ribs, it could have gotten embarrassing. Take as much time as you need. I have Tom and Tony coming up after lunch to brief me on their progress. I'll probably fall asleep again."

Susan had gotten a clean bill of health from her doctor. She felt good when she returned to the office. She went to the door and listened, sure enough Tony was droning on.

After another half hour, they both came out. Tony didn't even say hello. Tom lingered. When they were alone, Tom asked her if she was free one evening, if she would like to go out for dinner.

"Tom, are you finally asking me out on a date? I have waited for years for you to ask."

Tom's face turned beet red. He just stood there. Finally he said "Can I take that as a yes?"

"You sure can. I'm free tonight and tomorrow; the rest of the week through the weekend I have a girl's thing. Some of my old friends from Fort Bragg are coming up here."

"If tonight is alright, I'll make reservations. Would 6:30 –

7:00 be OK to pick you up?"

"Sure, you know where I live."

Tom left feeling like a high school kid. Susan was a nice lady and he was looking forward to it. It wasn't like he had been a monk; he had been seeing an old friend who worked for the FBI, but it had kind of turned into a brother-sister relationship after the heat of the sex had cooled.

When he got to the office there was an envelope lying on his desk.

"It looks like you've got a fan, a school kid from the printing on the envelope," said Tony.

Tom opened the envelope carefully and extracted a piece of paper. It was folded in two. He opened it. Two words were printed on it – "Roger Dunbar". Tom sat down at his desk and stared at the name. His mind was churning. Who was Roger Dunbar, and who had sent it? He looked at the envelope – the writing was that of a small kid or someone trying to write like a small kid. The same was true of the contents. Roger Dunbar. He wrote the name on another piece of paper and went out to his secretary and asked her to run the name.

The briefing upstairs had not gone well. George was in a foul mood and had told them both to put pressure on the relatives. Tony had then gone off on a tangent about what and who he thought had shot Mrs. Turner. He was back on the Special Forces trail. George had not been happy. The only good thing had been his date with Susan.

He went through his notes on the Turner case again. He was engrossed in it when his secretary came in and said there was nothing in the files on the name he had requested, but she had looked the name up in the phone book and there was an R. Dunbar, lives out in the high rent district. She placed the name, address and phone number on Tom's desk and departed.

Tom called the Turner relative who couldn't remember the name. The phone rang and was picked up just as Tom was getting ready to hang up. He introduced himself and asked if the name she couldn't recall was Roger Dunbar, and if she had sent him the name in the envelope.

"Why that's it," she sounded pleased. "The other thing and I don't remember if I told you, he was very rich. I hope I have been of some help. I haven't sent you anything."

Tom thanked her and said she had been very helpful, and hung up the phone.

He called Susan.

"Tom, here. Look I have to cancel tonight."

"Why, Tom, are you getting cold feet? I finally get you to take me out and you cancel. Why?"

"Look Susan, nothing could keep me from taking you out and I hope we can re-schedule. It's just that I got a break on the Turner case. George was not happy with our briefing.

"I understand, Tom. How did this break come about?"

Tom hesitated. "This is between you and me OK?"

"OK," said Susan.

"I got a name in the mail today. That's it, just a name that Mrs. Turner's relatives verified. It's going to take some time checking it out, that's why I canceled. I didn't want to be thinking about it during our time together. I want that time to be special."

"Me too, Tom. We'll make up for it."

Tom hung up. He didn't want to take Tony along or brief him for that matter. He buzzed his secretary and told her to lay on a car with a navigation system on it. He would need it in 10 minutes. Tony came over and asked if Tom needed him for the rest of the day, otherwise he would go and take care of some personal errands.

"No, go ahead. I'm going to look at some property in Virginia. It's time I got out of my old house. Besides, we have plenty of comp time built up, so have a good time."

Tony went back to his desk and dialed Diane's number. He knew she was off for the next two days and had hinted she wanted company. What she didn't know was that he had seen his doctor and explained his on again off again erection prob-lem. His doctor had written him a prescription for Viagra. He had tried it when he got home and 'bingo', it had worked like a charm, although he had to manhandle the erection, but it worked.

Diane answered the phone on the second ring. He had asked if she wanted company. She said "Yes, definitely," and for him to come over as soon as he could. He told her he'd be there in twenty minutes, could he bring anything, only himself had been her answer.

Tony rang the bell for her apartment and the door buzzed him in. He took the elevator up to the 4th floor and got out. He had already taken the Viagra and could feel its effect. Diane opened the door and invited him in.

She looked gorgeous in her white silk blouse and blue skirt. He noticed she didn't have anything under her blouse. He reached for her and gently pulled her into him. They kissed softly. Tony ran his hand down her back and felt her body. She responded and kissed him deeply.

"Are you sure you want to go there?" she whispered in his ear. "I don't want us to end up frustrated like last time."

"Believe me, Diane, I want to go everywhere. I feel real good."

He unbuttoned her blouse and carefully laid it on a chair. Her breasts drove him crazy. They were perfect. He felt himself throbbing. Diane stepped out of her skirt, no underwear; her red hair between her legs was like a red flag waved in front of a bull. They both undressed him and when she saw his erection she pulled him into the bedroom and laid on the bed waiting.

"I have never seen him that big before, Tony. God he is long."

Tony lay down next to her. She scooted down and rolled Tony on his back. She took him in her mouth and licked the small amount of lubricant that was coming out of his penis. Tony gently pushed her over on her back and started sucking her breasts. He moved down and ran his tongue between her lips. She had a delightful flavor that drove him crazy.

"Tony, if you move your tongue up a few inches, you'll find my clit."

Tony had never thought about the clit. He assumed it was in her vagina. He moved up and found a long protrusion. He started sucking it. Diane was moaning and squirming, pushing his head into the mound. He kept sucking until she screamed. It startled him and he stopped sucking, looking up at her. Her tongue was out, licking her lips and rubbing her breasts with her hands.

"Don't stop," she yelled.

Tony started sucking and she shivered, crying out.

"Tony that is the best thing that has happened to me," she said relaxing in bed.

Tony moved up, kissed her on the lips and she guided him into her. He thrust in gently and withdrew it slowly.

"Once you're in you don't have to be so careful," she told him. Tony thrust harder and in a few minutes Diane was having another orgasm.

"Hold him in there, don't move," she demanded.

He held her until she relaxed.

"What has happened to you, Tony? You are great. Let's try it from the back."

She got on her knees and hands and he thrust it into her. Seeing her red haired vagina made him crazy. He thrust it all the way and grabbed her by the hips and pulled her to him. He lost track of time. He just kept thrusting and she was crying and moaning. She orgasmed and he came right after. She collapsed and he remained on top of her, still hard inside of her. He rolled off and they lay on their sides.

"Well, this has never happened before. What has happened to you?"

"When I took your blouse off and saw your beautiful breasts, something happened to me," he said, gently stroking each breast.

"Hmm, can you stay the night?"

"You bet I can," he said, smiling at her.

She laid there while Tony went to the bathroom. He had actually hurt her. He was long and when he was behind her, it hurt, but nothing she was going to complaining about. My God, the times they were both ready and he couldn't get it in, and after all this time she had the nerve to tell him where her clit was. They were moving in the right direction.

Tom drove the car, heading over to the Virginia side and punched in the address for Roger Dunbar. This navigator business was great. He followed the directions and was soon at the house. He slowed a little so he could get a look at it. This guy was rich. He must have had two acres around the house. He could just make out a swimming pool through the fence in the back. What to do? He would return in the morning.

Tom got to work early. He went over the Turner file. He wanted to be familiar with everything in it so he wouldn't have to bring it with him. Tony arrived looking like he hadn't slept all night. Tom told him to get some coffee. They had an interview this morning. Tom called up to Susan and asked if she could schedule him and Tony in to see George first thing. She informed him that would be no problem, come up and wait for him. He should be back there any time now. Tom knocked on the door followed by Tony and walked in.

"Good morning," said Susan in a pleasant voice.

"It looks like one of you had a rough night."

George walked in and looked at Tom and Tony. He took a second look at Tony.

"What happened to you? If this work is getting too tough for you, I think I can transfer you to something less demanding." Tony didn't say a word. He poured himself another cup of coffee and took a Danish off the tray. George walked into his office and closed the door. He had to go over the night's faxes and emails before he got distracted.

"I didn't see Diane downstairs yesterday. She is the one with the beautiful red hair." She was addressing her comments to Tom. He looked at Tony who averted his gaze.

"I hope she isn't sick. She is such a nice girl," said Susan.

"She isn't sick. She has two days off. She had to work this weekend," said Tony chewing on another Danish.

"I'm certainly glad to hear that," said Susan as her intercom light went on.

"Send them in," they heard George say.

They both entered George's office and took a seat.

"What is going on?" said George.

"I've got the name of Mrs. Turner's friend here in D.C.," said Tom.

Tony almost spilled his coffee.

"So who is this mysterious Casanova?" asked George in a casual voice.

"His name is Roger Dunbar, have his address and phone number. We are going out to see him today, in fact, this morning. I'm going to give him a call first."

George stared at Tom.

"Is this the name the relatives came up with?" asked George.

"Yes and I confirmed his residence, drove by there yesterday afternoon," said Tom.

"Good work," said George in a quiet voice.

"Remember, he is only an acquaintance. Don't give him the 3rd degree."

"I just wanted to let you know before we went out there, "said Tom, getting up.

"OK. Keep me informed," said George, waving them out.

As soon as the door was closed, George used his secure line and dialed Roger. His wife answered.

"Get Roger on the line," said George.

Roger answered after a few minutes.

"You are getting company this morning," said George in an even tone.

"What are you talking about?" asked Roger in a groggy voice.

"Two FBI agents will call you in a few minutes and ask for an interview this morning."

"George, I swear I had nothing to do with it." Roger was panicking.

"Listen to me and listen good; don't deny you knew Mrs. Turner. Admit to the affair but also bring the following two names into the conversation – Peter Compton and Hank Wadsworth. Tell the two agents that Mrs. Turner was extremely afraid of them, something to do with Hank's son. Pete and Hank are old buddies, go back years, served in the Special Forces together. According to Mrs. Turner, Pete had threatened her. Pete's wife, now deceased, and Mrs. Turner were good friends and played golf together, but Mrs. Turner didn't trust Pete."

"OK, got it," said Roger, now more confident. "Anything else?"

"Leave my name out of it." Roger hung up.

Tom dialed but the line for Mr. Dunbar was busy. He pushed redial several times and finally got a ring. The phone was answered immediately.

"Roger here, how may I help you?"

"Mr. Dunbar, this is Tom Reed with the FBI. Can my partner and I come out to see you this morning?"

"Sure, come anytime, I'm home all day today."

"Thank you, Mr. Dunbar, we will be there within an hour." Tom hung up.

They headed out to Virginia and reached the Dunbar residence in an hour and fifteen minutes. Tom could have gotten there faster but it was good to keep a suspect waiting.

They pulled up the driveway and Tony whistled. "This guy is rich."

It was the first words he had said all morning. He had not asked Tom how he got the Dunbar name or anything about the case. Tom figured it had been a good night for him with the redhead

Tom rang the doorbell and a maid of Latin descent answered

the door. Tom introduced himself and Tony and said Mr. Dunbar was expecting them. They were led into a paneled den.

A short, chubby man got up from behind the desk, holding out his hand, greeting them both.

"Please sit down." Mr. Dunbar indicated two plush chairs.

Tom noticed that it placed him and Tony at a lower level than Mr. Dunbar who sat behind his desk. Interesting, he thought.

"Mr. Dunbar, can we record this or would it make you uncomfortable?" asked Tom.

"No, go right ahead – I'm a lawyer so I know how these things work."

"Thanks," said Tom. "It makes it a lot easier for us."

"Let me start by asking you if you know a Mrs. Turner."

"Yes, I do."

"What is your relationship to her, are you related?"

"I met Mrs. Turner at a party here in Washington. I'm a registered lobbyist so parties are part of the job, if you know what I mean. No, I'm not related to her."

"What was your relationship to her?"

"I had an affair with her both here and in Tucson, or rather Marana."

"How long did this affair last?"

"I would say about a year or so, no, it was more than a year."

"During this time did Mrs. Turner express any concerns to you? Was she afraid or worried about someone?"

"That's a tough question. I don't like to tell tales out of school, if you get my drift."

"Well let me phrase it this way. Did you introduce Mrs. Turner to any of your friends?"

Tom was looking closely at Mr. Dunbar.

"Well no I didn't."

A lie. Tom saw it in Dunbar's face, he was lying.

"OK back to the other question, was Mrs. Turner scared or did she at any time indicate to you that she might be in danger?"

"There was something that had happened to a young man

she had been seeing, he had killed himself and his father and a friend of his had threatened her."

"Did she have anything to do with this young man's death?"

"Not that I'm aware of."

"Oh come on," said Tony. If you are having an affair for over a year, surely she told you some things."

Mr. Dunbar was taken aback by Tony's outburst.

"Hey look, I'll be up front with you. Mrs. Turner gave me genital herpes and HIV. I infected my wife with herpes. She knows the whole sordid affair. If Mrs. Turner gave this young man something, I don't know about it. I didn't introduce Mrs. Turner to this young man or anyone else."

"Did you get mad enough to kill her or have her killed?" Tony was on a roll.

"I swear to you, I don't know anything about her being killed or who did it. You have to believe me. I'm getting out of this lobbying business. In fact I have already sold out to a law firm here in D.C. and the countries I represented have signed a contract with them. We have bought a house down in the Caribbean and are spending the winters down there. It's something I did for my wife who has been devastated by this affair."

"Are you keeping this place also and buying a place in the Caribbean? I knew the lobbying business was good but we are looking at some upscale property here. The place you are buying or have bought, where is it, and is it beach front?"

Mr. Dunbar turned pale. He looked from Tom to Tony who was asking the questions.

"I have managed to put a little aside over the years. This place is paid for."

"Did you pay cash for the place in the Caribbean or did you finance it?" asked Tom.

Tony looked at Tom, not knowing where this was going.

"Well, I paid cash which leaves me an annuity to live off of, and yes it's on the beach, and it's private."

The private part was an afterthought by Mr. Dunbar which

indicated to Tom that he was proud of it.

"Do you have any offshore bank accounts that you have not reported? Through the years we have learned that lobbyists have money placed in offshore accounts by the companies they work for." Tom asked in an even, quiet tone.

"Look, I don't know. If they have placed some money somewhere, I am not aware of it." Mr. Dunbar at this point was looking around the room like it was the last time he would see it.

"I think I have answered your questions and by the way, I was in Tokyo the night Mrs. Turner was killed. You can check with the airlines and this company – he produced a card – and from now on I'll have my lawyer present when you question me."

"Just one more question, Mr. Dunbar, and then we are finished and I want to say that you are not a suspect in Mrs. Turner's death," Tom said in a low, even voice.

"How did you learn of Mrs. Turner's death?"

Mr. Dunbar almost collapsed in his chair. There was a tic around his eyes and his demeanor had completely changed.

"Well, I read it in the newspaper," he said as if searching his mind.

"Thank you, Mr. Dunbar. We'll see ourselves out," said Tom as they got up and headed for the den's door.

"No, wait, someone told me she had been killed."

"Who told you?" asked Tom.

"I want to talk to my lawyer."

Tom and Tony headed out and got in their car. When Tom pulled out of the circular driveway, he looked at Tony.

"What do you think?" he asked Tony.

"He is lying and he knows a lot more. If we don't get him, the IRS will."

"Exactly what I was thinking. He has money stashed somewhere. My brother-in-law bought a place in the Caribbean on a private beach and when all the under the table to the local government was over the actual price of the house was just about three million."

They drove back to D.C. Tom was thinking that there was no reason to brief George unless he asked. They would let Dunbar stew. He would call Pete in Idaho and let him know that he had along with Hank been implicated by Mr. Dunbar.

He sat down at his desk and thought about this morning's interview. Tony had handled himself well. He was surprised. Maybe Tony ought to transfer over to the Attorney General's office, as a prosecutor. He dialed Pete's number.

"Pete here," he heard a groggy voice say.

"This is Tom, your friendly FBI buddy."

"Hey, I'm just having my first cup of coffee. What can I do for you?"

"Sorry Pete. I didn't think about the time difference. I thought I would bring you up to date on our investigation."

"Go ahead, it will be a while before Jane is ready with her homemade biscuits, ham and eggs and pancakes with home-made syrup."

"I should have placed you in leg irons and tied you to a tree up there. I had a package of Lance peanut butter crackers and day old coffee."

"Well, I always said it was a matter of priorities, good woman good food."

"I don't want to hear anymore, but I might take the next plane up there and munch on your scraps."

"You have to bring your own woman thought."

"You know Pete that is a distinct possibility. I have finally met someone I could settle down with, believe it or not."

"That's great, Tom. You deserve someone special. There is more to life than work."

Tom agreed and told Pete about Mr. Dunbar and what he had said. Tom felt there was someone else here in D.C. who had also known Mrs. Turner but warned Pete that if Tony gets his way, they might be up there again.

"The Dunbar name doesn't ring a bell, but now that you

mention it, Mrs. Turner was not available for golf on week-ends. They usually played 9 holes on Tuesday and 18 holes on Fridays. The last time she was at our house, a Friday night, she was catching an early flight Saturday morning, but I can't remember if she said D.C. or not. If as Dunbar said she was afraid of me, she had a strange way of showing it. I got several invites after her husband died but tactfully refused, used her close friendship with my wife as an excuse. Listen, and I'm reaching now, but Hank is over at Langley this week. Mrs. Turner was feeling no pain that Friday night and was talking about a lot of influential people she knew. She had Hank and me as a captive audience. She knew Hank was with the agency and asked if he knew a, and don't hold me to this, a Hampton or something like that. I think she was showing off. Ask Hank about it, his memory is better than mine. He, like myself, may have let it go over his head, but it's worth a try. Shit, Tom, I guess I'm getting old. We could have discussed this when you were up here. What's that, Jane? Jane says I'm not getting old. She must have burned a pancake or she wants to go shopping later on. But in all seriousness Tom, Hank was always better than me on the debriefing we had to go through when we came back from a mission."

"Thanks, Pete. I'll get in touch with Hank. He is in the Ops. Section, isn't he?"

"Yes – works for the old Burma Fox – you know who I mean."

"Yes, I know who he is and Pete, I hope you choke on your breakfast. My regards to Jane."

Tom wrote down Hampton. He dialed his secure number for Langley, a secretary answered. Tom asked for Hank Wadsworth. The person patched him through to another section and the person on the other end of the line asked Tom for identification. Tom gave him his code and said he was on a secure line. A few minutes later Hank answered.

"Hank, Tom here."

"Tom of the famous three letter unit."

"The same one, Hank. I just talked to Pete and I briefed him on our progress. I won't go into details unless you want to meet somewhere, but our D.C. connection, a Mr. Dunbar, named you and Pete as suspects in the case."

"Very interesting," said Hank.

"Pete mentioned a name that the deceased had talked to you and Pete about at a Friday night party at Pete's house, or should I say she let it slip. The name Pete remembered was Hampton. He said your memory was better than his."

"Let me think about this. I'm going to call Pete and together maybe we can come up with something. Tom, I think you and I better meet somewhere, the sooner the better. I have just completed a case that might interest you. Name a place in D.C. or Virginia and I would like, if at all possible, for it to be today."

"How about that little fish restaurant a block down from Walter Reed?"

"I know it, The Fish Net or something like that. Let's say an hour and a half?"

"Good," said Tom and hung up.

Tom sat and thought about the conversation. Hank was up front, that was sure, but he had a feeling when he mentions Hampton, Hank knew the name. He wanted to go alone. He informed Tony that he had a personal thing this afternoon and that Tony was free to do whatever. Tony was all smiles. Tom informed him that he expected him in good shape in the morning and for him to go easy tonight. Tony just kept smiling.

Tom went over the tape transcripts his secretary had laid on his desk in a large envelope. OK, he was ready. He drove over to Maryland and found the restaurant about two blocks down from the entrance to Walter Reed. He took a booth towards the back. It was a small all white tile restaurant that had been in business for as long as he could remember. He had been a patient at Walter Reed in 1969 and when he was mobile he and some other patients had gone down regularly. The shrimp was fresh and great. He had just sat down when Hank walked in. There were two other booths occupied towards the front.

Hank sat down and looked around. "Didn't this place used to have tables?" he asked Tom.

"Yeah, I think you're right, tile covered tables."

The waiter/owner came over and asked what they wanted.

"Do you still serve shrimp on newspapers?" asked Hank.

"Sure do."

"We'll have two dozen large shrimps and two drafts," said Tom. "Oh and the horseradish."

The owner yelled something towards the back of the restaurant and went behind the bar and drew two glasses of beer and placed them on the table.

"I heard you talking about the tables. You must have been here when my dad and mother ran the place."

"It was back in the 60's," said Tom.

"Yeah, that's about right. I should never have gotten rid of those tables, they were a lot easier to clean up."

The steamed shrimp arrived, heads and all. They twisted the heads off and peeled them. They were great.

"I just finished doing a background on a Japanese corporation. Lots of baggage. One of their subsidiaries is funneling money to the Mideast terrorist groups. Is Dunbar's first name Roger?"

Tom nodded his head.

"Well, Mr. Dunbar has at least three offshore banks he is putting money into, could be as many as seven. Sent the report to the Attorney General so you folks will have it in a few days. We can't investigate U.S. citizens in the states. The Polish corporation he also represents is owned by this same Japanese Corporation."

"He has sold his lobbying business to a local law firm and has bought himself a winter home in the Caribbean, lives in the high rent district in Virginia," said Tom. Tom also brought Hank up to date on their interview with Dunbar.

Tom told Hank about the Hampton name that Pete had given him. "The name is not Hampton, its Hamilton," said Hank.

Tom stopped eating and just stared at Hank. His mind was churning.

"Not only that, but Dunbar has steered quite a few stock tips to Hamilton, making him a rich man."

Tom was trying to digest this information and its implications.

The shrimp was consumed in silence.

"You know this places me in a difficult position and you know who Hamilton is don't you?"

"Yep, I do," said Hank finishing his beer. "I also know Hamilton was in Tucson the night Mrs. Turner was killed and he returned to D.C. the same night. Look at his alias name and expense voucher for the date."

"I know this comes as a shock to you, Tom, but he is a grown man and has been caught with his hand in the cookie jar. Be careful how you handle this, Tom. I would go to the Director of the internal review with this. His doctor is Hollingworth and Hamilton panicked when he heard his friend was infected, but he got a clean bill of health from Hollingsworth."

"One other thing, Tom, don't use my name. I had to cash in a few chits to get the information and it came from your organization." Hank placed some bills on the table and got up. Tom followed slowly. They thanked the restaurant owner and headed for their cars.

As soon as Tom got in his car he placed a call to Susan. She answered on the first ring.

"What can I do for you Tom?"

"I need to see you tonight."

"That sounds good. My girlfriends canceled, will be up next week. Same time as we talked about?"

"Yes, that sounds good. I'll see you then."

Tom hung up. Susan was smart and knew the Director's secretary. That could be an entrance for him.

He went back to the office and started typing his report. He made sure it was neat and to the point with all the T's crossed and I's dotted. Christ, he noticed the time. It had taken him longer than expected. Usually his secretary would type it but not this, it was too close. He placed the report in his personal safe and headed for his car. He would barely make it to Susan's. He knocked on her door and it was answered immediately. Susan was ready and didn't say anything until they got in the elevator.

"I thought you had stood me up again," she said with a smile. I didn't let you in 'cause I sensed your urgency and walls have ears, as they say."

Tom apologized and said he had gotten caught up in a case and lost track of the time. Susan squeezed his arm and said she understood. There was an old Inn down by Annapolis, was it too far for her, or did she have somewhere else she would rather go.

"You know there is an out of the way place off I-95 about 15 – 20 minutes away. The food is great and it's private."

"Tell me how to get there," said Tom. Annapolis was a little far.

They arrived and the place was almost empty. They picked a booth in the back and the waiter took their orders for drinks.

"You seem a little tense tonight Tom. Is it Roger Dunbar that's bothering you, or someone else?"

Tom stared at her. So Susan was the one who had mailed him the Dunbar name.

"How close are you to solving the case?"

"I have solved it," Tom said looking into her eyes. "Thanks for the tip."

Their drinks arrived and the waiter left menus for them to look at.

Susan smiles at him and held her glass up in a toast. They touched glasses and took a sip. "When this case is over I'm retiring," said Tom. "I have been here too long and it's time I sold my old rambling house and bought something smaller with some acreage around it. Some place where it's not so crowded and less hectic."

"I'm retiring also," said Susan with a smile. "It's time I sold my condo and moved up to the place my husband left for me. In fact, I sold my portfolio and invested in government bonds. I have already typed up my notice and filled out my retirement papers. It takes about a month to clear everything. It could get messy around the office in the next couple of months."

"You're right"

The waiter came back and asked if they needed some more time. They were both hungry so they ordered, Tom choosing the same as Susan.

They sipped their drinks.

"You know, Tom, I have been waiting for years for you to ask me out. What took you so long?"

"The rumor was that you were involved with your husband's old boss. I didn't want to get turned down. After my wife passed, I have led a pretty quiet life, not exactly a monk's life but quiet."

"Yes, I know," said Susan studying her drink. There are no secrets among the secretaries."

"Hmm, it sounds like you ladies are in the wrong profession. Have you considered intelligence?"

Susan laughed, "No we leave that to others.

"What are your plans after you retire, other than moving to your husband's place?"

"Well, I really don't know. I would like to get married again. I'm too young to dry up like a prune and I want to do some traveling and paint."

"Have you picked out a husband yet? Or am I getting too personal?"

"Not at all. I have my eye on a guy but I don't know him very well yet, but I hope to. What about you?"

The waiter brought their dinners along with the wine Tom had ordered. It looked delicious. They saluted with the wine and started eating. After a few minutes Susan said, "Well?"

"Oh! Marriage would be nice but things have happened so

fast with this case that I haven't had a chance to plan too much. I guess what I'm saying is there is someone but I don't know her very well yet."

"Would you like to know her better? You can't compare her with your deceased wife, but it could turn out good for both."

Tom held his glass up and touched hers and they took a sip.

"You have an appointment with the Director in the morning at 0700 hours, Tom."

He looked at her and said "Thanks."

"He is coming in early to meet with you."

"I hope I haven't over planned, and that you are prepared."

"No, I really appreciate it Susan. I didn't want to ask you. I know you and his secretary are close. Again, thanks."

They lingered over coffee and departed.

"Can I see your house Tom?"

"Sure, it's early. It's not far from here."

They drove out past Rock Creek Park and drove up to an area where Susan had never been. The homes were old but stately. Tom drove up a gravel driveway to a large two story house. She noticed the three car garage attached by a breezeway – extensive lawns from what she could see in the dark.

"My parents left me this. They lived here most of their lives. My father was an attorney here in D.C."

They went inside. Tom turned on lights. It was an orderly and well kept house.

"Don't tell me you do the housekeeping?"

"No, I have a woman come in twice a week. I haven't seen her since Christmas. I just leave cash out for her and when I come home it's gone. I can tell she has been here."

"Sounds like a good arrangement. It's a beautiful house Tom. I think you should double her salary."

They went upstairs. It had four large bedrooms, each with a bath. The master was huge, with a large bathroom. It was obvious that it had been remodeled.

"Do you want something to drink, a liqueur or something? "

They had stopped in the doorway to the bathroom. Susan turned and faced Tom. He was a head taller than she was. She just stood there and looked up at him. He took her in his arms and gently kissed her on the lips. Susan returned the kiss and they stood there not realizing what was happening or maybe they in their own mind did. He led her to the bed and started undressing her. She was beautiful and lay down on the bed naked. Tom removed his clothes and lay next to her.

He caressed her gently, she was in excellent shape. They kissed and he got on top and nuzzled her neck and breasts. He could feel her react. She spread her legs wider, he felt her mound and lips; she was moist. She guided him in. They made gentle love and she dug her nails into his shoulders as her tremors came, crying out softly, holding him tight. He came hard and he knew she could feel his semen enter her.

They lay side by side, Susan cuddled up against him.

"I have dreamt about this with you," she whispered.

"That makes two of us," he said fondling her breasts.

"Where do we go from here?" he said.

"That's up to you, Tom. I'll tell you now, I'm a needy person and I enjoy sex and from what you gave me tonight, I know we are compatible. You are a big man, Tom. You fill up my entire being. I have had men, Tom, but none the size of you. I wasn't sure it would fit at first."

"I wish you could spend the night?"

"No, that won't work. We both have plenty to do in the morning and although it's not late, we both need a good night's sleep and before this goes any further you and I have to talk about a lot of things. I have waited for years for this, and I want us to start out everything above board, okay?"

"OK, let's get you home. The bathroom has anything you need."

Susan cleaned up and was ready in a few minutes. They talked about different things on the way to her condo.

"Let me out here, I can manage fine," said Susan.

Tom double parked and got the door for her, taking her into the building and up to her floor. They kissed gently in the elevator. At her door he whispered in her ear that he loved her and always had. She looked at him and smiled giving him a peck on the cheek.

Tom drove home and went to bed - set his alarm for 0530. He didn't think he could sleep but the next thing he knew the alarm went off.

Tom arrived at the office – got himself a cup of coffee and took the documents out of the safe – he briefly went over them and took the elevator up to the Director's office. The secretary was there and told him to take a seat. She looked at him and told him the Director would be here any time.

The Director walked in, said good morning and motioned Tom to follow him into his office.

"Is it airtight?" he asked Tom.

"It will be when the documents from the Attorney General's office get here."

"A messenger brought them over last night."

"I would like to state that when this is over I wish to retire. George Hamilton and I go way back and have been friends. It was not easy for me to complete this. I have not said a word to him and that in itself has been tough."

The old Director looked hard at Tom and nodded his head.

"There is a summary sheet on top with times and dates."

The Director took the top sheet and looked at it.

"You have been an outstanding agent, Tom. You should have had your own division long ago, but I went along with your wishes, against my better judgment. You are what we used to call in the Special Forces, the kind of guy you wanted at your six o'clock, no better compliment could be had."

"I'll take this from here, you know the SOP. Take anyone who you might feel will be in danger and take off for an un-known destination. When you get there, call me at this number. I want you out this morning, along with the other people who have helped you."

Tom got up as did the Director and shook hands. When he reached the Director's secretary, she told him Susan had a rental car and was waiting at his house. Tom started to say something but she held up her hand and pointed to the door.

"What about George's confidential computer and his alias?"

"Everything was accessed last night and removed. Have a good trip."

Tom stopped by his office and checked his desk. He told his secretary that he had a case and would be gone awhile and headed for his house.

George walked into the office and found the replacement secretary there, who usually replaced Susan when she took a vacation or off for the day.

"Is Susan sick?"

"I really don't know, Mr. Hamilton. I got a call to cover your office this morning."

George looked puzzled and walked into his office. There were two agents waiting.

"Mr. Hamilton, please come with us," said one of the agents.

"What's going on?" George's demeanor changed. He knew what was going on. "Can I call my wife?"

"Later," said the same agent.

George was escorted up to the office next to the Director's. Inside were four men sitting around a table; there were empty chairs and he was told which chair to take.

The Director walked in, acknowledged the others around the table and directed his attention to George.

"This is a sad day, George. You have been around long enough to figure out what is going on." With those words the Director walked out.

Two days later, Tom and Susan were aboard a flight, heading for Salt Lake City and then up to Coeur d'Alene.

Susan had told Tom about her place up there that her late husband had left her. No one at work knew she owned the place.

It wasn't much she told him but she had renovated it over the year and it was quite comfortable. Tom patted her hand. She had also told him about George and their relationship over the years. He was surprised but not overly since he knew of agents and division heads who were seeing their secretaries. He had admitted to a short affair with his secretary but broke it off when she got married.

They changed planes and headed for Idaho. He told her there were some people he wanted her to meet.

They rented a car and stopped at a grocery store and picked up a few things. They would return in a few days to stock up.

On the way to her place, Tom said, "Take a left here." Susan slammed on the brakes and followed Tom's instructions. They drove under a sign that said "The Snake Ranch" and over a cattle crossing. They came to a large cabin and Tom got out. He walked up to the door and knocked. A man answered and stuck his hand out from behind a screen door.

Susan couldn't hear what they were talking about, but Tom came back and opened her door.

"Come on, I want you to meet someone."

Susan got out and walked with Tom up to the door. Pete and Jane greeted them and told them to come in.

"Pete, go over and get Cathy and Brian."

"Hell, I'll call." Pete went out and hit a triangular piece of iron hanging on a pole with an iron rod. It made a racket but got the desired results.

Susan could see a couple emerging from a smaller cabin. They walked in with Pete.

Susan and Cathy stood there and looked at each other. Suddenly they were hugging and saying, "Oh my God, Oh my God."

The others took seats in the living room and stared at them.

"I'm sorry," Susan turned to the others, "but Cathy and I go way back."

"Yes, we used to attend funerals together, a lot of funerals and then later we consoled each other," said Cathy with tears in her eyes.

"Oh, Susan, I want you to meet my husband Brian. Brian, Susan, a very dear old friend."

"Susan and I have met but I don't know if she remembers. I was saddened to hear about the Colonel," he said in a hushed tone. He was a real soldier whose toughness saved a lot of young lives."

Susan stared at Brian. "Command SMG Huff, how could I ever forget you and your people? You saved Sam at least twice that I know of."

"It's a small world Tom," said Pete. "Are there any more surprises or could we all sit down and talk about what brings you folks all the way up here?"

"Well, I own the Wilson's place about a half a mile from here," said Susan.

"You have had a lot of work done up there," said Brian. "I've driven by there and know some of the work crew. I was wondering who owned it. I've never seen anyone living there and the workmen didn't know the owner."

"Well," said Tom. "I called Pete here early one morning and he was waiting for his breakfast. I told him I would come up and eat the crumbs. He agreed but said I had to bring my own woman, so I did and here we are."

"Don't believe everything Pete tells you. He is about half truthful. He actually had me bent over the kitchen table and was not too pleased when the phone rang."

Everyone laughed. "You'll have to excuse me Susan, I'm trying to snag this guy so I never say 'no' to him, and he is coming around."

"I'll have to remember that," said Susan. "I'm sort of in the same predicament."

Everyone laughed again.

"How about a nice trout dinner here around five? That will give you two a chance to clean up and put your things away," said Jane.

"That sounds great," said Pete. "Brian and I'll go over and get some trout in the creek."

Tom and Susan thanked them and said they hadn't meant to bother them.

"No bother," said Cathy. Jane and I will do the heavy lifting while the boys are having fun at the creek."

Tom and Susan bid farewell and took off.

"That was a real surprise," said Susan, leaning over for a kiss. "I have known Cathy for years and knew of and met Brian several times. I'm glad she found someone nice, she had a rough time when Sam was killed."

Susan drove over another cattle guard and stopped in front of a beautiful cabin/house. Someone had recently oiled the logs and they glistened in the sunshine.

"This place is gorgeous," said Tom.

"I can't wait to see the inside," said Susan. She produced a key and they went inside.

"They have done a good job," she said looking around the living/dining room. All rough leather furniture, Tom was carrying her suitcases.

"The master bedroom is in there," she said pushing Tom in the direction of an open door. It was huge with walk-in closets and a large bathroom with a shower and a huge Jacuzzi tub. Tom went back out and got his baggage and brought the groceries in. The kitchen was stainless steel appliances and up-to-date counters. There was nothing lacking. Tom walked into the master bedroom. Susan was naked and putting away their clothes, placing the empty suitcases in a separate closet.

"We have six hours before dinner. Are you hungry or what?" she said, hands on her hips.

"What!" he said and started taking off his clothes. Susan hung his jacked and slacks on a hanger and was bending over placing his shoes in the closet with their clothes. Tom came up behind her and put his erection between her legs, grabbing her hips.

"My, oh my," said Susan, grabbing Tom's silky head and stroking it gently. They walked over to the bed and Susan laid down on it, feet still on the floor.

"I'm wet already but go in gently until my insides get uses to it."

She guided him in. He gently thrust and suddenly he was in her warm place. He reached under her and stroked her clit as he thrust in. Susan was starting to shake and cried out. He kept thrusting and pulling it out. She came again, this time hard and buried her face in the bed moaning. She collapsed and he came. Tom pulled out and lifted her onto the bed. They lay there, she in his arms.

"You are going to have to marry me, Tom. You have ruined me for any other man. I have had orgasms before but not this kind, and you are so gentle and loving with me."

"When Jane told us about Pete having her bent over the table, I was ready for you," he said laughing. "I think you and I can do anything and probably will. You're the first woman I have been comfortable with. It feels great."

"Hmm, I like to experiment, but for now I'm happy, very happy."

They fell asleep. Susan woke with a start. They had an hour to get over to the Snake Ranch. Tom was awake, he followed her into the shower soaping her all over and she him. He was erect. He placed Susan against the wall and spread her legs. This time he entered her fast and she cried out. She came and he right after. They stood not moving.

"God, Tom, if I wasn't so hungry I'd go back to bed with you."

He pulled out.

"Jesus Christ Tom, that's a dangerous weapon."

"And don't you forget it," he said kissing her wet face.

They arrived at Pete's place and entered the screen porch, Janet opened the main door and delicious smells wafted out at them. Brian and Cathy were there.

"We thought maybe you got hung up," said Cathy with a smile. The others laughed.

"It happens quite frequently around here. It must be the air," said Jane.

Susan blushed and laughed, "I guess we need to have a girl's talk so I know what to expect up here."

Drinks were passed and toasts were made. Tom brought them up to date on what had transpired. They all seemed surprised.

"We will have to go back when the trial comes up, or it could be handled by the Justice Department. We'll have to see. We both have homes back there, so we have to sell. D.C. is a rat race and we both need a change, and also retire."

"How did you find your place?" asked Brian.

"It's more than I expected. They did a fabulous job. I have to send them a bonus," said Susan.

"Well, don't come up here and ruin the economy," said Brian. "An agreement is an agreement. I'm sure they were well compensated from what I hear."

"I did 99% by mail – plans, contracts, etc. The foreman was an old friend of Sam's."

"We are happy you're here and hope you stay. We three can get into some real mischief," said Cathy, smiling.

"Tom, I wouldn't retire yet. You are going to need every penny you can lay your hands on. Brian and I are looking for jobs. I'll tell you, these ladies are hard on the wallet," said Pete getting a punch in the arm from Jane.

"Dinner is ready. Hope you like trout. When Brian and Pete go fishing, they go fishing, so everyone just take a set, I'll place everything on the table, and please, everyone, eat or we'll have fish for a week," said Jane.

"The air up here makes me hungry," said Susan.

"Well, not only the air," said Tom, "it's also the extra-curricular activities."

"That can get you a dry spell, Tom. No, I take that back.

I'm tired of dry spells."

They all laughed.

The dinner was great and they all had heady appetites. Susan was almost embarrassed by the amount of food she put away.

The ladies cleared the table and the men retired to the living room.

There was laughter and giggling coming from the kitchen. Jane was telling stories about when she and Pete came up and their first night here, how he had screamed and woken Cathy and Brian. Susan laughed so hard she had tears streaming down her face.

"Well, we weren't exactly asleep. Brian always insists on giving me a sleeping potion each night so I'll wake up refreshed in the morning. The only problem is, the sleeping pill is about this long." She held her hands apart in an exaggerated manner. There was another outburst of laughter.

Tom looked at Brian and Pete. "Have you checked their birth certificates? It sounds like a group of high school girls out there."

"Nah, let them have their fun. I enjoy laughter; it's music to my ears. You know the old saying, 'if our ladies are happy, everyone is happy'."

CPSIA information can be obtained
at www.ICGtesting.com
Printed in the USA
BVHW060759160819
555740BV00007B/50/P

9 781733 314909